"What the hell we gonna do when we get there?"

"Get rich," Tony said quietly. An astonished look was in his eyes, as if he'd never spoken such a thing out loud. Perhaps he didn't know it till he said it.

"Hey, I'm with you," cried Manolo, clapping his hands three times and thrusting a fist in the air in a gesture of triumph. "Hey, Cousin Tony, we gonna get us a yacht?"

"Everything, pal," said Tony Montana, his eyes still fixed on the far horizon. The chaos around him had vanished. He smiled at the open sea like an admiral. He clapped a hand on Manolo's shoulder. "We're gonna get us everything there is."

Scarface

A NOVEL BY PAUL MONETTE
BASED ON A SCREENPLAY BY
OLIVER STONE

B®

BERKLEY BOOKS, NEW YORK

SCARFACE

A Berkley Book / published by arrangement with
MCA Publishing, a Division of MCA Communications, Inc.

PRINTING HISTORY
Berkley edition / August 1983

ISBN: 0-425-06424-7

A BERKLEY BOOK ® TM 757,375
Berkley Books are published by The Berkley Publishing Group,
200 Madison Avenue, New York, New York 10016.
The name ''BERKLEY'' and the stylized ''B'' with design are
trademarks belonging to Berkley Publishing Corporation.
PRINTED IN THE UNITED STATES OF AMERICA

*To my mother and father,
forty years together and still counting,
and to Ethel Cross,
who taught me more about books than Yale did.*

Chapter One

IT WAS ALL noise and chaos in the harbor. To the sailors on the rusted shrimp boats, it looked like the start of another revolution. They lay at anchor for three days running, unable to maneuver in the crowded waters. Two days' catch rotted on the docks, ravaged by shrieking gulls, because the fish carts couldn't get through the mass of officials and huddling families. Yet none of the fishermen dared complain, for this was a government operation. They prowled the decks and drank rum in the waterfront bars, waiting. Normal life would start up again. It always did. People had to have fish, no matter who was in power.

All across Mariel Harbor, the sleek American fleet nuzzled among the tugs and scows. These were all private craft, customized yachts and blue-hulled sailboats, gaudy with teak and chrome, manned by overfed weekend captains dressed in polyester whites. The customs officials veered among them in Soviet-made gunboats, barking orders and assigning numbers, but it was no use. The Americans pushed and clamored. Fistfuls of bribe money lobbed through the air. The rich men's boats plowed through and hugged the docks. They were used to being served first.

The Cuban officials could not keep order. They had no army to back them up, because Castro didn't want a military profile. The exiles themselves were no problem. They stayed with their families and their meager luggage, glazed from the long wait in the hot spring sun. They waved and called out to their cousins and friends in the waiting boats, who'd crossed from Miami to bear them away to freedom. But they didn't surge forward, for fear they would rile the officials. The slightest false move, and they might be sent back to their desperate villages.

The problem was the demonstrators. Two hundred, three hundred strong, they swept back and forth along the pier, carrying placards and bawling. "Let them go!" they chanted. "Let the worms go!" They threw the exiles' luggage into the harbor. They grabbed up the stinking shrimp from the fish troughs and pelted several families. They jeered till the children cried. They were students, mostly, and the placards they carried— "Death to the traitors!"—were the mirror of those their older brothers carried, back in the days of the revolution. They had no politics, to speak of. It was just an excuse for a holiday, a chance to throw stones at the boredom of it all.

Yet the immigration officers made no move to restrain them, any more than they tried to restrain the American journalists, clicking their cameras and shrilling their questions in bastard Spanish. For this was a propaganda event. It had nothing to do with the pitiful exiles, yearning to join their kinfolk on the solid gold streets of Miami. It had nothing to do with the students, who already had an autocrat in power and thus didn't need to raise one up from the rabble. All of these were merely local color, immigrant and exile both. Only the officials, in their khakis and spit-shined shoes, badges gleaming in the noonday haze, dimly understood the larger purpose they all served. Because they were good bureaucrats, because they loved their government like a father, they knew they were doing their part to bring peace to the world.

For Castro was out to normalize relations with the Americans. In a gesture worthy of ancient kings, he had opened the harbor at Mariel and declared his people free to go. Some few, anyway. There were quotas, of course. Still, within seventy-two hours of his announcement, a flotilla of boats was on its way from the U.S. mainland. Three thousand boats in all, drunk on freedom and Carta Blanca.

Finally, after endless hours of triplicate forms and false alarms, a thin stream of refugees was permitted to gather at the end of the dock. The gleaming yachts jostled for position as the first was tied up to the piling. A couple of weeping refugee women reached out like beggars to the polished deck. The minicam unit from NBC-Lauderdale nearly trampled a child as it zoomed in for a close-up. All the hysterical energy of the last few days, the hope and terror and patriot zeal, was suddenly focused on that one spot where the first refugee would step off the dock into happy exile.

Nobody noticed the trucks. They came in a line between two warehouses, with armed police running ahead and behind. Five altogether, rumbling and grinding their gears, old trucks from the Second World War, probably Russian as well. It was a little late for the army. Most of the footage for the evening news was already in the can.

The police pressed the crowd back so the trucks could make the turn onto the pier. The guards who brought up the rear hurried forward as each truck braked. They released the chains on the tailgates, and the tailgates fell open with a grinding roar, striking the dock with a splin-

ter of wood and sending the rats in the pilings below
streaming into the water. Still the crowd didn't understand. They strained to watch the immigration men
check their final lists. They cavorted for the television
crews. They spat at the boats from Florida.

Had anyone peered into the truckbeds, it would have
taken several seconds to grow accustomed to the dark.
The steaming sun beating on the water had made them
all sea-blind. Perhaps they would have caught the stench
before they saw a thing. If pain had a smell, if madness
did, then this was how it stunk. Chains slithered and
clinked in the darkness. Here and there a groan went up,
but without any hope of mercy. Even the guards, as they
prodded and cursed, winced with a kind of shame, as if
they were horrified to bring what was in there out to the
light of day.

Now you could see them. They lay there stacked
together, their cheeks hollow, their eyes dead, manacled
wrists held out in front of them, pleading like the
damned. They were dressed in rags. Their heads were
shaved. Now, as they slowly disentangled themselves
and staggered forward, the sores stood out livid where
the chains had rubbed. They hadn't bathed in days.
They whined at the glare of the sun. They stumbled
down the ramp, dragging their chains. There must have
been fifty or sixty in each truck, but somehow, only a
couple had died of the heat. It wasn't till they began to
form lines, careful to do exactly what the guards said,
that one saw how tough they were. They were dirty and
vile, they had touched bottom—but they had no plans
to die.

What were they doing here? There must have been
some mistake. What kind of propaganda was this?

The demonstrators had seen them now. They shook
their placards and crowded forward, grumbling with
scorn and ridicule. The hollow men stood in ranks
beside the trucks, staring ahead unblinking as the

guards cut away the dead ones. The police held the students back, till they stood face to face with the line in chains. And the grumbling stopped. And the placards fell like broken kites. For the holiday was done.

Out on the end of the dock, an immigration official spelled out the procedure for the third time to the red-faced captain of a forty-foot boat called "Shangri-La," out of Sarasota. "We have you down for four families," explained the official. "This means you will take twenty anti-socialists as well."

"Listen, I can't handle thirty-five people on this boat. You want me to sink?"

"That is not an immigration problem," replied the other coolly. "The formula's fixed in Havana. Take it or leave it."

The captain had no choice. He came as a conquering hero, savoring the hero's welcome that awaited him back in Florida. He couldn't return empty-handed. Hordes of anxious relatives paced the port of Miami, praying for the safe return of the so-called "Freedom Flotilla." The captain cast an anxious glance along his shining deck. Inside the main cabin the luncheon table was set for six and getting cold. As long as they encountered no turbulence, he thought. The sky was blank, without a shred of cloud. As long as the refugees stayed where they were told.

"All right," he murmured to the bored official, trying to remember where he'd stowed his gun. Wondering what the hell these commies meant by anti-socialists.

Back by the trucks, a sergeant of police went methodically down the line, unlocking the manacles at each man's wrists. As he passed among them he spoke in a surly undertone, scarcely pausing to draw a breath. "Go on," he sneered, "go suck the tit of the bitch-whore America, you ugly bag of garbage. See what they do to you there. You'll starve in the streets, you pigs."

On and on he cursed them, rhythmic as a priest pass-

ing out the sacrament. None of the men gave a flicker of
response, for fear he would not release their cuffs. The
students watched with a kind of horrible fascination.
For a moment pity was in their eyes. But somehow the
contemptuous words of the sergeant taunted and teased
them, till finally they came to their senses. They began
to whisper to each other out of the corners of their
mouths. "Convicts," they said. "Traitors. Killers.
Perverts."

Soon they were jeering out loud, calling across the no-
man's-land that separated them from the men in chains.
The sergeant grinned when he heard the chorus, and his
rabid curses came faster and sharper. He had freed
perhaps fifty men from their chains. A hundred more
stood waiting, while others still spilled from the final
trucks. The free ones looked as chained as ever. They
stared across at the shouting students, not sure they
hadn't been brought here to be lynched.

The last truck disgorged its shame. These had to be
dragged out by the guards. They emerged like frightened animals, unchained because the chains were all
inside them. They wore hospital gowns. They carried
their dim belongings in pitiful bundles. These were the
hopeless mad, and as soon as the students saw them, the
fury of the curses grew. "Send them away!" the demonstrators cried. A shiver of exultation was in their
shouting now. At last they could rid the state of all its
tainted blood. Send away the sick. Send away the old.
There was no end to what they could purge.

The sergeant's eyes gleamed as he came to the next
prisoner in line. Before he inserted his key he yanked the
chain, and the manacles cut so deep that a ring of blood
blossomed at either wrist. The convict clenched his
jaws, but he gave no cry. "You too, Scarface," sneered
the sergeant. "Go lick the feet of the millionaires. Let
them grind their boots in that scum face of yours."

With that he flicked the key—once, twice—and the

manacles fell to the dock. And the scarfaced one, in the young angry prime of his life, kicked back his head and laid a full wad of spit in the sergeant's eyes.

"Fuck you and fuck Castro," growled Tony Montana.

The sergeant went white. The spit coursed down his cheeks like crocodile tears. He drew back his fist and landed a punch square on Montana's cheekbone, just at the tip of the scar. Montana didn't even seem to feel it. A curl of a smile touched his upper lip as he spoke again: "And fuck your Communism up the ass."

The quaking sergeant let fly with a second punch, an uppercut to the jaw. Montana hardly winced. He turned his head to the side and spit out a tooth and a mouthful of blood. The sergeant was crazy. He shoved Montana back, meaning to get him behind the truck so he could beat him to a pulp. But suddenly a rough hand clamped down on the sergeant's shoulder. "Leave it alone," snarled the captain of police. "Let's get them on the boats."

Reluctantly, the sergeant turned once more to the line of manacled men. The captain shouted through a bullhorn at those who were already free, ordering them to the end of the dock. "Keep your papers in your left hand," he commanded. "Once you set foot on a boat, you are no longer a citizen of this country. If you lose your papers, the Americans will shoot you."

The convicts moved along the pier, the students heckling on all sides. Most of these men had been in solitary, some for as long as five years, but they fell naturally into groups and gangs, banding together the way they did in the exercise yard or down in the mess. They weren't friends, exactly. Any one of them would have killed the man beside him for an extra packet of cigarettes. Yet they knew that safety lay in numbers, and nobody wanted to board a boat without some men he knew to back him up. They were going into enemy territory. They needed to be an army.

Only Tony Montana walked alone. Even in his broken cardboard shoes, his grimy shirt pocked with holes, his shaved head and his prison-gray skin, he walked like a prince, the rock of the hips and shoulders like a panther. His eyes were so pure in their fury, they looked as if they could burn through steel. He was twenty-five and rock-hard. He had made no alliances during his five years in jail, because he didn't need a blessed thing.

None of the other convicts had ever made a move on him. They gave him a wide berth, because they knew the type. A man who was going to explode one day, muscle and tissue and brain, a man who could live or die, take it or leave it, kill or be killed. The long thin scar that zig-zagged down his cheek like a bolt of lightning made men shrink and touch their faces, terrified of pain. Now and then you saw a man in jail who was born with nothing to lose. A man like that didn't make deals. He didn't sleep, and he didn't dream. He just waited for the next chance. And when it finally came, he'd kill the whole world if it stood in his way.

When Tony Montana reached the crowd at the end of the dock, his quick eyes took in the whole operation. A dozen refugees were already huddled on the deck of the first yacht in line. While the captain bellowed in protest, a score of convicts was led to the gangplank. The captain wouldn't let them on till the guns had been brought up from below. He even demanded manacles, but the immigration men stood belligerent. As the argument raged back and forth, Tony Montana wanted no part of it. He knew he would land in Miami branded as an un-desirable if he went over on one of the rich men's boats. He looked out to the harbor, beyond the yachts, search-ing among the American fleet for something big and ugly, where a captain wouldn't be so discriminating. His eyes picked out a fishing tub, proudly flying the stars and stripes. If he could just wait for that one, he thought—

"Hey, Tony," called a friendly voice beside him.

His fists clenched as he turned. He found himself face to face with a grinning man about two years younger than he—darkly handsome, lean and tightly muscled, with an irrepressible laugh and a streak of nervous energy that made him seem to dance in place, like a fighter. He thrust out his hand. Montana made no move to take it.

"Same old Tony, huh?" said the stranger with a laugh, withdrawing his hand but taking no offense. "Manolo Ray. The little fox, remember? I'm your fuckin' cousin."

Montana cocked his head. His eyes darted left and right, as if to make sure nobody had witnessed his being called by name. Then he looked Manolo up and down, noting how the younger man managed to look dapper, even in prison rags. Somehow he had convinced somebody not to shave his head. Montana could tell he hadn't been in long. He still had a little color.

"So what you been doin', kid?" he asked in a voice that was oddly gentle.

"I been over Guantanamo, workin' on a gang. They gimme two years for stealin' a car. Hell, it was ready for the junkheap. Fuckin' thing broke down right in front of a police station." Manolo threw back his head and laughed, as if his own bad luck never kept him from enjoying a good story. "I heard they was shippin' guys out to the States, so I ask the warden if I can go. He says I ain't bad enough. You gotta be scum of the earth. I'm scum of the earth, I tell him. He says no dice. Cost me six hundred bucks to convince him. How 'bout you, Tony? Where you been?"

"You still talk too much," Montana said.

"Yeah, sure," replied the other with a grin. "You want to make somethin' of it?"

For a moment Montana's face went blank, the blank men had kept their distance from for years. This was how he looked when he pulled a trigger. There must have been a hundred men in the crowd who'd have scrambled for cover if they'd seen him then. But they would have been wrong. All of a sudden he broke into a grin that was the mirror image of Manolo's. And he said: "Nope."

With that they fell into step beside each other and sauntered down the dock like a couple of swells out for an outing. The hundred men who'd have fled in terror at the look on Tony Montana's face would have learned something very important about him if they'd watched his meeting with Manolo Ray. For it wasn't just when he pulled a trigger. Montana went blank like a man disarmed when he cared about somebody. Just for a second, all his panther manner disappeared. He was defenseless. If someone had only seen it, he would have had something on Tony Montana. But nobody saw it.

"What boat we on?" Manolo asked him, as they sat on a coil of rope and watched the convicts file onto one vessel after another. Montana nodded out to the harbor, where the battered trawler rode the sluggish tide, waiting its place in line. Manolo, who had been staring greedily at the yachts, winced with sudden dismay. "Huh? You gotta be kiddin'."

"Better to be with a mob," Montana said, figuring the trawler would hold a couple of hundred easily. "We don't want to stick out."

"Well, I hope you can swim, amigo, 'cause that thing looks like it already sank."

"Don't worry, we'll get there," Montana replied, his jaw set grimly as he gazed out over the water, past the harbor light.

"What the hell we gonna do when we get there?"

"Get rich," said the other quietly. An astonished look was in his eyes, as if he'd never spoken such a thing out loud. Perhaps he didn't know it till he said it.

"Hey, I'm with you," cried Manolo Ray, clapping his hands three times and thrusting a fist in the air in a gesture of triumph. "Hey, Cousin Tony, we gonna get us a yacht?"

"Everything, pal," said Tony Montana, his eyes still fixed on the far horizon. The chaos around him had vanished. He smiled at the open sea like an admiral. He clapped a hand on Manolo's shoulder. "We're gonna get us every fuckin' thing there is."

They weren't really cousins. They grew up in the same Havana slum, in tarpaper shacks that lined an alley indistinguishable from a thousand others. The two boys were drawn together because neither one had a father. Both men had died in the revolution. Died on the right side, at least, in bloody guerrilla skirmishes high in the mountains. Their widows were due a string of medals and a proper pension, but only the medals had ever arrived. The slum alleys didn't look any different under Castro than they had under Batista. It was still just rice and beans, with now and then a hunk of dogmeat. The history they taught in the schools was changed, but nobody from the alleys ever went to school. The only thing a slum kid could aspire to be was a soldier. The good money that had filtered down in the old regime— to the pimps, the hustlers, the whores, the pickpockets —was gone with the gringo tourists and the high-roll gamblers.

When he was ten years old, Tony Montana loved nothing better than to sit in his mother's tiny kitchen, listening to his grandfather talk of the old days. The old man had worked as a doorman at the Cristobal Beach Hotel. When he spoke of the playboys and chorus girls, the Bentleys and the diamond chokers, he went into a kind of trance. He held up his head in a lofty way, and his gestures were grand, his manner elegant, as if he too had swept in every evening to lose a fortune at baccarat. Had Castro had spies in Mrs. Montana's kitchen, they would have arrested the old man as a genuine anti-socialist. Tony knew it had to be a secret between him and his grandfather. But his head grew full of visions, and he knew even then he would never rest till he found that lost and magic world again.

By the time he was twelve he had started to learn his trade. He and Manolo would take the bus to the garden quarters of the city, where the bureaucrats and the generals lived in the houses of the rich who'd fled the revolution. The two boys would talk their way into somebody's house, pretending one of them was sick. While the lady of the house administered bicarbonate of soda to Manolo, Tony would dart through the rooms and pick up whatever he could stuff in his shirt. The two boys came home from the suburbs laden down with bud vases and china figurines, little madonnas and cigarette boxes. Now and then Tony would bestow a trinket on his sister Gina, six years old, but he knew his mother would have turned him over to the local priest for punishment if she'd ever found out. So he horded his loot in the crawl space under the shack, counting it up like a king in his treasure-house, till he outgrew childish things.

They graduated to picking pockets. Manolo would sit on a bench in the fountained park in front of the shuttered art museum, sobbing as if his heart would break. When somebody stopped to comfort the child, Tony would slip out of the bushes and lift a wallet or snatch a purse. They made a fair amount of money this way, enough to keep them in beer and cigarettes, but somehow it never satisfied Tony. If he was going to steal, he wanted to steal from the rich. Pearls and gold watches and thick folds of cash—that's what he itched to grab hold of. He wasn't long for a people's republic.

When he was fourteen and Manolo was twelve, they joined a gang. Tony was kind of reluctant, but he knew he would end up a victim if he had no affiliation. They were mostly fifteen and sixteen, these kids, and what they specialized in was random violence. They would break a hundred windows at the Ministry of Agriculture. They slashed the tires on a fleet of Jeeps behind the army barracks. They lit smutty fires in back doorways. They threw live cats on the power grids, so as to throw whole neighborhoods into darkness. They loved nothing better than being caught in the act and chased through the streets. They called themselves The Devil's Cousins.

If someone had told them they were anarchists, undermining the revolution, they would have laughed till their sides hurt. The revolution had nothing to do with them. It was a delusion of their parents. They themselves were engaged in a far more serious matter, the business of not growing up.

By the time he was sixteen himself, Tony had grown more and more restless. He had long since proven himself as daring and destructive as the others, once almost losing an arm when a bottle bomb exploded too fast. The gang respected and included him, but only Manolo was close enough to tease him and make him laugh. Only to Manolo would Tony express his contempt and dissatisfaction. The Cousins were going nowhere, Tony said. He didn't want to end up drunk and married and dead before he was thirty. He had bigger plans.

"Hey, chico," he said, shadowboxing as he and Manolo made their way home one evening, "you think I wanna spend the rest of my life *here*? Hey, you gotta be kiddin'. I'm goin' where the money is. I'm gonna find me a princess and live in a fuckin' castle."

"Lotta princesses right around here," retorted his friend, eyeing a girl in the window opposite, lazily brushing her long dark hair.

Tony snorted contemptuously. "You think too small, chico. That's your problem."

Manolo wasn't listening. He'd caught the eye of the girl in the window, who smiled at him coyly as she pinned up her hair. Manolo hitched his thumbs in his belt loops and leaned casually against a lamp post, affecting a studied indifference.

Tony noticed none of this. He looked off into the middle distance like a seer in a trance. His fists were clenched, his forehead beaded with sweat. His voice quivered with passion as he whispered: "I'm talkin' princess, chico. You understand?"

He'd been spending time down on the docks, talking to the old fishermen about life in Miami. Everyone told him the same thing: Don't go over poor. Poor in Miami was just as bad as poor in the slum alleys. Don't go over without connections, or you'd end up picking lemons for a dollar a day. Tony listened carefully, filtering out the anti-American bullshit. He knew it wasn't hard to get across the ninety miles to Florida. An able-bodied man could make it with a forty-horse motor and a rowboat. But the more he listened, the more he realized he needed a stake. He had to have money to bribe his way in, or he'd just be another illegal alien, like some dumb Mexican farmworker.

So he hustled around on his own for a while, looking to make a connection. He only went out with the gang one or two nights a week, and they didn't like it, but Manolo managed to keep peace. Tony sniffed out the bar where the loan sharks gathered, the numbers runners and the bookies. This whole class of con men had been driven deeper underground by the ascendancy of Castro. They no longer sported in linen suits and Panama hats, with gold-handled canes and foot-long cigars. They had to dress down like everybody else. The flash went into the closet. But they made as much money as ever, because they provided essential services.

And they still needed runners and bagmen.

They started Tony small, selling reefers in the alleys. He had to carve out his own territory, and he worked on a fifty-fifty split, fifteen cents on a cigarette. Within six weeks he was dealing a couple of hundred a day, five hundred a day a month later. Most of his competition was old dopers who weren't looking to make much more than an easy buck or two, as long as they got their dope for free. Meanwhile, Tony was working the schoolyards. He worked out a special deal with an army corporal, splitting his own percentage so as to be the main conduit to the city barracks. He worked the chain gangs doing road work down by the harbor, selling in bulk to the prisoners. Then he cut the guards in and doubled his volume.

The wizened old crooks in the bar could hardly believe it. Marijuana was a small-time operation, scarcely worth the trouble of keeping the traffic flowing. It was more of a public relations gesture between them and the barrio, where they made money hand over fist on gambling and loans. So they saw right away that Tony Montana was somebody special. They offered him a bagman's slot in the numbers racket, where he'd have a good deal more responsibility and a lot less running around. They even implied that if he kept his nose clean, there might be a spot one day in the protection business. If a man could make a territory his and no one else's, he stood to make a fortune.

They were stunned when he turned them down. They might have even got angry, except Tony was a real smooth talker, even then. He knew the old con men were just like his grandfather, sighing for a lost world. All he had to do was tell them, very serious and man-to-man, that he only planned to work till he had a stake, that he wouldn't rest till he'd had a shot at Miami. What could they do? They understood that a man with talent had nowhere to go in Cuba. Crime needed freedom. The

States was the only place in the world where any man could grow up to be a President Carter, or an Al Capone at least.

So he worked for a couple of years in the streets selling reefer, moving ounces to his serious customers and a kilo every two weeks to the corporal. He brought in Manolo for the nickel and dime work, and he took a week's trip up into the mountains late one August, to watch the harvest and see how the crop was moved across the island to Havana. They were all just peasants at the growing end. He realized that if he had his own foreman in the fields, he could double the output next season. Then he'd take the plants right to the ocean and bring them around by boat, rather than rely on the cumbersome fleet of trucks that the mob had used for twenty years. But he kept his ideas to himself, so he wouldn't get overcommitted. He wanted to leave in a year. He mustn't get tangled in power.

By Christmas he had six thousand dollars saved. It was hidden in a biscuit tin in the crawl space underneath his mother's shack. The con men would have banked it for him, but he didn't trust them for a minute. His goal was fifteen thousand. He knew it would cost that much to buy ten thousand American dollars on the black market.

For her thirteenth birthday he bought his sister Gina a gold cross on a chain, for they were still Catholics, no matter how much the state disdained it. Gina wore the cross when she came into the kitchen for her birthday dinner. Her mother ripped it off her throat and flung it out the window into the open sewer that coursed through the alley. Nobody said a word. Tony brought no more presents home.

He figured he'd be able to leave by the following summer. Unlike Manolo, who spent every penny he made on the black market, buying American jeans and pointed shoes, Tony bought nothing for himself. It didn't even bother him. He had no eye on the present any more. Once he had made his place in Miami he'd dress like a prince—the waiting was almost pleasurable. No wonder he was such an easy target. He walked to the barracks that morning in February, the lemon trees heady with scent in the winter drizzle, a flour sack over his shoulder stuffed with weed. He walked like nothing could touch him. The gods' mouths must have watered, he needed to fall so bad.

He stood with the corporal in the stockyard between two trucks, counting out money. On the other side of the stockade fence was the riding ring. As the two men split up, Tony happened to glance through the fence. A spotted horse was trotting by, with a woman riding. She wore cream-colored jodhpurs and boots that gleamed. The silk scarf at her neck floated behind her like a trail of mist. Her sleek black hair tumbled to her shoulders. Tony stepped to the fence and gripped the chain links and stared at her. She passed without so much as a glance, patting the horse's neck and murmuring endearments. She seemed to have ridden out of a dream—or out of the past Tony had only heard about in stories. His knuckles went white as he held the fence, desperate as a prisoner, even as she turned the horse in a circle and trotted back toward him.

"I know you," she said with a teasing smile. "You're the boy with the drugs. You got any pills?"

Tony shook his head.

She sighed. "I can't sleep," she said, tossing her hair because it was hot, pulling the scarf from her neck. She said no more. The horse had scarcely broken stride, and now she clicked her tongue, and they loped away across the ring. It was five minutes before Tony let go of the fence.

He spent the whole day trading favors, till he found a pharmacist with a back door. He showed up at the riding ring the next morning at exactly the same time, and when she trotted by he held up a little bottle and shook it like a castanet. They grinned at each other. She leaned down and took the bottle through the fence.

"What else do you do?" she murmured.

"Everything," said Tony.

"Behind the stables," she whispered, not a moment's pause. "Three o'clock."

He was there by two, dressed in a fancy shirt of Manolo's. He paced the dusty road behind the stables, cursing himself for being a virgin. She drove up in an old Mercedes, and when he got in she said nothing, but started to laugh as they sped away. He thought she would never stop laughing. They passed through a neighborhood of old estates, many of them now given over to government operations. At last she turned in at an open gate in a high stone wall, and Tony got suddenly nervous when he saw the wide lawn and the great colonial mansion. Her laughter had dwindled down to a purr in her throat. Tony opened his mouth to speak.

"Don't ask anything," she said, not turning her head.

She led him through high cool rooms, the light kept out by wine-dark velvet drapes. The heavy old Spanish oak looked like the furniture of a palace. Up a spiral flight of marble steps, they came into a peach silk bedroom, with a canopied bed and a balcony overlooking a pond, where a pair of black swans drifted back and forth. She tore off Tony's clothes and then her own. She sucked him all over, biting and panting, and then drew him into her and rode him until she was screaming. There was no time to be a virgin.

And when it was over they took a long hot bath and did it again on the white-tile floor. She dropped him back at the stables at five o'clock. "Don't ask anything," she had warned him, and he followed it to the letter, as if the sorcery would break if he stepped outside the circle. He asked no questions even of himself. He told no one. He rearranged his schedule so he saw his

major customers at night. And he was there at the
stables every afternoon at three. She came to pick him
up perhaps twice a week. He never knew which days it
would be.

For weeks they didn't exchange a word, except what
they groaned in bed. Every now and then he would
bring her a gift—a scarf, a bracelet, a bottle of scent.
She smiled like a child, wide-eyed, when she opened
each package. She laughed with delight, no matter what
it was. Yet Tony never saw any of his presents again,
not on her boudoir table, not on her dresser, not in her
closet. It was as if she was hording them somewhere.

Tony didn't ask.

Six months went by, then a year. He had his fifteen
thousand saved. Was he going to Miami or not, Manolo
kept asking, who had taken over half the deliveries now.
In a month or so, Tony would say. It wasn't that the
dream was any less real; he stood ready to go on a half
day's notice. But it was as if he drew a blank every afternoon at three, and he could not leave till she'd
released him. She had become his dark angel, and how
he finished it with her was how he would finish the past.
Not just his own. His grandfather's too, and his country's.

Nothing seemed any different, that rainy Friday in
March. He brought her a càmeo, which she held against
her cheek with the same abstracted smile. She folded it
back in the tissue and laid it on the chaise. Then they
ripped off their clothes and went at it, seething and
moaning. There was always a kind of rage about it, as if
they were both groping to escape the questions they
swore they would never ask. And then they lay in the
bathtub, idly stroking one another's face. Because it
was always the same, it had become a kind of dream.

So when he knelt on the white-tiled floor, kissing between her thighs as she rubbed his hair dry with a towel,
he knew it was just the final beat of their wings. In a
minute they'd have to fly. It was twenty to five; the

clock was in his heart. So why, when he stood up and moved to the stool where his clothes lay in a heap, did she reach for his hand and draw him back toward the bed? The queerest, calmest smile was on her face. Wasn't it time that he asked that question? Why did he just go with her, and lay in her arms doing nothing while the minutes swarmed like hornets?

Her head rested on his chest. He could feel his own heart beating. For a moment he thought she was asleep; for a moment he thought *he* was. Then she suddenly drew in a gasp of breath, for no reason at all. Then the bedroom door flew open, and Tony looked over without surprise, as if fate would always break in unannounced and always find him naked.

He didn't get a very good look. It was a military man, bearded and dressed guerrilla-style, so there was no telling what rank he had. Somehow the woman slipped away. She didn't seem to be in the room at all. Tony leaped to his feet and grabbed a lamp, and the two men began to circle. The bearded soldier was spitting curses at him, but Tony hardly listened. He was amazed to see the man wasn't armed, not with a gun anyway. He must be very high up, Tony thought. He must be used to bodyguards. It was the first time Tony understood that fate itself could be unprepared. With the oddest sense of anticlimax, he saw he was going to survive this thing.

He swung the lamp back and forth as he edged to the door. He lifted it over his head to throw it, when the soldier suddenly ducked into the bathroom. Tony bolted. He crossed the hallway and leaped down the stairs, but he landed wrong on his ankle and pitched headlong. In a moment he lay in a heap at the bottom, one arm twisted beneath him. By the time he scrambled to his feet, he could hear the boots thundering down the stairs. Tony made it to the door, but he couldn't unlock it fast enough, his fingers were like jelly. He felt the soldier's hand clamp down on his naked shoulder and spin him around. He had no idea what the weapon would be, but he clenched his teeth because this was it.

Still gnashing his teeth with curses, the soldier drew his free hand behind his head. Tony saw the long curve of the razor. Instinctively he clamped his hands about his genitals. His blank, astonished face was the clearest target a jealous man could ask for. The razor whizzed in the air and sliced into his upper cheek, just missing the eye. It hit the cheekbone with a sickening clunk and went zigzag as it swept toward the chin. The pain was so intense, the gout of blood so thick, Tony could not even open his mouth to scream.

That was all the soldier wanted. As soon as he saw the gash he flicked the razor shut in its case and turned and walked heavily down the hall, as if it was past time for his whiskey. Tony stood in a daze with his hands to his face, trying to hold his cheek together. He knew the duel was over. He staggered back up to the bedroom and retrieved his clothes, snatching up the towel she'd dried his hair with to staunch the flow of the blood. He walked out without a backward glance.

And he staggered home on foot, hiding behind a hundred trees so he wouldn't be stopped for vagrancy. It was dark by the time he got back to the alleys. He crawled beneath his mother's shack to nurse his wound alone. When he woke next morning, an infection had already furred the edges. He needed forty stitches, and he was stuck two weeks in a hospital ward, his face so badly swollen he could only see out of one eye.

But he didn't care, and he didn't complain. All he knew was that he could kill now. It was as if he'd waited all his life to try the limit of his power. He finally understood what final act was needed before he could break away and claim his kingdom. The day he was released, he bought a forty-five automatic and a sawed-off shotgun.

He spent a day and a night high up in a coral tree

directly across the road from the mansion gates. The
soldier was driven away at seven A.M. and didn't return
till five in the afternoon. The woman went out twice in
the loud Mercedes, once in the morning to go ride her
horse, then again at three P.M., as if there was still a
chance that Tony Montana might yet be waiting behind
the stables. She returned alone. About nine o'clock the
army car emerged through the gates, with a soldier
driving who was scarcely older than Tony. The woman
and the bearded officer rode together in the back seat.
Once they had sped away Tony shinnied down from the
tree and went home, satisfied that he knew their every
move.

Still, he waited a few days before he acted. It was
almost as if he had put the revenge out of his mind as he
went about the alleys with Manolo, catching up on
business. He began to negotiate with one of the fishermen at the harbor, arranging to have a shrimp boat
ready on a day's notice. They would take him halfway
across the Florida Straits and drop him in a rowboat.
The outboard motor alone would cost him twenty-five
hundred dollars. He spent several evenings with the
gang, who stood in awe of the lightning scar and didn't
dare ask how he earned it. Manolo was relieved. He
thought Tony had finally come to his senses. He knew
none of the details, only that it was a woman and it was
over. They were in business again, he and Tony. They
swaggered like pimps down the alleys, and everyone
knew who they were.

Then, one evening about sundown, Tony got dressed
up fancy, in a white linen suit and a black silk shirt unbuttoned to the breastbone. No Panama hat, but even
so he looked like he planned to spend the night playing
baccarat, with a mink-draped chorus girl breathing in
his ear. He stowed the two guns in the gunny sack he
usually carried his weed in. He walked the whole way to
the mansion gates, because he was too proud to borrow
a car.

He waited beneath the coral tree till he saw the lights sweep down the drive. Then he walked across the street, pulling the forty-five out of the sack. The army driver must have seen the pale figure glimmering at the gates, but he kept on coming. As he slowed to make the turn, Tony walked right up and crouched as if he meant to ask some innocent question. The driver smiled, secure in the power that radiated from the general just behind him. He felt so safe he didn't even see the gun that Tony was raising in the darkness. If the woman in the back seat hadn't screamed he would have felt no terror at all. In any case, he was dead a second later.

At the first report of the forty-five, the bearded general began to scramble across the car, climbing over the screaming woman. Tony dropped the revolver into the sack and pulled out the sawed-off shotgun. He leaned in at the driver's window, pointing it into the back seat. There was the smallest pause as he watched them squirm and clamber to escape. It was as if he hadn't decided even yet who was meant to die here—her or him or both of them. As if he couldn't know till he'd come to the moment how to make his vengeance perfect.

His face went blank. He blew the general's head off.

Next morning he made his rounds the same as always. He and Manolo had breakfast in a rancid cafe, dealing reefer to kids and old servants, the latter left high and dry by the revolution. Then Tony picked up nine kilos at a cannery near the railroad yards, since he was now in a position to have a month's supplies forwarded to him. He stored them in the crawl space under the porch, beside his biscuit tin. Then he took a bus so as not to be late at the barracks, where he made his regular transfer with the corporal. As the corporal sniffed the goods and dipped a pinch under his tongue, Tony stared through the fence at the empty ring, completely dispassionate. He hadn't expected a rider, but he didn't care. He would have looked through her if she'd been there.

He turned back to the corporal with an automatic

hand out. The price had been settled for months; payment was always in tens and twenties. But the corporal only grinned at him. Then his eyes flicked once over Tony's shoulder, and Tony understood right there that fate was never finished. He was grabbed from behind, one at each arm, and dragged across the pavement to a police car, its red light blipping sullenly in the morning heat. Before two hours were up he was standing in front of a judge. The sentence was brief: six years at hard labor.

Tony never wasted a moment's time trying to second-guess it. He'd been wrong to assume that revenge was an end to anything. The war of passion was a war of attrition. Luckily, Tony was blessed with a gift for shedding the past. He worked like a stevedore on the chain gang, till he naturally assumed the position of lead dog. He slept hard, like a laborer, ignoring all the indignities of prison life. It had no psychic effect on him, because he managed to live in a state of suspended animation. No wonder he grew strong while the others weakened and went mad. He was asleep inside. Yet he waited for the next chance with a pure fury in his heart, but hidden and protected. All the while he was mesmerized, he was ready to spring like a cobra.

He had friends among the guards of course, who had served as his well-heeled middlemen in getting the dope to the cell blocks. They kept an eye on him, especially since Manolo had doubled their piece of the action. They made sure Tony Montana got a little meat every now and then. They kept him out of solitary. They made sure he wasn't one of the dozen men who died every week in the purges and rapes and interrogations.

Tony had been in for a year and a half when he got the word through the captain of the guard that he might have a chance at a transfer. Tony didn't care. One prison was like another. He didn't even want to work less, because hard work kept him numb. Then he found out that this other program would cut a year off his sentence, and he volunteered right away, without even asking what it was. Two nights later, the guard woke him up around midnight and led him through the yard to an armored bus. Thirty other convicts dozed inside.

They were driven to the northwest end of the island, to a vast tract of untouched country, swamps and grassy plains and rugged sawtooth mountains. The convicts were issued guerrilla fatigues and put through a course of basic training, a month of crawling on their bellies and hacking their way through pest-ridden jungle. Two men tried to escape. They were caught and used for a torture demonstration, then put out of their misery with a bullet in the brain. The convicts were not issued guns of their own till the final days, when they no longer dreamed of running away. All they wanted now was an enemy.

Tony didn't mind the rigors of training. He liked getting tougher and tougher. But he kept the same distance he'd always kept from the politics they fed him. To the commandos who ran the program, the whole world was a search-and-destroy mission. Dozens of governments needed pulling down. The fascist colonial powers must be slaughtered in their beds. Tony paid no attention at all as the imperialist conspiracy was blocked out on the map. He knew it was all crap. He figured in a couple of weeks he'd be doing guard duty down at Guantanamo and sleeping in a jail. He planned to cause no trouble at all—not till he had a chance to make a break for it.

It was midnight again when his unit was roused and hustled out to a grassy field. They were bundled into the bus with all their gear. About dawn they came out to a quiet harbor pocked with Russian gunboats. They were led down a pier to a sugar tanker. Then they were lowered into one of the holds, which stunk of molasses and hadn't quite been cleared of rats. The tanker groaned and shrieked at its fittings as it made for the open sea. The thirty men crouched in the darkness. Nobody told them anything.

Eighteen days they were prisoned there. Food was lowered in a basket, and water six times a day. Nobody came even close to dying, in spite of the heat and the reek of vomit and the rats that chewed through their sleeping rolls and nipped at their feet. They endured it as if it was some kind of final examination, at the end of which they would be certified at last. Tony had no problem with the discomforts of the voyage, but his heart sank when he realized they were a million miles from Miami. This far away, was there any place left to escape to?

They landed in Angola in the deep midsummer. After a day's briefing in the open air in the port city of Luanda, they were transported inland, six hundred miles by train to the high plateaus and coffee farms along the lush eastern ridge. They were billeted in a makeshift camp near the Zaire border and issued Russian rifles. Tony never really understood who was fighting whom. His own men were allied with the government forces, against an enemy in the north and another in the south. In any case it was civil war and none of Cuba's business, or so it seemed to Tony anyway.

Rumor had it that upwards of twenty thousand Cubans were now in place, fighting hand-to-hand in the bush. Tony's unit was meant to patrol the railroad, the so-called Benzuela Link, which carried Zaire's copper to the ocean. The revolutionary party in the south had taken to sabotaging the railroad line, effectively stopping the copper traffic for two or three months at a time. Most of the work was sentry work, but now and then one of the Cubans would step on a land mine, blowing himself to bits along with fifty feet of track. There were sneak attacks and skirmishes. Tony blew away four men one Sunday morning, as they knelt to poison the water hole that the government forces drank from.

There was no escape. They were too far inland. Tony grew less and less political, feeling more strongly than he had in Cuba that all parties were meaningless. He heard the propaganda from the north and the propaganda from the south, and it all sounded the same. He did not defend that two-mile stretch of track for a minute. He defended himself. He wished he would wake one morning and find they had all slaughtered each other, so he could walk untouched across the wild hills to the ocean, and there find a ship that flew no flag and sailed for plunder and nothing else. He began to think it was the distance he kept that kept him alive. Within six months, only nine of the thirty convicts were still alive.

Abruptly, one afternoon, they were herded together and bussed to an airfield. An Angolan colonel shook their hands as if they were heroes, while they filed into the belly of a B–52 that looked like it couldn't make it above the treetops. It almost didn't. It strained to stay aloft as it flew directly south along the veldt, the grass gone summer-gold and starred with galloping herds of zebras. The plane rattled its fastenings, like a Quonset hut in a hurricane. They landed that night on the bank of a river, and as they walked away from the plane toward the camp, a shell came singing out of the air and exploded across one wing. The plane keeled over.

They woke to a sneak attack. The fighting went on all day, all night. Tony understood even less what the sides were here. They were right on the border of Namibia. Angolan rebels, under the banner of UNITA, made raids across the whole belly of the country, as far north as the Benzuela Link. But there were Namibian rebels as well, based in the thick forests of the southern Angolan foothills. These made forays against their own government when they weren't fighting side by side with UNITA. Tony killed twelve men the first day. He was scared for the first time.

Four days in, it was clear that the Cuban losses were very heavy. Tony considered walking away from the

combat and hiding out in a cave. Then he got lucky. A
government lieutenant he'd saved from an ambush
when they were all up north suddenly had the young
Cuban summoned out of the field. He handed Tony a
packet addressed to a colonel stationed a hundred miles
downriver. As soon as it was dark Tony hopped a raft
and began to pole his way along the current. By dawn he
was out of the main area of battle, though he still had to
keep a lookout for the stray renegade. Cubans were the
white-faced enemy. It seemed everyone was out to kill
them.

He landed at dusk at the government camp, where
they ushered him blindfolded to the colonel's tent in the
forest. Tony presented his packet, and while he waited
beneath a monkey tree, an old woman brought him a
bowl of stew. He could hear the colonel and his men
arguing in the tent, but as he'd never yet got a grip on
the Portuguese patois, he could only guess he had
brought them a packet of trouble. About an hour later,
the colonel appeared outside and beckoned Tony over.

"Tell him," he said in his tortuous Spanish, "he'll
have his replacements within two days."

Perhaps it was the nakedness of his accent. Perhaps it
had something to do with a black man facing a white
man five thousand miles from home. In any case Tony
could tell he was lying. There would be no replacements.

They ushered him back to his raft and watched while
he poled away upriver. Of course he had no intention of
going back. The lieutenant would learn soon enough
that he and his men were backed in a corner, without
any hope of rescue. Tony went about a mile and
beached the raft, pulling it into the trees. Then he
doubled back and waited at the edge of the camp. He
was too good a guerrilla to be detected. When he had
calculated that the night guards were an hour from the
end of their watch, their heads nodding over their rifles,
he snuck around to the water's edge where the boats

were roped. He slipped away in a rowboat.

It took him two days to reach the coast. For the
longest time it was all jungle, with snakes dangling out
of the trees above the current and fat macaws bellowing
in the branches. At last he came out into a tidal plain
where the water buffalo dozed in the eddies. Scarcely a
sign of human life, except here and there a village on
stilts in the marshes, looking the way it must have
looked a thousand years ago. Tony hated it all. He
longed for the noise of a city, the crowds and the risks
and the scramble for power. He hated this empty virgin
land.

The port at the mouth of the river was only two
streets deep, barely civilized compared to Luanda. Yet
even here the architecture was a kind of colonial ginger-
bread, improbable and charming. Tony walked about
with a giddy sense of freedom, even though he had to
keep one eye peeled for the army police. From his days
on the docks at Mariel, he knew his way around a harbor. By midday he'd talked with a Spanish sailor who
told him the lay of the land. Most of the ships in the harbor had been waiting clearance for months, while the
paperwork piled up in the customs office. The customs
men had all been recruited into the army. Trade was at a
standstill. His own ship had finally received permission
to sail for the Mediterranean, full to the gills with hardwood and copra.

That night Tony rowed his boat across the harbor to
the Spanish freighter. He monkeyed up the anchor
chain, slipped onto the deck, and crabbed across to the
aft hold, where he lowered himself into a labyrinth of
mahogany logs. Exhausted, he fell asleep against the
rough and fragrant bark—and woke up two hours later
with a little scream, as a spider six inches across sank its
teeth in his shoulder.

He lay delirious with fever for three days, unable to
move. The heat was brutal in the hold, and he sweated

ten pounds and went into shock. The water was choppy in the mid-Atlantic, so the logs were always shifting and rumbling. A hundred times he was nearly crushed. He would have been dead for certain the night of the third day, except for a quirk in the transport of hardwood. They had to vent the hold a couple of times a week, so the wood gases wouldn't build up too much pressure. Rot would set in if the cargo was kept sealed. So they lifted the hatch.

If he hadn't been so sick, they probably would have thrown him to the sharks. After waiting two months for the clearance to leave, they didn't need any trouble with immigration. But they could see he was Spanish, and so took pity on him. They nursed him back with coconut milk. By the time they'd reached Gibraltar he was rational again. They told him they were bound for Marseilles. He hadn't ever so much as looked at a map of Europe, but as long as it wasn't Africa he was satisfied. The last few days at sea, he worked with the crew and got his strength back. Cuba seemed like a dream he'd had. The whole world on the other side of the fever was just a mass of shadows now.

When they docked in Marseilles, he stayed on board to help unload the cargo. When the immigration men came on to check the sailors' papers, he managed to slip away just as he'd arrived, down the anchor chain like a water rat. As he lay drying off in the sun at the end of the pier, he realized he had nothing. Just the second-hand clothes of a Spanish sailor. He would never go to Florida now, he thought. He would never see his family or his friends again. He thought of the fifteen thousand cash going moldy in the biscuit tin, and he laughed out loud. He'd never felt so free in his life.

He nosed around for a couple of weeks doing odd jobs on the docks, for bosses who didn't inquire too much about his credentials as long as he'd work for three dollars a day. He scaled fish at a cannery from dawn to noon, then spent the rest of the day wandering about, talking to the old fishermen in a kind of waterfront pidgin. After a while he was able to figure out where he was by looking at sailors' charts. He who had grown up thinking that Cuba and Miami constituted the major poles of the world now saw what a puny corner they occupied. The sailors pointed out Angola, and they pointed out Marseilles, and suddenly he had a new respect for the vastness of things.

He liked the restless feel of the port city, where it didn't really matter how much French you spoke, where nobody asked too many questions. He found himself an attic room in the house of a blind widow, and though he grew restless with the cannery work, he managed to steal a bicycle one day. This he used for long afternoon rides up into the hills, through the medieval perched villages to the monasteries and ruined castles that had lined this route since Roman times. For weeks he was content to be by himself, poking about like a tourist.

He learned just enough French to eat by. On Saturday nights he visited a waterfront brothel, where he paid nearly half his cannery wages to stay all night, always with a different woman. He wanted nobody else in his life just then, neither friend nor lover. If someone had pinned him down, he would have said he was resting. For once he had no plans to escape, or perhaps he was trying to give fate the slip. He even put on some weight. Where he'd come out of prison lean and tight, his face hawk-thin with its burning eyes, now he ate whole loaves of bread from the basket of his bicycle as he drove around. He guzzled forty-cent wine from a goatskin. From the look of him he was settling down to be a lazy Bohemian. After a couple of months he wouldn't have looked out of place with a sketchpad, wearing a beret.

But if anyone thought he had outgrown his ambition and put away his dreams, they were much mistaken. It

was just that for once he wasn't in any rush. It didn't
take him long to find out he'd landed in the heroin
capitol of the world. He was also smart enough to know
it wasn't in the same league as selling reefer in the slum
alleys. The market wasn't local at all. But he knew that
every operation of this kind needed runners and
bagmen, and they might be glad of a man without a
country, especially somebody trained to kill.

He went at it very, very slowly. He haunted the waterfront night after night, and gradually fell in with a
couple of street dealers, two-bit hoods no older than he.
He knew the type like the back of his hand. They had no
ambition except to get stoned and stay stoned. Tony
didn't push them. He simply let it be known that he had
some experience dealing weed and that he was always
open to a proposition. Then he sauntered away, prepared to wait for months if he had to.

Then things began to accelerate, as if fate had caught
on to his casual ways and decided to make him jump.
One morning at the cannery, word went around that an
immigration team was raiding along the docks, looking
for illegal aliens. The foreman tried to cut a deal with
Tony, proposing to get him a French passport on the
black market. Tony could see it was a setup, that the
foreman was probably in collusion with immigration.
He refused and quit on the spot. He didn't want a
passport anyway. He liked being unattached.

Because of the heat from immigration, the job market
suddenly dried up. Now Tony had no choice but crime.
For a couple of days he picked pockets in the city parks
and cased a few shops and banks, but his heart wasn't in
it. He grew wistful for the days when he and Manolo
used to talk their way into the houses of the rich in
Havana and pocket everything that wasn't nailed down.
There he had had his first real taste of privilege. That
was what he wanted now, more than he wanted to shoot
up a bank and paw through bags of currency.

Restless and brooding, he stopped on his way out one morning to ask the widow if she needed anything. Almost in spite of himself he'd permitted a certain friendly intercourse between them. Perhaps he'd let down his guard because she was blind: there was no way she could finger him. He was almost shamefaced when he did errands for her, as if he feared somebody would notice and accuse him of being a good boy.

He found her out in the kitchen yard, washing clothes in a big tin tub. As they exchanged a few minimal words of French, he happened to glance along the clothesline. Billowing there and drying in the sun was a whole wardrobe of priest's vestments—cassock and surplice and collar, hand-edged linen, richly brocaded capes shimmering with Easter. When Tony asked where it all came from, the blind woman proudly explained that she worked in rotation with three other women of the parish to keep the monsignor spotless.

Without even really thinking, Tony walked to the end of the line and lifted down a black cassock. The widow noticed nothing as she hummed along at her work. Tony plucked a couple of collars off the line, called good day to his landlady, then raced back up to his room. The cassock was still faintly damp under the arms and along the hem, but he couldn't wait. He pinned the collar in place and ducked into the widow's bedroom to borrow her Bible. Then he was off to the western edge of the city, where the white-walled villas were tiered above the sea on the first flank of the Riviera.

It was as easy to get in as it used to be when Manolo feigned a stomach ache. In halting French, his black eyes rapt with saintliness, Tony explained he was taking up a collection to build a children's hospital. The deep-tanned Riviera matrons, wearing halter tops and bubble glasses and heavy gold bangle earrings, had just enough reflex left from all that convent training that they couldn't turn him away. They ushered him in, running

upstairs to grab a robe and fish some bank notes out of
their Hermès wallets. And quick as a cat thief Tony
would dart through the downstairs rooms, pocketing
silver and bibelots.

As he staggered home that evening, the pockets of his
cassock laden down with treasure, he was totally exhila-
rated. He set out all his loot around his room, not
bothering even to think about what he should take to
the pawnbrokers. Of the cash he'd collected for his
bogus charity, he only kept a few hundred francs. The
lion's share he brought next morning to the church near
the docks, depositing it in the poor box when nobody
was looking. He knew he was just being superstitious,
but also he seemed to want to prove he was in it for
something besides the money.

His act got better and better. He mesmerized the
women of the villas—it was almost always a woman,
whose husband was out making his fortune or dawdling
with his mistress. They begged Tony to stay for lemon-
ade. They served him lunch on their dazzling terraces,
with a view out over the Mediterranean that seemed like
a kind of sin it was so gaudy. They couldn't have been
more well-mannered in the presence of a priest. All their
virginal modesty seemed to come back to them. Uncon-
sciously they began to confess, spilling out the misery
and boredom of their lives to the dark-eyed Spanish
priest with the dueling scar and the air of a pirate.

Tony never tired of it, and more curiously still, he was
not overcome with desire. Even without the protection
of the cassock, he wouldn't have made a move to seduce
even the most beautiful of them. Perhaps his experience
with the general's woman had left him gun-shy. Yet he
seemed to be after something deeper than pleasure. For
this was the princess class that lived in the villas above
the sea. He saw them in all their splendid isolation, ac-
coutred in limpid silks and lying about in rooms cush-
ioned like a jewel box.

What was he after? Was he there to learn how their men kept them, so he would know when he came to occupy a castle of his own? Or did he really want to know what the boredom was like—the long afternoons on the telephone, the desultory shopping—so as to be sure it would never happen to any woman of his?

He couldn't say. All he knew was, he had to go back to the villas day after day. He'd ring a new doorbell and wait, a shiver of excitement creeping up his spine, till the door was opened by some new vision of sultriness, her lips wet with longing, a restless glint in her haunted eyes. Meanwhile, his room grew cluttered with treasures. Every surface was covered with clocks and china dogs and silver ashtrays and jade figurines. Tony could have opened a pawn shop himself. Every now and then he would give a trinket to one of the whores, but otherwise his store of riches seemed to have no plan, no scheme, no purpose.

He developed such a perfect air of detachment, the hoods on the docks began to be drawn to him. When he drifted about the waterfront bars at night, no longer a priest but still somehow desireless, the small-time gangsters bought him drinks and hinted at certain deals. Tony kept his distance, not yet ready to commit himself till someone made him an offer he couldn't refuse. He was no more interested in getting too involved with any particular criminal than he was with any particular woman. He still went to the brothel on Saturday night, and still he demanded a new girl every time. None of these could remotely be called a princess.

Tony Montana was a happy man that rainy afternoon when he passed the sweetshop. He had just changed out of his priest's attire, having spent the morning with the wife of an industrialist, wandering through her rose garden. He had a meeting that night with a dealer who was going to introduce him to the next link up in the chain of command. There was a chance to do some runner work over the border into Switzerland. Tony had everything in place. For once he was not the prey of forces, but had set things up so he was free of everybody else's needs.

In the sweetshop window was a tray of marzipan fruit —strawberries, figs, apricots. He smiled, remembering the widow's passion for candy. On an impulse he headed inside, patting the pocket of his sailor's pants and realizing he had no money. He chuckled softly, since for once he'd had no thought of stealing. But the old proprietor was busy, weighing chocolate for a bunch of kids, so it was the easiest thing in the world for Tony to lean into the window and scoop up a handful of marzipan. He stuffed his hand in his pocket, turned around and slipped out the door—right into the arms of a scowling cop.

It seemed like a joke. All right, the cop had seen him red-handed through the window, but it was only half a franc's worth of candy. Tony could hardly believe he was being led to the station. As they bore down the street, the gendarme tugging Tony along by his cuffed hands, Tony threw back his head and laughed at the craziness of it all. He wasn't even worried when they fingerprinted him and stuck him in a detention cell with a lot of drunks and pimps. Tony Montana was a secret now. They couldn't possibly stick him with a ten-cent crime.

But they left him there for a week, till he started to fight with the drunks and pimps and hollered at the guards. He finally thought he'd got somewhere when a fleshy man in a self-important suit came swaggering down the hall and let him out. Tony began to complain about his rights, and the man cuffed his ear and sent him sprawling. "Shut up, Tony Montana," he sneered. "You got a one-way ticket to Havana, compliments of the French government. Save your breath for Castro."

All the way back in the plane, Tony kept revolving it over and over in his mind. He couldn't believe they'd tracked down who he really was. He thought Tony Montana had disappeared in the hills of Angola. Tony Montana had died on a ship in the mid-Atlantic. It was something to learn, that the world had a network subtle enough to pick up a nobody. Your store of treasures didn't help you a bit, nor your best disguises, nor all the princely women who'd told you the story of their lives.

It was the last thing he would learn about the world for the next five years. Back in Havana they put him on trial for twenty minutes—desertion—and then he was sentenced to twenty years. Twenty years was life these days. Nobody lived past forty in a Cuban jail, not since the revolution. Tony Montana, the one they would call Scarface, was led away in a stunned silence. The key that turned in the lock was forever.

Only Tony Montana himself knew there would be a next chance. He couldn't have learned what he'd learned for nothing. A man who had a destiny had to have three chances. And so he waited, month after month. He needed no one. He wanted nothing. All he knew was this: his apprenticeship was done. When he next got out he would own the world, or leave it in ashes before they'd ever take him again.

Chapter Two

THE WIND HAD been rising all night in the Florida Straits. By dawn the waves were fifteen feet, and only the barest bruise of day got through the moiling clouds. Lightning shot the sea, and the thunder fell like bombs. The trawler had gone astray about two A.M., but the captain didn't find out till after five, when he came up to relieve the drunken sailor nodding in the wheelhouse. Now the captain sat at the shortwave, probing a break in the static. With so many overfilled boats in the Straits, he doubted the Coast Guard would answer a "Mayday." But he knew every groan in his ship, and it felt like she might break up from the strain and the extra weight. He had a boat for maybe sixty. There were two hundred and thirty-four people aboard.

Most of the refugees were huddling on the deck. They held to their families in pitiful clumps, the thin blankets tented about them soaking wet from the spray of the waves. A toothless retard, half-naked, his shirt draped around his head, capered around the deck, giggling and pointing a finger at the storm. The men with their families shoved him away, and he caromed from group to group, spinning his laugh like an incantation. Every time the ship rose up on an angry swell, a chatter like a tribe of monkeys rose from the crowd on deck. There was panic, but they didn't dare move for fear they would be thrown overboard.

Tony stayed close to Manolo, right up at the prow of the ship. The younger man lay curled and shivering on the anchor chain. He'd been vomiting his guts out all night long. At each heave of the ship he groaned and cursed, but softly, like a man praying. He had no strength left to shout. Tony, meanwhile, leaned out over the rail of the ship, dousing his face in the sea spray. He laughed at the power of the storm. He almost seemed to be urging it to greater heights, shouting into the wind as if he was master of the revels. He dropped to Manolo's side and shook him.

"Whatsa matter, chico?"

"I wish I was back in my cell," said Manolo, moaning through gritted teeth. "I miss the cockroaches."

"Hey, babe, this is good for you. Clean out your system. In a month you'll be eating lobster. Steaks this thick," he said, holding his thumb and forefinger four inches apart.

Manolo retched. With a shaking hand he fingered a small Negrito charm on a chain around his neck. "We've had it, Tony," he whispered. "Yemaya is angry with us."

"Oh shit, not you," retorted Tony with disdain. He'd managed to duck the Afro-Catholic malarkey all the while he was growing up, but the prisons were rife with it. Men in cages needed their mystic fix. Tony looked down at the cheap glass charm—Chango, god of fire and thunder, his sharp teeth glinting, his eyes rolling deliriously, head crowned in gold. Chango had no power on the sea. The sea was Yemaya's kingdom.

"Help me, Tony, while we still got time. All we

need's a pin. Little rouge—little eye shadow. Ask one o'
them broads." His trembling hand gripped Tony's
shirt. He was practically crying.

"Knock it off!" cried Tony, pulling away. "I don't
go for that mystical shit. It's your fear talking, chico.
You make your own fate. There's no such thing as gods.
You hear me?"

As if in answer, the mainmast shuddered and began
to crack. Planks flew up from the deck, and deep in the
belly of the ship timbers began to rend. The captain
came scrambling out of the wheelhouse. He looked up
at the mast and slowly crossed himself. The refugees
had scattered from their huddles. Screaming and stam-
peding, they raced for the rails. Their eyes were riveted
on the quaking mast, trying to gauge where it would
fall. A huge wave broke on the starboard side, sucking
ten people into the sea.

Manolo rose to his knees and drummed his fists on
Tony's hip. "See what you did!" he bellowed. "Yemaya heard you! Take it back!"

Tony stood with his feet apart, his gaze wild as he
searched the deck. He seemed to be the only one still
upright. The others just clung to the rails and pleaded at
the sky. Those who'd lost their relatives to the surging
of the waves raged and gnashed their teeth. Nothing
could comfort them. Tony saw a couple of sailors cutting free the lifeboats below the wheelhouse, close under
the swaying and splintering mast. He reached down and
dragged his raving cousin to his feet.

"You shut up now, chico. We're getting off this
tub."

He gripped Manolo about the shoulders, and they
lurched across the heaving deck. Another wave hit them
broadside. Tony and Manolo went sprawling, and another handful of refugees tumbled into the sea. One of
the lifeboats sprang loose from its fittings and slid down
the deck. Only one boat still held in its ropes, ready to
be launched to the open water. Tony crawled to it, one

hand gripping Manolo's collar. The younger man had passed out.

The mast came down with a shattering roar, crushing the wheelhouse, cutting a horrible swath along the port side of the prow. Several refugees were pinned. Others were knocked in the water. Now they could hear the tearing down below, as the bones of the ship broke up and the sea began to pour. Tony hauled Manolo into the lifeboat. He beckoned to several people at the rail, but they were in shock. Only the quick and the strong made their desperate way to the safety of the dory. Ten or twelve had clambered in when the last rope snapped, flinging the lifeboat over the side. It smashed into the water.

Tony grabbed the rudder. One of the sailors took the oars. The sea was so rough, they were pulling away from the trawler fast. The air was thick with the shriek of refugees, as those in the water struggled to stay afloat. Several of the men in the lifeboat reached out over the sides to the women and children, hauling aboard perhaps twenty in the first chaotic minutes. Tony tried to keep steering in a circle, but a wave would nearly swamp them and toss them aside. When he next caught sight of the trawler, it was a couple of hundred yards away. It still held together, but even in the gale-force wind Tony could hear the wail of surrender rising from its deck.

A strange and giddy laugh made Tony turn his head. The toothless retard had just been fished from the water. Practically naked, he stood in the lifeboat and clapped his hands, swaying to the beat of the storm as if it was music. Everyone else looked half-dead with grief and exhaustion. An angry sailor, outraged to hear such levity, grabbed the retard around the neck and made as if to toss him back in the water. Only a brutal cry from Tony managed to stop him. The retard subsided and sank to the floor of the boat.

There was nobody left in the water. Though they

peeled their eyes and circled about, they saw nothing in the stormy waves. It was as if Yemaya had sucked them down to her dark cave at the bottom. Tony's jaw was grim as he looked at the pitiful band of survivors—twenty-five, thirty at most, in a boat that would have held fifty. Manolo stirred below him and opened his eyes. He looked around gravely at the shivering refugees, then up at Tony. His eyes asked the question he couldn't speak: *We gonna make it?* Tony nodded.

Suddenly one of the sailors let out a cry. He was pointing at something far out in the water. Tony squinted into the wind till he saw it: a boy, holding tight to a scrap of timber, bobbed up and down in the waves. In a flash Tony had shifted course, and the sailor at the oars poured on his strength. A shout of hope went up in the boat. Everyone's eyes were fixed on the figure of the boy. It was as if they could endure their losses if only they could be granted this one small reprieve.

The boy had seen them now. They shouted and waved encouragement as the lifeboat closed the distance. Manolo manned a second pair of oars. It seemed they would make it in time, in spite of the surging waves. They were only fifty feet away. Now Tony could see the look of shock and numbness in the boy's white face. He had reached the end of his strength, and he didn't seem able to focus on his rescuers. The refugees kept calling, as if they could will the life back into him. Thirty feet now. Twenty-five. The boy let go of the timber and slipped beneath the surface.

A wail of pain went up in the lifeboat, twin to the wail that rose from the deck of the trawler. The rowers' faces were beet red as they strained against the sea. the boy's face broke the surface; one hand clutched the air. Tony roared a curse of rage at the raw, indifferent sky. He suddenly felt he was going to explode. He tore off his shoes, jumped up on the gunwale, and dove into the whirling current.

He hadn't swum in five years, since the languid days

in the harbor at Marseilles. If he'd thought about it, he would have realized there was no way he could swim in such an angry sea. But he didn't think; he just moved. He reached the spot where the boy went down. He was just visible beneath the surface, adrift and not even struggling now. Tony went under and dragged him up. He was deadweight as he choked to breathe. Tony crawled back toward the boat with his one free arm. All the refugees were shouting with joy. Manolo grinned at the rudder, shaking his head at his crazy friend.

Then the sea did a curious twist, like a woman turning restless in her sleep. Where Tony had been a bare ten feet from the boat, suddenly it was twenty feet. A whirl-pool seemed to have caught at the boat, so Manolo couldn't keep it steady for the rescue. A wave slapped Tony and left him gasping. He realized he hadn't much strength at all. The boy was conscious, but he couldn't help. Tony paddled frantically to stay afloat. Over the crest of the waves he could see the lifeboat drifting off. The refugees watched in stunned silence. The cheering had stopped.

The retard stood up in the stern and started to laugh again. They turned on him now as if they would kill him for sure. He thought it was all a game. He pulled from beneath the rear seat an inner tube, black rubber and spattered with patches. He whirled in a pirouette and flung it with all his might. It needed the strength of a madman. The inner tube dropped to the water a couple of yards from Tony. The cords were standing out in Tony's neck as he groped toward it. In the end the sea took pity on him and waved him the last few feet. He grabbed it. The boy climbed onto it.

A wild hurrah went up in the lifeboat. Manolo had to shout them down, or they would have tipped it over. The retard kept on twirling, lost in a gleeful jig, but Manolo let him go on dancing. He knew good luck when he saw it. He sent up a silent prayer to Yemaya, as he watched Tony clamber up into the tube and settle the boy in his lap. They were drifting further and further off. Tony waved once, and Manolo waved back. They would not meet again till God knew where. But yes, they were going to make it. Nothing could stop them now.

The trawler did not break up. It shipped an enormous amount of water, but it was stubborn, having outlived twenty years of hurricanes in the Straits. Powerless, it drifted west till it ran aground in the Keys. Twenty-nine people were lost overboard, another thirty-two recovered from the lifeboat. It was hard to be sure about the numbers, since the captain's list was lost when the wheelhouse was crushed. The U.S. agencies had lists of their own, but they'd proven to be notoriously inaccurate. Enormous changes had been made at the last minute, when the boats were being loaded in Havana. In the case of the trawler, they had to trust the refugees themselves for the information. This only made the bureaucratic tangle more of a nightmare than it usually was.

Fortuitously, the lifeboat came to rest at Miami Beach. The storm ended just before dawn, and they rolled in on a beautiful set of breakers, beaching right outside the Fontainebleau Hotel as the sun poured in from Africa. Manolo and thirty others stepped from the boat onto their new homeland. They walked up the powdered beach to the hotel's outdoor terrace, where the early risers were just ordering breakfast under yellow and white umbrellas. The refugees stood in a line at the terrace wall, gaping at the splendor. The maitre d' called the Miami police, the police called the INS office, and within two hours the Cubans were on their way in a bus to the Key West Naval Station. But not before they had ruined the breakfasts of a score of well-tanned lawyers and doctors.

Tony and the boy—his name was Paco—were blown like a leaf before the wind, but they never fetched up on land before the storm was done. They bore west for a while in the wake of the trawler, but every riptide sent them zigzag. Every capricious gust tossed them back a mile for every two they traveled. When the storm did a turnabout, shifting east and blowing the lifeboat towards Miami, the inner tube seemed to ride a hundred whirlpools. By midday the next day the sky was blue, and the swell of the ocean had dwindled to a whisper. The inner tube floated in the stark noon light, its two occupants fast asleep, the eight-year-old curled in the man's arms like a kid brother.

A Coast Guard chopper spotted them as it swooped low over the emerald waters, looking for boats gone astray in the storm. Paco and Tony woke up to see the chopper descending like some vast prehistoric bird, whipping up the water as it drew close. Then it lowered its hooks, and a loudspeaker barked instructions, in English and then in Spanish, till Tony had secured them both in a sling. They were winched up into the belly of the craft, and it rose to a most majestic height and headed north-northwest.

It touched down on the wide lawn at Key West Naval, about two hundred yards from the mess, where the processing of the refugees was proceeding at an inchmeal pace. Four or five long lines trailed out into the yard. Though a squad of Coast Guard and INS officers worked to keep the lines orderly, several hundred refugees were clamoring to find their families and friends, many of whom had been separated when they were assigned to boats. But a certain hush came over the crowd when the chopper landed, as if they thought some bishop or politician had come to give a speech. Tony and the boy stepped down, flush with a sense of importance. They crossed the lawn, ignored the lines, and walked right into the building. Nobody stopped them.

Tony had already figured Paco to be his ace in the hole. If he said they were cousins, there would be a lot less likelihood of their finding out he was a convict. He sized up the row of tables along the wall as if it was a

gauntlet he had to run: Immigration and Naturaliza-
tion, Customs, Public Health, FBI, then a scatter of
church and relief organizations. His arm around Paco's
shoulder, Tony cut into the Public Health line between
two fretting families. They were all so scared, they
looked like they thought they were going to be shot if
they made the slightest wrong move. All over the room
were TV crews, doing interviews with any refugees they
found who could speak a little English.

"There is no vegetables, there is no meat," cried a
vehement woman, clutching a baby as her husband
stood mute beside her. She spoke right into the camera,
ignoring the blonde who held out the microphone, as if
she thought this testimony would ensure her citizenship.
"Two kilos of rice a month. No milk. The Russian
shoes cost ninety dollars. My husband he drive a bus, a
hundred dollars a month. How can we live?"

Arguments broke out everywhere. A young black
refugee railed at the glazed official at the INS table. He
shook his papers angrily in the official's face. "*Mira!*
Why you not listen? I am not prisoner, I am electrician.
Look this," he shouted, holding up a square of cardboard. "Union card. Emmanuel Rojas. No prisoner."

"Yes, Mr. Rojas," the official replied. "These docu-
ments are easily forged. Step this way, please." And he
prodded him into the FBI line. The rule was very simple:
all young men were convicts until proven otherwise.

Someone had gotten hold of a portable radio. A salsa
beat played loud and hot. In one corner of the mess, a
church group had set up a food dispersal. Refugees
clustered around, pushing and shoving. Each went away
with his first American ration of Dr. Pepper and Ken-
tucky Fried Chicken. Nearby, an obvious transvestite in
a clinging gown and white-blonde wig, a sort of Cuban
Dietrich, attempted to perform a song for the minicam
unit from Channel 4. When the crew turned away to
look for more political matters, Dietrich tore off his wig
and began to shout in Spanish. "They ask for iden-

tification wherever you go. There is no freedom—there is nothing there. Everyone is the same, is boring. We have to steal to live," he said with a passionate dignity. But the unit had already moved on, because it didn't exist unless it was in English.

Tony had almost reached the Public Health table when he heard a cry of joy from the INS line beside him. Paco suddenly bolted. A man darted forward and grabbed the boy up in his arms. An uncle. The pair danced in a circle, laughing with relief, and then the boy pulled the man over to meet Tony, all the while pouring out the story of the rescue. The uncle shook Tony's hand with both of his, thanking Tony effusively. "You are a saint," the man said brokenly. "Anything you ever need. My name is Colon, Waldo Colon. Anything."

A moment later they'd said goodbye, and Tony was all alone. A male nurse stepped up to examine him, shining a light in his eyes. Blood pressure. Pulse. The nurse peeled back Tony's lip to check his teeth, as if he was a horse. Then Tony stepped up to the table for the first interrogation. The official jotted down a straightforward medical history, seeming to scarcely pay attention. Then at the end, kind of casually, he said: "What prison were you in?"

"No prison," retorted Tony. "My wife and children are here in Miami. They're waiting for me."

"Mm," the official murmured, checking out Tony's short haircut, the drab of his clothes. He beckoned an FBI agent, who asked Tony to follow him. They went back of the tables to a makeshift office fashioned out of hospital screens. Two men sat at desks six inches deep in records. Cigarettes dangled from their mouths, and each sipped often from a coffee mug. They looked as if they were trying to mimic each other. The one on the left glanced through Tony's medical file and then smiled at him, addressing him in Spanish.

"So what'd you do in Cuba, Tony?"

"Construction business," said Tony Montana precisely—in English. Not even much of an accent.

"Where'd you learn English?"

"I go to the movies," he said with a grin. He had studied two years with an old priest in the next cell. It was the first instance of self-improvement among the convicts that the priest had seen since the revolution.

"Got any family in the States, Tony?" asked the man on the right.

"No, nobody," Tony said, abandoning the story of the wife and kids as being too complicated.

"Ever been in jail, Tony?"

"No, never."

The man on the left slurped his coffee and checked a list in his hand. Dryly he asked: "You ever been in the crazy house?" Tony laughed contemptuously, not deigning to answer. And the man continued: "How about your sex life, Tony? You like guys? You ever dress up like a woman?"

"Fuck you," said Tony Montana.

The two men laughed and lit cigarettes. They tilted back in their chairs, looking him up and down. Tony tried to think what power they had. They couldn't send him back, could they? They couldn't turn away refugees. That's what America was for.

"So where'd you get the beauty mark, Montana?" asked the one on the left, trailing a finger down his own smooth cheek. "Eatin' pussy?"

"Knife fight," Tony said. "When I was a kid. You should see the other guy."

The one on the right stood up, breaking the symmetry. He came around the desk and held out his hand, as if he meant to congratulate Tony. Tony made a move to shake, but the agent gripped his wrist and held it up. "And this?" he asked, pointing at a small tattoo between the thumb and forefinger. A heart with an arrow through it.

"That's for my girlfriend."

"Girlfriend, my ass." He dropped Tony's hand and turned abruptly back to the table. His partner looked puzzled. The one who had noticed the tattoo puffed with pride as he straddled his chair. He savored the notion of being one up on his fellow agent. "Some kinda code they use in the can," he said. "I seen it when I was stationed down there. Some of 'em got these pitchforks on their hand. They're the hit men. You can't believe how much they kill each other—like animals. I never seen a heart before."

"You want to tell us what it means, Montana?" the other asked briskly, furious at himself for his ignorance. "Or you want to continue this up at Fort Chaffee?"

"Listen, you got it all wrong," said Tony smoothly. "All I was in for, see—they gimme two years for possession of American dollars. See, I was planning to get a boat and come across to Florida. I hate Cuba. You understand? I'm a political prisoner."

The two men laughed, and the one on the left said: "That's funny, that's good. Real original."

"It's true!" cried Tony threateningly, stepping forward and slamming his hand on the desk. The two men didn't move a muscle. "You gotta have dollars, or you can't get anywhere. I want to *make* somethin' of myself here. I got about two thousand bucks off a Canadian tourist, but it turned out to be a trap, see—"

"What'd you do, mug him?"

Till now there had been a certain back-and-forth, as if the three of them were involved in a highly delicate negotiation. In the end they might have let him go. But now Tony lost all sense of the game. He sneered at them, and he bit off his words like a snarling dog. "Hey, what's it to you if I fuck Castro, huh? What would you do? They tell you all the time what to think, what to say. You wanna be a sheep, like everybody else? *Puta!* You gonna work your ass off fifty years and never own nothing? Whaddaya think I am? I'm no little *puta* of a thief. I'm Tony Montana, and I'm a freedom fighter got kicked out of Cuba. And I want my human rights just like President Jimmy Carter says. Okay?''

The two men turned to each other. They smiled sardonically. The one on the left offered the other a cigarette. They put their Winstons between their lips, then the one on the right flicked his Zippo and lit both. Each took a nice long drag. The one on the left nodded toward Tony. "Carter oughta see this human right," he said.

"I'll tell you somethin', Tony," drawled his partner. "We've heard all the crap before. We're up to our knees in it. From what I can gather, Castro's been cleanin' out his sewers."

"We're gonna send you up to Fort Chaffee for a while," said the first. "Let 'em do a little observation. See if they can figure out what rock you crawled out from under, before we let you loose with the other animals. Hey, Jack," he called to the guard who was standing just outside the partition, "this one's goin' to summer camp."

Tony stood tall and arrogant. "You send me where you like," he declared. "Nothing you can do to me Castro has not done already."

And he turned and joined the guard and strode out of the makeshift office like a king in exile. The two officials boiled inside as they watched him go, wishing they had the power to punish, like a proper inquisition. There was a ruckus as the next one was being brought in. He reached out and punched Tony's arm. "Hey, cousin," he said, as Tony spun around with both fists raised. It was Manolo. The two men laughed, though the guards restrained them from embracing. No words were necessary. Tony was led away, and Manolo stepped in to face the two men at the desks.

"I wanna go where he goes," said Manolo, jerking a thumb over his shoulder.

"Don't worry, pal," said the one on the left, swilling a gulp of coffee.

• • •

Of one hundred and twenty-five thousand Marielitos who made it to Florida, it was discovered that perhaps one in five had a criminal record. At Fort Chaffee, Arkansas, where thousands were interned for several months, the whole ragtag bunch of them—perverts and murderers, liars and thieves—came to be known as "Los Bandidos." As if they constituted some enormous gang about to be set loose on an innocent land, like a plague almost. The only thing the bureaucrats knew how to do was waste time, pushing their papers around and keeping the refugees contained while somebody in the State Department tried to think of a diplomatic way of sending the scum back home. Meanwhile, the ex-cons at Fort Chaffee began to band together, dealing and threatening and vying for power, the same way they had in the jails of Havana. In fact the place was very like a jail, except the facilities were better.

Every Saturday night they saw a movie, as if the brass at Fort Chaffee was trying to instruct them on how Americans conducted themselves on a weekend. There were other things to do besides brawling and stealing hubcaps. Thus they were herded together in the outdoor amphitheater. Popcorn and Cokes were passed out. Tonight they were watching *The Treasure of Sierra Madre*. Some dimwit lieutenant had decided it sounded vaguely south-of-the-border and thus might soothe the exiles. Unfortunately, the print was badly damaged, and anyway most of the Cubans had seen it before. So they yammered back at the screen and jostled and hooted among themselves. Bogart was all alone, talking to himself. In a minute the bandits would get him.

"Conscience," Bogart said. "Conscience, what a thing. If you believe you've got a conscience, it'll pester you to death. But if you don't believe you've got one, what can it do to you?"

Manolo and Tony sat in the front row. Manolo

chewed gum and wore dark glasses. His hair was slicked
back like a punk. From the black market that flourished
in the camp he had managed to acquire a pair of Levis
and a tee shirt that said: "Fuck off and die." Tony,
beside him, sat hunkered down in his seat, riveted to the
screen. He didn't even hear the noise and catcalls erupt-
ing from the crowd around him. He still wore the same
prison fatigues he'd arrived in, the arms of the shirt
cut off at the shoulders, the pant legs frayed at the
bottom. Most of the men at Fort Chaffee had accepted
the bounty of one or another well-meaning church
group, and now they were dressed in hand-me-down
double-knits, golf pants and bowling shirts. The pure
American Synthetic. Next to them, Tony looked like a
revolutionary. Well-fed and muscular now, working out
at the base gym every day, with his hair grown long and
his scar to flash, he was a curious mix of dangerous
forces. Half pop star, half guerrilla general.

Bogart died his lonely death, and the gold blew away
like a dream across the shimmering Mexican desert. As
the film flickered out, the crowd of convicts raced for
the exits. Saturday night could begin in earnest now.
Stashes of rum and PCP, weed and Vitamin Q, would
be broken out of their hiding places in the barracks. The
guards knew better than to enforce the letter of the law
all the time, and besides, the guards had astral planes of
their own to reach on Saturday nights.

Tony sat mesmerized in his seat, till the amphitheater
was nearly empty. Manolo kept shaking his shoulder.
Finally he stood and stretched, rolling his shoulder
muscles like a panther, and the two men sauntered up
the steps and out to the base proper. Manolo walked
with his hands in his pockets, very laid-back, like a
young buck out for a little action. Tony danced a bit like
a fighter, shadowboxing the humid air. He seemed
about to burst for nervous energy. Suddenly he went
into a gangster slouch and punched Manolo's arm.

"Thought you could screw Fred C. Dobbs, huh?"

The words curled out of the corner of Tony's mouth. It was a near perfect imitation. "Well, you got it wrong, didn't you? Ha ha ha!"

Manolo laughed back at him. "Me, I'd'a got away with the gold," he said, cocky and young and uncomplicated.

"You see how he's always lookin' over his shoulder?" asked Tony, darting an exaggerated look behind him. "Just like Tony Montana, huh?"

"You're a lot better lookin', chico."

"Don't trust nobody, Bogart. Don't trust women. Don't trust his own gang." Tony's eyes narrowed to slits as he took in the noisy, crowded street before them. It was hard to tell if the impersonation was over or not. "Don't got nobody," Tony whispered. "Just himself."

"Yeah, real paranoid," retorted Manolo, starting to walk again. "That kind kills himself. Don't matter who pulls the trigger."

Tony caught up with him. He was all loose and relaxed now, like he'd just worked out. "Never happen to me, baby," he said, nudging Manolo's shoulder. "That's one thing I'll never be. Never be crazy."

"Oh yeah? How do you know? Fuckin' jungle out there, *makes* people crazy."

"I know," said Tony, "that's all." The mimic was gone from his voice now. He spoke as if all his treasure was here, in the real world. He was icy clear. The only reason Tony Montana looked over his shoulder was to make sure he was still far ahead of everyone else. And he always was.

The gray and tin-roofed barracks lined the street on either side. Lights out was officially eleven P.M., but no one was watching the clock tonight. The summer air, not so much as a breeze for days, hummed with mosquitoes and a salsa beat. Clusters of men crouched in the dry grass strips in front of the buildings, tossing dice. Somebody was singing and playing a banjo, a sharp hot love song full of revenge. Various drunks reeled up and down the street, talking to themselves. Every now and then a fight would break out between two of them. A knife would flash, a stab in the arm or a slice across the face, but nothing serious. It was too hot. They were too drunk to care.

As Manolo and Tony drifted through, nodding here and there but not stopping at any one group, a pock-faced punk named Chi-Chi sidled across their path. "Hey, Manny," he said with a lazy smile. He was ripped to the tits.

"Hey, Chi-Chi. What's goin' down?"

"Usual shit, man. You want some peanuts?" He thrust a hand in his pocket and drew out a fistful of pills, yellows and reds and big fat whites.

Manolo shook his head. "No thanks, pal. I got so wasted the other night, I thought I died. I just come up for air."

All this while, Tony stood patiently by, not even appearing to listen. He watched the banjo player across the way, as if he cared very much how the song turned out. Chi-Chi seemed to know better than to offer the pills in his direction.

"How 'bout a little snatch?" Chi-Chi asked Manolo. "Pussycat name Yolanda just roll in."

"Oh yeah?" said Manolo. "What she look like?"

"She look like you, 'cept she got a snatch."

"Sorry, Chi-Chi," Manolo laughed. "I think I'll pull it myself tonight."

"If you get stoned enough," said Chi-Chi, carefully plucking a yellow pill from the pharmacopoeia in his hand, "you don't even notice who you're doin' it with." He popped the pill into his mouth and hiccuped as he swallowed it.

Tony had had enough. As the two men continued to talk, he wandered away down the street. A hundred yards farther on was the center of what they called "the boulevard." In the alleys beside the mess hall was the thriving heart of the black market, where the portable stalls on Saturday nights sold toiletries, clothing, cigarettes, booze. Here the traffic in transvestites was conducted by a gang of professional pimps, whose patter and swagger were broad as Miami. The "girls" were dressed to the teeth. As Tony ambled by, one of the marketeers called out hello, but he didn't stop.

On the steps in front of the mess, a couple of young guys still in their teens were tossing a frisbee. Across the glass doors of the mess someone had spray-painted "Viva Carter!" In the gravel yard beside the steps was a row of telephone booths, each with its door removed. Here stood a patient line of about a dozen refugees, each with a pocket full of dimes. They would stand at the phone for hours, these types, poring through the well-thumbed pages of a Miami telephone book, trying to make a connection with somebody on the outside. Now and then one of them would strike gold, hooking up with an uncle or a cousin. With a sponsor, chances were fifty-fifty that a man could be released from the army base. The hope of it kept the refugees in the phone line feeding in dimes and quarters day after day, as if they were playing a slot machine.

As Tony passed by, a handsome young man with a bushy head of hair screamed into one of the phones and slammed it down. He turned away in disgust, only to find Tony grinning at him sarcastically. "What's so funny?" asked Angel Fernandez in broken English. "You know how many goddam Fernandezes they got in Miami?"

"Hey Angel," Tony said gently, "maybe after twelve years you got the wrong number or somethin'. People like to move around, ya know."

"Lousy country," Angel said disgustedly, shaking his head as he moved off toward the alley to buy a pint of rum.

Tony knew Angel would be back in the booth tomorrow. More than any of the rest of them, Angel longed to reunite with those in his family who'd fled

Cuba during the early days of the revolution. Angel was as innocent as his name. His two years in prison had somehow not hardened him like the others, and Tony felt very protective toward him. Even angry like he was now, Angel was a sweet-tempered kid. There wasn't a lethal bone in his body. Angel Fernandez was a kind of good-luck charm to Tony. Made him feel life wasn't quite so full of scum.

"Hey sugar," called a dusky voice beside him. Tony turned and stared at a bone-thin transvestite in a slit skirt, with a bust like a shelf in a tight-fitting blouse. He was smoking a cigarette, standing against the wall because he was still a little wobbly in high heels. He couldn't have been more than eighteen. "My name's Lena," he said. "You want a piece?"

"Thanks anyway, honey," Tony threw back at her. "I'm savin' it for my wedding night."

She leaned forward into the light. Even under the makeup, you could see the shadow of a beard. "I bet you love to take it, baby, doncha?"

There was a moment's dangerous silence, during which they simply stared at each other. Then all of a sudden they started to laugh, both of them. The sleek transvestite blew him a kiss and wobbled away to cruise the street. Tony winked as she passed him. He didn't care what people did. He had no moral problem with anybody here, not the dopers or the pimps or the drunks or anyone else. People ought to do what they liked. Tony was sure as hell going to.

"You're too hot-headed, that's your problem," Manolo said, rejoining him now by the phone line. "Creep had some information. Guys tell him stuff so he'll give 'em pills."

"So what's he hear that I don't hear?"

"Up in Washington they're tellin' Carter that nine out of ten of us is real bad news. They say they're gonna ship us back."

"Listen, I read the papers, asshole. You think I don't

know that? Immigration's startin' these hearings. 'Exclusionary,' they call 'em.'' Tony looked bitterly at the boulevard, where the scum of the earth cavorted. They all seemed weirdly content to live by the freedoms of this new jail. It was a hell of a lot better than Cuba. "We gotta get outa this hole," Tony said, "before they start havin' 'em here."

"Chi-Chi says a lotta shit went down in a place called Pennserania. Riots—fires. Things are gonna pop here, Chi-Chi says."

"Pennsylvania," said Tony precisely, who had heard the guards talking about the trouble at Indiantown Gap. "What's Chi-Chi got, crystal balls? *I* coulda told you we're gonna have a riot."

Manolo's voice rose an octave. "You think they're gonna let us out after that? Shit, they'll throw the fuckin' key away."

"Hey chico, this is America," Tony said softly, as if he was trying to explain it to a child. "They got lawyers here. They got a ACLU, gives medals to guys like us. Castro don't want us back. What are they gonna do with us, put us in a gas chamber? They're stuck with us, okay?"

"Yeah, well what if we gotta sit here another six months?"

"You worry too much, Manolo. That's *your* problem." He shadowboxed about his friend, throwing punches and stopping just short of Manolo's nose. "We'll find somethin'," he said. "There's gotta be a ticket outa here. You just gotta be ready. Get in shape, ya know?"

With that he turned and sauntered down the street again. Manolo, never one to be left behind, caught up with Tony and fell into place beside him. He liked nothing better than to hear Tony counter all his fears. As they approached Barrack 9, where the two of them slept, they came up to a group of very hip types who were dressed as slick and punk as Manolo. Here the beat

wasn't salsa. It was all Blondie and Pat Benatar. These
guys were ready for the real America. Tony, still exploding with nervous energy, began to swing when he
heard the sound. He snapped his fingers and rolled his
hips like Presley, till the punks applauded.

Everybody loves him, thought Manolo. *He can go
anywhere. And he don't even care.*

Tony did a back-pedal, light on his feet. He smiled at
Manolo and then began to sing. The imitation was
awful this time. "Love you love you baby," Tony
crooned. "Give it up give it up give it up."

He danced till the punks had gathered around him.
Where a moment before they had all seemed blurred
and bored and slightly exhausted, now they clapped and
laughed as if they'd really heard their own music for the
first time. But as soon as he had them, Tony stopped.
Waving vaguely, he sauntered up the steps of the
barrack, almost like it was past his bedtime. Some
things, it appeared, were only things of the minute. He
had graver matters to ponder now. It was as if he didn't
even see what effect he'd had on the group around the
radio.

Manolo, hurrying to catch up with him, realized a
man like Tony had no limits. All he needed was a ticket
out of here, and he'd take possession of the world as if it
was his birthright. Manolo's head grew crowded with
loot and power and dazzling women. He seemed to
understand that Tony was going to deal him in, no matter where it led, perhaps because Manolo knew what a
right-hand man was for.

That was who got the tickets.

Later on that night, when most of the *bandidos* of Fort
Chaffee were either passed out cold or huddled in the
alleys beside the barracks, losing their shirts at craps,
Tony appeared once more in the doorway to Barrack 9.
He walked alone through the near-deserted streets of the

army base, till he came again to the row of telephones beside the mess. The frantic calling was over for tonight. It was too late to be dialing New York and Miami, waking people up with a lot of wrong numbers.

Tony pulled a bunch of quarters from his pants pocket and laid them on the metal shelf under the phone. Then he drew from his shirt pocket what looked like a tattered card. On one side a telephone number was written in pencil. Tony dropped in a coin and dialed a Florida number. As he waited for the connection to go through, he flipped over the card—which turned out to be a snapshot, frayed at the edges and flaking. It was his sister Gina, long long ago, standing in front of the shack in the tarpaper alleys of Havana. She was grinning and pointing at her feet, showing off a pair of new shoes.

The phone began to ring far away, and for a moment Tony's face was full of repose. For once he looked young, without the impulse to dart a nervous glance over his shoulder. The phone was answered on the fourth ring. A sleepy woman's voice said: "Yes? . . . Hello? . . . Who is it?"

Tony did not reply. He stared at the snapshot as if he was hypnotized. The woman called out to somebody else: "It's nobody, Mama. Go back to sleep." Then she hung up.

Tony smiled. He replaced the receiver carefully. Then he slipped the snapshot back in his shirt, next to his heart, and stepped out of the phone booth. He strolled back through the empty streets to his barrack, hands in his pocket, kicking a stone. A rapt expression was on his face. He looked like he'd just finished talking to his girl. No, it was more than that. He looked like he'd just made love.

They couldn't escape, that was for sure. Oh, they could get over the wall all right, but then they'd be driven underground. Before they knew it, they'd end up in some slum alley without a chance in hell. The point was to get a green card, but it seemed to have to do with who you knew, and Tony and Manolo didn't know anybody. Not Out There. Because his English was so good, Tony wrote long letters to various social service organizations asking for work, but apparently Cubans were sent to the bottom of the pile, because he never heard anything back. Meanwhile, the situation at Fort Chaffee deteriorated by the day. The penned-up refugees were brawling among themselves, close to riot. All it needed was a match.

One hot afternoon, in the outdoor boxing ring behind the gym, Tony was putting away his fourth opponent in a row. His white satin trunks soaked with sweat, his face beet-red in the headgear, Tony shuffled and feinted, digging in and battering a young punk who was twenty pounds heavier than he was. Thirty or forty ex-cons stood around watching the fight, shouting encouragement to one or another of the opponents. A lot of money rode on the match. The odds were 5:2 against Tony, simply because he'd been fighting for two and a half hours. They didn't see how he could keep it up.

The punk lumbered across the ring, looking to land one elephant paw in Tony's face. Tony danced left, then right, then tore into the guy. He landed a rain of punches on the solar plexus, finishing with an upper cut to the jaw. The punk went down like a fallen tree. Out cold.

"Okay Tony, knock off," said the referee as he checked the K.O. He was a corporal who was getting twenty percent of the take on Tony.

"C'mon," said Tony roughly, "gimme another bum. I'm hungry."

The corporal shook his head. Tony turned away, muttering curses, and threw off his headgear and tossed his gloves. As he ducked between the ropes, Angel came over to tell him they'd made four hundred dollars. Tony laughed and spit out a mouthful of blood. "Maybe I should stay in here for good," he said, as Angel patted him dry with a towel. "I could become a millionaire."

Suddenly Manolo came running out of the gym, waving and smiling. Though a group of Cubans were clustered around to shake Tony's hand, he shrugged them off along with the towel and walked across the yard to meet his friend. They jogged together along the track so Tony could warm down.

"You ready for the good news?" asked Manolo.

"You got me a bout with Sugar Ray Leonard."

"Better," he said. "We're outa here in thirty days."

"Outa here where?"

"Miami," retorted Manolo. "And that includes a green card. We got it made, chico."

"Yeah?" Tony stopped jogging and shadowboxed for a moment. "What do we gotta do for it? Go to Havana and put The Beard away?"

"No. Somebody else."

Tony looked startled. "You're kiddin'," he said, then after a moment: "You're not kiddin'."

"Guy named Rebenga. Emilio Rebenga."

"Yeah," said Tony, "I think I heard of him." He began to walk back in the direction of the gym, as if all he wanted right now was a shower. He hadn't said yes or no yet about killing Emilio Rebenga.

Manolo was waiting for him beside his locker when he stepped out of the shower room, shaking his head like a dog. As he dried himself, Manolo kept talking. "He's comin' in today, Tony. Castro just sprung him. Chi-Chi says he was top dog in the secret police in the old days, but then he and Castro had a big fight, and Castro put him away."

Tony's face was completely neutral. He stood at the cracked mirror across from his locker and methodically combed his hair. He hardly seemed to be listening to Manolo.

"Anyway, when Rebenga was in power he tortured some guys. Real nasty stuff. Includin' the brother of some rich dude in Miami. Guy wants the favor repaid. What do you think?''

Tony finished combing his hair. He drew his fatigues from the locker and pulled them on. Manolo didn't push him. He waited as Tony laced up his shoes. At last Tony turned to him. "If he was just a communist," Tony said, "I'd prob'ly nail him for the fun of it. For a green card, I'll slice him up like a loaf o' bread if they want."

Manolo grinned. "What kinda knife you want?''

"Stiletto."

"You got it. What else you want?''

Tony checked his hair in the mirror one more time. He stretched his shoulders in his old gray shirt like a rich man shrugging in a raw silk jacket. "You think you can get me a riot tonight?" he asked. "I might want to make a little noise. And hey, Manny, you tell your guys we don't leave here without Angel."

Manolo nodded and went away like he was walking two feet off the ground. He took the four hundred dollars from Angel and went to the alleys and picked up, besides a sharkskin jacket and a pair of boots, a pearl-handled knife. By the time he got back to Tony, about four hours later, he had spoken to several gang leaders and set up a midnight operation. The gangmen were looking for any excuse to explode, and if Tony Montana needed a decoy to cover the killing of a Party cop, they were more than glad to oblige.

Manolo and Tony took a leisurely walk past the INS office just as Emilio Rebenga was being brought in. He looked about five feet tall beside the two agents who led him up the walk. He was bald on top, and he wore thick glasses. He kept looking nervously left and right, as if he was scared that the agents would turn on him. As the trio passed into the building, Tony spat in the dirt at his feet.

It began to rain about five o'clock, and dinner was

served in the mess. Emilio Rebenga, who had no
friends, took his tray to the very last table, where only
the retards sat. He was just beginning to eat his apple
pie when Tony Montana sidled up and bent over to
speak. Instinctively Rebenga flinched. Tony said: "You
ever hear of a guy name Edouardo Tice?" Rebenga's
face went blank, and Tony barely stayed two seconds. It
was as if he knew that Emilio Rebenga would have to
think long and hard to remember. In any case he didn't
eat the rest of his pie.

The rain got worse around ten o'clock. Rebenga lay
on his bed in Barrack 4, staring at the ceiling. Suddenly
he sat bolt upright. His eyes were wide with fear as he
looked around the room at the hundred refugees he
didn't know. He spent the next half hour trying to think
of a place to hide his money and papers. He had worked
out a deal for a green card that would get him sprung
from Chaffee tomorrow afternoon. He only had to survive the one night. About eleven o'clock he began to
talk to a guard about getting some extra protection.
They dickered a while over the price, but couldn't reach
a proper compromise. At eleven-forty-seven Emilio
Rebenga ran out of time.

Six hundred refugees erupted from the barracks and
stormed the main gate. "Libertad!" they shouted.
"Libertad!" They had even managed to make some
banners out of bedsheets, emblazoning their cry for
freedom in raw red paint. One of the men in the phone
line had placed a call to Channel 6, Little Rock, and a
minicam unit arrived about ten minutes after the start of
hostilities. Emilio Rebenga ran up and down Barrack 4,
trying to decide where to hide his money. He was practically bouncing off the walls, he was so nervous.

The refugees threw stones and debris from the roof of
Barracks 9 and 10. The guards were managing to keep
several hundred at bay at the main gate, but refugees
had snipped through the chain-link fence in a dozen

places. Thirty or forty were already running away down the highway. The base had just decided to break out its squad of police dogs when Tony Montana appeared in the doorway of Barrack 4.

Rebenga froze. He was backed into an alcove beyond the rows of bunk beds, between the TV set and a pinball machine. Tony called out in a neutral voice, like someone announcing the rules of a game: "I come from the brother of Edouardo Tice." Then he stalked the room, as the noise outside grew to a clamor. Loud-speakers blasted warnings. The dogs were yapping as if they were after a fox. Rebenga fell to his knees beside the TV set. He'd been a dead man since dinner time. Now he was so scared, he only had the wit to pray that it wouldn't be long and slow, like the death of Edouardo Tice.

Tony reached the lounge area. He danced on the balls of his feet and tossed the knife from one hand to the other. His lips were parted in a kind of smile, and he hissed between his teeth. It sounded like someone had lit a fuse. Rebenga, who hadn't been to Confession in thirty-eight years, clasped his hands before him and started whimpering in Latin. Tony darted in like a sword dancer and sank the stiletto in just below the right lung.

In Barrack 6 they had just set fire to their mattresses. The smell of gasoline was heavy on the hot night air. Someone had turned a radio on, and salsa blared in the flames. Tony stabbed him in the belly, in the shoulder, and by then he was down. A deep thrust to the back of the neck, like a bullfighter, and it was over.

Tony wiped the blade on the man's shirt and walked away with a blank face. He could have done it with a single stab, of course. Till now, he had always tried to kill with a bullet to the brain. But it was as if for this, his first murder in America, he needed to leave a signature. He would not let them ignore him. He would make them pause for a moment's silence when they heard about the death of Emilio Rebenga. Tony walked out of the barrack as if he had killed some monster who barred the gate to his freedom. In the red light of the riot he stood like a conqueror. The choke of mace was swirling in the air. The refugees were being driven back. Only Tony Montana had won tonight.

Chapter Three

MIAMI STEAMED IN the August heat. Neon rippled the boulevards, shimmering like a mirage that had gone too far, till the eye had lost the power to make it disappear by going close. Miami hadn't changed in twenty years, except to get worse and worse. It was Vegas without the games. The lobbies of the big hotels still had a turquoise and orange patina, no matter how beige they were painted. Miami had stopped in the fifties, like a rich old bag with a lot of money her old man left her, spending it all on plastic surgery, tucking and snipping and ironing out her face till it looked like somebody'd died inside. The nights were slow and unbearably hot. You could only survive in Miami by revving up, and you took whatever was available—speed, coke, bennies, booze, broads. It was said there were those who didn't need any of that, who lived in Miami as dull and plain as if they were living in Kansas City, but they were a dying breed. And they never went out at night.

Southwest 8th Street, Little Havana, was what you might call the middle of the night. "Calle Ocho," the street of bad dreams. Anything could happen, and anything did. Life wasn't worth two plugged nickels, but oh was it gaudy. The Havanito Restaurante, 8th and Ocean, was the perfect symbol, for it lay at the heart of the dream. Revved up was the only way to go at the Havanito Restaurante. Some people swore it didn't even exist in the daylight, when the sun came up like a giant lizard and swallowed your brains. Havanito was all shimmer—a whore on her third Q and her fourth trick of the evening. Totally wasted. Totally gone.

The parking lot was crammed with Cadillacs and Continentals, many of them repainted and customized for twice what they cost when they tooled out of Detroit. Young Cubans in flashy nightwear, gold-thread jackets and diamond solitaire pinky rings and alligator shoes, sat with their strapless dates in leatherbound convertibles, while the carhops brought out trays of hot fudge sundaes and banana splits. The ice cream stand at the Havanito Restaurante hadn't served a child in years. This was late-night ice cream, for those who were so whacked out on drugs, so starved to death on vodka, they just had to have a little something smooth. They pigged like kids at a birthday party.

Inside, the Havanito Restaurante was a glitter dome, walled with mirrors and hung with enough chandeliers to light a stadium. The decor was Spanish-Moorish, naugahyde for days. At three A.M. every table was taken, and a glance around at the diverse beasts of the night showed what a serious social function the Havanito played in the life of Calle Ocho. The pimps and the dealers had come to the end of another long day of entrepreneurship, and now at last they had a chance to show their colors and vie for the glitter crown. Here among their own.

The waitresses moved like well-oiled troops, back and forth to the kitchen. Steaks and lobsters were the order of the day at three A.M., though most of the diners were

so coked up they hardly took a bite. It must have been
the swankest garbage in Dade County, though the waitresses had learned to doggy-bag the lion's share of it,
going home at dawn with pounds and pounds of sirloin
and lobster tails under their arm. Not that the tips
weren't fabulous. If he liked your attitude, a Calle Ocho
dealer thought nothing of laying an extra hundred on
the bill. If only everyone in Miami could have worked at
the Havanito Restaurante, there wouldn't have been
any poverty at all.

That's what it looked like out in the glitter dome,
anyway. Back in the kitchen things were a little different. In the scullery corner, where Tony Montana
scrubbed the grease off a million pots and Manolo
loaded the cavernous dishwashers, life was still lived at
$3.50 an hour. They'd been out of Fort Chaffee for four
weeks now, and they used up the cash they got paid for
the hit just getting to Miami. They were bunked with
two others in the extra room of a cruddy apartment
behind an outdoor market where chickens were sold. It
smelled like the slum alleys of Havana. The job at the
Havanito Restaurante was the best they could get. All
the refugees they talked to told them to shut up and be
grateful.

"All I can say is," Tony shouted over the noise of the
running water, "your big shot friend better come up
with somethin' quick, or I'm gonna rob me a bank. I
didn't come to this country to break my achin' back."

"He's comin', he's comin'," Manolo shot back.
"Trust me, will ya?"

When the mountain of pots was finished, they were
both drenched in their long white aprons, as if they'd
been caught in a storm at sea. They lit cigarettes and
took a break in the linen closet, peering out through a
cubbyhole into the main dining room. At table after
table they could see young Cuban guys in fancy clothes
and lots of gold, chiquitas curled beside them on the fat

banquettes, their bodyguards just across from them, missing nothing as they watched the room.

"Look at that chick, man," Manolo whispered, nodding at a booth not ten feet away. "Look at them knockers."

"Yeah, look at the goon she's with," retorted Tony sullenly. "What's he got that we don't got?"

"Money, chico. Lots and lots o' money. Coke money."

"Junkies," sneered Tony. "They got no fuckin' character."

He reached to stub his cigarette in the ashtray propped on Manolo's knee. In the dim light of the closet, Tony saw his hand all shriveled white from the dishwater. A curious mix of associations flashed across his brain. He recalled his grandfather, grabbing Tony's wrists and staring into his palms as if the old man was a fortuneteller. "You got good hands, boy," he said. "Someday they'll be picking gold right off the street." He thought of Bogart, mosquito-bitten and backed to the wall, all the gold slipping through his fingers like water. He saw his own hand gripped around the stiletto, cutting the world to bits so it would look at him and quake.

The door to the closet swung open, and Jimmy Lee, the Rastafarian salad chef, stuck his nose in. "What you boys smokin' in here?" he asked, his tongue licking at the corners of his mouth. His hair was in dreadlocks, and he had to wear it piled up under a net. He looked like Aunt Jemima.

"We're just tootin' a little Co'Cola," Manolo said.

"You wish, honey," Jimmy Lee answered dryly. "You got company out back. Looks like he died six months ago."

Manolo gripped Tony's arm: "El Mono's here!"

Tony gave a small groan, as if he couldn't take anyone seriously who sported a moniker. He walked through the kitchen behind Manolo, affecting a certain indifference. When they stepped out into the alley, Manolo went right over to where two men stood leaning against a burgundy Coupe de Ville. Tony hung back to check it all out. El Mono, "the Monkey," lived up to his name. He was nervous and crooked and feverish, seeming to smoke about three cigarettes at once. His face was pocked and pitted like the moon. The other man, Martin Rojas, was an amiable, heavy-set man with a receding hairline. He looked like an off-duty cop.

"Hey Omar," Manolo said, using the Monkey's real name as he shook his little paw, "how's it goin'? This is my friend I told you about—Tony Montana. He cut up Rebenga good. Hey Martin, meet Tony."

The two men looked Tony up and down. Tony nodded curtly and stepped forward. Somehow he made it seem as if he had stepped away. Omar said: "You can handle a machine gun?"

"Sure," said Manolo. "We was both in the army. Tony, he fought in Africa."

Omar's eyes flicked from Tony to Manolo: "Be at Hector's *bodega* Thursday. Four o'clock. We'll pick you up. You get five hundred each."

"Hey!" cried Manolo, like it was a gift. "What do we gotta do?"

"We gotta do a boat, that's what we gotta do." Omar's voice was completely neutral. He revealed exactly nothing.

"Okay, let's do it," said Manolo, smiling and nodding gratefully.

Suddenly Tony's voice broke in: "We heard the going rate on a boat's a thousand a night."

Omar grinned. "Yeah, well first you gotta work your way up to five hundred." He dropped his cigarette butt in the dirt and ground it out with his ratty tennis shoe. He began to walk around the car to the driver's side.

Tony took another step forward. Martin's body

seemed to tense, as if he stood ready to crouch and fight. Tony said: "What'd I do for you guys in the slammer, huh? Was that dominoes or what?"

Omar grinned a little wider, as if some private joke got better and better. His grin was the most simian thing about him. He looked like he'd just eaten a banana. He turned to Manolo. "What's it with your friend, chico?" he asked pleasantly. "Don't he think we couldna got some other space cadet to do that hit? Cheaper maybe?"

Tony shot back: "Then why didn't you?"

Manolo said: "Hey, it's okay, Omar. He'll do it."

Omar opened the door of the car. Martin got in on the passenger's side. Omar continued to address Manolo. It was as if Tony wasn't even there. "Just be happy you're getting the favor this time, chico," said the Monkey, nervously jingling the keys in his hand. "And tell your friend not to give us no trouble, or he'll get his head stuck up his ass."

He slipped into the car. He was so hunched over his head barely came above the steering wheel. The Cadillac came to life with a roar, and they screeched off up the alley, Manolo raising his hand to give them a last wave. Tony turned on his heel and strode back into the kitchen. Twenty more pots had been stacked in the old steel sink. Tony slipped the damp apron over his head and began to scrub savagely. Those pots were going to shine like silver before he was through.

The convoy headed down the empty highway. They'd just crossed over the bridge to Bahia Honda Key. It was two A.M. Tony Montana drove the lead sedan, with two other cars tight behind him. Martin Rojas sat in the passenger seat, muttering into a Gabriel walkie-talkie, radius thirty miles, forty on the open sea. Several voices crackled through the static. "Okay twelve, keep

coming," said one. "All clear, tango sierra." Martin let
out a string of numbers in Spanish. A second voice
spoke through the darkness: "We love ya, twelve. No
mosquitoes here."

At an order from Martin, Tony turned off into a
mangrove swamp. The road was rutted and full of puddles. Hundreds of crabs were scrambling across it. The
tires of the convoy crushed them into the mud; nobody
even felt them. They twisted through bushes that
scraped the sides of the car, over roots and shell pits that
jarred their teeth, till they veered toward a light and
burst through into a clearing. A heavyweight North
American moving van stood foursquare in the brush
above the beach. Twenty men carrying machine guns
stood guard all around it. It couldn't have driven in
through the swamp. There had to be a real road on the
other side of the clearing. It occurred to Tony that his
own convoy had been brought in roundabout, so they
wouldn't be able to find the place again.

At the water's edge, a fleet of perhaps a dozen racing
boats was being revved. Omar sat in an open Jeep on the
beach, supervising the operation. He had a radio
operator working shortwave beside him. All the guards
around the van, all the men in the boats were dressed in
olive fatigues. To Tony, it had the look of a paramilitary encampment, just prior to debarkation. On
Martin's orders, he drew up the sedan beside the Jeep.
The two other cars parked just behind him. He was told
to grab his weapon and get out and wait.

His gun was the prettiest thing Tony had ever packed.
It was an Ingram Model-10 machine pistol, with folding
butt, capable of firing eleven hundred rounds a minute.
Ten inches long. Came with a nice suppressor. You
could slip it in a briefcase easy, a purse even. Tony and
Manolo had each been issued an Ingram just before the
convoy took off from Miami. They would have to turn
them in when the operation was done. But right now, as

Tony stood by the car and hefted the thing, he felt as if he was holding the future in the palm of his hand. It felt terrific.

He exchanged a glance with Manolo, who stood by the car behind him. They were clearly very impressed by the scope of the operation. They listened as the radio operator worked the shortwave. "Intersection twelve September and fifteen October," said a voice off the dark ocean, "we're twenty-one karats west of you." The operator leaned into his mike. "Check twelve," he said. "We got a bullfrog croaking around at thirteen October."

Tony turned to check out the moving van and was startled to see two cops in uniform walking towards the Jeep. Omar turned from his charts to greet them. They all shook hands. "So what's happening, Omar?" asked the fat one.

"Everything's cool, Charlie," replied the Monkey. "Got a big Jamaica wind tonight. I figure we need about six, seven hours."

The fat cop whistled. "Frank's gettin' up in the big league, ain't he? Whatcha doin' weight-wise?"

"Twenty-three, twenty-four tons," said Omar.

"Okay, Omar," the second cop said. "No problem this end. We got you covered all night."

Omar reached into the back seat of the Jeep and grabbed up two paper sacks. He handed one to each of the cops. The fat one opened his, glanced inside, then stuffed it into an airline bag he carried in one hand. The second cop turned his over to the first, as if the fat one was the banker. They glanced around approvingly and made off again in the direction of the van. Tony pretended to be looking somewhere else.

The boats went out in ranks of four, like a show at Cypress Gardens. Magnums, Scorpions, Performers, Novas—Omar's men had no special preference when it came to boats, not like they had for guns. They swept

out into the Caribbean, steady at sixty for about ten
minutes. Tony was in the first rank, sitting in a white
vinyl bucket seat beside Martin. The driver was a blond
kid, looked like a surfer. At a signal Tony did not pick
up, the four boats cut their engines and came to a halt.
Martin opened a briefcase fitted with an electronic system. He unwound a long antenna cable and dropped it
in the water. A numbering system began to flash red on
the monitor. The driver was standing up now and studying the ocean through a nightscope. Martin listened
through headphones and studied the monitor as Tony
dragged the antenna through the water, circling the
boat. Suddenly a beep went up from the briefcase.

"There," said Martin, and flicked on a microphone.
He read out a group of coordinates to the fleet of boats
around him.

They started west-southwest at quarter speed, and
after about five minutes they saw the freighter looming
under the moon. She was a hundred and ninety feet, a
Panamanian V-8 built in the forties. She looked like
an ocean liner next to the racing boats that soon were
buzzing like hornets about her bows. Tony's boat was
a typical hauler: twenty-eight feet, with twin 450
Chryslers. Stripped of galleys and bunks, it could haul
up to five thousand pounds of weed.

Dozens of sweating men on the freighter's deck began
off-loading the bales into the racers. They worked by
the light of flashlamps, moving the bulky burlap out of
the holds, along the decks, and onto the pulleys that fed
down to the haulers. Tony, looking up at the sailors
who worked the pulleys, saw black Jamaican faces.
Most of the sailors were stripped to the waist and
wearing bandannas. Once Tony thought he saw the captain: an enormous man, about six-foot-six, wearing a
red motorcycle helmet.

The loading took two and a half hours. Then the racing fleet took off for Bahia Honda, each boat stacked

to the gills with bales of weed. When they reached the clearing in the mangrove swamp, a human chain of workers started heaving the bales from the boats up into the van. Tony and Manolo and three other guards stood by and kept watch. As each boat was unloaded, Tony noticed that the crew hauled it up the beach, where somebody with a big tin can would stand on the tilted deck and douse it with liquid. Tony couldn't fihure out what was happening, till the smell of gasoline was wafted toward him in the offshore breeze. He couldn't believe it. They were going to *burn* these boats? What for?

It was dawn before the van was completely loaded. The boats were all clustered high in the sand at one end of the beach. As Tony and Martin moved to the sedan, the two cops lit a torch and set the boats on fire. The first explosion was enormous, lighting up the clearing like the sun that had not yet risen. Tony had been very good all night; he hadn't asked a single question. But his frown was so anxious as he watched the boats explode in flame, easily a half million dollars in hardware, that Martin volunteered a curt explanation:

"They're stolen. We can't take 'em back. Too easy to trace."

Tony nodded. The van pulled out of the clearing and headed for the highway. Tony's convoy cut back through the swamp the way they came. For several hundred yards, Tony could still see the flames in the rear-view mirror. The waste was so astonishing, he couldn't even fathom it. He thought of the high-roll gamblers his grandfather used to tell him about, who blew a hundred grand in a single night at the blackjack table. He cradled the Ingram in his lap, sorry he had not had a chance to fire it. He thought of the men at the top, so rich they could burn it, and he raged inside with a wild impatience.

He wanted it now. He wasn't going to wait any

longer, and he wasn't going to start at the bottom
either. As he turned onto the highway and began the
long drive back to Miami, he realized he'd have to
mount an operation of his own. Whatever it took. Whoever he had to step on. At last he'd reached the place
where the streets were littered with gold. He'd seen it
now. All he had to do was scoop it up.

Two days later Tony and Manolo were walking down
Ocean Avenue, all duded up. Manolo had dragged Tony
along when he went to blow his five hundred, and he'd
even convinced Tony to toss out his fatigues and spring
for a decent suit of clothes. Just now they were dressed
in peacock shirts and tight-fitting pants, and they
walked past windows reeking with prices, pointing at all
they wanted.

Actually, Manolo was doing most of the pointing.
Tony was pretty subdued. They left a window full of
color TV's, and the next one down was a bank. Through
the ice-green glass, the workers and customers of the
Banco di Venezuela passed back and forth through the
air-conditioned reaches. Manolo ogled the lady tellers.
Tony checked out the guard's weapon.

"Twenty-five tons," he said, "figure ten million
bucks. What do we get? A lousy five hundred." This
was not the first time he had said it. It was beginning to
sound like a broken record.

"Yeah, but it's like I keep tellin' you, Tony. They got
the organization."

"I got more brains than that fruitcake Omar. His
organization can eat my dick. If you weren't suckin' up
to him all the time—"

"Look, chico," interrupted Manolo, ignoring the
bait, "you mind if we just get started? They'll cut us in.
There's enough for everyone."

"You sound like a goddam communist. I say we get
our own stash. Sell direct."

Manolo didn't seem to be paying attention. He took a step back so he could check his hair in the window. "How we gonna do that?" he asked. "We don't got any money. Hey Tony, I just fell in love."

He turned to look at the girl he had glimpsed reflected in the window. She had just stepped out of the bank and was walking in their direction. Hot Cuban girl, spike heels, in a tight skirt and lacy blouse that left nothing to the imagination. Though she pretended not to look at them, she was eyeing Tony and Manolo from the moment she caught sight of them. She stopped and opened her purse, pouting her lips as she fished for something, but really just to give them a better look. She pulled out a stick of gum, unwrapped it, and popped it into her mouth. Then she started walking again, like she meant to pass right by.

Tony stuck out his chin and said: "Hey baby, wanna fuck?"

She didn't even break her stride. She lowered her eyelids and swiveled her head toward him as she passed. "Turn to shit," she said.

Tony burst out laughing. Manolo was livid. "How you gonna score that way?" he demanded, slapping at Tony's head. "You don't got any finesse. Watch me." And as Tony looked over at him he opened his mouth, stuck out his tongue, and wiggled it up and down, quick as a baby bird.

"—the fuck was that?" asked Tony, laughing.

"You don't know nothin' about chicks, do ya? That always works. Chick sees that, she *knows*. They can't resist it." And he did it again, licking the air at sixty miles an hour, his eyelids drooping—as if he were crouched between a woman's legs, drinking her in. Tony laughed so hard, he had to hold his sides. "You laugh," said Manolo. "Chicks see me, they start pullin' their panties off, right in the middle o' the street."

"Okay, Romeo," Tony said, nodding down the sidewalk, "do your stuff."

She was a tall cool blonde in a silky dress, and she'd
just come out of a jewelry store. Very high-class. As she
approached along the sidewalk, she didn't even see
Manolo and Tony slouched against the bank. They
simply didn't exist. Manolo wasn't fazed. He flicked an
imaginary speck of lint from his iridescent shirt, and he
followed right behind her as she passed. He caught up
with her at the corner, where she paused to wait for the
light to change. She glanced up at Manolo as he stood
beside her. Manolo's back was to Tony, so all he could
see was the blonde's face. A puzzled frown came across
her features. She leaned forward, embarrassed, and
said: "I beg your pardon?" Like she was dealing with a
deaf mute.

Manolo did not reply. He must have redoubled his ef-
forts with his tongue, for now the blonde looked quite
alarmed, as if he was having an epileptic fit. Tony was
weak with laughter, watching. Then all of a sudden she
seemed to get it. Her mouth dropped open. The blood
drained from her face. She opened her purse and pulled
out a small revolver. Manolo bolted. He ran by Tony,
and Tony chased after, shrieking now with laughter.
They ducked in an alley and didn't stop running till they
came out into the next street.

"Bitch!" said Manolo. "Cunt's prob'ly all sewed
up."

Tony grinned. "I told you, chico, you don't understand this country. To get a woman you gotta get
money first. Then you got power. And when you got
power, that's when they want you. Not before."

As they crossed to the opposite curb, a car ran the
light and nearly clipped them. They both turned and let
out a string of obscenities. Affixed to the car's rear
windshield was a sticker with the image of the stars and
stripes. It read: "Will the last American leaving Miami
please bring the flag?" Tony and Manolo threw the
finger and walked on into a shopping arcade. Speakers

were blasting country-western out of a gaudy electronics store. Street vendors were selling burritos and waxed-paper cones full of fried shrimp. They sat on a bench between two planters full of dead bushes and litter.

"Okay, so where do we get the money?" Manolo said.

"I been talkin' to this guy," said Tony. "Nick the Pig. Moves a lotta cocaine." He paused, as if to give Manolo a chance to protest. Manolo said nothing. After watching Tony hustle himself a place with the dealers of Havana when he was just sixteen, Manolo knew better than to ask how Tony had met this character. Tony always found them. "He says he's got some keys comin' in tomorrow afternoon. Ninety percent pure shit. He'll let us in on a key for thirty grand."

"Thirty grand! Where the hell we gonna get that?"

"So I says Nick, I tell you what. I'll give ya twenty up front and the other ten on consignment. That means we pay him when we sell it."

"Yeah? So?"

Tony stretched and yawned. He snapped his fingers, and the boy selling shrimp looked over from his cart, a rickety homemade affair under a beach umbrella. Tony nodded at the tray of greasy cones. The boy scooped up a fresh batch and brought it over to the bench. "That's a buck fifty," he said, handing it over to Tony. Tony dug a five out of his pants pocket. He nodded the boy away when he tried to make change. The boy blushed with gratitude as he turned back to his cart.

"So he says okay," said Tony, popping a shrimp in his mouth. "Nice guy, Nick. Not too bright."

"Oh yeah? What's he bein' so nice for? He tryin' to go to heaven?"

Tony flared. "Hey, Manny, if he's messing with me, I'll nail his head to the wall. You got that clear?" Manolo was silent. After a moment Tony held out the bag of shrimp, and Manolo took one. "I figure we put a full hit on the key," said Tony. "Then we got two keys. We distribute the shit to our ouncers . . ."

"What ouncers?"

"Our gang, jerkoff."

"What gang?"

Tony gave an impatient sigh. "Marielitos," he said. "Angel, Chi-Chi, Gaspar, Hernando—all them guys who can't get jobs. We'll have our own distribution, right on the streets. At eighty bucks a gram, we stand to clear fifty G's on the first buy. Then we cut a new deal with Nick, and we're in for two keys. Then four. Then eight. Can you count that high, chico?"

Manolo nodded. He didn't say anything for about a minute, just kept nodding. He seemed lost in the higher mathematics of it all. Then he said: "So where do we get the first twenty thou?"

Tony grinned. "Where does anybody go when they need money? The bank, right?"

"What bank?"

"Oh, I got a nice bank picked out." He popped the last shrimp and tossed the greasy paper into the planter. Then he stood up and began to walk away. Manolo had to run to catch up.

"Okay, Tony, we'll try it. But we gotta plan this thing. Real careful."

"Yeah, yeah, I got lotsa plans," said Tony. They reached the curb, and he grabbed Manolo's arm and darted through the traffic. "We gotta hurry," he said. "They're pickin' us up in half an hour."

There was no point trying to make an objection. Tony had it all worked out—or not worked out at all, but you couldn't stop him once he had it in his head. They went into a discount gun shop and picked up five cheap hand-guns for a hundred and thirty dollars and change. They waited on the corner of Brickell Avenue, Tony eating a bucket of fried chicken, till a beat-up Monte Carlo, its muffler shot to hell, lurched to a stop beside them.

Angel was driving, with Chi-Chi beside him in the front seat and Gaspar in back. Chi-Chi was wrecked on something—PCP, it looked like. Manolo and Tony hopped in beside Gaspar, and the car went weaving back into traffic.

Tony directed Angel to a busy shopping mall, where a small branch of the Bank of Miami was tucked between a Baskin-Robbins and a video-game arcade. Tony had noticed the place when he tracked down Gaspar and Chi-Chi playing Pac-Man in the arcade. He never even bothered to walk in and check the layout. All he knew was he needed a small bank. The robbery would take care of itself. He must have had a wonderful intuition for the American system, for when he and Manolo and Chi-Chi burst in, leaving the others out in the car, the bank's sole guard, a retired postal worker, surrendered in two seconds flat.

The tellers and customers were ordered to the floor. As Tony and Manolo shoved the manager back to the safe, Chi-Chi was left to cover the huddling victims. As they watched Chi-Chi weave with double vision, the gun in his hand veering wildly, they hugged the floor and shook with fear. Tony cursed the manager as he fumbled with the combination. When the cash stocks were finally revealed, Tony could see there wasn't much more than a few thousand.

"You cheap sonuvabitch!" snarled Tony. "This all you got?"

"Sir, I can't control the currency supply. Every week the Federal Reserve—"

"Shut the fuck up. Gimme this," he ordered, tugging at the watch on the manager's wrist. Manolo came hurrying in from the tellers' windows, where he'd scooped up a couple of thousand. He snatched the cash from the drawers in the safe, then turned to Tony. It was time to run.

But Tony was twirling the manager around, checking out the cut of his suit. "I want this too," he said gruffly. "Take it off."

"Hey man, what are you doin'?" Manolo shrieked.

There wasn't any rushing Tony. As the manager, quaking, removed his jacket and pants, Manolo ran out to the main room to help Chi-Chi. Perhaps a half dozen people had wandered into the bank during the robbery, and they too now huddled against the floor. Manolo stood at the window, nearly jumping out of his skin for nerves, and watched for the arrival of the police. Out in the Monte Carlo, Angel and Gaspar appeared to have fallen asleep.

At last Tony emerged from the manager's office, spiffy in a three-piece glen-plaid suit and tie. Manolo beckoned him frantically, but he took his time, glancing from one to the other of his victims to see if there was anything still worth taking. Chi-Chi staggered out to the car, dropping a bag of change as he got in. Immediately he passed out, and Angel and Gaspar scrambled to pick up the rolls of coins from the pavement. Manolo stood at the door of the bank, hollering at Tony to hurry. Tony grinned and saluted his victims, thanked them for their time, and sauntered toward the door.

"C'mon, will ya!" Manolo shouted. "What are you —crazy?"

"You gotta take your time, chico. You never enjoy it otherwise." He turned to survey the room once more, while Manolo gnashed his teeth. "Hell, I never robbed a bank before. It's like poppin' another cherry, huh? You get on your deathbed, chico, this is the stuff you remember."

And with that, almost reluctantly, he followed Manolo out, and they jumped into the Monte Carlo. As Angel left the parking lot and disappeared into traffic, Manolo did a quick count. " 'Bout eight grand," he said, weary and frustrated. All he wanted was a drink. Chi-Chi was still dead to the world, and Angel and

Gaspar were passing a reefer. Tony glanced mildly out
the window, as if all he cared about was the view. "Next
time," Manolo grumbled, "we'll plan it first."

Tony stirred from his reverie. "Let's get the rest of it
now, huh? Long as we're in the mood."

Manolo sputtered in protest, as Tony nudged Angel
and pointed to a parking lot on the right. Angel swung
the Monte Carlo wide and headed in. It was a supermarket—medium-size, its plate-glass windows plastered
over with notices announcing sale items. Young housewives and old pensioners trundled in and out, pushing
carts. It was mid-afternoon busy. Not the best time for
a hit, as Manolo seemed to be trying to tell Tony,
pummeling his shoulder with both fists, cursing the
half-assed risks they were taking. Tony was already out
of the car, stuffing the gun in his pants, not even telling
them who was to follow, who to stay.

He walked in the automatic door and stood near the
registers, glancing around till he saw the manager. Impressive in the suit, he walked through the crowd of
housewives—short-shorts and halters—and drew his
green card out of his pocket as he approached the whey-
faced manager. Tony flashed the card once in the
fellow's face, then slipped it back in his pocket.

"Sergeant Montana," Tony said in a hushed voice.
"Metro Dade Homicide. Looks like there's a security
problem here. We better go back to your office."

"Homicide!" gasped the manager, as Tony prodded
him down the aisle. He was shaking as if he expected to
be accused of the murder himself.

They reached the cramped back office next to the
loading dock. Tony closed the door behind them and
drew down the shade. The manager was wringing his
hands.

"Maybe I should call the district office," he said.

Tony pulled the snub-nosed pistol from his pocket.
"All right, short stuff," he said, "I want all the cash

you got. No bullshit, or I'll drill a new hole in your head, *comprende*?"

"But I can't," the manager squeaked, looking as if he was about to fall on his knees. "It's all in the safe. I don't have the combination."

"Then you better get a drill. We got all the time in the world."

As the sweating manager rooted in his tool box, Tony bent to the floor beneath the desk and dismantled the alarm button. Meanwhile, the Marielitos had got their act together and entered the front of the store, waving their guns and shouting. Manolo was furious with Tony, but he methodically cleaned out the cash registers as Gaspar and Angel shook down the terrified shoppers. Manolo sent Gaspar out to the car with the loot in a paper bag, mostly so he could check on Chi-Chi, who looked like he'd fallen into a coma. Angel covered the clump of shoppers, an unwieldy bunch of whimpering women, as Manolo ran back to the office to get Tony.

The manager sat at his desk, looking miserable and doomed. Tony had taken the drill from him because he was so ineffectual. The safe was a joke, just a thin steel door in the wall with a flimsy deadbolt. As Manolo came racing in, the drill bit through and sprang the lock. Tony opened the door. He grinned.

"Well, well, well," he said, reaching in for a fistful of cash.

"Tony, we can't keep the doors locked out there. People startin' to bang to get in. They've prob'ly called the cops already."

"Relax," said Tony, tumbling the money into a wicker basket. "This ain't the movies, chico. It'll take 'em an hour to get here."

Manolo seethed and grumbled as Tony cleaned out the safe. When he was done, he reached for the phone on the desk, dialed "O", and waited to speak to the operator. Manolo looked puzzled. "Get me the police," said Tony into the phone, then handed the receiver to the manager. Tony winked and slipped out of the office, Manolo at his heels. "You crazy idiot," Manolo spat at him. Tony laughed.

Towards the front of the store, he stopped at the produce section and grabbed up some peaches and apples. He stowed these in the pockets of his suit. Gaspar ordered the shoppers to the floor, and Manolo unlocked the front door. The circle of people waiting to get in fell back with a gasp when they saw the guns. Manolo held the door open, and Tony sauntered out. As his gang ran for the car, he grinned at the little crowd and reached into the wicker basket he carried under one arm. He pulled out a handful of ten-dollar bills and flung them in the air. As they floated to earth, the crowd went into a greedy scramble, fighting and shoving. Tony walked on to the car. Somewhere down the street they could hear a siren. Tony climbed into the back seat, and the Monte Carlo peeled off out of the parking lot.

Manolo leaned over the front seat. His face was red. There were flecks of foam at the corners of his mouth. "What are you tryin' to do, asshole?" he yelled at Tony. "You want to go to jail, go by yourself!"

Tony couldn't stop laughing. He rolled down the window beside him, reached into the wicker basket, and tossed a handful of bills out into the traffic. He couldn't stop laughing.

It was a grungy motel about two blocks off Calle Ocho. The swimming pool was green with slime. You expected to see a gang of rats sunning themselves on the patio. Actually, the rats were all in their rooms, scratching their fleas or comatose, gnawing the cardboard furniture as they waited the fall of night. Nick the Pig had lived at the Poinsettia Beach Hotel for six years, Room 9. Since he cleared about eighty thousand a month profit, he could have lived in a condo in Hallandale, with a nice view out over the Inland Waterway. But he was a very simple man, was Nick the Pig. Money meant nothing to him. The deal was what it was all about.

Room 9 smelled like the linen had never been changed since Nick moved in. Fast-food cartons and empty Fritos bags littered the snot-green carpet. Nick sat in the tiny room's only chair, all three hundred pounds of him, counting out Tony's money in thousand-dollar piles on the yellowed sheets. It was difficult for him to breathe. He was sweating buckets, though he was dressed in only his undershorts, as big as a tent and just as unwashed as the sheets. Tony and Manolo stood by the window, which was only open about four inches, but any air at all was better than the stink of Nick the Pig.

"Okay," said Nick, as he finished the final stack of twenties. He reached under the bed and pulled out a clear polyethylene package of coke. He turned with a grunt and laid it on a table piled with dirty paper plates. There was a pharmaceutical scale on the table, three-posted with stainless steel trays. Tony nodded at Manolo, who crossed to the table to check the weight.

"Hey, you like Quaaludes?" asked Nick. "Real cheap. I got twenty-six thousand I gotta move today. I'll give you five thousand for a buck and a half apiece." He pointed across the room at a stack of cardboard cartons. Plastic bags stuffed with pills were visible in the topmost carton.

"Not now," said Tony. They had no money left.

"Why don't you just take one o' them bags," said Nick the Pig. "It's on me. You keep it for personal use. Make the girls go crazy."

"Thanks," said Tony, "but I don't use that shit." Manolo nodded. They had a full kilo.

"Don't do drugs, huh?" Nick was startled and very pleased. "Me neither. That's how come I stay so healthy." He let out a huge guffaw, shaking his jowls and his stomachs. As Tony and Manolo moved to the door, Nick waved. "Y'all come back real quick now," he drawled. "People real hungry out there. We gotta feed 'em."

Tony had arranged for the Marielitos to meet him that afternoon, so they could break it up into ounces. With the last of the supermarket money, he had rented a small furnished apartment in the middle of Little Havana—an apartment suddenly vacated by a call girl whose body had not yet surfaced in Biscayne Bay. Tony had had enough of sleeping in a bunk in somebody's sister's apartment. In a couple of hours he had tossed out the call girl's teddy bears, her thirty pairs of heels and her books of poetry, and installed a pinball machine in the bedroom and a stereo system big enough for a ballroom, the latter ripped off from a discotheque by Chi-Chi, in one of his rare lucid moments. The Monte Carlo belonged officially to Angel, but now that Tony had the drugs, it was at his disposal twenty-four hours a day.

They cut the coke with a base of boric acid, using for filler an inert substance normally bonded for vitamin pills. In its loose state, it had the exact look of Peruvian flake, the Dom Perignon of the coke trade. Manolo had rounded up seven dealers, all from among the Cuban ex-cons, many with years and years of drug experience. In turn, these dealers all had several contacts in the growing underworld of Little Havana. The newly arrived refugees were setting up very impressive careers as suburban burglars, bank robbers, muggers, pimps, pickpockets. They were beginning to make good money, and the first thing they wanted to do was get high.

When the dealers arrived, they were surprised to find the coke already broken down into grams. A thousand tiny inch-high bottles covered the dining room table. Tony explained that he wasn't giving it out in ounces because he didn't want them cutting the shit any further. It was important to build up steady customers. He wanted people to consider his product top of the line. He had learned this back in the old days in Havana, when he used to issue reefers to his dealers in the slum alleys. It was cutting off your own nose to try to pad the coke too much. Tony lectured his men with the fervor of a sales manager. He promised terrific bonuses for volume. He stopped just short of a retirement plan.

He had roughly calculated that it might take a couple of weeks to deal the whole kilogram. After all, they couldn't sell to anyone else's clientele, lest they make the wrong kind of enemy before they'd established a beachhead of their own. Tony knew how high the murder rate had risen on account of cocaine. Riddled bodies were always turning up in the trunks of white Eldorados. The dealers were made to understand that they had to move among their own, a gram here and a gram there, feeling their way to a market. Tony knew that a certain number of Cuban crooks were pulling off beautiful heists. The traffic in stolen cars alone had tripled in the month since the first wave of refugees was released from Fort Chaffee. Still, Tony figured it would take a few weeks before his dealers could feel them out and prick their fancy.

It didn't work out quite the way he figured.

They moved the coke so fast, it was gone in four days. Unfortunately, so were three of the dealers. Tony had trusted Manolo's previous relationship with these men from the streets of Havana, where Manolo had continued to run the marijuana after Tony was sent to jail. It didn't seem that a man could disappear in Little Havana. Tony had figured that if any of his dealers tried to double-deal him, he'd track them down and blow them to smithereens. But these three were in it together, and they fled Miami altogether when they double-crossed Tony Montana. Some said they'd gone to New York. Worst of all, they got away with twenty-six thousand dollars of the coke money.

Tony was still reeling from this betrayal when the fourth of his seven dealers didn't show up one night with eighteen hundred in cash. Manolo was sure he'd run to join the others in New York, and this was especially galling, for the man had been Manolo's cellmate in Havana. Manolo wanted to go rough up the guy's brother, see if they could get some information. Tony stayed calm and made a couple of calls. Around three A.M., somebody told him his dealer was down at the morgue. He'd been shot by a cop who was on the take to four different coke kings. This cop had been looking for a nice drug killing for months, just to take the pressure off. As soon as the cop found out that Tony's dealer had no connections, the dealer was a dead man.

The cops might have even come down on Tony himself, if he hadn't been quick to lay a couple of thousand around the district. In any case, ten days after he bought the key from Nick the Pig the dope was all gone, and Tony barely had enough cash to cover the ten he still owed Nick. His rent was paid up for two more weeks, and he managed to come out of the fiasco with a couple of thou in his pocket, but he sure as hell wasn't the drug king he'd imagined he would be.

Anyone else might have given up right there. Perhaps the coke business was a closed system, involving so many bribes and safeguards, such an endless seesaw of loyalty and revenge, that the little guy stood no chance at all. Most other men who'd been burned like that would have had too much pride to call up Omar and ask to be hired on for another caper. Not Tony. The fate of his first kilogram he chalked up to experience. He convinced Omar that he had his organization now, available for anything. Tony was born with a deeper pride than the sort that needed swallowing. He knew what

kind of men the coke kings wanted. He sold himself to
Omar with that winning mix of guerrilla tough and
hustler's charm. You couldn't turn him down.

Omar blew his nose on the other end of the line. Then
he said: "Call me tonight. I think I might have something."

Tony hadn't had a break in weeks. The other
Marielitos either got stoned, or they went with Calle
Ocho women. Tony stayed clear of it all. He appeared
to need nothing to stroke his ego. Thus it was doubly
strange that afternoon to see him get dressed in his
banker's suit, spiffing up as if he had a date. Manolo,
who lay in bed half the day drinking beer and watching
the tube, asked him where he was going. Tony didn't
answer.

"Hey," said Manolo, "you better be back by nine.
Omar's gonna be countin' on us."

"I'll be back," said Tony, closing the door behind
him. Even slightly drunk, Manolo knew it was the first
time Tony had ever held something back.

Tony wound his way through the lower-middle-class
neighborhoods of Southwest Miami, past lookalike
yards and bungalows. He kept glancing down at a scrap
of paper on the seat beside him, on which was scribbled
an address. The houses were resolutely neat, with
plaster Madonnas in blue-shell grottos set out on the
clipped Bermuda grass. Tony drew the Monte Carlo up
to the curb in front of a peeling stucco cottage, with
rusted screens and a cracked sidewalk and a bower of
sweet magnolia on a trellis above the front door. It
seemed a most unlikely place to be dealing dope or anything else.

Tony grabbed up a paper sack beside him, combed his
hair in the rearview mirror, and proceeded up the walk
to the door. As he rang and waited, he could see
through the screen to the living room, where a waist-
high black Jesus stood in the corner. Garish religious

paintings were fixed to the walls. The furniture was threadbare, but the place was very clean. A stout woman with a powerful face, slightly hobbled by a touch of arthritis, came in from the kitchen, wiping her hands on a dish towel. The setting sun was behind Tony, so she couldn't see him clearly. She opened the screen door with a puzzled smile. She waited for Tony to speak. Then all of a sudden she realized.

"Hi, Mama," said Tony. "Long time."

She didn't speak right away. She raised a puffy hand to his face and trailed a finger down along the scar. She seemed to withdraw inside herself, though she gave no outward sign of this except for the slightest lowering of her eyelids. Then she said: "They don't let you write in jail, huh?"

She stood aside to let him enter. He didn't offer to kiss her, nor she him. She didn't ask how he had found her. She'd been living here now for four years, under the name of the long-lost cousin who'd helped her flee. Tony set his package down on the sofa but made no move to sit himself. For a minute the two of them stood in silence, and perhaps it would have ended there, with him leaving his presents and hurrying away, if Gina had not come in from work.

"Whose car is that?" she called as she ran in, shaking the heat from her long dark hair.

The older woman drew in her breath. Tony and Gina stared at each other. He grinned. "Last time I saw you you looked like a boy," he said.

"Tony!" she cried, and threw herself in his arms. He twirled her in a circle, the two of them laughing brightly. He was astonished by her beauty—the slim and graceful figure, the dusky skin, the large-lidded eyes. He held her at arm's length and beamed with pride. She tossed her hair and pranced about him, just as overwhelmed as he. Their mother slipped quietly out of the room, back to the safety of her kitchen.

Tony moved to the sofa and reached into the paper bag. "I got somethin' for you," he said, drawing out a box with a velvet ribbon. He handed it to Gina.

"Oh Tony, Tony," she whispered, her voice choking with tears. She fumbled with the ribbon. "I thought we'd never see you again."

"Can't keep a good man down," he said, his own voice husky now. He looked gravely down at the box as she slipped the ribbon off. She opened the lid and lifted the layer of cotton. Then she gasped.

It was a locket ringed with diamonds. Tony scooped it up and held it close, so she could read the words engraved on the brushed gold surface: "Hello again, little girl." Gina laughed through her tears as he undid the clasp and fastened it around her neck.

"Hey, Mama," he called, "you think I forgot you?"

He fished a second package out of the bag and walked to the door of the kitchen. His mother stood at the stove, wiping the porcelain surface with a dishcloth. When she didn't turn around, Tony undid the ribbon and opened the box. He drew out a gold chain from which hung a gold cross. As he walked to the stove she stood perfectly still. She almost seemed to flinch as he clasped it around her neck. Gina came into the kitchen laughing.

"It's beautiful, Mama! Look at mine." She strutted back and forth, but the old woman didn't crack a smile. "Don't be such an old sourpuss, huh? *Tony*'s home. Make him a little supper, huh?"

Gina had pressed the right button. Though Tony protested that he couldn't stay, the old woman put the light on under the chicken and rice. Gina retrieved the bottle of champagne from Tony's paper sack, and the two of them sat at the kitchen table, catching up. Mama would not take a glass of wine, and she wouldn't join in on the toasts to America, but Tony could tell she was listening to everything they said.

"So Mama does piecework," Gina said, "and I work parttime at a beauty shop. Hiram Gonzalez—his father had a barbershop in Havana, remember? Hiram's been very good to us. He lends me the money to go to night school. In two years I get my cosmetology license, and by then I'll be making enough—"

"Hold it, hold it," Tony said, waving his hand to stop the excited flow of her words. "Things are gonna change around here. I got a good job now. Mama don't have to sew in no factory no more." He reached in his pocket and pulled out a wad of cash. He peeled off a bunch of hundreds. He could feel his mother staring at it. "I made it, Mama. I'm gonna be a big success in America. I didn't wanna show my face till I was sure you'd be proud of me." He stacked the hundreds neatly. There must have been about a thousand dollars. "This is for you, Mama," he said, pushing the stack to the center of the table. " 'Cause I'm your son."

At last the old woman left the stove. She crossed to the table and picked up the money. For a moment it seemed she was going to stuff it in her apron pocket. But she shook it in his face and hissed at him: "Who'd you kill for this?" Gina rose and tried to grab her mother's arm, but the old lady slapped her away. "What is it, Tony? Banks now? You shoot people down in the streets?"

"Hey, Mama," he said, "this ain't Cuba. Things are different here. I work with this anti-Castro group. I'm what you call an organizer. We get a lotta contributions. I'm a politician, Mama."

"You're scum," snapped the old woman. "Just like all the other punks."

Gina was nearly hysterical. "What are you saying, Mama? He's your son!"

"Who do you think you are, you don't say a word for five years, then you show up here and throw money around." The old woman had switched to Spanish now, and the accusations tumbled out. "You think you can buy us with jewelry, huh? You look like a pimp. Some punk's going to shoot you full of holes some day, and I'm not going to cry for you Tony. Not any more. I cried my life away in Cuba. I don't need your money. I work for my living. You leave us alone." She was panting now, and her breast heaved with passion. Tony and Gina sat silent, their faces filled with an inexpressible sadness. Mama tossed the bundle of bills into Tony's lap. "And I don't want you around Gina either. I'm not going to let you destroy her. Get out of here now, before I call the cops."

There was a moment's stunned silence. Then Tony stood up, and the money fluttered to the floor. Mama was trying to unhook the chain, but it wouldn't come, and she started to cry in frustration. "Okay, Mama," Tony said gently. "Okay, I'll go." And he turned away without even looking at Gina, because he thought he couldn't bear it. His face felt burning hot as he banged the screen door open and strode down the walk to his car. He sat behind the wheel for a moment, looking completely blank.

Gina ran out and crouched by the car. "Don't listen to her, Tony. She don't mean it."

"Hey, it's okay," he said. No emotion at all.

"She's got a lot of hate in her. Give her time. She'll come around."

"I don't got much time," he said with a dry laugh.

She gripped his shoulder through the window. "I know you done some bad things, Tony. It don't matter to me. You listening? You're my blood. I don't want to lose you again." She leaned in and kissed him.

"Don't worry, honey, I'll keep in touch. You use that money in there, okay? Help Mama out. I'll call you."

As he drove away he watched her through the rear-view mirror, waving from the curb. His throat got thick for a moment, and then he turned the corner. It was a mistake to come at all, he realized that now. He'd just been looking for a little place to breathe. But if he wasn't going to get it here, then he'd have to wait till he made it to the top. All the more reason to go for it. It was just as well to know what you had to do without.

Home had nothing to give him any more. It was weakness and doubt that had brought him there. By the time he turned once more into Calle Ocho, he felt lucky to have all that behind him. Home. Family. Hadn't he always known the safe life was for little men?

Oh he'd take care of Gina, all right. He'd make sure she was a fairy princess before he was through. But his heart beat fast to get on to the next appointment. He had his destiny to tangle with, the shape of which now flashed across his mind like a shooting star. The risks. The chases. The desperate men. He loved it all, as deep as he loved the gold.

He didn't need anyone else.

Chapter Four

THE MESSAGE WAS brief, delivered by a woman's voice Tony had never heard before: "Meet the Monkey in the parking lot. Ten o'clock." And then she hung up.

It was already quarter past nine, but Manolo had alerted Angel and Chi-Chi to be ready to go on a moment's notice. Tony swore they'd be left behind if they were ripped, so they were all clean when they tumbled into the back of the Monte Carlo. There was a palpable air of excitement in the car. Tony was driving, and Manolo beside him kept flipping the radio, looking for a salsa beat. The parking lot the woman had mentioned was the one at the Havanito Restaurante. It was the street-side office of the coke trade. No dealing was done there, just high-level meetings. As the Monte Carlo turned in among the Continentals, Tony Montana's gang swelled with the pride of having arrived.

Omar stood by a row of phone booths, puffing on a cigarette. Beside him stood a bodyguard, six-foot-six, who looked like he had an IQ of about thirty. Tony got out of the car and left the other three to wait for him. Omar smiled and shook his hand warmly, as if there had never been any tension between them.

The deal was this: two kilos of cocaine, to be picked up at a motel in Lauderdale. Colombians, Omar said. They swore they could deliver fifteen kilos a month, but their references were spotty. No one in Miami had ever dealt with them before. Tonight's buy was a test case, and if it all went as planned, Tony could count on a regular run with these guys. Once they got up to the full fifteen a month, Omar was willing to cut Tony in on a percentage of the coke, say five percent. Omar handed over a bag of cash in hundreds, authorizing Tony to go no higher than twelve thousand a key.

The unspoken thing about it all was this: Colombians were animals.

Tony nodded and walked back to the car. "We been promoted," he told the others as he drove out onto Calle Ocho. The pay for the evening's pickup was a cool three grand. Angel and Chi-Chi whooped it up in the back seat, because now they could buy a color TV. Only to Manolo did Tony murmur that they would be dealing with Colombians. Manolo grimaced and whistled under his breath. Then he shouted at Angel and Chi-Chi to shut up.

They pulled off the highway into Lauderdale about eleven o'clock, just as the night was waking up. Traffic jammed up on the strip, as the neon clubs on either side opened their doors to the glitter crowd. Young girls in packs prowled the sidewalks. A blonde in a high-collared silver lamé jumpsuit cavorted on the roof of a parked Ferrari. Macho hoods passed by in their Lamborghinis and Porsche 911's, honking their horns in appreciation. Angel and Chi-Chi gaped at the girls, moaning and grumbling obscenities.

To break the tension, Manolo nudged Tony's arm. "Hey Tony, you been practicing?" Tony turned with a puzzled look. Manolo stuck his tongue out and flicked it a mile a minute. "You gotta practice, chico," he said. Tony burst out laughing. "Gotta stay loose," said

Manolo, whirring his tongue and groaning with pleasure.

About four blocks further along they saw the bright
yellow lights of The Sun Ray Motel. At least it was right
on the strip. The blinking neon was almost cheerful as
Tony pulled into the lot and parked around the side, by
the dumpsters. He handed the bag of cash to Manolo.
"You and Chi-Chi stay here," he said. "Anything looks
funny, I'm in Room 18. Give it ten minutes max, then
you better come get me. Money stays here till I come out
and get it. Nobody else."

Angel was so excited he forgot his gun in the car, and
they had to come back and get it. For a second there
Tony thought he should take Manolo in instead, but
then Angel would have been disappointed. He wanted
very much to prove himself as something more than a
driver. In the last few weeks he seemed to develop a kind
of hero worship toward Tony. Of course Tony was flat-
tered, but he also saw it as a challenge, a test of his skill
as a leader. He felt good being Angel's hero.

As they walked through the rancid lobby and down
the dirty orange hallway, Angel fingered a pendant that
hung from a chain around his neck: Chango, God of
Fire. More than any of the others Angel kept about him
a whole junkheap of charms: red and white beads, black
hand pendants, silver bangles, all to ward off evil
spirits. Where all of these things usually angered Tony,
with Angel they seemed just another mark of his gentle-
ness and innocence.

"It's gonna be fine," said Tony, nudging Angel with
his elbow as they came to Room 18. They exchanged a
brief grin. Then Tony gestured for Angel to stand back
with his hands in his pockets, one hand on his gun.
Tony turned and knocked.

The door was opened casually by an ugly squat
Colombian, about five-foot-four, face covered with
warts like a toad. The Toad and the Monkey, Tony
thought. The man smiled and nodded at him, his bug

eyes taking in Angel who hung back in the corridor. Tony spread his arms to indicate he was clean, then stepped by the Toad and into the room. On the blue and orange bedspread sat a tough-looking little chick in a miniskirt—expressionless eyes, red fingernails, short boycut hair. The Toad eased the door closed, leaving Angel in the hallway.

"Mind leaving that open?" Tony said. "I gotta keep an eye on my brother. My mom's real strict."

The Toad shrugged and left it a few inches ajar. "No problem," he said. "This is Marta."

"Nice legs," said Tony.

Marta nodded woodenly. She did not get up. Her eyes kept flicking to the television set, perched on the bureau across the room. She was watching the "Cable Newswatch."

"I'm Hector," said the Toad.

"Yeah, I'm Tony Montana. Omar sent me."

Hector gave a mock gasp. "Oh, I thought you were the guy with the pizza," he said. He laughed, but Tony didn't. Neither did Marta. "So, you got the money?"

"Yeah, you got the stuff?"

"Not right here," said Hector. "I got it close by."

"Ain't that a coincidence?" retorted Tony. "That's where the money is too. Close by."

"In the parking lot?"

Tony didn't answer. Hector seemed to get jittery all of a sudden, and he went to the door and peeked outside at Angel. He seemed satisfied that everything was quiet. He walked across the room, blocking the TV screen as he poured himself a vodka. He held the bottle up and turned to Tony, but Tony shook his head. Hector drank and said: "Where you from, Tony? Cuba?"

"What's the difference where I'm from?"

Hector chuckled, as if Tony had told a joke. "I like to get to know a guy I'm doin' business with," he said.

"Well, I don't."

"Hey, loosen up, Tony. Marta's got real bad nerves,

don't you, honey?'' Marta said nothing. She stared at
Hector's belly, as if she could see the TV through him.

"I'll loosen up as soon as you start doin' business and
stop fuckin' around, Hector. Where's the stuff?''

Hector smiled at Marta, as if he would let her answer.
Suddenly Tony heard a door slamming somewhere out
in the hallway. Angel shouted "Tony!'' Hector leaped
for the open door of the bathroom and disappeared as
Tony reached down to his ankle to grab his Baretta. He
spun around and reached for the door. Then he heard a
click behind him. "Stop right there,'' said Marta, in a
voice that could have drawn blood.

Slowly Tony turned, raising his hands to the ceiling.
She was holding a .44 Magnum, leveled right at his abdomen. Hector peeked out of the bathroom, saw that
everything was under control, and stepped back into the
room with a satisfied grin. The door was pushed open
behind Tony, and two sullen Colombians shoved Angel
in. They carried Ingram machine pistols with silencers.
Neither one could have been older than twenty. With
their straight black Indian hair cut across their ferret
eyes, they muttered to Marta in swift Colombian slang.
You could tell from the way they held their guns how
careless they were about killing.

"Hey frog-face,'' Tony sneered at Hector, "you just
screwed up real bad. You steal from me, you're dead.''

Hector snatched the Baretta from Tony's upraised
arm. He shrugged as if to say it didn't matter, dead was
all the same to him. He sounded almost bored as he
spoke his ultimatum: "You gonna give me the cash,
Tony, or you want me to kill your brother first? Before
I kill you, that is.''

"Try sticking your head up your ass,'' said Tony.

Hector shrugged again, then turned and unleashed a
stream of hard Colombian slang on the two goons. One
of them grabbed Angel and shoved him toward the
bathroom. Angel managed to turn and give Tony a
fearless look, as if to show him how tough he was. The

Colombian dragged him into the bathroom, while his partner stooped beside the bureau and picked up a coil of rope. Marta opened the suitcase on the bed. Clearing away some oily rags, she pulled out a portable chainsaw.

Tony could hear the two men in the bathroom tying Angel up. Angel swore a blue streak till they muzzled him with a strip of adhesive. As Marta attached the chain, Hector returned to his drink and drained it. Nobody seemed to have anything left to say to Tony. Tony kept counting the seconds in his head, screaming inside for Manolo. One of the goons came out of the bathroom and turned up the volume on the TV set. A little blonde pork-chop on the screen was chirping the details of a major drug crackdown.

Marta handed the fully assembled saw to Hector. She then returned to the suitcase and pulled out a voltage adapter and a long extension cord. She disappeared into the bathroom. Hector followed. The goon came forward and grabbed Tony, holding his Ingram tight to Tony's temple as he pushed him across the room. When they reached the bathroom the goons stood on either side of him, holding his arms and the guns to his head, forcing him to look.

Angel was hanging suspended from the shower bar. He dangled from the ropes like a puppet, and his legs straddled the bathtub. Though the tape covered most of his lower face, the horror was plainly visible. His eyes bugged out, and his skin was chalk white. He gave off a queer sour smell, as if the sweat that drenched his shirt came pouring right out of his gut. Hector was dead serious. He connected the voltage adapter and plugged the saw in the wall socket.

"No!" screamed Tony. "Let him go—you can have the money."

One of the goons slapped a piece of adhesive across his mouth. He struggled and kicked, but they held him so tight he couldn't move.

"Course we can have the money, Tony," said Hector with maddening calm. "But I don't like your attitude. Omar thinks he can fuck with us, don't he? He thinks we're a buncha spics, right?"

Then he smiled amiably and flicked the switch. The chainsaw roared in the tiny bathroom. Marta was crouched up against the wall beside the toilet, watching like a zombie as Hector approached the bathtub. Angel was having some kind of convulsion. Hector reached up with the saw and sliced his arm off at the elbow. Blood spattered all over the room, but only Hector was close enough to be doused with it. The feel of it slick on his face, sopping his shirt, seemed to fill him with exultation.

Angel dangled by one arm. Mercifully he had passed out. The other arm was still tied to the shower bar, swaying like a piece of meat on a butcher's hook. Tony writhed with rage in the grip of the goon Colombians. The roar of the chainsaw was deafening. Hector stepped forward again, studying the body with a strangely abstract gaze. He reached to cut off the right leg, the same side as the severed arm, but then some grotesque sense of balance seemed to possess him, and he turned instead to the left leg. It took longer to cut than the arm.

When he was finished he stepped back and flicked the chainsaw off. The silence was the most awful thing just then. Hector turned and stared at Tony, who had ceased to struggle in his captors' grip. The hate in Tony's eyes would have turned another man to stone. Though his mouth was still bound with the tape, he made it clear he would go to the end of the world to wreak his vengeance. No wonder Hector nodded at the goons to string him up. He couldn't let Tony go now, or else he was a dead man.

The one goon stepped forward and loosened the strap that Angel swung from, and the body tumbled into the bathtub, a heap of bleeding flesh. The other goon started to bind Tony's wrist with a length of rope. Daintily, Marta moved away from the toilet, tiptoeing as she walked across the bloody floor. She exited into the bedroom, where the TV was blaring the weather now. She turned down the volume as if she had a headache. She would turn it up again as soon as Hector was ready to cut.

Hector, meanwhile, stared at himself in the mirror above the bathroom sink. He seemed to take enormous pride in the blood that drenched him, the weapon he carried. He caught Tony's eyes looking at him with murderous hate, and he smiled. He spoke into the mirror, almost gently: "Coke's not for nice guys, Tony. Coke's about blood."

Suddenly there was the sound of a gunshot out in the hall, and the door to the room came splintering open. In the split second before Manolo opened fire on Marta, Hector's eyes went wide with surprise as he looked in the mirror. The last thing he saw was the blaze of triumph on Tony's face. Then everything fell apart.

Marta dove for the bed where the Magnum lay. Manolo shot twice and hit her in the eye and the abdomen, and she crashed onto the bed face-down, as if she'd suddenly got real tired. One of the goons erupted out of the bathroom, spraying the room with his Ingram, but Manolo was already crouched by the bureau and fired once, blasting the guy's stomach and crumpling him to the floor.

In the bathroom, as soon as he heard the first shot, Tony had spun around on the goon who was tying him up. He kneed him in the gut and slipped the rope around his neck. Now he stood back against the wall, lifting the guy off his feet with a stranglehold. Hector flicked on the chainsaw and tried to slash at Tony, but Tony held the goon in front of him like a shield. Hector didn't care. He began to slash at the goon instead, as if he could cut him away from Tony. Manolo appeared at the

bathroom door, holding the Ingram. He raised it to
blow Hector's head off when Tony shouted: "No! He's
mine!"

Hector turned and slashed at Manolo, who jumped
back out of the doorway. Then Hector backed away
past the sink and slid open the bathroom window. The
goon was screaming in Tony's arms, though he made no
noise on account of the rope. He bucked and twitched
with his slash wounds, so that Tony couldn't free himself to go after Hector. Hector held the chainsaw against
the window screen and ripped it across. Then he
dropped the saw and dove through into the alley.

Just then the goon passed out from loss of blood.
Tony let him fall to the floor, picked up the Ingram
beside the tub, and snarled at Manolo: "Finish off this
motherfucker!" Manolo was standing in the doorway
again, gaping open-mouthed at the body in the bathtub.
Tony didn't stick around to hold his hand.

He dove out the window after Hector, landing in a
rolling somersault and springing to his feet like a tum-
bler, running full-tilt already. Hector, squat and slow,
had just reached the end of the alley and turned into the
parking lot. As Tony came to the corner, Hector was
scrambling between parked cars, trying to get to his
two-toned Cadillac.

Tony didn't hurry now. The Ingram swung lightly at
his side. The neon bathed him as he stalked through the
lot. Several tourists had seen him now, and they ran
screaming into the lobby, where several others were
streaming in from their rooms, having heard the explosion in Room 18. Tony had no thought of the cops.
Revenge was all that mattered. Hector had reached his
car now, but there was no way the Cadillac would get
past Tony. He'd blow all the tires out. He'd blow the
windshield. Hector was his, that was all there was to it.

Hector might have thought he had a chance, as he
tore the car door open and fell into the seat. He was
probably gambling that Tony wouldn't open fire on a

public street. He was full of delusions, Hector. And worst of all, he'd forgotten the car keys.

Tony strode forward between two rows of cars. He could hear a lot of shouting from the lobby. He was twenty feet from the Cadillac when Hector opened the door and got out. He was holding up his hands and waving, like somebody trying to stop a speeding car. He bawled at the top of his lungs: "We can make a deal, Tony!"

Tony loved the feel of the Ingram as he raised it and squeezed the trigger. And kept squeezing. It was astonishing how many bullets the gun could spit. Hector's whole body began to dance. Tony raked the barrel back and forth across the Colombian's belly, unloading the whole clip, methodically blowing the man apart. Hector's eyes were still staring in horror as the last breath of life burst from his blood-specked lips.

Even the traffic in the street stopped, forty, fifty feet away. The tall cool figure of Tony Montana, the one they would call Scarface, stood bathed in neon yellow, holding a smoking gun. It said something about the gaudy night along the boulevard that he looked just then like a man who'd broken clear. The Monte Carlo came careening around the corner, Manolo yelling from the driver's window, but for the moment Tony heard nothing. He looked down at the Ingram pistol, weighed the heft of it in his hand, then reached to his ankle to see if it fit his holster. It did. He checked the cuff of his jeans for a bulge. He seemed satisfied.

The Monte Carlo lurched to a stop. Manolo jumped out, threw open the back door, and growled at Tony in a voice that was hardly human. Tony turned and ducked into the car, easy as a millionaire. The traffic stood still to let them peel out, and they tore off like an ambulance. The air was already shrieking with sirens as the reaper, Miami-Dade division, came racing in with the body bags.

Manolo was panting and shaking so hard, it sounded

as if he was having a coronary. He drove through two
red lights in a row. Chi-Chi, who had seen nothing, was
so jumpy beside him he seemed to be having with-
drawals. Manolo took a wide curve to get off the
boulevard, gunned across the pavement and knocked a
mailbox over, then lurched back into the street. About
two blocks later they shrieked to a stop beside an
exhausted playground. Manolo slumped to the wheel,
still shaking so hard it was almost a fit.

Tony sat silent in the back seat, breathing evenly as he
stared out at the empty playground. His face wore no
expression at all, and it almost seemed that his heart
must be as dead as his eyes, that he'd grown so hardened
he couldn't feel any more. But then he leaned slightly
forward and laid a hand on Manolo's quaking shoulder.
Right away Manolo stopped gasping. The fit seemed to
pass.

"What happened? What happened?" Chi-Chi kept
whispering it over and over, first at Manolo and then at
Tony. Frantically he dug his hands in the pockets of his
jacket, as if he'd lost his stash.

Suddenly Manolo shook free Tony's hand, reached
over and smashed a fist in Chi-Chi's face. "Shut the
fuck up," he snarled. Chi-Chi whimpered into silence.

Nobody spoke for a moment. Tony was boss; the next
move was his. There was an implicit assumption here
that their survival depended on following orders. The
whole reason for having a boss was to get through a
crisis like this. After half a minute Tony spoke: "Turn
around. Go back to the motel."

Manolo questioned nothing. If it seemed like madness
to return to the scene of the bloodbath, he kept it to
himself. As soon as they turned onto the boulevard,
they could see the flashing lights blocks away. As they
approached closer, traffic was being diverted away from
the Sun Ray. Its parking lot was jammed with patrol
cars, blinking red and blue. They had enough firetrucks
backed up into the street to put out a forest fire. Tony

directed Manolo to turn into a gas station just across from the Sun Ray. They drew to a halt beside a bank of phone booths.

Tony grabbed up the canvas bag of cash and stepped out of the car. He moved to the phone booth, dropped in a dime, and dialed information. "Sun Ray Motel," he said. As he dialed the number the operator gave him, he looked across the street toward the motel. There must have been a hundred people milling about in the lot, hookers and drunks and runaways and tourist couples in polyester finery, all of them clustered around and gaping at the sheet-covered remains of Hector. In the lobby a team of paramedics attended to several people who'd fainted from shock.

A rattled voice answered. "Sun Ray, may I help you?"

"Yeah, Room 18 please," Tony said.

Miraculously, the desk clerk put the call through. Perhaps any semblance of normality was welcome. Equally extraordinary, somebody actually answered the phone. "Carlson here," said a grim and ashen man who'd clearly had enough of Room 18.

"Yeah, is the lieutenant there?" asked Tony.

"Just a second."

As Carlson went off to get him, Tony could hear a lot of commotion through the line. People shouting, people crying. Someone who sounded like the motel manager was shrilling his own innocence. Then a new voice came on the line. "This is Highsmith," it said.

"Right," said Tony. "You think I could have a word with you, Lieutenant?"

"Who *is* this?"

"I think you got something of mine."

A half second's pause. Then Highsmith continued, very very cautiously. "And what might that be, Mister . . . ?"

"Montana. Tony Montana. I'm up from Miami."

"I see. What is it you're looking for, Mr. Montana?"

"Suitcase. Brown suitcase. It was on the bed. Course, somebody mighta moved it—"

Highsmith interruped coldly. "I think you've made a mistake, Mr. Montana. That object you're talking about is mine now. If you're smart you'll get lost before I start tracing this call."

"Now ain't that a funny thing, Lieutenant. I coulda sworn this bag I got right here belongs to you." There was silence now on the other end of the line. Tony smiled as he continued. "I'm tellin' you, it's got your name all over it, Lieutenant. We musta picked up each other's bag by mistake."

A pause. Then Highsmith's voice dropped to a murmur. "Where are you calling from?"

"I'm right across the street, Lieutenant. You can't miss me. There's a whole row o' telephone booths."

"If this is a double-cross, Montana, I'll cut your fuckin' nuts off."

He hung up. As Tony replaced the receiver he glanced across at the car. Even from this far away he could see that Chi-Chi was shooting up. Manolo sat slumped in the driver's seat, too staggered himself to stop Chi-Chi. Watching his helpless friends, Tony could feel his own eyes go suddenly hot with tears. He thought how Angel trusted him. Of all of them Angel was the one who would have been content to be nothing more than a dishwasher. He only came along because of Tony. He would have done anything for Tony.

With furious concentration Tony shook the tears away. He hawked and spat in the gravel outside the booth, forcing the thought of Angel from his mind. Love nobody, that was the rule. Everybody got killed in the end. He squinted across the street, following a big-bellied man in a baggy suit as he strode out of the lobby, carrying a suitcase. The man ducked into an unmarked cop car and drove across the motel lot, veering among the several cruisers and the paramedic equipment, nosing through the crowd and out to the street.

As Highsmith pulled into traffic, he glanced across at Tony in the phone booth. Their eyes met, as cold and deadly on one side as the other. Tony thought he was going to lose him, for the cop car kept traveling past the gas station. Tony watched it drive away up the boulevard, and he was suddenly weary from all the botched negotiations. Trust nobody, he thought as he stepped from the phone booth.

Then he noticed the cop car turn into a driveway a couple of hundred yards down the road. It waited with the motor running. Tony sprinted across to the Monte Carlo, jumped in the back, and ordered Manolo to drive. Ten seconds later they pulled into the driveway beside Highsmith's car. They were right next to a drive-in bank window. A big yellow sign proclaimed: "Instant Cash!"

Tony got out of the car and went around to the driver's side of the cop car. Highsmith leaned his elbow on the car door, pointing a gun straight at Tony's belly. Tony smiled as if the gun wasn't even there, but he stopped about five feet from the car. He held out the canvas bag. "Hi, Lieutenant. You recognize this?"

Highsmith growled: "What about all that mess back there, Montana? You think I need to come out eleven o'clock at night so I can get the dry heaves? What the fuck are you guys doin'?"

Tony shook his head gravely. "Colombians, Lieutenant," he said. "Should never have happened. None o' this. Like I said, I work out of Miami, and I'd be glad to give you a call whenever I got business in the area. Frankly, I could use the protection. You know what I mean?"

Highsmith studied him up and down. Then, almost reluctantly, he pulled in the gun and placed it on the dashboard in front of him. He grabbed the suitcase, opened the car door, and got out. Still grumbling a bit he said: "Yeah, well I'm sure we can work out something."

"Why don't you gimme your card, huh?" said Tony
smoothly, holding out the canvas bag.

There was one last moment's pause, as if Highsmith
needed to take a breath before he entered the big time.
Then he reached for the canvas bag, and once he got a
good grip on it, he dropped the suitcase on the ground
between them. He tossed the canvas bag into the car.
Tony made no move yet to pick up the suitcase. Highsmith reached into the inner pocket of his seedy suit,
which looked like it cost ten bucks with the tie thrown
in, and drew out his wallet. He slipped out a card,
smoothed it a little, and handed it across to Tony.

Tony beamed like a salesman. "Hey, this is great."
He jerked a thumb down the boulevard toward the
motel. "Listen, Lieutenant, *my* people don't live like
that. I think we can run this business like professionals.
You know what I mean?"

Highsmith nodded. "Sure make my job a whole lot
easier, Montana."

"Tony. Call me Tony."

"Tony," said Highsmith gravely, and the two men
shook hands. Almost shyly now, Highsmith got back in
his car. He kept his eyes on the rearview mirror while he
backed out, as if he was ashamed to look at the man he
had just made friends with. Only when the car had
pulled away up the boulevard did Tony reach for the
suitcase and bear it across to the Monte Carlo.

When they jimmied it open, they found six kilos.

They drove right back to the Havanito Restaurante.
Omar wasn't even there, just his lunk bodyguard, who
spoke no English. He had the three thousand cash in an
envelope, but Tony wasn't interested. He demanded to
speak to Omar. Reluctantly, the bodyguard moved to
the phone booth and dialed a number. Tony grabbed
the receiver.

"You get the stuff?" asked Omar, clearly annoyed to
be called away from his dinner.

"Yeah, I got the stuff, asshole," Tony said coldly. "But somebody screwed up real bad. One o' my men got carved."

"Hey, I'll check it out right away," said Omar, jittery now. "I'm sorry, Tony. Why don't we double that fee for the night's work, huh? Lemme talk to Honorato." Honorato was the moron bodyguard.

"No thanks," Tony said.

Omar's voice was suddenly hard: "Tony, you can't keep the yeyo. It ain't yours. I don't care who got killed."

"You don't understand, do you, Omar? You just lost your place in line. I'm givin' the stuff to the boss— direct. Now where do I find him?"

Omar paused. The toughness was gone when he spoke again. "Yeah okay, Tony. We'll go see Frank, huh? You do good work. I been tellin' Frank."

"Don't kiss my ass, Omar. You might get an infection. Where is he?"

"Don't worry, I'll set it up. I'll get right back to ya."

"You do that, Omar," said Tony, and hung up in the Monkey's face.

He waited in the booth and lit a cigarette. Though he only had about a hundred dollars to his name, he wasn't going to take the three thousand. He was in for bigger stakes now, and they knew it. Omar called back within three minutes. A meeting had been set up for nine the following evening. Tony wrote down an address on Brickell Avenue in South Miami. Omar was desperately friendly.

They didn't dare go back to the apartment. They took a room in a hookers' motel and watched television all night long. Chi-Chi nodded out early. For a long time Tony and Manolo didn't speak at all. They shared a couple of six-packs of beer and kept their thoughts to themselves. They both knew Angel's body would lie unclaimed in the Dade County morgue, because he had no

immediate family. After all those thousands of phone
calls from Fort Chaffee, he'd never succeeded in finding
the right Fernandez. He would be buried in the same
paupers' graveyard where all the rest of the coke murders ended up.

About four A.M. Tony told Manolo to get some
sleep. There was no way anybody could track them
down here. Manolo stood up and walked heavily to the
bed, where he lay down beside Chi-Chi. Tony thought
he'd fallen asleep, but after a couple of minutes he said:
"Hey Tony."

"Yeah, chico?"

"I don't wanna die that way."

"Yeah, I know. Me neither. Go to sleep now."

But Manolo couldn't let it go. "Why'd it have to be
him? He was such a little guy, Angel. Wouldn't hurt
nobody."

Tony turned in his chair and fixed Manolo with a
steely look. His voice hardened. This was the boss talking now. "Look, it's over, okay? We'll be more careful
now. I won't let it happen to us. You got my word.
Okay?"

"Yeah, sure," said Manolo quietly, as he curled up
under the covers and shut his eyes.

Tony turned back to the television, where a rerun of
Bewitched spilled its canned laughter into the room. All
of a sudden the tears were in his eyes again, and this
time he didn't will them away. His face was impassive as
the tears streamed down his cheeks. Though he wasn't
good with words, a voice inside him began to speak his
sorrow. Silently he talked to Angel till the first pink of
dawn streaked through the venetian blinds. He was
sorry he was such a lousy hero. Sorry he couldn't protect his men. Sorry most of all that he still had such a
hunger to be a king—a hunger that seemed obscene
now, with Angel lying dead in Room 18.

About six o'clock he finally passed out in his chair.

The suitcase lay open on the floor beside him, all its packets of snow gleaming in the dusky light. The test pattern buzzed on the TV screen, blank and empty as the godless day that broke outside like a fever.

That evening, Tony and Manolo drove to the high-rise district surrounding Brickell Avenue, adjacent to Coconut Grove and Coral Gables. This was the real money. They met Omar in the fountained lobby of a twenty-six-story condo complex. Four or five heavily armed security guards monitored every move and called ahead to make sure Mr. Lopez was expecting them. With the coke money in South Miami rising as far as the penthouses, these condo complexes had started doubling their security. A guard went up in the elevator with them. Another guard was posted on the top floor, walking the hallway with a German shepherd.

Omar and Tony and Manolo were let in at the double doors of Apartment 2620. A hefty, Indian-looking bodyguard named Ernie led them across a mirrored foyer to a two-story living room with a drop-dead view of the city below. Ernie had rabid eyes, and he looked about as friendly as a Doberman. Manolo gaped at the swank surroundings, the white carpet and the coral upholstered chairs, the antique painted furniture and wall cases full of pre-Columbian art. Tony tried hard not to look cowed by it all. He stepped to the terrace doors and looked out at the glittering city, with the black expanse of the ocean beyond. He still held the suitcase in his hand.

"On a clear day you can see Havana," said a gravelly voice behind him.

He turned to greet Frank Lopez, who had just walked into the room and was already heading for the bar. He was hearty-looking and big-boned, and the Cuban-Jewish mix in him made it hard to pin him down, nationality-wise. He had a wide handsome face and bushy, curly hair. About forty-five. He wore a blue cashmere jacket with a red silk pocket square, and supple Italian shoes made of lizard, so that Tony felt suddenly cheap in his own punk clothes. Lopez did not greet Omar, or even acknowledge the existence of anyone in the room except Tony. To Tony he said, clinking ice in a glass: "So, what are you drinking, Tony Montana?"

"Whatever you're makin'," said Tony.

"Call me Frank, Tony. Everybody calls me Frank. My little league team—the monsignor—even the prose- cutors. They all call me Frank." He turned with two glasses of smoky Irish whiskey on the rocks. He handed one to Tony, then waved his hand at the bar, as if to indicate that the others could get their own. He took a deep drink, clapped Tony's shoulder, and led him toward the terrace. Tony still held the suitcase.

"Omar tells me good things about you boys," said Frank.

"Yeah. Omar."

"Not to mention the job you did for me at Fort Chaffee," Frank went on. Tony was thrown. The shock must have shown on his face, because Frank laughed. "You didn't know that was for me, huh? That sonuva- bitch Rebenga killed my brother. Fuckin' commies. They ruin the world, ya know? Anyway, Tony, I'm grateful to you."

Tony set the suitcase on the floor. He took a swallow of his drink. "Don't mention it," he said. "I enjoyed it."

"And about last night, Tony." Here Frank sighed and shook his head. It sounded like he'd been thinking about this stuff all day. "Never shoulda happened. We shoulda checked 'em out better."

Tony said nothing. The two men drank and looked out at the city. When Frank spoke again, his voice had deepened further. The preliminaries appeared to be over. It was amazing how little attention was paid to the six kilos. Half a million dollars worth, and it seemed just then like nothing more than a ticket to bring these two men together.

"I need a guy with steel in his veins," said Frank. "I need him close to me. Guy like you, Tony. Most o' these guys, they're fuck-ups."

"Yeah, well . . ." Tony shrugged, as if to say he couldn't decide a thing right now. But he knew inside it was the interview he'd been waiting all his life to happen. He said: "This is the kinda business I been lookin' for. It's like I got a feel for it."

"I know you do, Tony. I could tell that the minute I saw you." He clapped Tony's shoulder again. In some way or another, they had stated the parameters of a deal. "Okay, let's take a look at the stuff."

He snapped his fingers at Ernie and pointed at the suitcase. They weren't taking anything away from Tony. It was purely a matter of summoning a servant. Ernie picked up the suitcase and hauled it over to the dining room table. Frank beckoned to Omar and Manolo, introducing himself to the latter with the flash of a grin and a firm handshake, but treating him too like a hired hand. Omar he paid less heed to than the girl who scrubbed his toilet. Only Tony did he treat as an equal. They stood in a half-circle around the table, and Ernie lifted the lid of the suitcase and stepped back. Frank felt one of the plastic bags with a practiced hand, as if to check the texture of the drug. He sighed and looked up at Tony.

"Men get killed for a thousandth of this," he said. "You know what I'm saying? There's a thousand dead men in this suitcase." He shook his head sadly, not expecting a reply. "You're a real pro, Tony. You didn't have to bring it all in. I was only buying two keys. You coulda kept the rest. I never woulda known the difference."

"Stuff's no good to me," said Tony dryly. "What do I want to piss it away in the streets for? You're the one with the system."

Frank raised his glass. "You stay loyal like that, you move up in this business. You move up fast. Salud!" Tony lifted his own glass and nodded curtly. The two men drank. Nobody else did. Frank laughed: "Then you find your biggest headache's figuring out what to do with all the cash."

"I hope to have that problem real soon," said Tony.

"Sooner than you could ever imagine, Tony. In your wildest Cuban dreams." He seemed to be somewhere else for a moment, even as he smiled at Tony. Then he shook himself and bellowed at Ernie: "Where the hell's Elvira? Go get her, will ya."

As the bodyguard padded off down the interior hallway, Frank stepped away from the table. Tony followed him back to the terrace. Omar and Manolo were left to their silent cocktail. Tony had no idea where Frank came by the paternal attitude toward him, but he didn't much care. He knew he could use it. Frank gave an exasperated grunt and said: "She spends half her life gettin' dressed, the other half gettin' undressed. What does that say, huh?"

"I guess you gotta catch her when she's naked."

Frank laughed richly. Tony couldn't figure him out, and he hadn't been able to discover much about Frank Lopez, not in Little Havana. The hustlers and dealers of Calle Ocho only knew Lopez as a figure of mythic proportions. He'd fled to Florida at the start of the revolution. Then he got right into heroin, from the street up. Now he was solely into coke, being one of the first to see that the clientele was a whole lot classier, besides which they paid their bills, besides which they weren't mugging old ladies to feed their habit. Frank was one of the men who made drugs look clean—as clean as any other business anyway. Yet Frank Lopez had always lived aloof from Calle Ocho, even when he lived there. Nobody really knew him. It was said he was responsible for the key contact in the police department that made the rise of the coke trade possible.

"How long you been here, Tony?"

"Month."

"Well, see," said Frank with a swell of pride, for all the world like the president of the Chamber of Commerce, "you made it this far already. There isn't one in a thousand gets this far."

Tony shrugged. "No time to waste. Hell, Angel thought he had a hundred years."

There was a commotion down the hallway, a woman's voice swearing a blue streak at Ernie. Tony could hear them approaching, the clack of the woman's heels on the parquet floor, but he didn't dare turn around till Frank did. Frank seemed almost hypnotized by him as they stood looking out at the view. Tony had never had a father, but he'd felt a queer tightness in himself ever since he and Frank started talking. It was as if someone was trying to mold him.

"I don't see the Duchess of Windsor," said a woman's voice behind him, icy with contempt. "Who's so important I gotta hurry, huh?"

Frank and Tony turned around. She was so beautiful Tony almost winced. White-blonde, her hair tumbled to her shoulders, framing the perfect oval of her face. She was wearing a burgundy silk dinner dress that cost about two grand. She was long and lean, and she'd clearly been seducing men since she was in the cradle. So quintessentially American she made the rest of them look like kitchen help.

"It's ten o'clock, honey," said Frank, ignoring her cussedness. "We're gettin' hungry."

"You're always hungry," she replied wearily, as if the whole subject bored her to tears. "You should try starving for a while, like the little children in India. Be good for you.'' The voice was lower class and rich at the same time. You couldn't pin it down. She walked and talked like a gun moll, but she carried her head like a princess.

"Want you to meet a friend of mine,'' said Frank, reaching out to take her hand. "Tony Montana, this is Elvira.''

"Hello,'' she said, her eyes flicking over him, quick and disinterested. She looked down at Frank's hairy hand clasping hers, then went on half to herself: "Tony Montana. Sounds like something with Cagney in it.''

"No,'' said Tony quietly. "Bogart.''

She glanced up, surprised. A fleeting smile rippled across her lips. They locked eyes for a moment, and the room was suddenly filled with silence. She broke it herself, quickly, as if she couldn't bear it. "So where we going?'' she asked.

"I thought we'd head over to the Babylon,'' Frank said. He had just pulled a wad of cash from his pocket, and he fluttered it like a deck of cards, as if to make sure that he had enough for the evening.

Elvira sighed. "That's where we always go,'' she said to Tony. "Anyone wants to kill Frank, they can always find him at the Babylon. Right, Frank?''

"Yeah, go get your coat, huh?'' Frank returned the roll of cash to his pocket as Elvira drifted across the room to a large buffet. She pulled open a drawer and drew out a beaded handbag. She checked out her looks in the gilded mirror above the buffet, darting a split second's glance at Tony. Tony didn't think Frank had heard her remark about the killing, but when she sauntered back to them he drew her close and kissed her neck. "As long as it's in your arms, darlin', I'll go out seein' stars.''

"Here, put this on,'' she said, as she pulled a stream of diamonds from the purse. Frank took the necklace and stood behind her to clasp it in place, and all the while she stared into Tony's eyes, as if to say "Can you do this?"

An ink-green Rolls Royce was waiting for them in the driveway outside the building. Frank drove, with Elvira beside him. Tony and Manolo and Omar were lined up in the back seat. There was no room for Ernie, so they drove away unguarded. Not unarmed: every single one of them packed a gun, Elvira included. Frank kept up a running commentary as they drove through Coconut Grove, talking to Tony in the rearview mirror. He seemed to know some millionaire or celebrity on every block, and he pointed to their various houses with pride, as if they were all members of some exclusive club Frank Lopez ran. Perhaps they were all his customers.

Twice during the ten-minute drive, Elvira drew a small vial of cocaine from her purse. She tapped the powder out on the back of her hand between her thumb and forefinger, and then she snorted it. The first time she held the vial over her shoulder after she was done, offering it to anyone who wanted it in the back seat. None of the men in back made a move. They acted as if they didn't even see it. The second time she didn't offer.

At the Babylon Club they trailed past a long line of cars in the driveway, every one of which seemed to be a Porsche or a Bugatti or a Corniche. The public was not invited. When Frank turned the keys to the Rolls over to the carhop, Tony recognized the man as an ex-con from Havana. The carhop recognized Tony too, but as Tony didn't acknowledge that fact, the carhop didn't so much as smile. Tony was higher up than he. The gulf could only be bridged from Tony's side, and Tony had all his bridges full right now.

They went up a wide staircase, Frank and Elvira in front, regal and swank and very much a couple now that they were in public. Tony half expected a brace of photographers to appear at the top of the steps to record their entrance. The doorman, all braided in gold, ad-

dressed Frank by name. As soon as they entered, a man
in a tuxedo approached them. He and Elvira kissed
cheeks, then he shook Frank's hand. Omar and Manolo
and Tony hung back in a clump, as if they were in-
truding.

The interior was built to have the feel of three or four
plush apartments running together on several levels.
The angles were daring, the walls awash with mirrors.
From where they stood in the foyer, they looked
through a jungle of tropical plants to a swimming pool
with a dance floor cantilevered above it. Bars were
perched on several balconies, and in every spare nook
and cranny were video games, slot machines, and pinball. The tuxedoed man led Frank and his party through
a garden of earthly delights toward the restaurant.

The Babylon Club appeared to be the nighttime capitol of South America. The crowd was a mix of Cauca-
sian and Latin, mostly young, mostly rich, mostly coked
to their eyeballs. The twenty-piece band was playing
to a heavy black beat—"Partying Down Tonight." The
waitresses wore little pillbox hats, sequined halters, and
the barest hot-pink shorts over black net stockings and
heels. Rich young men, a lot of them Cuban, huddled in
groups of three and four, putting deals together. They
seemed to be trying to outdo one another with the gold
chains and the diamond rings.

Altogether, it made the Havanito Restaurante look
like Howard Johnson's.

They were shown to a table on a balcony above the
dance floor. As soon as Elvira sat down, a woman
across the way waved to her and rubbed her nose. Elvira
excused herself, and she and the other woman walked
off to the ladies'. Frank ordered two bottles of champagne, Dom Perignon '64, so they wouldn't have to
wait when they finished the first one. Then he ordered
three ounces of caviar. The music was much too loud
for them all to talk in a group, so Omar and Manolo
were left to themselves on the dance floor side of the

table. Manolo ogled the girls miserably, wishing he could put down his glass and cut in. Frank leaned back in his chair against the wall and motioned Tony to do the same. It was easier to talk flat up against the wall. There was a dead space or something.

"All right, Tony," said Frank with a smile, "now I'm gonna tell you who the big guys are." He nodded across the room to a large table near the bar. "That guy in the purple shirt, that's Ronnie Echeverria. Him and his brother Miguel they got a huge distribution setup. Controls every gram that goes into Houston and Dallas. Then over there, with the redhead"—he nodded toward the end of the bar, where a hulking man had his hands all over a gorgeous girl—"that's Gaspar Gomez. Very bad news. He'd kill his own mother if the price was right. Stay away."

Tony took it all in as they went around the room, shifting his gaze from one drug king to the next, filing it all away. He couldn't figure out why Frank was telling him all these things, but he knew it was a rare opportunity. There was something curiously modest about Frank as he detailed the names of the dozen or so men who controlled the cocaine traffic. He seemed to be making a statement about the limits of his own power. Each man had his territory. Nobody sought to be king of kings.

". . . the fat guy with the chicas—over there, with the eyepatch—that's Nacho Contreras. El Gordo. Wouldn't know it to look at him, but he's got more cash than anybody in here. A real chazzer. You know what a chazzer is, Tony?"

"No, Frank, what's a chazzer?"

"It's Yiddish for pig. It's a guy he's got more than he needs, so he don't fly straight anymore. You hear what I'm sayin'?"

"Yeah, I hear you."

"Too many chazzers in this business, Tony. They're the ones you gotta watch out for. If they can cheat you out of an extra dime, they'll rip you and flip you and crack your skull with a stick, for the pure *pleasure* of it.'' Tony could not remember when he had heard anyone speak so intensely about life. Then he did remember: his grandfather. This was like his grandfather. "See it all comes down to one thing, Tony boy," said Frank, and it didn't sound patronizing either, "don't ever forget it. Men are greedy. Not all of them, but the ones who are get all twisted up inside. They can't get enough. They're so hungry they'll gnaw off their own fingers.''

"Enough of what?" asked Tony.

"Enough you name it. Toot. Cooz. Money. Lesson number one, huh?"

Frank reached over and squeezed Tony's hand. The grip was intensely strong, yet there was something trembling in it. Again like his grandfather, Tony thought, though Frank could hardly be older than forty-five. What was he doing sounding like an old man?

"Lesson number two," said Elvira, and they looked up to see her standing beside the table, one hand on her hip and looking saucy. "Don't get high on your own supply." She paused for a beat. The two men said nothing. Then she said: "Isn't that right, Frank?"

"Whatever you say, baby," retorted Frank, not really paying attention.

"Course, not everybody follows the rules," Elvira added, sliding into the chair beside Frank. She held up her empty champagne glass, and the headwaiter fairly leaped across the room to grab the bottle and fill it for her. Out of the corner of one eye, Tony saw Ernie standing on a balcony above and to the right of them.

Frank spoke to the headwaiter: "How much does this stuff go for, Calvin?"

"Five hundred fifty a bottle, Mr. Lopez." Calvin sounded proud.

"Imagine that, Tony," said Frank, one hand scratching the gray at his temple. "For a bunch of grapes. It's like toot, for Christ's sake."

Elvira leaned across the table and tapped Tony's hand with her cigarette lighter. "In France it costs a hundred," she said, "but don't tell anyone in Miami."

Frank laughed. "Yeah, well it costs a little more to serve it to this crowd." And he waved a hand around the gaudy room at the royalty of the coke trade. Then he picked up his glass and toasted. "To old friends and new friends," he said with feeling.

They all drank. Tony and Elvira stared at each other over the rims of their glasses. A glittering young man was passing the table and bent down and whispered something into Elvira's ear. She turned with a laugh, and the two of them huddled together, gossiping. He looked like a faggot. Frank paid no attention to him but leaned back once again in his chair. Tony followed suit.

"So how do you like the high life, kid?"

Tony took a swallow of champagne. "I may never drink Thunderbird again," he said.

Frank guffawed. "Hey, wait till we get you some new threads. You think you like five-hundred-dollar wine? Try a fifteen-hundred-dollar suit. You feel like you own the world."

"I never thought bein' rich could be so expensive."

Elvira now stood up and walked away to dance with the young man. They continued to laugh uproariously at some private joke between them. Frank drew a cigar case from his breast pocket and offered one to Tony. "Cuban," he said. Tony took one and let Frank light it for him. Frank didn't seem to look at Elvira at all. Tony couldn't stop looking.

"I'd like you to handle some stuff for me, Tony," Frank said, and immediately Tony grew alert. "Work with Omar here, I know he's a putz, but he's tough when he's gotta be. We're doing a pretty big deal in a couple weeks. Running a bunch of mules out of Colombia. You ever done mule work?"

"Sure," said Tony, not wanting to reveal his ignorance, and figuring he had a couple of weeks to learn.

"You do good on this, there'll be other things."

"How much is in it for me?"

"You'll be real busy for a couple weeks," said Frank. "Why don't we say fifty grand? You pay your partner here outa *your* pocket." He puffed on his cigar and watched the smoke drift up toward the ceiling. "Now that's enough business. Why don't you dance for a while? Then I'll order some steaks."

Tony was about to protest that he didn't need to dance, meaning he didn't want to dance with anyone else but Elvira, when he noticed Frank exchanging glances with a Mafia type at the next table. Tony was being dismissed for the sake of a high-level meeting. He stood up from his chair and decided he'd go play pinball. He didn't want to pick up a chick right now, and watching Elvira was driving him crazy. Manolo stood up to follow Tony—anything not to have to sit by Omar.

Frank called out as they left the table: "Hey, Tony, cut in on her, willya? She's had enough fag-talk for one night."

Tony nodded. He made a move to walk down to the dance floor when Manolo gripped his arm. "What the hell are you doin', chico?" Manolo asked sharply. "You gonna mess with the boss's wife?"

"He asked me to dance with her. I just do what I'm told."

"Dance with her, chico. Not too close. This is our big chance, you dig?" Manolo's eyes swept the room. He was dazed by the flash and power of it all. "Don't start walkin' no tightrope, Tony. Life's dangerous enough as it is."

They split off in different directions, Manolo to one of the dusky bars where the girls were bored and ready. As Tony walked onto the dance floor, he glanced around to see if Frank was tracking him. But no—Frank sat huddled with the hood from the next table, figuring something out on a piece of paper. Tony strolled across and tapped the shoulder of the elegant man dancing with Elvira. He looked up with an expectant smile.

"Piss off," said Tony.

The young man paled. Though he squirmed at the thought of a fight, he did not let go of Elvira. He made a move to put her behind him. She laid a hand on his arm and purred: "It's all right, Jason. He's one of Frank's thugs." Jason's lip curled with disdain. He murmured something to Elvira that Tony didn't catch, then clicked his metaphorical heels and melted into the crowd. As Elvira raised her arms to Tony she said: "So you can dance, can you? I thought all you could do was kill people."

In fact he was no great shakes as a dancer. They swayed to a Billy Joel beat, but they didn't move very far. They were staring into each other's eyes again, both of them smiling ironically. "Who said I was a killer?" asked Tony.

"Nobody, I just guessed. The hot-looking ones are usually real good with a gun. But maybe you're just another dealer, huh? Another dumb-ass dealer."

"Elvira what?" asked Tony.

"Elvira Saint James."

"Sounds like somethin' you eat in a fancy restaurant. Where you from?"

"Baltimore," she drawled with a sleepy smile.

"Where the hell's that?"

She cocked her head and studied his face, to see if he was kidding. He wasn't. She laughed deliciously. "It's in the northeastern United States, about four hours from New York. You've heard of New York?"

"Yeah, once or twice."

"My ancestors disembarked in Baltimore in 1689," she said, her voice gone singsong now, as if she were teaching grammar school. "You know—on one of those quaint sailing ships. From England."

"Kinda like Columbus, huh?"

"Yes, kind of like that."

"What'd they come over for?" asked Tony. "They owe money?"

Elvira shook her head. The diamonds on her neck shone like sunlight on the sea. The perfume she was wearing drove him nuts. Like roses and lemons mixed. "Religious persecution," she said.

"Ah," he exclaimed, as if he'd just put it all together at last. "Ain't that a coincidence. That's just what I was thinkin' when I met you. I says to myself, I bet she's a victim of religious persecution."

"Mm, and you look like you work for the White House."

He grinned and moved in closer. He didn't bother to look again in Frank's direction, since Frank didn't watch Elvira. Maybe that was the problem between them. Tony said: "Me, I'm just like your relatives. I come over on a boat too."

"Oh, so you're part of the Cuban crimelift, are you?" She shook her hair, and her eyelids drooped with irony. "As if Florida needed more scum."

Tony's eyes went hard for a second. He knew it was only a brutal joke. From the moment they met, they'd agreed implicitly to say just what they pleased. Besides, she'd made it clear a moment ago, talking about Baltimore, that class meant nothing at all to her. Yet he saw how far he had to go to acquire the kind of power that would draw her to him. He didn't doubt he'd get it eventually, but he wasn't sure if she'd wait. That he simply had to have her he'd known for an hour now, since the second he laid eyes on her. He wished she wasn't a junkie, but it didn't matter. Having her was what mattered.

"Put it this way," Tony said. "I came here for political reasons. Like I want to be king, and you can't be king of a communist country."

"You can't be king of America either," retorted Elvira dryly. "I think maybe you need a few history lessons. The county probably has a night school. Lots of chiquitas, I bet.''

"You don't know nothin', honey," said Tony, grinning tightly, one hand gripping her waist as if he would lift her off the ground. "There's hundreds o' kings in America. You married one, for Christ's sake."

She jerked in his arms. He thought she was going to stalk off, but she didn't. "We're not married," she said. "I don't believe in marriage."

"Baby, what have you got against the world? You look like a million bucks. You got enough bread to pick your nose with. Don't you get laid or something?"

Now she tried to pull away, to haul off and belt him. This was a little more tricky. A scene might make even Frank look up. They were dancing close to the band, and Tony glimpsed a side door, the musicians' entrance. He whisked Elvira out, waltzing her even as she beat a fist against his chest. Suddenly they were out in a quiet corridor. She fought like a cat, snarling and scratching.

"Easy, easy."

"I get laid when I like," she hissed through gritted teeth. "But I don't fuck ex-cons."

Now Tony was laughing. "I think we were made for each other, baby."

She was furious. Her green eyes flashed with contempt, and she tossed her head with huge disdain. "You know, you're even stupider than you look. Let me give you a crash course, José, so you know what you're doing around here. First of all, who, where, and how I get laid is none of your goddam business. Second, don't call me baby, I'm not your baby or anybody else's. Third, there's no bread. My parents pissed it all away. Why else do you suppose a ninth generation Baltimore junkie would be living with a spic Jew drug king? And dancing with jerks like you. You got the picture now, José? Good, now buzz off."

She slammed his chest a final time and turned and stormed away. Tony chuckled with pleasure as he followed her. She headed past a bank of slot machines, paused for a brief second at the entrance to the restaurant, then changed her mind and headed for the ladies'. Tony didn't think twice. As soon as he saw her disappear through the restroom door, he headed in after.

A woman fixing her lipstick in the mirror gave him a bored, dead-eyed look. On downers probably. Elvira was just going into one of the stalls when she caught sight of Tony. She groaned with exasperation. Grinning, Tony strode across the white-tiled room and prodded her into the stall. She was laughing in spite of herself, but she was still angry. He crowded inside with her and latched the door.

"Can't you take a hint?" she asked.

"Guess not."

He sidled close and stroked her hips, but she hardly noticed. She was reaching down the front of her dress, from which she drew out a small brass vial the shape of a rifle bullet. She tapped it against the palm of her hand, then flicked the top and pushed it up his nose. He snorted. She poked his other nostril, and he inhaled even deeper. Then he watched her do herself, as casually as if she were touching up her makeup. The stuff was so pure he could feel a throb of numbness just behind his eyes. He laughed and leaned forward to kiss her neck.

"There," she said. "You satisfied now?"

"Are you kidding?" he mumbled, his tongue against her throat. Already he was pulling her dress up her legs. One hand groped between her thighs. She scrambled away, but the space was tight in the stall, and he wouldn't quit.

"No!" she seethed, once more trying to beat him away with her fists. But he had her pinned to the wall now, one hand gripping her hair as he kissed her, the other hand grazing the mound of Venus. Outside the stall they could hear two women, laughing as they entered from the club. Elvira grunted and struggled, but she didn't cry out. She leaned forward, gripping his head, as if she was going to whisper a curse in his ear. She bit it instead.

Tony howled and leaped away from her, crashing against the side of the stall. She shook the dress so it fell to her knees again. She tossed her hair, then tucked the vial of coke back in her bra. Tony stood there watching her, stunned, one hand cupping his ear. She pulled open the stall door, took a step out, then stuck her head back in. Haughty and hard she said: "Don't get confused, Tony. Rule number three."

She slammed the door and left him in there. He rubbed his ear for a moment, turned around and un-zipped his fly, and urinated loudly in the bowl. He didn't bother to flush it. Then he pulled the door open and stepped out of the stall, only to find the two women washing their hands at the sinks, trying not to look at him in the mirror. Elvira had vanished. Tony sauntered across to the outer door, saluting the women as he went.

He wandered from room to room till he found Manolo, who'd wedged a girl in at the end of one of the bars and was putting the moves on. Tony tapped him on the shoulder and motioned him to follow. They went back to the table and sat down to eat their thirty-dollar steaks. Frank wanted to hear all about Cuba, and Tony obliged him, spinning out a good anti-communist line. He kept one eye on Elvira the whole time, as she picked at her food and pushed it around her plate. She ap-peared to listen to nothing that Tony said, laughed at none of the jokes, and barely looked up when Frank ad-dressed her. When a girlfriend stopped by the table to chat, she turned her back on all the men. Then a few minutes later she escaped to powder her nose with a couple of other girls, not even bothering to excuse her-self.

Tony nodded to Manolo, and they said a brief good-night to Frank. He wanted her to come back to the table and find him gone. That way they would avoid a stiff

and public goodbye, and maybe she'd be a little hungry
to see him again. Frank didn't seem to mind their sudden leaving. He was accustomed to men who had midnight appointments and other fish to fry. He clapped
Tony warmly on the back and welcomed him once again
into the organization.

"You remind me a little of me, Tony, when I was
your age. You're always thinkin', aren't you?" Frank
laughed and shook his head with obvious affection. "I
like a man who never stops. I think we'll be doin' a lotta
business, you and I. Take care now."

Tony and Manolo shook Frank's hand. Nobody
shook Omar's hand. Then they left quickly, Manolo
giving one last lingering look around at the Babylon and
its smoldering women. They got into a cab and headed
back to Brickell Avenue, to pick up the Monte Carlo.
Manolo waxed eloquent about the club and the girls,
imagining what it would be like when he and Tony could
go there on their own.

Suddenly Tony interrupted. "How 'bout the chick,
huh?"

"How 'bout her?" Manolo asked cautiously.

"Hey, she's in love with me, chico."

"Bullshit. How you know that?"

Tony grinned as he watched out the window, where
the palm trees and the big pastel estates of Coral Gables
passed before them like a dream come true. "The eyes,
Manny," he said. "Them green eyes don't lie."

Manolo grew tense. There was a thin edge of hysteria
in his voice as he reached over and gripped Tony's arm.
"Forget it, pal, okay? That's Frank Lopez's lady. You
stay away. You wanna get killed?"

Tony shook him off. "What are you, kiddin'? Can't
you see how soft he is? Too much booze, too much
blow. He lets a cuncha tell him what to do." He
shrugged and grinned again. "Frank Lopez, big fuckin'
deal."

They were silent after that, as they retrieved the Monte Carlo and headed home to the dead hooker's apartment. They hadn't slept in thirty-six hours, and now they crashed for twelve. Their dreams were palpable matters now, specific and gaudy and finally there within reach. For Manolo it was the big bucks and the power to spend them at the Babylon, with a gorgeous woman draped on either arm. For Tony it was his princess, come to life at last. They slept as if they needed all the sleep they could get, for they knew what they wanted now, and they knew they would have to fight like hell to get it.

Suddenly tomorrow was a whole new deal.

She was telling the truth about the nine generations. Her Saint James ancestors had fought in the Revolutionary War, right alongside George Washington. For a while after the War of 1812, they had owned about a quarter of Maryland, which they farmed like proper gentlemen, keeping about three thousand slaves. Later on there was a Saint James in Lincoln's government, an Under-Secretary of State for European Affairs. This Abner Saint James explained to the family in no uncertain terms that the three thousand slaves at Summerset, the Saint James farm in Maryland, stood in the way of his own advancement. Thus were the slaves freed a good two years before the Emancipation Proclamation.

Unfortunately, the farm fortunes dwindled accordingly. Vast tracts of land had to be sold off. Worse still, Abner's sons were aesthetes. The elder one exiled himself to France, where he squandered huge amounts putting on ballets that kept the people away in droves, mostly because the prima ballerina had no talent except of the carnal sort, which she only revealed in the confines of Mr. Rufus Saint James's bedroom. The younger Saint James poured all his money into founding the Baltimore Symphony. By the turn of the twentieth century the Saint Jameses were the poorest rich people in America.

Luckily, the next generation produced a winner. Mortimer Saint James graduated from Johns Hopkins, set up a small laboratory on the much-diminished family farm, and tinkered away for a couple of years. He emerged one morning shouting "Eureka!" He'd invented a completely new steering pin for the automobile, stronger and tougher and cheaper, and within six months he had sold the patent to Walter Chrysler of Flint, Michigan, thus ensuring a new lease on the Saint James fortune. Mortimer retired at the age of twenty-five, married a second cousin, and tinkered purposelessly for the next half century.

He produced one daughter, Alice, the first girl child in the Saint James line since the Revolution. This Alice was blonde and had green eyes. As soon as she was old enough she moved from the dreary hills of western Maryland to New York City, where she settled in Greenwich Village just after the Second World War. She had obviously inherited something of the impresario urge from her Saint James forebears, for she soon became involved in the theater, with a vengeance. She married a passionate drunk named Edgar Vale, who believed it was his mission to bring the avant-garde to the masses.

Alice and Edgar mounted two or three productions a year, hugely elaborate and rococo, of plays so obscure and Rumanian that even the translators didn't understand them. Nobody ever came to see them either, but nobody ever said art was easy. Alice and Edgar produced and drank, produced and drank, till they'd finally exhausted all the steering pin money. The morning after the flop of their final production—*While Nero Fiddled*, nine hours long, with a cast of sixty-six, in which the only line of dialogue was "Lost, all lost," in a hundred and nineteen languages—Alice and Edgar limped home to her ancient baronial lands in Maryland.

Which lands were mostly suburbs now, and mostly in the hands of others.

With what little remained of the family fortune, Alice and Edgar settled down in a lopsided stone house on the western edge of Baltimore. The house had once been part of the slave quarters of the Saint James plantation. And there Alice and Edgar produced their truly final production: a child they called Elvira. After that, they turned all their considerable creative energy to drink. They drank whole vats of gin and lay abed for days at a time, while the last of the Saint James monies evaporated into thin air.

Somehow Elvira Vale managed to grow up. She toddled off to the public school, not feeling very different from her friends, some of whose blue-collar parents were as drunk as her own. She did not pay much attention to her mother's incoherent tales of the previous eight generations. All she knew was this: she would flee the gray suburbs of Baltimore as soon as she could; and no matter what, she would never marry. Elvira Vale, growing up as she did tough and lower-middle-class, was not really aware of the three things rooted in her blood.

First was the desire to flee Maryland, which her people had been doing for generations. Second was the love of the theater, which had funded all those ballets and wrong-headed plays. Third and most significant was the love of intoxication. The Saint James family had been drinking for three hundred years.

Yet the day that Elvira left Baltimore and went to New York, she was eighteen years old and was sure she had no past at all. As if life were out to prove this point, Alice and Edgar had died within six months of each other. Liver complications. As soon as Elvira had buried them, there seemed no reason to finish high school. She had a friend who'd gone to Manhattan to be an actress/model, which meant Elvira not only had a place to stay but an in in the business as well.

She worked as a waitress for about a year, first at a Walgreen's in the garment district, then at a late-night hangout on 45th just off Broadway, where most of the waitresses hooked on the side. Everybody hooked on the side, Elvira soon found out, including her girlfriend from Baltimore. It turned out a girl made better connections hooking than she did in a dim-lit restaurant, though the chances of being "discovered" were about equal in both professions.

Elvira appeared in a couple of Equity-waiver plays, which meant she didn't get paid. The productions took place in spaces that didn't even look like theaters. Forty folding chairs were grouped around a makeshift set, and hardly anybody ever sat in the forty seats. But Elvira managed to meet a lot of feisty independent girls, and they helped her get a portfolio together and introduced her around to the modeling agencies. Now and then she'd land a couple of hours work and actually get paid, but nothing ever really led to anything concrete. More often than not the agencies told her she was too pretty. Pretty was not the right type that year.

So she hooked a little. The girl she shared the apartment with on 59th and Second Avenue introduced her to the man who ran her "agency," an outrageous queen who looked and acted like Divine out of drag, whose name was Norman Desmond. Norman set the girls up on very Class A dates—the theater, dinner at Sardi's afterwards, and then a couple of hours' sex in a midtown hotel, usually the Hilton. Elvira always wondered if Norman didn't have a contract with the Hilton. The john paid a hundred and twenty-five, of which the girls received seventy-five. This was in the late seventies, when three hundred a week still bought you some time.

Elvira hooked maybe twice a week, and the johns were as predictable as the Hilton. Midwest; in for a convention; got it up fast and popped their load in ten minutes. It was very, very easy. But Elvira also had dates of her own on Friday and Saturday, with powerful men who worked like bandits in the cul-de-sacs of Manhattan, managing real estate and making book and selling information. Men who weren't exactly gangsters but just about. They took her out very fancy, to hundred-dollar dinners and dance places that didn't even open till two A.M. A weekend went on all weekend.

And she didn't really drink much. Just a beer. Just a double Stolichnaya on the rocks, which she sipped all night. But she did try a little cocaine when they had it. She never took as much as the men did, and anyway she didn't like the way it made her nose run. She hated being hung over. But the thing about cocaine was this: though people always said it was libido-suppressive, it made Elvira horny. The weekend men were very aggressive types, and they wanted to jump into bed three or four times a day, as if they had to make up for lost time. Elvira tended to feel smothered by all that desire, abused even. But if she tooted a little coke she figured what the hell and went in for some kicks of her own.

By the time she was twenty she'd become aware that certain girls in the actress/model class had made it to the top. They no longer needed a waitress job on the side, and they even stopped hooking except for an occasional regular. Luck and the right connections had led them into modeling gigs where they could pull down five hundred dollars a day. They no longer had to rely on their Saturday dates to provide them with cocaine; they had their own supply. These were girls who had come to the city at the same time Elvira did, and somehow they'd gotten ahead of her.

She began to get impatient, panicky even, fearful that she might end up just another hooker. Her roommate, only three years older, no longer even talked about actress/model matters. Hooking had ceased to be part-time. Elvira began to look at herself in the mirror and wonder if she was losing her looks. How long did pretty last anyway? Twenty-five? Not thirty. Deliberately she began to cast about for a way out. It was time she found some security. She zeroed in on her johns and Saturday gangsters, looking for a proper situation. She fantasized about finding one who would set her up in a swank apartment and be away on business two out of every three weeks.

She settled for Harry Sullivan, mostly because it got her out of New York, which had come to seem like a dead-end trip. Harry was a Hollywood producer. Though Elvira could never get it clear what he was a producer *of*, there being no correlation between the projects Harry talked about and what actually opened in theaters and showed on CBS, still he seemed to have a lot of money. And though he was manic and a lousy drunk and his skin was pocked and he bragged too much, he had a passion for "saving" girls like Elvira. He whisked them away from the hand-to-mouth and the degradation of whoring. He kept them safe in his house in the Hollywood Hills, coddling them and showering them with gifts.

Why not? Elvira knew it wasn't going to be forever. She knew she was only the next in line in a man's elaborate dream-life; but then, that's what a pretty girl always was, in her experience anyway. At least she didn't have to deal with Norman Desmond any more. And once she moved to Los Angeles and Harry gave her her own gold American Express, she was doing a hell of a lot better than seventy-five bucks a throw. Harry only required it once a week, and he didn't even have any kinks to speak of.

It was practically a dream come true, except for one thing. She missed the cocaine. Harry was pushing forty-five, and he was a drunk of the old school, Irish and red-faced. He didn't indulge in the white lady, and neither did his old-school friends. Not that Elvira couldn't live without it; not that she was an addict or anything. Cocaine wasn't heroin. It was simply her drug of choice, and she found she missed the couple-of-grams-a-weekend men she used to see in New York.

And in spite of the Spanish bungalow with the oval pool and the drop-dead view of the city lights, in spite of Harry's Eldorado and the charge account at Neiman's, Elvira began to see that, by Hollywood terms at least, Harry Sullivan was middle-middle at best. She watched the pretty girls—no prettier than she—exit the stretch limousines and enter the swank restaurants, laughing and tossing their sunstruck hair. Elvira felt the same pang of distance that she used to feel in New York when she caught a glimpse of a star model ducking into Studio 54—the signature models, rich and free, with faces kings dreamed of. But whereas in New York there was always the chance that the next connection would land her in clover, in Hollywood she was just another housegirl, wandering around a swimming pool. It was worse than being married, if she wasn't going to be very rich.

It was around this time, as she turned twenty-one, that she started to call herself Elvira Saint James. She had never felt the need of the nine generations before, but now she figured a measure of class was every bit as important as pretty, especially if she meant to find a zillionaire. In the back of her mind she decided she would probably do best with somebody even older and more old-school than Harry. As long as he had a fortune that could choke a horse, it didn't matter how middle-middle he was at heart. Thus she began to flirt boldly with Harry's set, casting about for the right situation.

At the same time she reactivated her modeling career. Harry wouldn't have allowed her to do it for the money, but she convinced him she simply needed to get out and do something—*anything*. She had a whole new portfolio made up, and she carted it around to the agencies and soon lucked out with a lucrative stint as a hand model, painting her nails for a TV spot that flashed her image into millions of homes for weeks on end, though only as far as her elbows.

But it wasn't the work that drove her. She wanted to get back in the hustle, meet the girls who were trying to break in, find out who they were dating. Within a month she was part of a nice little group, and of course they introduced her to their coke connection. It was as natural as sharing the name of one's hairdresser, or one's gynecologist. And anyway, Elvira didn't spend very much, only what was left over from what she made as a model. Say a gram a week. It took the edge off the weekend nights, when she went out to long dreary restaurant dinners with Harry and his friends from the slow lane.

For a while it worked very well, this living a double life. She spent her days with the girls and her evenings with Harry and never really had to be alone. She'd always hated to be alone. The only problem was, she wasn't in love. Listening to the other models spill their stories of the men who obsessed them, the ones who fucked them over and the ones who swore they'd kill them if they looked at another man, Elvira wondered if she hadn't made a secret vow against love as well as marriage. Every other pretty girl she met was a deep romantic, with one eye always on the door, waiting for her prince to come riding in. Elvira hated to think she was a cynic. She was sure it was only that the right man hadn't come along yet. She more or less hoped he'd wait till she'd got herself settled down with a rich man. She was certainly too much a realist to suppose the prince and the zillionaire were one.

Six months later she was up to two grams a week, still a very manageable amount, and in any case the dealer wasn't out to screw the girls. That is, he *was* out to screw the girls, but not out of money. He sold them snow at eighty dollars a gram, a good twenty-five percent below retail, and all they had to do was go to bed with him now and then. Elvira didn't mind a bit, since sex and cocaine went together so well. "Like gin and tonic," she used to tell the other girls. And the dealer liked her attitude so well, he began to give her Quaaludes free.

She started to sleep like a baby.

Unfortunately, she also started to fight with Harry. She made scenes at the table in the boring restaurants, disdainful of all that sloppy Irish drunkenness. She flirted with every man who looked twice at her, just to get Harry upset. And he wouldn't fight back. He developed a wounded, long-suffering look like a beaten puppy, and the more Elvira raged and threw tantrums, the more did Harry shower her with middle-middle presents. He begged her to tell him what she wanted.

She wanted a better deal. She was sick of everyone and everything, and the only thing that made sense any more was her temper, which flashed like a brush fire at the slightest provocation. She blew up at salespeople and sent the maid away in tears. She stalked out of a restaurant in Beverly Hills one night, flinging a drink in Harry's face just because he happened to ask her why she kept going to the bathroom. It was none of his goddam business. If her dealer was feeling romantic and wanted to lay a free gram on her, why shouldn't she blow it all in one night?

She didn't even bother to retrieve her coat as she left the restaurant. She hurried away along Rodeo Drive, high as a kite, convinced she would never return to Harry Sullivan again. You had to close a door before the next one opened. By the time she reached Wilshire Boulevard she realized she didn't need anything but the clothes on her back and the half gram in her purse. It was as if she was daring the world to show her something new. She'd cut her losses, just as she had in Baltimore and later on in New York. She'd never felt as free as she did that night.

She stood on the corner of Wilshire and Rodeo, waiting for the light to change. A limousine drew up at the curb beside her, its windows black and impenetrable. Suddenly one of the windows purred open, and a dark-eyed man with bushy hair, exuding money and power like radiation, leaned out and said: "You need a lift?"

"I'm not hooking, if that's what you mean," said Elvira.

"Don't worry, I'm not paying," said Frank Lopez with a grin. "But you look like you need a lift. How far you going?"

Elvira gave a short laugh. "About a million miles," she retorted dryly.

"Now ain't that a coincidence," he said, swinging the door wide. "So am I."

Even as she ducked inside she knew it was not about love, not for her anyway. The moment she laid eyes on him she knew he would fall in love with her. It might have seemed appropriate to wait a little bit, having just walked out on Harry not fifteen minutes before. But she knew instinctively that Frank Lopez, whatever else he turned out to be, would never be middle-middle. And though she didn't expect to love him, it didn't mean she didn't want him. For there was an immediate chemistry between Elvira and Frank Lopez, and not just of the carnal sort. She smelled the cocaine on him ten feet away. He might not be a prince, but he sure as hell had a princely stash.

He was there in L.A. trying to set up a distribution scheme, since Hollywood was the next stop for much of the coke that funneled through Miami. The scheme didn't take; the action in coke was still fundamentally local, outsiders not welcome. So the only thing Frank had to show for the trip was Elvira Saint James. She really meant it when she said she was free to go. She did not have to stop anywhere and pack a suitcase. She didn't have to make a phone call or arrange to sublet her apartment. She left L.A. without a backward glance.

They'd been together two and a half years now. He loved her as much as she'd thought he would—no more, no less. He was crazy busy setting up his empire, and he only really needed her when the rest of it got to be too much. Which wasn't very often, and usually involved a week's vacation—baking in a boat off Eleuthera, pouring money down the drain in Vegas, buying up half Manhattan. Day to day, mostly they stayed out of each other's way. They went out on the town at night, but only from eight to eleven. Elvira had safe men—colleagues of Frank's, the occasional gay tennis pro—who squired her around if she felt like dancing late.

But they did enjoy what they gave to each other, and they savored it more and more, the longer they were together. To Frank she was like a goddess. She spent her beauty recklessly, and she left a trail of gold when she walked. She worked on that; she made it happen. Hours she spent perfecting her beauty—her hair, her skin, her clothes, two hundred pairs of shoes—and because he loved the movement of her, she walked beside him in a trance of sensuality.

What he gave her was the money, the chance to indulge without limit. Without even the limit of decency.

They were thus the perfect couple the night that Tony walked into their lives.

Chapter Five

MIAMI INTERNATIONAL WAS having a bad day. A torrential rain the night before had caused considerable runway flooding. The winds were gusting heavily in the west, and there was a wind shear alert off and on all morning. The planes inched along through two-hour lines. A DC-10 bound for Houston had just been commandeered by a Cuban national with a bottle bomb. He wanted to go back. The air conditioning had broken down in the International Arrivals Building, and when they finally got it back in service after three and a half hours, they managed to short the computers at customs. It took triple the time to check a passport.

Pan Am 91 from Bogota was two hours and sixteen minutes late landing. The lines at customs snaked a hundred yards down the halls. Tony Montana, in a three-piece silk-and-linen blend, with a diamond on his little finger, kept glancing down at his watch, almost as if he was timing something. He carried a brown glove-leather attaché case, chock full of invoices that proved what line of work he was in. He was the epitome of the young ethnic American businessman, heavily into import-export. On the way up, of course.

At last he stepped up to the counter, where a chunky, sullen customs officer gave him a frigid look. "Mind opening that, sir?" he said. The "sir" was in quotes.

Calmly Tony zipped open the attaché. As the officer probed among the papers, Tony glanced at the next line over. A fat woman pushing a baby carriage had just stepped up to the counter. A squalling child with a toy panda sat in the carriage. The officer waved them through without even demanding to look in the woman's purse. Behind her was a nun in a full white habit, holding all her papers neatly in one hand. She too was waved on through. By this point Tony's official was ransacking the attaché, trying to find a false bottom. Of course there was none.

At last the official looked up, seemingly annoyed not to have turned up any contraband. He handed Tony a slip of paper on which his rights were printed, and then he said: "Would you please step into that room over there, sir?" Tony sighed wearily. An old man on crutches was waved through the line right behind him. An armed customs agent came forward and escorted Tony into the interrogation room.

He was asked to strip for a body search. As he removed the fifteen-hundred-dollar suit, they asked him questions about his four days in Colombia. He answered flatly, as if the whole thing bored him. He stood there in his underpants while the sub-agents went through his pockets and felt along the seams. They tapped at the heels of his shoes, looking for a hollow spot. The interrogating agent couldn't crack his alibi. The import-export papers were all in order. Reluctantly they handed him back his suit, and Tony asked cheerfully: "You sure you don't want to stick your fingers up my ass?" Nobody laughed.

Tony left the interrogation room with a wonderful

spring in his step, as if he'd just gotten a clean bill of
health from his doctor. He didn't seem bothered at all
by the long wait. Neither did Manolo, who sat reading
the papers in Omar's Cadillac, the radio and the air conditioning turned up high. When Tony got in, they drove
back to Calle Ocho, now and then laughing out loud at
how easy it all was.

They parked in front of a nondescript little bungalow,
the yard overgrown with crimson poinsettias. This place
had been Omar's stash house for almost two years,
which practically qualified it for a brass plaque above
the door. A stash house was usually good for about two
months. Omar admitted them, puffed with pride, as if
he'd just negotiated a dangerous run from Bogota himself. His woman was cooking a big celebratory supper in
the kitchen, and the smell of spicy Cuban food per-
meated the house.

In the living room, waiting patiently for Tony's
arrival, were the fat woman with the baby carriage, the
nun, and the old man on crutches. Tony and Manolo sat
on the sofa, and the mules handed over the goods.
Manolo used his pocket knife to rip open the panda,
while the little kid shrieked in protest. A candy bar was
produced to mollify him. Half a kilo was tucked in the
panda's belly. Tony, meanwhile, was methodically dis-
mantling the baby carriage. The aluminum handles were
hollow and filled with coke in long plastic tubes. Omar
knelt in front of the old man and carefully sawed
through the cast on his leg. A kilo was banked and
padded along the inner face of the plaster. The nun
slipped out of her habit like a stripper. Two kilos were
strapped to her body.

The fat woman took the diapers off the baby, revealing a thick packet of the drug that had come through
unscathed, in spite of the wet. The ex-nun had now
moved to her suitcases, where she unpacked half a
dozen crude religious statues. Tony gathered up the
painted ceramic virgins, carried them into the bath-

room, and smashed them in the tub. Then he lifted the bags of cocaine out of the rubble. By the time they were done, they had eight kilos stacked on the coffee table in the living room. The mules were each paid five hundred in cash and told to report again the following Monday, when they would be issued their tickets back to Colombia, this time to smuggle out dollars.

Tony sat sprawled on the sofa, staring happily at his loot. He had engineered the whole operation in Bogota. Hired the mules. Packed the drugs. Figured out all the disguises.

"You were only supposed to bring in six," said Omar, frowning as he checked the glassine bags.

"Yeah, well I haggled them down," said Tony.

"You're not supposed to make deals," snapped Omar. "You just do the transport."

"I don't think Frank'll throw out the other two kilos, do you?"

Nothing more was said about it, though relations between them remained barely polite if not strained. It was growing increasingly clear to Tony that Omar was nothing more than a middleman. He brought in men for various operations, but good men were not exactly hard to find, with the pool of new blood from Cuba. Everyone else did the legwork and the mulework. Omar just seemed to sit at home, making telephone calls every couple of days to Frank. Tony was annoyed that he'd had no chance to speak to Frank himself since the night they'd talked at the Babylon Club. The first half of the fifty thousand was paid promptly, in crisp new twenties and fifties, but Omar was the contact.

Worse than that, Tony had had no word of Elvira in almost three weeks. The day after he met her, he was talking to his sister on the phone, and it turned out Gina was best friends with the girl who worked daily for Frank Lopez. This Beatriz had reported that Elvira left that morning on a Caribbean cruise. So Tony couldn't follow up their meeting with a call. Beatriz had promised to alert Gina as soon as Elvira returned, but apparently there'd been no word. Tony had no one to talk to about it. The whole subject freaked Manolo out, and nobody else could be trusted not to tell Frank.

He'd been glad of the chance to go to Colombia, just to get his mind on something else. For a few days after he returned he was busy around the clock, dealing out the shipment. Nick the Pig had been brought in on Tony's recommendation, to do the package delivery in the ghettos. Frank had been using a two-bit redneck who watered down his stuff and screwed his clients so bad the market had virtually shriveled up. Nick had a solid list of rich black pimps, and Tony went with him when he made his route, in order to get acquainted with the regulars.

Tony enjoyed the delivery phase, because it gave him access to so many different worlds. He and Manolo were sent one morning to a brokerage house in the financial district. They were ushered into the plush office of a hotshot junior partner, Mr. Reeves, where they turned over a manila envelope with twenty-eight grams in it. Mr. Reeves himself would do the distribution among his own people. He handed over a personal check to Tony, laughing as he checked his package, clearly feeling he was part of a great and dangerous adventure. Tony got him talking about the market, asking a hundred questions of his own about investments.

He delivered to two law firms and a judge's chambers. He dealt ten grams to the maitre d' of a class A restaurant in one of the big hotels, who insisted that Tony sit down for a lobster dinner. People were always delighted to see their dealer, assuming they were all paid up. They liked Tony right away, because he was so much more presentable than most of the goons Omar employed. He didn't make them feel they were dealing with a gangster. His manner was suave, his dark good looks memorable. They told him things about themselves. He seemed to want to hear everyone's story.

Within two weeks he had dealt two kilos himself, with
Manolo assisting, and received the second payment on
the fifty thousand. Omar had swallowed his personal
problems with Tony, since all reports from the field
were so positive. As Omar turned over the checks to
Tony, he indicated that Frank was prepared to let him
do the next Colombia run as well, with a good chance
now that the work would be regular, say a run every six
or eight weeks. If Tony worked steady from run to run,
he'd gross maybe a quarter of a million a year.

Not bad, considering that just two months ago he was
making twenty-four dollars a night washing dishes.

Tony and Manolo moved out of the hooker's apartment into something much more substantial, two bed-
rooms and a balcony with a view out over Biscayne Bay.
Fifteen hundred a month, furnished. No lease, of
course, since in their business a man could be broke or
busted overnight. There were landlords who were sensi-
tive to these variables, and they charged a little bit more,
say thirty percent above the market, but they asked no
questions at all.

Already they had so much money they didn't know
what to do with it. Manolo filled a closet full of clothes
and went out on dates nearly every night, treating his
friends to dinner at the Havanito Restaurante. Chi-Chi,
whose cut was a good deal smaller, spent most of it
buying back drugs off the street. He lived in a squalid
little room off Calle Ocho and freebased the night away.
Tony did a lot of flashy shopping of his own and sent
racks of beautiful clothes to Gina, but he knew he was
hoarding his money for something. He was waiting for
Elvira to come back, to see what would turn her on.

It was while Tony was down in Bogota on his second
trip that Manolo met Gina. She came by the apartment
to show off a dress Tony had sent over. They only spent
a shy ten minutes together, but Manolo neglected to
mention it when Tony returned. It was Gina who
blurted it out on the phone, pumping Tony with ques-

tions about his easygoing sidekick. Tony was curt.
When he hung up he went right to Manolo and con-
fronted him with it.

"She's not for you, chico," he said. "I don't want
her mixed up with a guy who might get chewed up by a
chainsaw. You dig?"

"Yeah, yeah," said Manolo, who'd known exactly
how Tony would react. "You can't hide something that
gorgeous, you know. You think I'm the first guy's
noticed her?"

"I'll worry about that," retorted Tony. "When she's
old enough, we'll find her a nice doctor. Or maybe a
stockbroker."

"She ain't a nun, Tony. She's lookin' for a party, just
like everybody else."

They dropped it. Tony decided he had to keep in
closer touch with Gina. He called her the next afternoon
and started grilling her about her boyfriends. She
laughed it off, berating him for treating her like a child.
He started in to lecture her when she suddenly interrupted. She'd seen her friend Beatriz the night before.
Elvira was home.

It was one o'clock. He had a dozen deliveries to make
that day, but he managed to palm a few off on Manolo,
a few more on Nick the Pig, and he had the rest done by
three. He drove to Brickell Avenue and waited outside
in the Monte Carlo. He had no idea what her schedule
was. She might only go out in the evening, for all he
knew, and even then only accompanied by Frank. He
couldn't call. He couldn't leave a note. With so much
time gone by, he hadn't a clue where things stood between them any more. He had no other choice but to
count on his luck.

About ten after four the Rolls was brought around to
the portico just outside the main entrance. She appeared
out of the elevator in a white silk dress, dazzling next to
her Caribbean tan. She was alone. Tony let her get into
the Rolls and drive out of the driveway and turn right

toward Coral Gables. Then he gunned the Monte Carlo and tailed her for about two blocks. At the next intersection the light had just gone red. Elvira slowed the Rolls to a stop. Tony tapped his brake and rammed her rear bumper, not very hard. She leaped out of the Rolls cursing, her eyes blazing. Tony got out grinning. She didn't appear surprised.

"You idiot," she said, but not without amusement. "What are you trying to do now?"

"I thought you might like to go for a ride."

"In that?" she retorted disdainfully, pointing at the Monte Carlo. "I think I'll pass. Besides, I have to go get my hair done."

"Why? It looks great the way it is."

She shrugged. She didn't seem to mind at all talking in the middle of the street. There wasn't much traffic, and the cars funneled by them easily enough, but they must have wondered how these two could stand there chatting after one of them had just rear-ended the other. "Nothing better to do," Elvira said.

"So why don't we go for a ride?"

"As a matter of fact I was thinking about you," she said. "When I was in the Bahamas." She gestured down the street, more or less in the direction of the ocean. "I realized there was something I forgot to ask you."

"So ask, why don't you?"

"How'd you get this?" She reached up a manicured finger and drew it down along the scar, barely touching it. "It's very sexy."

Tony smiled. "Somebody's husband."

"Oh." She shook her head and clucked her tongue. "See why I don't believe in marriage? Too damn bloody. Where should I leave the Rolls?"

He pointed to a parking lot across the way, in front of a Pizza Hut. She got back in the car and pulled it in. People in Miami had gotten used to seeing Rollses at Pizza Huts. It was a whole new breed. The Rollses of Palm Beach, purring down Worth Avenue with the chauffeurs in gray livery, wouldn't have been caught dead at a Pizza Hut, of course, but they couldn't hold back the future either. Elvira seemed to delight in the incongruity as she left the car and trotted across the street to the Monte Carlo. Tony thought his heart would stop, she was so beautiful running towards him.

"Have you got a towel or something?" she asked when she opened the door. The seat was in fact very grungy. The Monte Carlo looked like it was owned by farmworkers. There wasn't anything handy to lay down for her, so he unbuttoned his rayon short-sleeved shirt with the tiger on the back and slipped it off. He spread it on the worn and oily seat beside him, and she got inside.

She immediately turned the rearview mirror toward her and checked her face. Tony had already peeled out into traffic, hunkering down to look out of the side mirror. She tilted the rearview back in his direction and slumped against her door and gave him an antic look.

"So," he said as they slipped onto the expressway, "how was the Caribbean?"

"Real pretty."

"I come from the Caribbean, you know."

"I know," she said. "Did you used to hang out on the beach half-naked, toking on a little joint?"

"Uh huh. No joint, though."

"Oh, right. You're the dealer who doesn't get stoned. I think you do it just to be ornery."

"What's ornery?"

"Trying to rape girls in the ladies' room, that sort of thing." The car was stuffy. She opened her window and held her head so the wind blew in her hair. "Where are we going?"

"Looks like I'm going to need a new car," he said, "if we're going to be taking a lot of rides."

"We're taking *this* ride," she replied precisely. "I wouldn't make any plans if I were you. I never make plans."

"What kinda car you like?"

She shrugged, as if to say she could no longer be sure of anything she liked. "My father used to have an old Jaguar," she said. "When I was a little girl."

He took a downtown exit, making his way to Sarasota Boulevard, where the auto dealerships were lined up for several blocks. When he pulled into the Jaguar place and parked the Monte Carlo outside the main entrance, the salesmen on the floor looked pained. As Tony and Elvira walked in, Tony shrugging into his tiger shirt, the sales manager approached with barely concealed contempt. They paid no attention, they were having too good a time. He showed them four or five sedans, none of which piqued their fancy till they came to a bright red XJ–6.

"I think this is you," said Elvira.

Tony stalked around it, then got inside and ran a hand over the leather dash. He leaned out the window and beckoned her over. "You like it?" he asked. "I mean, is it you?"

She shrugged. "Bit loud, I suppose. But yeah, it's real cheerful. You look like a million bucks in it."

Tony grinned and got out. The sales manager was sort of wringing his hands, looking out the window as if he could will a nice white businessman to come in and buy a car. Tony had to tap him on the shoulder to get his attention. "Uh—excuse me. How much is this car?"

"Twenty-eight thousand," said the manager, thin-lipped and arrogant. As if to say: "Out of your range, pal."

Tony reached into his front pants pocket and pulled out a wad of cash, as casually as if he carried it around all the time, though he'd retrieved it a couple of hours ago from the coffee tin where he had it stashed. It was all in thousand-dollar bills. Tony started peeling them off, and the manager, pale and stunned, held out the palm of his hand so Tony could count them out. Elvira looked on with vast amusement. When Tony had handed over the twenty-eight bills, he asked the manager to double-check. With shaking hands the manager did a recount, all the while fawning on Tony, promising him they could have the car ready to drive away by noon the following day.

"No way," said Tony. "There's some custom work needs to be done. Can you do it?"

"What sort of custom work?" asked the manager with a gelid smile.

Tony walked along the side of the car, pointing here and there at the body. "Get this whole section bullet-proofed," he said. "Here and here. And I want blackout shutters. Bulletproof window in back. Tint all the windows except the front, I don't like bein' looked at. Then I want one o' them radio scanners, you know? The best they got, so I can pick up flyin' saucers if I have to. You got all that?"

"I think so," said the manager wanly.

"We're gonna need fog lights. Case we take a little vacation in a swamp." Tony turned to Elvira, who stood with her arms folded, enjoying it all as much as he. "Am I forgettin' anything?"

"How about machine-gun turrets?"

"Nah," he replied with a shake of his head. "With the Ingram, see, you don't need a turret." He turned to the manager. "Do ya?"

"Uh, no—I suppose not." The manager stood there stupidly, holding the twenty-eight thousand. He looked like he'd never seen cash before. He was a whiz at explaining financing, but he seemed to have no patter that fit the current situation. "These extra . . . features," he said. "They'll cost you quite a bit."

"How much?" retorted Tony, starting to peel another G-note off his wad.

"I simply couldn't tell you," said the manager, anxious and rattled. "I'll have to get hold of a specialist. This just isn't usual."

But he had a sinking feeling that it was going to be. He ushered Tony into his office and made him sign the ownership papers. When he asked for identification, Tony produced a Florida driver's license and his green card. The manager may have seen a green card before, but he'd certainly never sold an XJ-6 to someone who carried one. He promised to have an estimate on the extras by tomorrow afternoon. No, Tony did not have to give him any more money right now.

He walked Tony back to the Monte Carlo. Elvira was standing beside it, smoking a cigarette. With a growing sense of disbelief, the manager watched Tony remove his shirt and place it on the greasy seat so Elvira could sit. As Tony got in and they drove away, the manager gave a weak wave, as if he'd just lost a sale.

"You move real fast, don't you?" she said. "Maybe too fast."

"I been waitin' a long time. Where to?"

"Back to the car. I still have to get my hair done."

"When will I see you again?"

She laughed. "You don't need to see me. You just bought a new car. You're going to have girls coming out of your ears."

They were on the expressway. The traffic was heavy and dirty. Rotten motels lined either side of the road, looking out on the stream of cars. The city seemed as grungy here as the car they were driving in. Elvira in her clean white dress was like a creature from another planet.

Tony turned to her. His face was grave, his eyes burning. "I been waitin' a *long* time," he said. "The minute I laid eyes on you, I was crazy about you. The *minute*. You understand?"

She was startled at the nakedness of it. She lowered her head, embarrassed, and fished in her purse. She brought out a vial of coke and a tiny silver spoon. "Get your own girl, Tony," she said quietly. "I'm not available."

"You just figure out when I can see you again."

They drove on in silence. She took a toot of the coke

in either nostril. She didn't bother to offer him any. She dropped the vial back in her purse and idly licked the little spoon. She gave a dry laugh: "Did I ever tell you I was born with a silver spoon in my mouth?"

Tony didn't answer. He just kept driving. His face was completely blank.

Arnoldo Sosa was surely the most glamorous man in Cochabamba, Bolivia. But he would have held his own in Monte Carlo too, or Acapulco or even London. He was a playboy of the old school, about six-foot-two with black wavy hair, Fernando Lamas the year he married Esther Williams. He had a lean athletic body and a Copacabana tan; and he favored polo shirts and pocketless pants, so everyone would see for himself. On his right wrist (on his left was a Rolex) was a big-linked gold ID bracelet, with "NOLDO" written in diamonds.

Accompanying Sosa everywhere was a man whom even Sosa called the Shadow: a thin, intense, venomous-looking Hispanic in his mid-thirties, with the look of death in his smashed and stitched-up face. The Shadow always stood slightly behind the person or persons addressing Sosa, in a sort of garotte position. He stared down anyone who might glance in his direction with a look that could turn a man to stone. Sosa himself was full of a wild and passionate energy. He didn't need drugs; he was high on money. Because of the Shadow, it was very difficult to muster the same intensity as Sosa. You were too busy wondering if you were going to have your windpipe severed. This was deliberate.

Still, Omar had a much worse time of it than Tony. Since he was so nervous to begin with, he could hardly stand still when the Shadow was in the room. Omar looked like he itched all over. But then, he'd had a bad time of it ever since they left Miami. Sick in the plane to Bogota. Groaned all the way from Bogota to La Paz. Sick all over himself in the helicopter ride up the mountains to Cochabamba. Besides, he was tense and annoyed just being with Tony. He hadn't wanted to bring him along at all, and he'd tried to convince Frank that Tony was too impulsive, that he couldn't shut up, that he paid no attention to forms. Frank was insistent. Tony had done such a good job on his first three runs to Bogota, it was time to move him closer to the source. Frank wanted his input.

So that is how Tony Montana happened to be walking through a coke factory with the biggest playboy in Cochabamba, maybe in all of Bolivia. The four of them —Sosa first, then Tony and Omar, with the Shadow so close behind them they could practically feel his breath on their necks—walked through the processing lab, following the drug from step to step. There were four black coal-fired stoves, each with a massive iron kettle on the flame, bubbling with coca paste. Chemists in white lab coats worked side by side with mute, barrel-chested Indians. Along one wall was a row of brick ovens, where the refined cocaine was dried.

Tony missed nothing. He felt as if he was being let in on the secrets of some vast magician.

"So between here and my other factory," said Sosa, "I can guarantee production of two hundred kilos— that's refined—two hundred kilos a month. Problem is, I got no steady market. Some months I can't move fifty keys, other months I gotta do two, three hundred. Crazy, huh? How can you do business that way?"

"Hey, I know what you mean, Mister Sosa," Omar replied unctuously. "We got the same problem up in Miami. Month to month, you never know what the demand's gonna be."

Sosa gave him an icy look, as if to say he didn't need another parrot. In his limp suit, with a wet cigarette clamped in his nervous fingers, Omar was hopelessly out of his league. He'd been one step behind from the moment he staggered off the helicopter. But Tony still held back, letting the two of them talk. He paused for a moment at a long table just beyond the ovens. The Shadow stopped beside him. Refusing to be intimidated, Tony pinched up a sample of the dried coke and snorted it up his nose. He smiled at the dead-eyed Shadow, to show that he liked the product. He said in a low voice: "Somehow, pal, I don't think you and I are gonna get along."

As he caught up with Sosa and Omar, he realized the Bolivian was wasting no time. He was already talking the deal. "What I'm looking for," he said to Omar, "is someone to share the risk. Like I want a guarantee. Say a hundred and fifty kilos a month."

"Well, that's an awful big commitment, Mister Sosa." Omar was so nervous his fingers were shaking around his cigarette. "It's too bad Frank can't be here to discuss it in person."

"It certainly is," replied the Bolivian with a trace of sarcasm. "I would have liked to meet him. I thought I was going to."

Omar seemed not to know what to say. Tony took a step forward. "He wanted to meet you too, Mister Sosa. But he's got a trial comin' up. It's not so easy for him to get outa the country right now."

"Mm," said Sosa, for the first time taking a good look at Tony. At least this one wasn't shaking.

"But don't worry," continued Tony. "Omar and me, we got the power to make a deal. Frank's real serious about his relationship with you. He respects you very much."

Omar's eyes went wide with shock. He was speechless. Sosa visibly relaxed his hostile stance. He suggested they move on to lunch. The four men exited the factory, which looked from the outside like an oversize Quonset hut with a row of brick chimneys along one side. The jungle came right up to the building on two sides, and there was a wide grassy field in front. Half a dozen trucks were parked there, ready for transport. Sosa led the way to his Jeep. The Shadow drove, and Omar sat beside him. Sosa rode in the back seat with Tony.

They made their way down a tortuous winding road with deep canyons on either side. The Andes rose around them, green and empty and jagged, alive with birdsound. The road passed under an arch of black-green trees with twisted trunks that oozed gallons of yellow pitch. At last they came to a "gate," a camouflaged spot where a group of guards stood watch, peering out of the bushes onto the paved main road. These guards were dressed in quasi-military gear, and each held a submachine gun. They parted a curtain of branches, and the Jeep turned onto the road, heading up the mountain.

Sosa asked Tony how he'd come into the business. Tony gave him an animated account, telling stories of his reefer days, of his time in Angola and then Marseilles. Sosa listened with interest, delighted by Tony's enthusiasm and sense of adventure. About two miles up the road they entered Sosa's compound, where a vast and improbable colonial mansion perched on a high plateau, ringed by terraced gardens and overlooking a giant panorama of mountain and canyon.

They left the Jeep in a shaded portico and proceeded down a high vaulted interior hall to the dining room. It was cavernous, the walls hung with huge paintings from the Spanish classical period, portraits of princes and allegorical extravaganzas. The long table was set at one end for three, with an ornate candelabra, gold-rimmed dishes and heavy silver. The Shadow sat by himself in a corner beside the mantel, arms folded and staring out the windows at the mountains. Omar and Tony sat on either side of Sosa at the head of the table, while a stream of servants brought in course after course. They ate in regal silence for a while. Three different wines were served.

At last Sosa turned to Tony. "If Frank Lopez can guarantee me a hundred and fifty kilos a month for one year," he said, "plus an escrow account in dollars in the

Bahamas for fifteen percent of the action, well then I could sell him a key as cheap as nine grand." He drained the last of his Chateau Lafite. "He'd have to pick it up here, of course."

Omar couldn't stand the pressure any more. He blurted out: "But if we do that, then we take all the risk of delivery ourselves. Besides, we'd have to cut out the Colombians. You know what that means?"

Sosa seemed offended to be asked such questions. Tony spoke up with a shrug. "It means we go to war with 'em," he said. "So what? They're all animals anyway."

Sosa smiled. "If we cut out the Colombians," he said carefully, "we take risks on both sides."

"We'd have to split the risk," said Omar, scrambling to find a negotiating posture he could defend. "If you could guarantee the delivery as far as Panama . . ."

Sosa laughed. "Panama? That'd be fifteen grand a key."

"Fifteen grand!" cried Tony. "You gotta be kidding, Sosa. We still gotta take the stuff in. You know what it's like in Florida these days? The Navy's all over the place. They got frogmen. They got EC-2's with satellite tracking. They got Bell assault choppers, up the ass they got 'em. It's not easy any more, y' know. It's no duck-walk."

There was a pause following this outburst. Omar was horrified. But Sosa seemed to take it all with a bemused smile. He liked Tony's intense and impulsive manner. Once again he ignored Omar and turned to direct his next proposal to Tony. But suddenly there was an interruption, as an aide came in from the hallway and nodded to Sosa. Excusing himself, Sosa stood up from the table and moved to join the aide at the end of the room in the bay window, near where the Shadow was sitting. The aide was a tall black man with close-cropped hair and horn-rim glasses. He looked peculiarly intellectual in the circumstances. He engaged Sosa in a low and murmurous conversation.

Omar leaned across the table to Tony. He whispered: "Shut up, will ya? I'll do the talking."

Tony shrugged. "Talk faster, then."

The horn-rimmed man gave a paper to Sosa, and as Sosa leaned over to sign it, the aide happened to glance down the dining room table. When his eyes fell briefly on Omar, he gave a small start. His eyes narrowed as he tried to put something together.

Omar said to Tony: "You just leave it to me. Wait'll I tell Frank how you been buttin' in. He'll have your ass."

Tony shrugged again. At the other end of the room, Sosa returned the signed document to the black aide, who whispered something in Sosa's ear. Sosa hardly reacted at all. His eyes darted down the table to Omar, then he nodded and waved the aide away. He glanced down at his Rolex as he returned to his place at the table.

"Where were we, gentlemen?"

"Panama," said Tony. "You're looking for a partner."

"Look, Mister Sosa," said Omar, fuming at Tony's interruption, "we're gettin' ahead of ourselves here. I come down to buy two hundred keys. That's it, that's my limit. I got no right to negotiate for Frank on anything larger than that. Neither does Tony, I don't give a shit what he says. So why don't we . . ."

"Hey Omar," said Tony, "why don't you let the man finish? Let's hear his proposition."

Omar's nerves exploded. He half rose out of his seat and spat the words across the table. "You got no authority here! You don't know what you're talkin' about. I started you in this business, Montana. Maybe if you shut the fuck up you'd learn something."

Tony remained completely calm. "Listen, Omar,

Frank's gonna love this deal." He glanced at Sosa. "*If* you guarantee it as far as Panama. Nine grand a key, no more."

Omar was speechless. He had no control over Tony, and he knew it. He turned to Sosa and practically pleaded. "Look, if you want I'll go back and talk to Frank about this. It's just not something I can do on the phone. You gotta try to understand my position. Tony here don't got no responsibility. *I* do."

"Okay, okay," said Sosa, suddenly adopting a conciliatory tone, as if Omar had been through enough. "Why don't you go right now? My chopper can take you to Santa Cruz. I've got my own jet there—you'll be in Miami in five hours. Talk to Frank, see what he says. You can be back here for lunch tomorrow."

"But—but—what about the two hundred keys?"

"Consider that deal made." Sosa stood up. Omar and Tony followed suit, for there didn't appear to be any room to refuse. "I want you to leave your partner here," continued Sosa. "He and I can work out the Panama route."

Omar and Tony exchanged a troubled look. Suddenly it seemed to both of them that Tony was in some danger. But after all, they weren't on the best terms themselves, Tony and Omar, and anyway Tony was much too tough to balk at this point. So they walked Omar out through the garden to the wide west lawn, where the chopper was already whirring. Omar seemed almost delirious at the thought of getting away. He didn't even show surprise when he saw the horn-rimmed aide sitting beside the pilot. He shook Sosa's hand and nodded to Tony. The noise of the chopper was much too loud for them to talk. Omar stepped inside. Tony and Sosa stepped back.

They'd forgotten the Shadow, who'd crossed the lawn ten paces behind them. Now he stepped past Tony and Sosa and hoisted himself through the chopper's opening, just as it started to lift off the ground. The ripple of a puzzled frown crossed Omar's face.

As Tony and Sosa made their way back to the house, Tony could see a woman on horseback emerge from the trees at the far end of the lawn. An image from deep in the past flashed across Tony's mind: the soldier's wife who used to pick him up in the afternoon behind the stables. His scar tingled for a moment. Sosa led him to an outdoor gallery off the dining room, where the servants were laying out coffee and fruits. Tony grabbed up a peach and bit into it. He watched the helicopter disappear over the mountain's rim.

He turned and looked at Sosa, as the playboy poured out the coffee. All day Tony had been aware of Sosa's elegant manners, his tailored clothes and refined tastes. He knew that Sosa kept apartments in New York and London and Beverly Hills, that he bred race horses and collected paintings in the six-figure range. If Tony felt like a two-bit hood the night he met Frank Lopez, he felt doubly so here in the presence of Arnoldo Sosa. He longed to possess this kind of sophistication. No detail escaped his notice. It was as if he was memorizing the other man's life, so he could some day reproduce it in a kingdom of his own.

"Hey Noldo," he said, playing the name like a chess move, "you know why us Cubans are all screwed up?"

Sosa smiled as he spooned in sugar. He didn't seem to mind the familiarity. "Why, Tony?"

" 'Cause the island's in the Caribbean, the government's in Russia, the army's in Angola, and the people all live in Miami."

Sosa threw back his head and laughed. Tony flushed with pleasure. Just then he felt like Sosa's equal, or at least that there was a chance he would one day close the gap. For this was the life he wanted, down to the tassels on Sosa's lizard shoes. He stood taller, trying to mimic the other man's posture. He held his cup precisely the way Sosa did.

"Very good, Tony," the Bolivian said. "I'll have

to remember that." Suddenly he looked over Tony's shoulder with an expectant smile. "Now you will meet my queen," he said, not without irony.

Tony turned as the horse and rider cantered up the lawn. They came to a halt just beyond the gallery. A servant walked out and took the reins as the woman dismounted. An exotic, dark-eyed senorita, haughty and strange and distant. She carried a riding crop, which she flicked against her leg as she approached.

"Gabriella—my rose," said Sosa, almost quivering with pride. "How was the trail?"

"Dusty," she replied, not even glancing at Tony. "We were up in the north pasture. The grass looks awful—needs more sheep."

"I'll see to it."

Already she turned to go. "We have the Rinaldis at eight," she said, unutterably bored.

"Gabriella? I want you to meet an associate of mine. From Miami. Tony Montana . . ." He motioned the two of them together, though neither moved an inch. "My fiancée, Gabriella Sardina."

"Hello," said Tony.

She nodded briefly, completely uninterested. Then she went away into the house, and Sosa watched her go with a strange and wistful look on his face. He seemed totally unaware of how rude she'd been. He suddenly looked very unlike a playboy. In spite of the lean and powerful body, Tony could see he was forty-five. He wasn't young any more.

"I like you, Tony," he said, moving to pour another cup of coffee. "You don't tell lies. It's too bad the same thing doesn't hold true of your partner."

"Huh? What are you talkin' about?"

"Omar," said Sosa. "He's scum." Tony looked bewildered. "My associate recognized him. They knew each other several years ago, in New York. He was an informer."

Tony bristled. "Listen, I don't know anything about that."

"I know you don't, that's why I'm telling you." Sosa's voice was calm and friendly. "Omar put Vito Duval and the Ramos brothers away for life. My associate barely managed to escape. Omar was a fool not to recognize him today."

Instinctively Tony looked up at the sky, just in time to see the helicopter come sailing over the mountain again. It was still pretty far away, but Tony could see it was trailing something from a rope or cable, as if it had just picked up someone stranded in the jungle. He turned with a questioning look to Sosa, who was smiling and holding out a pair of binoculars. Tony took them and trained them at the mountain, where the chopper was sweeping down toward the lawn.

"Garbage must be eliminated," said Sosa.

Omar hung by his neck from the end of a thick fisherman's rope. His face was blue, and his tongue lolled out. He hung like a broken puppet. Then the body hit the ground as the chopper came in for a landing. Tony lowered the binoculars. Sosa watched him closely for a reaction. Tony looked back at him, no emotion at all. Sosa moved to refill his coffee.

"So how do I know you're not a nark, Tony?"

He lifted the cup to his lips with an almost feminine delicacy. Out on the lawn they could hear the chopper's rotors winding down. In a sudden flash of temper, Tony walked up and batted the cup out of Sosa's hand. It smashed on the tiles at their feet. A look of panic crossed Sosa's face. The servant woman behind the table went scurrying into the house.

"Listen, you jerkoff," Tony barked, "I never hit on anyone in my life didn't have it coming to him. You hear me? All I got's my word—and I don't break that for nobody. I never trusted Omar. Like you say, he's a piece o' garbage. For all I know he's the guy who set me up and got my buddy Angel killed. That's history. It's a tough business, right? Omar's dead. I'm here. You wanna go on with me, you say so. You don't, I walk outa here—and you can kiss my ass."

There was a sound of running behind them. The Shadow had bolted out of the chopper as soon as it touched down. Now he tore across the lawn, as if he knew his boss was in grave trouble. He was ready to break every bone in Tony Montana's body. Sosa and Tony faced each other grimly. In a moment Tony would have to turn and fight the Shadow. He was a bare ten feet away when Sosa held up a hand and stopped him in his tracks.

"It's all right, Alberto. Leave us."

Obediently the bodyguard turned and trotted back the way he came. Sosa stepped over the litter of broken china and poured himself another cup of coffee.

"I think you speak from the heart, Tony. But I say to myself: What about this Lopez? He has *chivatos* like that working for him, his judgment must stink. I say to myself: What other mistakes has this Lopez made? How can I trust this organization? You tell me, Tony."

"Hey, Frank's real smart," said Tony. "Don't blame him for that animal. It could happen to anyone—even you. I'll talk to Frank myself. I'll fix it up between you. We gotta make this deal."

Sosa smiled. He motioned to Tony to sit down and passed him the bowl of fruit. Out on the lawn they could see three of Sosa's paramilitary guards carrying away the remains of Omar, the man they called the Monkey. Hummingbirds buzzed the jasmine plants that bowered over the portico.

"As far as Panama, then," said Sosa. "Thirteen grand a key."

"Ten," said Tony.

"Twelve."

"Eleven."

Sosa smiled and drained his coffee. He set the cup

and saucer down on the table. He reached out with both hands, as if to show he had nothing up his sleeves. Tony reached out his own hands, crossing them so he could grip Sosa in a double handshake. They sat hunched forward in their wicker chairs, holding the grip for a long moment.

"Eleven, then," said Sosa. "I think we're going to be doing business together for a long time, Tony."

"That's the way I want it, Noldo."

They let each other go and leaned back in their chairs. Their eyes stayed locked together. When Sosa spoke again, it was with the oddest tenderness. "Just remember, Tony," he said, "don't fuck me. Whatever you do, don't ever fuck me."

At the end of the lawn, the guards tossed Omar's body over the edge and down the canyon. Already the scavenger birds were gathering, wheeling in the sky.

The Lopez Bakery was a model operation. Housed in a white-tiled deco building on Tallahassee Boulevard, it employed thirty-five Cuban refugees—the old school of refugees, who'd fled the mother country in the first days of the revolution, fine upstanding American citizens all. You could eat off the floor of the Lopez Bakery. Men in white aprons and bakers' hats bustled back and forth with long wooden shovels, setting the dough in the wall ovens and bearing away the fragrant loaves. The Lopez Bakery specialized in delicious, crunchy soda crackers, of a kind that the Cuban community remembered fondly from the old days. But they made wonderful tarts as well, and wedding cakes and poppyseed rolls. It was a picture-book operation, with gleaming white trucks in the driveway and vigorous, grinning drivers to do the deliveries.

No wonder Frank Lopez had received so many citations. In his tidy office on the upper level, with a big picture window looking down on the bakery proper, the

walls were chockablock with plaques and mementoes.
The Chamber of Commerce, the Small Business Admin-
istration, the Better Business Bureau, the Elks, the
Rotary, you name it—nothing they liked better than to
take a tour of the bright and fragrant premises of the
Lopez Bakery. It was the classic American success story,
immigration division. Along one wall, between a Cuban
patriot flag and the stars and stripes, was a row of
photographs: Frank shaking hands with JFK; Frank
shaking hands with LBJ; Frank shaking hands with
Nixon; Frank shaking hands with Jimmy Carter.

No one was shaking Frank's hand just now. He
stormed around the office, hollering and shaking his fist
in the air. His bodyguard Ernie stood impassively in the
corner. Tony and Manolo sat in two chairs drawn up to
the desk. Manolo was kind of hunkered down, wincing
a bit in the face of Frank's explosion. Tony sat with his
arms folded, a patient look on his face.

"What are you, *nuts*, Montana!" roared Frank,
banging his fist against the wall. "You go and make an
eighteen-million-dollar deal without even *checking* with
me! I've had people tortured for less than that!"

"Hey, Frank, it's a money machine," said Tony.
"Eleven grand a key, we can't lose. We make seventy-
five million in a year. That's serious money, Frank."

"Oh yeah? And what's Sosa gonna do when I don't
come up with the first five million, huh? Send me a bill?
I'll tell you what he's gonna do. He's gonna send hit
squads up here, that's what."

He groaned like a man in pain and banged the wall
again. All the photographs jumped, and the one of
Nixon went cockeyed. Ernie flexed his fingers, as if
waiting for an order to strangle someone. He didn't care
who.

Tony shook his head and sighed, like he was terribly
disappointed. "Frank, you don't realize. I'm in real
tight with Sosa."

"You know what this trial is costing me in legal fees,

Montana? A fuckin' fortune, that's what. Now they got this new racketeering law says they can take it all, every penny I ever made, back to the year one!" Frank swept a bunch of papers off his desk and onto the floor. The unfairness of things was insupportable.

"So you're short a couple mill," said Tony. "So I'll make some moves on the street for you. We can get a mill here, mill there. Everyone's gonna want a piece o' this. Kinda like a syndication, ya know."

Frank shot him a cold-blooded look. "You been makin' some moves on your own, have you?"

Tony shrugged. "Hey, I keep my eyes open."

"Oh yeah? What do your eyes say about the Diaz Brothers, what about them, huh?· What about Gaspar Gomez? What's he gonna do when you start moving two thousand keys on the street next year?"

"Fuck Gaspar Gomez. Fuck the Diaz Brothers." Tony was surly now and impatient. He stood up and faced Frank across the desk, and perhaps for the first time both of them realized Tony was a couple of inches taller. "What'd they ever do for us? We'll bury them cockroaches."

Frank just stared at him for a minute. He was breathing heavily from all that rage, and there was confusion in his eyes. He'd been in this business for fifteen years, and he knew the young man in front of him was the wave of the future. He didn't want to be scared. He wanted to go with the crazy risks and maybe end up with the world in his pocket. The anger began to fade in him, and he sat heavily in the desk chair.

Tony sat casually on the corner of the desk. "Look, Frank," he said, "it's time. We gotta expand. The whole operation." His voice was gentle and coaxing. "New York—L.A.—Chicago. We have to set a mark of our own, Frank, and enforce it, whatever it takes. We gotta think big."

"Like your friend Sosa, huh?" Frank sounded weary. "Maybe this is his idea. He's a greaseball, Tony.

He's a snake, that's what he is." But somehow there wasn't much conviction in his curses. It was as if he didn't expect to be believed. He was like a father whom nobody listened to any more, whose sons were too busy getting laid. "You don't trust a guy like that," said Frank. "Maybe I made a mistake sending you down there. Is that what happened to Omar, Tony? Did he know something he wasn't supposed to know?"

"Are you saying I'm lying, Frank?"

Ernie moved a step out of the corner. Manny's hand slipped off the chair arm and hovered at his jacket pocket.

Frank spoke carefully. "Let's just say I want things to stay the way they are. For now, Tony. Stall the deal."

There was a long pause. As the two men stared in each other's eyes, Tony knew Frank knew Tony had given his word to Sosa. There was a break about to happen here. Maybe it wasn't irretrievable, maybe they just had to sleep on it. Maybe they still respected each other enough.

All Tony said was: "Have it your way . . . boss."

He turned to leave, beckoning Manolo to follow. It seemed there would be no final word. They reached the door, Tony opened it, then stood back to let Manolo go through. Frank called out on the spur of the moment. He almost sounded sad, except the words were so hard.

"You know I told you when you started Tony, the guys who last in this business are the guys who fly straight. Real low key. Real quiet. The guys who want it all—the chicks, the champagne, the flash—they don't last."

Tony paused to hear it all, but he didn't look over at Frank. And he didn't nod at the end or wait a respectable interval. He just walked out and shut the door. If he seemed angry at anyone at all, it was Manolo, who stood in the outer office looking bewildered and frightened. Tony batted him on the side of the head and headed for the elevator. He banged the button and banged the wall beside it, and Manolo tried to steer clear of his fury, which only made Tony snarl at him. They went down in silence.

The doors opened, and they walked through the bustling bakery, skirting a cartload of rolls as it dollied out to the trucks. It wasn't till they'd gained the street that Manolo could speak. He didn't care how angry Tony got. He still couldn't understand why everything fell apart up there.

"What's he gonna do, Tony?"

Tony spun around as if he was going to jump his friend. His eyes were slits of rage. "You mean what are *we* gonna do, chico," he said with a sneer. "We're gonna get Frank Lopez, that's what."

Chapter Six

EIGHT DAYS LATER Tony and Manolo were sitting in a plush waiting room. Everything was either gray or lavender, and even the walls seemed to be carpeted. Both men were decked out in suits and ties. Manolo carried the attaché case on his lap, perched on his knees as if he was expecting dinner on a plane. Tony read the sports page, grumbling because there wasn't enough soccer coverage.

They were waiting to see George Sheffield, a tough and grizzled lawyer whose reputation was nearly legend among the coke kings, several of whom he had managed to keep out of jail, in spite of crimes too numerous to list. He was on retainer to five or six Cuban gangsters. His methods were entirely unorthodox and certainly illegal, but he had so many murderous friends, nobody dared to question his arrangements. Besides, so many lawmen were on the take to him, there was scarcely anyone left to ask the questions.

Tony's appointment was for three P. M., and he didn't get ushered in till after four, but he kept his temper. He understood there were men that even kings had to go to hat in hand. He had pulled a lot of connections just to get this meeting. He had meanwhile taken his cut of the last Colombia shipment in coke. Frank was more than glad to lay a couple of kilos on him, because his own distribution was thrown into chaos by Omar's sudden demise. Tony and Manolo had spent the whole last week dealing the coke with Nick the Pig.

They'd had to be very careful not to intrude on Frank's client list. Moreover, they still had to keep their commitments to Frank, so it meant that some days they were out on the street twenty or thirty hours without a break, peddling grams. They had to get coked up just to keep going. For the first time since they started in the business, they began to look a bit green about the gills. Despite the three-piece suits and the attachés, no one would have mistaken them now for anything else but dealers.

A blonde and shapely secretary who was clearly getting it from the boss led them into Sheffield's office. The lawyer didn't even look up from his papers at first, as he spoke into the phone with a hoarse and gravelly croak. His eyes were heavy-lidded and yellow; they seemed cigarette-stained like his fingers. As Tony and Manolo sat down he put out his fortieth Camel of the day, swore into the phone, and hung up abruptly. He ran a hand through his thin red hair and looked warily at the two Cubans.

"So who's Tony Montana?"

"That's me," said Tony. "This is my partner, Manolo Ray." No response. "They tell me you're the best lawyer in town."

Sheffield snorted and reached for a Camel. "Did they also tell you how expensive I am?"

"Yeah, sure. It's like they say—if you gotta ask, you're outa your league."

"J.P. Morgan," Sheffield said. "A personal hero of mine. So you read American history, do you? What've you done lately to get *your* name in it?"

Tony laughed. "Not much yet. But I'm thinkin' of expanding my operation, see. Go independent. Get my own distribution system. Make my deals right at the source. From what I understand, the first thing I need is a class act like you on the payroll. You know, to advise me—just like you do those other guys."

"What's your time-frame?"

"Now," said Tony.

Sheffield took a deep puff of his cigarette. Then he coughed till it seemed he would spew his guts out. He hawked noisily into his handkerchief. Then he spoke, his voice heavy with sarcasm. "We start with a hundred grand," he said. "Cash. On the table." His rheumy eyes took on an arrogant glaze, as if to say: "Come back when you're ready to play hardball."

Tony nodded at Manolo, who flicked open his briefcase and drew out an envelope. He handed this over to Tony. Tony reached in and grabbed four wrapped stacks of thousand-dollar bills. There were twenty-five bills to the stack. Tony butterflied and fanned the money, as if to make a ritual show of its all being there, and he laid it in a pile on Sheffield's blotter. When Tony looked up, Sheffield was smiling broadly.

"I guess I got the job," said the lawyer.

Tony waited in the Jaguar. He'd made no attempt to conceal the car. It was visible from all twenty-six floors of the condo complex across the street. A limousine was waiting under the portico. After Tony had been sitting there about ten minutes, he saw three men emerge from the condo building: Frank Lopez, Ernie, his bodyguard, and a third man Tony had never seen before, a burly man with a slight limp. They all climbed into the limo, and it drove away, passing so close to Tony that Frank could have reached out the window and touched him. But Frank was too busy talking to the third man. And

Ernie, who was paid to watch for people like Tony, was already deep in the funny papers.

Tony left his car and walked across to the entrance. The day guard by the elevator knew him of course and merely nodded as Tony stepped in and pressed 26. When he reached the floor, the guard with the dog nodded like a buck private in the presence of an officer. He almost saluted. Tony walked up to Frank's door and rang. He expected a servant, at least the maid, and he was momentarily startled when Elvira herself opened the door.

"You just missed Frank," she said flatly. The flatness did not conceal her surprise. She wore jeans and was barefoot. Her body was beautiful, her face tired.

"I didn't come to see Frank."

Her eyes flared with annoyance. "This is not the time or the place," she said, already closing the door. "Next time make an appointment."

He stuck his foot in the door and blocked it and bulled his way into the foyer. She didn't put up any fight. She covered her face with her hands and groaned with exasperation, sick of this game. "I got something important to tell you," Tony said gently. "Why don't you make some drinks and act normal."

"Sure," she said, turning wearily toward the living room. "Why not? We're all normal here."

She walked across to the bar, reached down two glasses, and poured two fingers of Chivas Regal in each. She opened the small refrigerator beneath the bar to get ice, then seemed to decide it was too much trouble, and banged the door shut with her bare foot. She turned to hand him his drink.

"So tell me, how's crime?"

"I heard you was up in New York," said Tony. "All by yourself."

"It's none of your business who I was with."

"Me, I been down to Bolivia."

"So I understand," she said, seeming to get more hostile with every remark. She made no move to sit down but leaned against the bar in a defiant pose.

"What else do you understand?"

"I understand you and Frank have done your last deal together."

"I guess so," said Tony. "We ain't formally concluded anything, but . . ." He shrugged and shot her a sly grin. "Makes things a whole lot easier, don't it?"

"Does it?"

He raised his glass in a toast. "Here's to the land of opportunity," he said. She clinked glasses with him, and each took a belt of the scotch. She did not return his grin. She seemed to be waiting for him to make his point or leave, she didn't care which. Out of the blue he said: "Do you like kids?"

"I don't know. I guess so."

"Good. Cause I like kids." Suddenly he got very awkward. He moved a step closer to her, but then she seemed to freeze a bit, so he moved a step away. The grin was gone. His voice was husky as he spoke. "Look, here's what I am," he said. "I climbed up out of the gutter. I'm not the smartest guy in the world, but I got guts and I know the streets and I'm makin' the right connections. All I need now's the right woman. Then there's no stopping me. I'll go all the way to the top—really *be* somebody. Like Frank y'know, with the charities and committees and stuff, but even bigger." He laughed awkwardly. "Tony Montana, huh? Immigrant refugee makes good. That's me."

Elvira looked vaguely stunned, but she said nothing. Perhaps there was pathos in her eyes. Mostly she looked convinced he had just arrived from the moon.

"Anyway," Tony went on, "what I came up here to tell you is . . . uh . . . I'm in love with you." They both looked away from each other. There was something almost apologetic in Tony's voice. He seemed to understand it would be so much simpler if love had not come into it at all. "I know things right away," he said. "The first time I seen you, I knew you belonged to me. It's like we're two tigers, y'know. And there's no other tigers left." They looked at each other again. Her face was very, very quiet. It was hard to tell if she was angry or sad or what, but she wasn't happy. He said: "I want you to marry me. I want you to be the mother of my children."

For a moment they stood in a stunned silence. Then she shook her head with a mournful little laugh and moved to the end of the bar. "Tony, Tony," she said, softly reprimanding him as she opened a drawer and pulled out a mirror about six inches square. "I already told you. I don't believe in marriage."

"But this is different."

She set the mirror down on the bar, then fetched a vial of cocaine from the drawer. She unscrewed the cap and began to tap out lines on the mirror's surface. "It's never different," she said wearily. "And what about Frank? What are you going to do about Frank?"

"Frank's not gonna last," he said, a trace of pity in his voice. "You know that."

She had four lines laid down, each about two inches long. She set the vial down and retrieved a short glass straw from the drawer. She leaned down and tooted one nostril, then stood up with her eyes shut, holding the bridge of her nose.

"I'm not lookin' for an answer now," he said. "Just think about it, will you? You and me, we could . . ." His hands fluttered in a futile gesture. He couldn't find the words.

She leaned down to do the other nostril but suddenly had to sneeze. She tried to hold it in, pinching her nose as she let out a little squeak. And now there was blood in her hand, and she threw her head back as she reached for a Kleenex. Tony stepped toward her, reaching out both hands as if she was going to fall.

"Please," she said, daubing her nose with the tissue, "just go now, will you?"

He nodded gravely. Whatever she liked. "I'll be back," he said, and turned and strode away to the door. As he closed it behind him he began to whistle softly. All the way out to the car, all the way back to his place he was in a drunken good mood.

After all, she hadn't said no.

He went out again at four o'clock, and this time he took unusual precautions not to be followed. He drove around the block three times, idling under a tree till the street behind him was empty of traffic. In a way it wasn't odd that he should be so secretive. After all, he had appointments with dangerous men all day long; and he often returned with fifteen or twenty thousand in cash on the seat beside him. But even this did not explain the curious shyness in his face. He almost looked embarrassed, the way another man might look as he snuck out to buy a dirty magazine.

He drove down 17th Avenue to Shenandoah Park. He pulled into the driveway of a three-story tenement, where a bunch of Cuban teenagers were tinkering at a '58 Chevy. They watched in awe as Tony parked the Jag. He waved to them as he trotted up the steps to the back door. Then he disappeared inside and climbed two flights to the top floor. There was a noise of laughter and an accordion playing behind the door at the top of the stairs. Tony knocked.

The door opened, and a burly man threw up his hands and hooted with delight when he saw who it was. He shouted back over his shoulder: "Hey, it's Tony!"

He beckoned Tony into a large and crowded kitchen, where a group of eight or ten children was seated around the table, sporting party hats and eating hot dogs. They cheered when they saw Tony, and Tony laughed and shook his fists in the air like a boxer. An enormous Spanish woman stood at the stove, and another man perched on a stool, playing the accordion. Tony waved at all of them, then crouched to the table beside one of the kids. "So tell me," he whispered, "how old are you? 'Bout nineteen, huh?"

"No! Ten!" cried Paco Colon, throwing up ten fingers for emphasis.

"No kiddin'," said Tony. "You coulda fooled me." He drew a thick envelope out of his pocket. "You think you can use these?"

Paco Colon, the boy that Tony had plucked from the sea, who had drifted all night in his arms, asleep in a raging storm, now tore open his birthday present. Inside the envelope were tickets to a half dozen Dolphin games, tickets for the whole Colon brood that sat around the table. Paco waved the tickets in his hand, shouting excitedly. Then all the children cheered.

Waldo Colon set down the accordion and went to the refrigerator to get Tony a beer. Waldo and his wife Dolores had taken in all his sister's kids, for she had been one of the missing off the trawler. They were a dozen now, uncles and cousins and the aged grandmother, all living somewhat helter-skelter in the third floor tenement overlooking Shenandoah Park. Tony had tracked them down about a month ago, remembering the promise Waldo Colon had made to him when he retrieved his nephew at Key West Naval.

Anything Tony ever needed. Anything.

Tony chatted amiably with Waldo and Dolores, sipping his beer and pleading he was too full to eat. They asked him about his business, and he replied evasively, for as far as they knew he made all his money in import-export. They tried to fix him up with a date, listing all the eligible girls they knew around the neighborhood. He declined, laughing heartily at their insistence that he needed a woman to fatten him up.

Suddenly there was a commotion in the parlor. A

tremendous roar and a stamping of feet. All the children squealed and held their breath. Then a gorilla appeared in the doorway, beating its breast like King Kong. The children shrieked with excitement as the gorilla lumbered around the table to Paco's place. He picked the child up bodily out of his chair and held him over his head, roaring triumphantly. Paco was giddy with laughter. The gorilla lowered the child onto his shoulders and pranced around the kitchen as the other children cheered.

Finally Paco gripped the gorilla's neck and yanked. The headpiece came off. The kids whistled and banged the table when they saw who it was: the toothless retard, the one who had thrown the inner tube to Tony and Paco. Now that the jig was up, he lowered Paco to the floor, unzipped the stuffy suit, and stepped out and bowed. As the children applauded, he walked over to Tony and spoke a laborious hello. Though he had a severely cleft palate, he talked with greater precision now, for the Colons had enrolled him in special classes at a rehabilitation center.

"Hello, Ricardo," Tony said warmly, shaking the young man's hand.

Tracking this one down had been a good deal more difficult. Tony had had to bribe an official at INS, and even then it took two weeks of poring over medical charts, for he didn't even have a name to go on. Eventually he found him in a public sanitarium in Sweetwater, thin and terrified and strapped to a bed, covered with sores. Three more bribes were required to spring him. And most important, Tony had had to convince Waldo Colon to take in another child, this one twenty years old.

Waldo and Dolores had not even had to discuss it. They nodded yes before Tony finished asking the question.

Now Tony visited once every couple of weeks, usually unannounced. But today was special, Paco's birthday.

They all grouped around the table as Dolores bore in the cake, decorated yellow and blazing with candles. They all sang at the top of their voices, Tony included. He could only stay another few minutes, for he had another delivery to make before sundown. He would press an envelope of cash into the hand of the protesting Waldo on his way out, as he always did. Meanwhile he laughed and sang with the others, all his problems forgotten.

As soon as they finished their cake, he would give the kids a boxing lesson.

The Babylon Club was hopping like Saturday night as Tony and Manolo drove up. Tony turned the Jaguar over to the carhop he used to play cards with in jail, palming him twenty bucks as he shook the guy's hand. Tony and Manolo, both in tuxedos, made their way through the crowd on the steps and entered the glittering foyer. The Babylon was always jammed, always fast and wild, but some nights it seemed to go over the edge, till the air itself crackled with something like an electric charge. It had to do with a conjunction of the music, the drugs, the carnal desires, and maybe even the moon. Whatever it was, it was turned up high tonight.

As soon as he saw them, the maitre d' hurried over and shook both their hands. He led them through the milling crowd at the bar and into the restaurant. Tony nodded to several people as he made his way to the perfect table just above the dance floor. He ordered a vodka tonic. Manolo had scarcely sat down when he started looking around for a woman. Tony was too busy thinking. He had a hundred details to sort out about sending a team of mules out of Panama. Seeing Elvira this afternoon had made him glad, but also terribly impatient. As he waited for his drink he pulled apart a book of matches, idly watching Manolo as the latter scanned the crowd on the dance floor.

Suddenly Manolo's mouth dropped open. He looked

like he'd seen a ghost. Tony's eyes swiveled to the dance floor. Like a laser he spotted his sister Gina, in a black crepe dress he'd sent her himself. She was dancing with a flashy young Cuban in a burgundy velvet suit, big diamonds on both of his pinkies. Instinctively Tony rose in his chair, his hands curling into fists.

"Easy, Tony," said Manolo, "it's okay, it's just a disco for Chrissake."

"Who's she with?"

"What do you give her money for, if you don't want her to go out and have fun?"

"Who is he?" asked Tony again, but beginning to calm down now. The waiter arrived with the drinks, and he sat.

"Some kid, he works for Luco."

Just then Gina turned in their direction. Her eyes widened when she spotted them, but she quickly waved and grinned at them. Manolo waved back. Tony nodded. The guy in the burgundy checked them out.

"Keep an eye on her, will ya?" Tony grabbed his drink and stood up. It was time to work the room, see who he needed to make an arrangement with. He was damned if he was going to sit and watch like a chaperone. "Make sure he don't dance too close," he called over his shoulder to Manolo.

"Sure, Tony."

Tony crossed toward the bar. He saw two of Echeverria's men huddled over their beers. Echeverria did a lot of trade in Panama red, and Tony was sure they'd have a good update on the customs situation. One of the men looked up and waved to him. Tony headed over. Then suddenly someone stepped in front of him and laid a hand on his arm.

"Hello, Tony. You remember me?"

Tony turned with a white flash of anger, ready to fling his drink in the guy's face. He jerked his arm away. The guy was paunchy, and his face was red and veiny from too much booze.

"Yeah, sure," said Tony, simmering down. "Mel Bernstein, right? Homicide. Everyone knows you."

"That's right, Tony. I think we better talk." He gestured toward the quiet end of the bar and made a move that way, but Tony stood his ground a moment longer.

"Talk about what? I ain't killed anybody lately."

"No?" said Bernstein dryly. "Gee, that's a relief. How 'bout ancient history, Tony? How 'bout Emilio Rebenga? Seems to me you're forgettin' a whole bunch of Indians at the Sun Ray in Lauderdale."

Tony laughed. "You know, Mel," he said, "whoever's givin' you your information must have a lot of trouble talkin' with his head up his ass."

Bernstein leaned close and breathed in Tony's face. He smelled of garlic and rotgut whiskey. "Are we gonna talk, Montana, or am I gonna bust your spic wiseass right here?"

Tony didn't argue. He followed Bernstein to the end of the bar, noticing just at the last that Bernstein walked with a slight limp. He flashed on the man he'd seen get into the limousine with Frank. They took the two last stools in the corner, and Bernstein ordered a double Four Roses rocks.

"The news on the street is you're bringin' in a lot of yeyo, Tony. Congratulations. You're not a small-time hood any more. You're public property, and the Supreme Court says we can invade your privacy." It all sounded very friendly, like the grin of a shark.

"No kiddin'," said Tony, cocky again. "How much we talkin'?"

"Well, let's see now." Bernstein pulled a Bic out of his shirt pocket and slid the paper napkin out from under his drink. He scribbled a figure and passed the napkin to Tony. It said "25,000."

Tony snorted. "I still think you're havin' an information problem, Bernstein. I don't even get my first shipment from Panama till next week."

"Bullshit. You pulled in a hundred and eighty grand in the last ten days."

No question about it, Bernstein's information was getting better and better.

"How 'bout I give you ten?" said Tony.

Bernstein bristled. "Whaddaya think, I'm havin' a sale? I want twenty-five by tomorrow morning, and that's just for openers. Maybe you'll have to eat hot dogs for a week, but I'm sure you'll make it up. Everybody's doin' real good. Ain't no recession down here."

Tony knew there was no room to argue. Bernstein could bust him in five minutes flat, tie him up in a trial that could cost him a quarter of a million. He was just getting started, he couldn't afford the hassle. He lit a cigarette. "What do I get for my money?" he said. "Protection?"

"*Protection?*" Bernstein was flabbergasted. "What do you think this is, New Jersey? You protect yourself, asshole. Believe me, if you're like the rest o' these guys you'll be dead in a year." He downed the last of his drink and signaled for another. "Let me tell you how the system works," he said, and in a grotesque way he sounded almost avuncular, like he was a high school coach. "It's a trade-off, see. You feed me a bust every now and then. Or maybe you call me if there's a homicide, and when me and my boys get there we find a little present. Other day a Cube got clipped in Miami Springs, we found a hundred grand cash underneath him. Safe to say robbery wasn't the motive. No use turning it in, the state'll just spend it on niggers."

Tony was gripped by the purest stab of hatred. He felt an almost physical hunger, as if he'd never be satisfied now till he'd torn the man's face off. A list began to take shape in his head of those he would one day eliminate. The list was still hazy, just the one name at the top—Mel Bernstein—but he suddenly knew it would be a whole list before he was through. And whatever happened, they would never kill him till he'd got through his list.

"Works the other way too," said Bernstein, positively cheerful now. "We tell you who's moving against you. We shake down who you want shaken down. Course we collect. Hey, we're eight guys. Professional work, Tony. When we hit, it hurts." It sounded like he was advertising laundry soap.

"I'm real impressed. Is all of America this wonderful?"

"Just the colonies, Tony. Just where the spics have taken over."

They both downed their drinks. They ordered another round. In fact they were both lucky, because neither one could kill the other. They needed each other too much.

"So how do I know you're the last cop I gotta grease?" asked Tony, wondering now who else Frank was going to pull down on him. "What about Metro, Lauderdale, DEA? What rock are *they* gonna crawl out from under?" It was abundantly clear that Bernstein came from the same neighborhood.

Bernstein shrugged. "That's *your* problem, José. We don't cross no lines." He drained his third drink in ten minutes as he stood up. "Look at it this way: I got eight killers working for me. If their reputations are compromised, their careers are gonna suffer. Which means their *families* are gonna suffer. Which means they're gonna make *you* suffer." He started to turn away, but something dawned on him. "Oh yeah, and two of my boys got a vacation coming up. Throw in two round-trip tickets to London, okay? First class. They're real nice guys."

Tony just stared at him now. Bernstein loved it. He reached out a hand and patted Tony's cheek. "I like the scar. Just like Capone, huh? Real nice touch. But you oughta smile more, Tony. Enjoy yourself. Every day above ground's a good day."

With that he winked and limped away, waving to two

or three men in the crowd as if he was a politician, which he was. Tony sat there brooding. It wasn't the money. It wasn't even that there were cops who had to be dealt in at every turn; that was part of the racket. No, it was Frank who was troubling him now. He didn't think he'd have to go up against Frank so soon. If it had come to that, there was going to be blood.

Tony looked up, and his eyes drifted back to the dance floor. The burgundy suit was snuggling up to Gina as they danced. One hand was on her ass. Tony's jaw tightened, and he stood up ready to barrel over and flatten the guy. But he'd hardly taken a step when something drew his eye to the entrance of the bar: Elvira had just walked in.

She wore a long slinky sequined dress, coral-colored, and her hair was up with gardenias in it. She paused in the doorway and looked around. Ernie was just behind her. Frank was slightly off to the side, his ear being bent by the owner. Tony moved toward her, he couldn't stop himself. As soon as she saw him coming she glanced with a worried look in Frank's direction, almost as if to warn Tony. But Tony didn't take the hint.

"Well hello," he said. "Did you think about what I said?"

She shook her head. "I never remember what anyone says." Already Frank was eyeing them. He didn't like what he saw.

"Why don't I give you a hint? Coupla little kids—big mansion—happily ever after. Is it comin' back to you?"

"Please Tony—"

But Frank was there now. He was grinning, but there wasn't anything happy about it. "Hey Tony," he said. "Long time, huh? When are you gonna get your own girl?"

Tony looked him right in the eyes. He said evenly: "That's what I'm doing, Frank."

The grin faded. Ernie seemed to hover a little closer.

Frank grabbed Elvira's arm. "Then go do it somewhere else, Tony. Like get lost."

Elvira said: "Frank, he was only—"

"What was that, Frank?" Tony cupped his ear like a deaf man. "I don't hear so good sometimes."

"You keep it up, Tony, you won't be hearing anything."

He made a move to push by Tony, dragging Elvira into the bar. Tony took a step right and blocked them. Ernie reached into his jacket.

"You gonna stop me, Frank?"

Frank's whole body seemed to shake with rage. A snap of his fingers, and Ernie would have drawn his gun. But this was between the two of them. "You're fuckin' right I'm gonna stop you," he said. "I'm givin' you orders, Montana. Blow. Now."

Manolo was suddenly there beside Tony. One hand was in his pocket, and he faced down Ernie grimly. Frank let go of Elvira and pushed her away. *Something* was about to blow, but it wasn't Tony.

"Orders?" said Tony. "There's only one thing gives and gets, *gusano*. And that's balls."

At that moment, it seemed amazing that the Babylon Club could go on dancing and drinking. All that laughter and hustle, and nobody even half-aware they were about to hit an iceberg. Ernie and Manolo now fronted each other like a mirror image, in an ancient pose of warriors. Tony and Frank looked ready to fight with their bare hands. It was Elvira who stepped between them.

"This is so fucking ridiculous," she said, contemptuous of all of them. "I wanna go home and get stoned, if you don't mind."

Somehow the spell was broken. She stalked away to the foyer, beckoning for her sable wrap at the cloakroom gate. Frank turned immediately to follow her, fishing in his pocket for a fifty to tip the shaken maitre

d' who'd been waiting to show him a table. Ernie was
more reluctant to go. He'd had his finger on the trigger
for half a minute, and to break off now was like coitus
interruptus. Yet he had no choice. He shot a final murderous glance at Manolo and turned to follow Frank.
Manolo gave an audible sigh.

"What was that all about?"

"Scum put Mel Bernstein on me," Tony said. He
headed back to the table, Manolo nervous beside him
and firing questions. "Had to be Frank," said Tony.
"Who else knew about the Rebenga hit? Omar's fer-
tilizer, ain't he? Frank's just lettin' me know what kinda
weight he can pull."

Manolo was actually sweating, as if he'd been dancing all night long. "I don't know, things don't look so
good here, Tony. Why don't we put off the Panama
deal. Get outa town for a while, y'know, go up to New
York?"

Tony shook his head. "Too cold. I like the weather
here." Suddenly his eyes darted to the edge of the dance
floor, where Gina and the burgundy suit were arm in
arm and laughing as they headed up the stairs to the
lounges. Abruptly Tony stood up from the table.

"Where you goin' now?" asked Manolo, bewildered.

Tony didn't answer. He strode across the dance floor,
knocking a couple of people out of his way, who swore
at him as he gained the stairs and barreled up two at
a time. He reached the landing, but neither Gina nor
the burgundy suit was visible. Tony plowed right into
the ladies' room. Several women ducked or dove for the
stalls, as if they were used to jealous lovers spraying the
powder room with bullets. In a flash Tony could see
that Gina wasn't there, and he stormed out as suddenly
as he'd stormed in.

He crossed the hall to the men's room and threw the
door open. Three men were lined up at the urinals,
minding their own business. There were two stalls at the

end of the room, and under the door on the left two pairs of feet were clearly visible, a man's and a woman's. Tony raged across the room and hit the door with his shoulder. It crashed open, revealing Gina just as she was about to snort a spoonful of coke. The burgundy suit stood behind her, running his hands along her ass and kissing her on the neck.

They were both thrown off-balance as Tony exploded into the tiny space. Gina screamed. With a single blow to the head Tony dropped the burgundy suit to the floor. He began to kick at the guy's face.

"Tony, stop!" she cried. "What are you doing?"

He whirled around and grabbed her hand. "What am *I* doing? You goddam whore, what do you want with this shit, huh?" He ripped the vial of cocaine from her fingers and scattered the drug all over the floor of the stall. Then he dropped the vial in the toilet. The burgundy suit had scrambled to his knees, and with one hand Tony lifted him onto his feet. He was chalk-white. "You get the hell out of here, *maricon*, I'll kill you the next time!" Then Tony threw him out of the stall, and he tripped and fell heavily against the sink, splitting his lip open.

"Fernando, don't go!" cried Gina. She began to beat at Tony with her fists.

Tony turned and pinned her against the wall of the stall. Fernando crawled to his feet and staggered out of the men's room. Everyone else had already split. Manolo now rushed in.

"You think it's cute, huh?" sneered Tony, holding her as she struggled and tearing the crepe at her shoulder. "Somebody puttin' their hands all over your ass in a toilet. Is that how you want to grow up?"

"It's none of your business, Tony," she spat at him.

"The hell it isn't! Three-dollar hooker, that's all you are! Snorting shit like the rest o' these pigs!"

Manolo hovered at the door of the stall, trying to

quiet them down. The owner would probably be up in about two minutes, and they'd already had enough trouble.

"What are you, a priest?" shrilled Gina. "A cop? Look at *your* life, Tony. You can't tell me what to do!"

Manolo said: "Let me take her home, Tony."

Tony seemed shocked by the savagery in Gina's voice. He loosened his grip, and she slipped away from the corner. He probably would have let her go without another word just then, but she wasn't finished. Taunting and contemptuous she said: "I'll go out with who I want, Tony. And if I want to screw them I'll screw them."

His face went pale with outrage. He lunged at her and smacked her face. She tried to run across the room, and he dragged her back by her hair. She tripped and fell in a heap, sobbing. Tony stood over her, desperate and confused. Manolo pushed him aside and knelt to console her. Now the door to the corridor was opened gingerly, and the maitre d' stuck his head in.

"Get her outa here," said Tony to Manolo, his voice cracking with something like grief. And he walked away, shoving the maitre d' aside as he exited into the corridor. The little crowd of spectators parted to give him room.

Gina did not stop crying till Manolo had taken her down the back stairs to the parking lot. He settled her into his Cadillac and headed for Little Havana. He couldn't think of a thing to say, and he made it clear by his mildness that Gina owed him no explanations. But once the tears had stopped, she spoke in a voice taut with anger: "He's an animal, isn't he? Mama's right. He hurts everything he touches. I don't care if I never see him again."

Manolo said with a shrug: "He loves you, what do you want. You're his kid sister."

"He still thinks I'm fifteen, doesn't he? Just because he's been in jail for five years. Can't he see I grew up?"

"You're the best thing he's got," said Manolo gently. "He don't want you to grow up to be like him. So he's got this father thing, wants to protect you . . ."

"Against *what*?" she retorted irritably. She pulled a brush from her bag and began to stroke her hair. It crackled with electricity.

"Guys like the jerk you were with tonight."

"Don't *you* start now, Manolo," she said. "I like Fernando, he's fun. Knows how to treat a woman."

Manolo looked pained. "Come on, Gina, what kinda future's he got? He's a bum. You oughta go out with a guy who's goin' somewhere."

She gave him a peculiar look. "Like who?" she said carefully.

"I don't know. Doctor—lawyer—that kind." He eased the Cadillac next to the curb in front of the bungalow. His face crinkled up in a friendly smile as he reached across to open her door.

She grabbed his hand. "What about you, Manolo? Why don't *you* ever take me out?" He let her hold his hand, but his face reddened, and he looked away. "I see the way you look at me," she said. "How come you don't ask?"

He chuckled nervously. "Hey, Tony's like my brother," he said. This wasn't really an answer. Perhaps what he meant to say was that Tony wouldn't like it. Considering what a lady-killer he was at the Babylon Club, his shyness was startling, though no less endearing for that.

"You think about it, okay?" said Gina, raising his hand and kissing the tips of his fingers. " 'Cause I'll tell you something, Manolo. You don't know what you're missing."

She slipped out of the car and hurried toward the house. As he watched her fumble with her key in the yellow porch light, he felt an awful sinking in his heart. He had loved her since the day she came in laughing to visit Tony. And he knew that Tony would not allow it.

It frightened him to have to keep secrets from Tony, almost as much as Tony himself had begun to frighten him, with all his deals and his hunger for power.

Manolo would have been quite content to be a small-time hood, living his life in a quiet bungalow like this one, curling up with a girl like Gina. Instead, wherever Manolo looked they seemed to be in way over their heads. The money was big, all right, but the simple life he harbored deep inside receded further and further with every passing day. He drove away heartsick, convinced that no matter how successful he and Tony became, he would never have what he really wanted.

When Manolo moved to take care of Gina, Tony walked downstairs again and headed for the bar. He had been through three interruptions now—Mel Bernstein, Elvira, and Gina—but he was no less intent on talking to Echeverria's men about the situation in Panama. The two were sitting just where they had been, nursing their eighth or tenth Dos Equis of the evening. They greeted Tony warmly, for Echeverria, their boss, had been one of Tony's marijuana contacts in the old days in Havana. They regaled him for ten minutes with their exploits on a trawler full of fifteen tons of weed. They weren't cokeheads, they were potheads, and thus they were mild and rather befuddled, gentle as golden retrievers, at least among friends.

Tony began to question them about Panama customs. His first shipment from Sosa would arrive in Panama City in the next three days. Tony would fly in and set up the mules. He had a list of about fifteen names, local Panama hoods who would find him mules by the truckload. Apparently there wasn't a soul in Panama who wouldn't sell it for five hundred dollars. Tony ran through the list with Echeverria's men, feeling them out about each of the gangsters, finding out who he could really trust. Customs, it seemed, was no problem. There were three or four men who had to be bribed, and by international standards they were still refreshingly cheap.

Tony loved this part of an operation, the trading of information and the sizing up of men. His own personal problems seemed to vanish, at least insofar as they took the shape of Bernstein, Elvira, and Gina. Just then he was sure he could handle all of them, Frank Lopez as well. He felt this assurance much more acutely when he wasn't actually facing the people themselves. By working on his power base, by getting his deal to run without a hitch, he was building himself a position in which all personal frictions would naturally resolve themsélves. It was as if he thought he could drown them in champagne.

In any case, he was feeling on top of the world by the time he had worked his way around the bar, talking with this one and that one. The men in power were eager to talk to Tony Montana, who'd struck a new kind of deal in Bolivia. The hustlers wanted to bask in the glow of his self-assurance. It must have been after two when he finally went back to his empty table to have a last drink.

The dancing had stopped and the band packed off, but the night wasn't over yet. The night was never done at the Babylon. To the lush strains of Sinatra's *Strangers in the Night*, the deep-tanned owner appeared on the stage, picked out by a pin spot. He tapped his microphone and said: "Are ya all high enough?" A wave of cheers and applause rose from the darkened restaurant and bar. "Good, good. 'Cause we got something real special for you. We found him stoned in the jungle, and we're sending him back right after the show. From Caracas, Venezuela, ladies and gentlemen, we present with great pride"—a roll of drums—"*Octavio!*"

The spotlight shifted and picked up a sad old man at the corner of the stage, enormously fat, with a Quasimodo mask covering his head and neck. The coked-up

audience broke into rhythmic applause. Many of them
were from Caracas themselves and knew the act backwards. With a red bulb for a nose, the fat man gyrated
grotesquely to the Sinatra song. The crowd began to
laugh, and the music suddenly shifted beat to *Saturday
Night Fever*. Octavio began to shimmy, shedding the
stuffing out of his clothes, his big eyes staring mourn-
fully.

Tony watched in a kind of brooding silence, all alone
like the clown himself. Octavio tore his head mask
off, revealing a young white-painted face with large
blackened eyes. The crowd was laughing, and in fact the
gyrations were very funny, but there was something
hypnotic as well about his dancing, some deep ritual
yearning. He was stripped down to leotards now, thin
as a stick, and he began to pull girls out of the crowd
to dance with him. They bounced around like yoyos.
Everyone was laughing except the clown and Tony.

As he watched the figure of mockery, the pin spot
shining on the sad white face, Tony began to feel a sort
of prickly heat at the top of his spine. The disco beat
was frenetic, the whole room caught up in hilarity. And
yet there was another rhythm here, moving in the
darkness. Tony cocked his head, as if he didn't quite
believe what his antenna was picking up. He caught a
glint of metal out of the corner of one eye—

And suddenly dove for the floor.

Machine-gun fire ripped through the upholstery just
where his torso had been, smashing the mirrors behind
the table. The crowd erupted in screams. Tony rolled
and grabbed for the Baretta at his ankle. He knew he
was hit in the shoulder. He lunged under a table as the
bullets kept coming. He could tell from the spurt of fire
there were two of them. He got off a shot and hit one of
them in the chest. The gunman staggered across the
disco floor, spraying the walls and ceiling with a final
volley as he fell.

The crowd exploded for the exits, trampling one

another. The second gunman was crouched behind an overturned table, trying to pick off Tony as he scrambled behind the bar. A wounded woman in the middle of the floor was screaming, and the maitre d' was pleading for a short cease-fire so they could drag her to safety. But they weren't playing by the Geneva conventions. The gunman sprayed the fleeing crowd with bullets, as if to make them exit even faster. Tony popped up from behind the bar and fired twice, hitting the gunman in the hand, which made his trigger finger wilt.

Tony bolted for the door. His tuxedo seemed to be in tatters, his left side drenched with blood. Dozens of partygoers had taken cover in the foyer, but most had already fled into the night. Tony ran out crouched, holding his shoulder. He sprinted across the parking lot to the red Jaguar, praying the keys would be in the ignition. He was just reaching for the door when another burst of fire off to his right made him duck. There was a third gunman across the way, standing beside a black van. Tony fired his last shot and made the guy sprint for cover.

Then he tumbled into the Jaguar, reached under the seat, and pulled out his Ingram pistol. The key was in the ignition. It flashed through Tony's mind how dumb these hitmen were not to strip his car. He gunned the engine and lurched across the parking lot. As he passed the main entrance to the club, the man he'd wounded in the hand was running out. He got off a wave of bullets, but they ricocheted off the armored side of the Jag. Tony roared out into the street.

Or course the van came after him. Tony could see it in the rearview mirror, about a block behind him. It had stopped to pick up the second gunman, who now leaned out of the passenger's window, waiting for a shot at Tony. Both cars ran a red light, then another. Luckily the streets were quiet because it was so late. The van was souped up like crazy, and it was gaining. The gunman fired a volley, trying to explode the Jaguar's rear tires.

The bullets reverberated along the armor plating, till Tony's teeth were rattling in his head.

The two cars were nearly abreast when Tony took a corner on two wheels. A wino was just stepping into the street, and Tony hit the brakes and swerved to miss him. The front bumper of the Jag bashed the van. The gunman was struggling to put a new clip in his gun. The Jag and the van shrieked down the street, the van edging over to ram the car again and again. Tony pulled a lever, and the bulletproof blackout shutters whapped down across the side windows. The van was trying to cut him off, push him onto the sidewalk. The gunman aimed his fresh-armed Ingram and blasted out Tony's windshield.

The Jag leaped the curb and careened down the sidewalk. The van slowed to watch him crash, but Tony kept his hold on the wheel. He drove the car onto the street again. He tapped the lever, and the blackout shutters whirred partially open. As the van came abreast of him, Tony laid the Ingram across his arm and sprayed the field with lateral fire. The gunman in the passenger's seat ducked, but the driver wasn't so lucky. His head exploded like a watermelon. The van went berserk, roaring across the street and up the sidewalk, smashing through the plate-glass window of a hardware store. It burst into flames.

Tony was a mess, and so was the car, but he couldn't stop here. He cut away from the main drag and headed back to Calle Ocho along quiet suburban streets. The hole in his shoulder wasn't going to kill him, but it hurt like hell. He couldn't go to a hospital—too many questions. He didn't dare go home, since he couldn't be sure they weren't staking it out. He decided the only safe place was Nick the Pig's.

It took him a good half hour to get there. Most of the cuts on his face and hands—from the blowing of the windshield—had stopped bleeding. Even so, he looked like he'd lost a fight with a grizzly bear. His shoulder slumped as he staggered out of the car. His white tuxedo shirt had turned a ghastly crimson. When Nick opened the door to let him in, wearing only a pair of drawers the size of a tent, Tony pitched forward into his arms, as if he'd finally reached a place where he could let go.

Nick carried him over and laid him down on the sofa. It was quarter to three, but he made a couple of calls and managed to have a med student there within half an hour. As the student cut Tony's tuxedo off and began to dress the wound, Nick called Chi-Chi and Martin Rojas and told them to report to his place pronto. Tony sipped at a glass of hundred and fifty proof rum. He was weak from loss of blood, but the wound wasn't deep. The bullet had gone right through. Even as the student stitched him up, he was on the phone trying to track down Manolo.

At first he wasn't certain they hadn't got to Manolo first. There was no answer at the apartment. He called a couple of dealers who worked for them, and they managed to come up with last names for the girls Manolo was seeing. A couple of dead ends, till finally a girl named Miriam answered and said: "Yeah, he's here. Who's askin'?"

When Manolo grabbed the phone, Tony could tell he was wired on coke. As soon as he heard what had happened, he freaked out. He clamored to apologize, like none of it would have happened if he hadn't left Tony alone.

"Look, chico," said Tony, "just get your fancy clothes on and meet me outside the bakery in forty-five minutes. Now move your ass!"

He hung up the phone and grunted as the med student pulled the last stitch. Nick the Pig paid the student four grams and let him out just as Chi-Chi and Martin arrived. Tony got dressed quickly in the clothes Chi-Chi had brought. His face was slightly pale, and he winced as he slipped on the shirt, but he was as ready to go as ever. Revenge was a wonderful cure.

"I'm bettin' he's not heard anything yet," he said to Nick. "Gimme forty-five minutes, then call him. All you say is you're one of the guys at the club. Say you just heard about the van, and the word is I got away."

"No problem, Tony."

Chi-Chi and Martin followed Tony out to the car. Before he got in he walked around the Jaguar, checking the damage and shaking his head. Chi-Chi suggested they take the Monte Carlo, which he and Martin were driving now, but Tony seemed to feel it was a point of pride that his car was still running. They drove away like battered warriors, flags still flying.

It was getting on close to four-thirty when they pulled up across the street from the Lopez Bakery. Manolo was already there, standing beside the Cadillac and nervously looking left and right as he puffed on a cigarette. When Tony got out of the Jaguar he tried once again to apologize, but Tony silenced him with a playful cuff on the side of the head. They left Martin outside to cover the street. Tony had guessed right that there would be no extra guards at the bakery, since the war had been meant to be fought and won and finished with at the Babylon. Tony and Manolo and Chi-Chi went around to the back of the building, where the bakery trucks were all lined up. A couple of people had already reported for work to start the ovens, but they were busy inside. The three men moved up the outdoor fire escape and jimmied the door at the top.

As they made their way down the dim corridor, they could see the light spilling out from the half-open door of Frank's office. As they edged closer, guns drawn and at the ready, they could hear Frank bellowing into the phone.

"What?! You gotta be kiddin', aren't ya? It was three to one. Junkie dopes!" He slammed down the phone and turned to someone in the office. "They screwed it up. Don't anything get done right any more?"

A muffled voice said something like: "There's always

another day. At least you scared the shit out of him.''

"Did I tell ya 'bout my softball team?'' asked Frank, as if the hit on Tony Montana was just another hassle he'd have to deal with later. "They won the division. We're goin' to Sarasota for the State Championship. How about that?''

"That's great,'' said the muffled voice.

Tony pushed the door open and stepped inside, leveling his gun at Ernie before the bodyguard could make a grab at his jacket. Manolo and Chi-Chi sidled in behind Tony. They stood on either side of him, their guns at ease, but the firepower was enough that Tony could lower his own gun to his side. Frank sat stunned at his desk. Across from him in an easy chair was Mel Bernstein, cradling a bourbon and water in one hand. Mel looked double-stunned.

"Congratulations, Frank,'' said Tony. "What'd you do, pay off the umpire?''

Frank recovered beautifully. He frowned with concern at the cuts on Tony's face, the arm in the sling. "Jesus, Tony, what happened?''

"Sorry I'm dressed so casual, Frank. They ruined one o' my fifteen-hundred-dollar suits.''

"Who?'' Frank demanded, clearly outraged. He sounded ready to track them down himself.

"Hitters,'' said Tony flatly. "Never seen 'em before. Hiya Mel. What do you think?''

"I don't think nothin', Montana. I think you better develop some eyes in the back o' your head.''

"Hey Tony,'' said Frank, "I bet it was the Diaz Brothers.'' He slammed his fist on the desk in fury. It was like he always said: the business was full of scum. "Sure it was. Who else, huh? They got a beef goes back to the Sun Ray job.''

"Maybe so,'' said Tony. There wasn't the shred of emotion in his voice.

Frank laughed nervously. Nothing was funny. "All that matters is you made it,'' he said. "We'll take care o' those guys. I'll see to it myself.''

Tony stepped forward and sat on the edge of Frank's desk. "That's okay," he said. "I'm gonna take care of this myself.''

There was an awkward pause. Manolo and Chi-Chi stood as before, feet apart, their Ingrams cradled in their arms, in a paramilitary posture. Ernie's eyes kept darting from one to the other of the intruders, as if he was looking for a chink in their armor. Mel sat back and sipped his drink. He was keeping a very low profile. What was happening here, he seemed to be saying, had nothing to do with him.

Frank spoke up in a halting voice: "Well . . . uh . . . so what are the guns for?"

"What for?" asked Tony. "I guess I must be paranoid, huh?" The air seemed to grow more tense. Suddenly the phone rang. Nobody made a move to answer. It rang again. "Why don't you pick that up, Frank? Might be a deal.''

"It's Elvira," he said, the slightest note of warning in his voice. "She can't get to sleep. Too much coke.''

It rang again. Tony reached for it. "I'll tell her you're not here," he said.

Frank's hand shot out and grabbed the phone before Tony could touch it. He lifted it to his ear, his lips quivering with anger because he couldn't seem to control this scene. "Hello? Hi, darlin'." As he listened he played with the papers on his desk, neatening them into piles. "Yeah, well, I should be home in about an hour. Why don't you take a Quaalude, huh?" He opened a box of cigars and offered them up to Tony, as if they were having the most normal meeting imaginable. Tony shook his head. "Just sit tight till I get there, honey, okay? We'll watch the sun come up. Okay? You take care now." And he hung up the phone with a gentle smile, as if he'd proven something important to himself, if not to Tony Montana. He looked up at Tony now with perfect self-assurance. They could resolve whatever they had to, surely. Like a pair of gentlemen.

"Frank," said Tony, "did anyone ever tell you you're full o' shit?"

"Huh?" Frank's smile had not quite faded. Perhaps he hadn't heard him right.

Tony reached forward and grabbed Frank by the collar of his shirt. He dragged him out of the desk chair and hauled him across the desk, sending the papers flying. "You know what I'm talkin' about you worthless cockroach," Tony said. Behind him Manolo raised his gun and pointed it at Ernie, who was quivering to move in on Tony. Mel sat perfectly still.

"Tony, no!" Frank was scared. He couldn't work up any anger now, and a whine began to worm into his words. "You gotta listen, please."

"You remember what a chazzer is, Frank? It's a pig who don't fly straight. Just like you."

"Why would I hurt you Tony? I brought you in!" It was hard for Frank to talk, splayed as he was on his stomach, the heel of Tony's hand pinning his neck to the desk. "I gave you your start, you're my brother," pleaded Frank. "I believed in you!"

Tony leaned down and spat the words in his face. "I stayed loyal to you, Frank. I made what I could on the side, but I never betrayed you. *Never*. But you . . ." Here he drew back and spat for real. "A man ain't got no word, Frank, he's a cockroach!" He squashed an imaginary cockroach under his thumb, right in front of Frank's eyes. Then he pulled him further across the desk, till he was flailing.

"Mel! Mel!" cried Frank. "Do something, please!"

Mel sat as impassive as ever. "It's your bed, Frank," he said. "You lie in it."

"Please Tony, gimme a second chance! Ten million —I'll give you ten million bucks right now. I got it in a vault. In Spain. It's yours, all of it. We'll get on a plane." He was squealing now like an animal, his voice broken by sobs. It seemed he was about to mess his pants.

"You know what your problem is, Frank? You don't got any guts." Tony lifted his hand from Frank's neck, as if he couldn't stand to touch such cowardly flesh.

Now Frank groveled. He clasped his hands and pleaded, his whole body quaking with terror. "You want Elvira, Tony? She's yours, okay? I'll go away, Tony, I'll disappear. You'll never hear from me again. Just gimme a chance, Tony, gimme a second chance. Please."

Tony stared at him with disgust. All the men in the room seemed embarrassed by the spectacle. Even Ernie. Frank scrambled to his knees, sobbing freely now. He was like a specimen of something vile, set out on a laboratory table as a group of indifferent scientists stood around observing. Nobody else made a sound.

"I don't wanna die, Tony, I never did nothing to nobody. Please . . . please."

"Yeah you're right, Frank," Tony replied with a sneer of disdain, "you always had somebody else do it for you." He turned to Manolo. "You mind shooting this cockroach for me?"

"Nah," said Manolo, stepping past Tony to point-blank range.

"Tony, no!" cried Frank, as the first *whump* of the silencer sounded. The bullet caught him square in the chest; but even as he gripped his heart, trying to hold the blood in, he kept shaking his head in disbelief. Manolo fired a second time, then a third, and Frank keeled over backwards off the desk. The last look on his face was pure astonishment. The body crashed to the floor.

Tony swiveled his eyes to Mel Bernstein, who still remained calmly in his chair. "Don't worry, Tony," he said. "I didn't see nothin'."

"Oh yeah? What were *you* doin' here, Mel? Sellin' tickets to the policeman's ball?"

"I told him it didn't make sense, Tony. Why's he wanna clip you when we coulda had you working for us instead?" Mel shook his head and grimaced with distaste. "But I guess he got hot, y'know, about the broad. He messed up real bad."

"Yeah, so did you Bernstein," Tony said coldly.

Bernstein shot a look at Tony's eyes. Still he sat casually in the chair, still holding the drink in one hand. With Frank dead and the others standing around, he looked to be the senior officer of the group. But for the first time there was worry in his glance. "Careful, Tony," he said. "Don't go too far."

"*I*'m not goin' anywhere, Mel. *You* are." He raised the gun.

Mel leaped to his feet, the blood draining from his face. He wasn't a whiner like Frank. He wasn't the sort who made deals. In a perfectly rational voice he said: "Hey c'mon, what is this? You can't shoot a cop."

"Is that what you are, Mel? You coulda fooled me." He fired one shot, muffled by the silencer.

Mel took it right in the gut. He dropped to his knees on the floor and looked up stunned. "Lemme go, Tony," he whispered. "I can fix things up." Still he was not pleading. This was the voice of reason.

"Sure you can, Mel. Maybe you can fix up one o' them first-class tickets—to the Resurrection. So long, Mel," he said with a tight grin. "Have a good trip." And he fired twice more till Bernstein slumped against the desk, his eyes still open, stunned as ever. Tony turned toward the door.

"Hey, what about him?" asked Manolo, gesturing towards Ernie with his Ingram.

Tony looked at the bodyguard, who waited stoically by the far wall where the Little League pictures were hung. Tony cocked his head and studied the man, as if he had never quite taken his measure before. There was no question that Ernie was a dead man. All Tony had to do was nod. But he seemed to appraise the bodyguard's

skill in a purely objective way. Till now he had never felt
the need of a personal bodyguard. He understood instinctively that the only kind worth having was one who
owed you his life, who would thus be loyal as a blood
brother. You needed a man who would die for you.

Tony flashed a friendly smile and reverted to Spanish.
"You want a job, Ernie?"

"Sure, Tony."

"Good. Come see me tomorrow."

"Thanks, Tony."

Tony nodded and turned to go. Manolo and Chi-Chi
didn't follow; they knew they were meant to stay and
torch the place. Tony clanged down the steps of the fire
escape, breathing deep in the chill dawn air. The eastern
edge of the sky was already mackerel gray. He trotted
around to the front of the building, ignoring the pain in
his shoulder. He crossed the street and gave the signal to
Martin to carry the box of explosives up to the others.
As Martin retrieved it from the back of Manolo's car,
Tony jumped into the Jaguar and peeled off.

It was sometime after five-thirty when he pulled up in
front of the condo complex on Brickell Avenue. The
doorman looked with dismay at the battered shape of
Tony's car, but he nodded with crisp respect as soon
as he recognized Tony. The guard on the twenty-sixth
floor was fast asleep. The police dog wagged his tail at
Tony. He had to ring the doorbell twice before she
finally answered. Her hair was disheveled, and she wore
a silk nightgown. Apparently she'd been able to get to
sleep after all.

"Tony?" she asked, like she wasn't sure, even with
him standing there. "What happened?"

He reached out and grabbed her hand, then stepped
in and closed the door. He drew her across the living
room toward the terrace. She didn't protest. He slid
open the glass door, and they stepped outside. The sun
was just appearing over the brink of the ocean, yellow

and liquid and throbbing with light. The wrinkled sea went from pewter to blue.

"Where's Frank?" she asked quietly.

"Where do you think?"

They watched the sun for a half-minute more. She touched his cheek with a light hand, feeling of each cut as if she was tracing a line on a map. He could smell her perfume, faint from the night before.

"What do I do now?" she asked.

"Go pack your stuff. We're going home."

She nodded and moved past him into the apartment. Tony stepped to the balcony rail an ' looked down at the dawn-streaked city. Lights still winked in a thousand buildings, as if they were not yet sure of the sun. At the corner of Brickell Avenue, a bright-lit billboard perched on a six-story building. "THE WORLD IS YOURS," it proclaimed, and below that: "Pan American. To Europe, Africa, South America."

Right now it is, thought Tony. Right now was all he could be sure of. Because he knew that violence would go with him now like a shadow, he understood that the present was where he would live for the rest of his life. He had no other choice.

He turned from the rising sun and went inside. He wandered through the expensive rooms of Frank Lopez's penthouse. He found her in the bedroom. A couple of suitcases lay open on the bed, and she stood at the door of a room-size closet, looking so bewildered it was as if she had amnesia. He walked up behind her and stroked her shoulders. The clothes were hung in double rows, a dress for every day of the year, another for every night, it seemed.

"I don't know what to bring," she said. She sounded sadder about the business of packing than she had about Frank.

"Doesn't matter," he said gently. "I'll send Nick up tomorrow. Just take what you need right now."

She turned to look into his eyes, searching there for something she couldn't seem to name. He couldn't be sure how drugged she was, or what the drug was at this hour. 'Ludes, probably. She said: "When I met him I didn't bring anything. We just ran away." Her gaze seemed to sharpen now. She looked at him so piercingly it scared him. She whispered: "Do you understand?"

"Look, you're tired—"

"I always run away, Tony."

She stared in his eyes a moment longer, as if to give him the chance to back out now before it was too late. To break the silence he leaned forward and brushed her lips gently with his. It wasn't quite so forward as a kiss. It demanded nothing. As he drank in the smell of her she pulled gently away. She moved across the room to the table beside the bed, where she opened a drawer and drew out an eighth of cocaine. Then she walked to the door and out, without a backward glance.

By the time he followed her into the living room, she was already out the apartment door and drifting toward the elevator—still barefoot, still in her nightgown. She had apparently taken him at his word: all she needed right now was her coke. Tony ducked into a closet and grabbed the first thing he saw, a full-length lynx coat. Then he walked out of the apartment to where she was waiting by the elevator, patting the snout of the guard dog and murmuring endearments. Tony left the door of Frank's apartment wide open, figuring the cops would be here before long. The twenty-sixth floor guard was still sound asleep in his chair at the end of the hall.

Tony slipped the coat over her shoulders as the elevator arrived. They stepped inside, and the dog whined slightly, as if he understood that the mistress of 2620 would not be coming back. They descended in silence, but she nuzzled close to Tony, burying her face in his chest. As he held her in the rippling fur he felt an incredible surge of power, as if the elevator were shooting up like a rocket instead of bringing them down to the ground.

When they stepped out into the lobby, the guards on duty didn't bat an eye. They were too well bred to stare at her naked feet. As she glided across to the glass doors, Tony's protective arm around her shoulders, she waved vaguely, a little girl's goodbye. Then she and Tony passed out into the driveway.

As they headed to the Jaguar an old pensioner, out for his morning jog, stopped to buy a newspaper at a vending machine on the curb. He watched the two figures approach the car. He didn't seem to notice how rumpled Tony looked, his arm in a sling and one eye puffy, any more than he noticed the battered condition of the Jaguar. What the old man riveted on was the sleepy figure of Elvira, barefoot and loose in the voluminous coat. He felt a terrible pang of jealousy as he watched Tony help her into the passenger's side. They had clearly stayed up all night, partying and making love. The old man felt like an old fool as Tony revved the Jag and gunned off up the street. He felt as if his life had been a bust.

And whoever they were in the Jaguar, it seemed the world belonged to them.

Chapter Seven

IT ALL WENT even faster after that. The moment the news got out that Frank was dead, several of the major dealers made contact with Tony. He was able to work out a consortium that would guarantee Sosa his hundred and fifty kilos a month. The other dealers were more than glad to take Tony's terms, since they feared they would meet the same fate as Frank Lopez if they didn't get in with Tony right away. It had always been an unwritten law among them that none of the others would kill them once they'd become a king, at least not until all avenues of deal-making had been exhausted. Tony was something they'd never seen at the top before. He didn't care how high up somebody was; if they stood in his way they were dead. He shot first and asked questions later, but not many.

There were perhaps twenty coke kings in the Dade County area at the time that Tony Montana blew away the Lopez empire. There was no hard and fast set of rules as to when a man became a king, no code of chivalry, no book of princely goals, not even a financial requirement. One simply knew. Most of these men had hit the boom time at about the same time that cocaine itself did—suddenly, explosively. They were weed dealers making a cool million a year for three years running, with a sideline in coke, and suddenly coke went through the roof and they were pulling in fifteen, twenty mill a year. Tax-free. Down to their toes they didn't want to lose this Midas life. Keep the peace at all costs, they figured. There was enough for everyone, by which they meant enough for the twenty or twenty-five of them who'd clawed their way to the top of the snow-capped mountain.

Tony was merely offering them a terrific investment, after all. Sosa's price was better than anything they could do. They put up all the front money, Tony put up none, and they split the coke in equal shares. Tony got about a fourth of it. Broken down into grams, it worked out to roughly 37,000 units a month. Much of this was job-lotted to smaller dealers, so Tony was taking in maybe sixty dollars a gram. Two-point-two million a month, and the whole structure was in place within four weeks, since Tony was able to take over the lion's share of Frank's client list. Some of the clients he parceled out to his partners in the consortium, just to keep everyone happy.

The work was staggering, of course. Tony was on the phone to Sosa in Bolivia twice a day, trading all the latest rumors as to busts and bribes and traffic foul-ups. He had a payroll of forty, from the bone-thin pharmacist who cut the coke to the Marielito punks who bagged the Quaaludes and ounced the marijuana, for Tony quickly saw that he had to diversify his product. A couple of times a month he would find himself on a jungle airstrip two hours' flying time from Bogota, negotiating with wild men in ruined double-breasted European suits, while an ancient B-26 was being loaded in the background with bales of marijuana. He practically commuted to Panama City.

With the help of George Sheffield, Tony set up the

Montana Realty Company in Little Havana for the laundering of funds. This was a storefront operation, and it offered wonderful bargains to the Cuban population. Blocks of bungalows were saved from the condo developers and made available to blue-collar workers who hadn't had a proper home since they fled Cuba at the start of the revolution. Tony got an overnight reputation for generosity and civic duty. Within weeks the Chamber of Commerce was itching to give him a plaque.

Then they set up the Montana Diamond Trading Company, in a cubbyhole office above a drugstore on Calle Ocho. Here they could launder massive amounts, as they tapped into the international gem market and opened a phony office in The Netherlands, as well as several bank accounts in Basil. Things went like clockwork at the money end.

Still there were problems. Gaspar, one of the original gang, was ambushed one night and blown up in his car; and they never found out who did it. The little dealers were always shooting each other for petty cash, and in order to keep things quiet, Tony was caught in an enormous spiral of bribes among the cops and judges. The newspaper headlines grew more and more lurid: "Raid Nets 100 Million Dollar Cocaine Stash"; "135 Drug-Related Homicides So Far This Year." There was a *Time* magazine coke cover. The Feds appointed commission after commission to make it all stop. They had no real effect, of course, but they made things very complicated.

Tony bought an old mansion in the most exclusive section of Coral Gables which had been Wasp since the days of Ponce de Leon. It had acres of lawns and a boat dock on a canal and beautiful stands of live oak hung with Spanish moss. Tony surrounded the whole property with a sophisticated electronic fence, and he sent in crew upon crew of workers to rejuvenate and swank up the old white-columned house. While the ringing of hammers went on inside, Tony erected a big neon sign on the front lawn. "THE WORLD IS YOURS," it said.

During the months of reconstruction Tony and Elvira lived in a posh marina on Biscayne Bay, on a fifty-eight-foot boat that Tony picked up for a steal in Panama. That is, he literally stole it, as reprisal against a Panamanian official who screwed up a customs operation that left a dozen mules in jail. Neatly lettered along the hull was the boat's new name: *Elvira*.

The lady herself had gone into a long funk following the death of Frank Lopez. For weeks she never left the yacht, but could be seen leaning over the rail for hours at a time, staring out at the waters of the bay as if she was on a cruise to nowhere. Tony was so busy getting his empire into place that he only saw her late at night, when she paced their gaudy silken cabin, all wired up from the day's cocaine and rambling out the story of her past. She didn't seem to mind Tony's presence, though she hardly seemed to focus on him. She was even crazed to make love, and they did so every night, but especially then she was somewhere else, lost in a furious reverie that sometimes left her sobbing when she came.

Tony didn't mind. Now that he possessed her he was full of an extraordinary patience. He could see what a wrenching, broken life she'd led—betrayed by her bankrupt parents, drifting from one bad man to another, stoned on her drug of choice since she was eighteen—and he knew it would take some time before she understood she was safe at last. What he really meant to do was restore her to her heritage. None of the mess and chaos of her life had destroyed the royal lineaments in her face. All she needed to rule was the kingdom of his heart, and together they would triumph. He could not be king without her. Power was not enough.

Meanwhile he filled the yacht with presents. During the week of her birthday she found a Cartier box on her breakfast tray every morning, two hundred thousand dollars' worth of her birthstone—diamonds, of course

—before the week was out. She smiled in a dreamy,
melancholy way as she opened each, and she always
wore the day's jewel to bed that night when they turned
to make love. She seemed to understand that in some
things Tony was determined to outdo Frank. When she
wouldn't leave the boat, streams of salesmen would
arrive from various pricey stores, laden down with
boxes. If she wouldn't go shopping, the shopping would
come to her. Her vials of cocaine were refilled every
morning, no questions asked.

It was Tony's idea that they get married. She had
never been coy about it, maintaining staunchly since the
day they met that marriage wasn't for her. Tony had
been in business about three months, they were due to
move into the mansion in a couple of weeks, and he
started to push the notion. She didn't say yes, but she
didn't say no. Perhaps she was beginning to recover
from the past. She was even willing to go out again, and
they dropped by the Babylon several nights a week,
where the rest of the cocaine royalty paid them court.
They were beautiful to look at then, and they sometimes
caught themselves looking at their reflection in the
smoky mirrors that lined the walls. Then they would
wink and smile through the mirror, as if they were in-
vincible.

One day she opened one of the boxes from the stores,
and in it was a bridal gown. She put it on and drifted
about the boat for several hours, standing again at the
rail and looking off to sea as if somebody had jilted her.
When Tony came aboard late that night, she was lying
in bed in the gown, propped against the pillows and
reading *Rolling Stone*. A string of lines was tapped out
on the coke mirror on the bedside table. Tony shot her a
questioning look, and she shrugged her puff sleeves and
said: "What the hell, let's do it."

He poured money into it. He had the garden of
the mansion entirely relandscaped to accommodate
two hundred guests, hauling in truckloads of white

rose bushes and shrill albino peacocks. A caterer was brought from New York. An organ was installed among the live oaks. Limousines were sent for all the guests. To the neighbors it looked like a convergence of funerals backed up along the street, but then they were so upset about the neon sign, which showed no sign of being removed, they weren't awfully rational when it came to the Montana place. The neighborhood had gone downhill with the force of a nuclear bomb.

The guests were in any case a motley assortment, emerging from the limousines looking like pimps and hookers, bodyguards at their sides, bulges in their pockets, rather as if they had come to attend a convention of Murder Incorporated, South Florida chapter. It was a brilliant thing Tony had done. There had not yet been a big family celebration to bring together the cocaine overlords. Echeverria came, and the Diaz Brothers with their chorus girl wives. It didn't mean they wouldn't open fire on one another before the week was out, but the event somehow defined them all as a social class of the highest blood. Tony's wedding marked the occasion of his ascendancy among the kings, all in recognition of the dramatic boost he had given the local economy by dint of his deal with Sosa. The overlords let it happen because they needed a charismatic figure, and Tony was their JFK.

Fifty of the men sitting on pink satin folding chairs on Tony's lawn, then, were gangsters of one stripe or another. Gina, whom Tony had set up in a beauty salon of her own next door to Montana Realty, beat the bushes all over Dade County and came up with a list of relatives or pretty near, neighbors from the slum alleys of Havana, even the nun who'd taught Tony his catechism. Mama had finally agreed to come at the last minute. It was her stated intention never to set foot in Tony's house, but after all the wedding was in the garden.

Elvira was represented, except for some few girl-

friends (cokefriends, more accurately) and a couple of
pansy dance partners, by a single Maryland aunt, Miss
Theodora Evans. This estimable lady, who owned a tiny
bookstore and art gallery in Annapolis, had been the
black sheep of Elvira's family when such things mattered, her reputation mostly founded on a two-weeks'
indiscretion with a flaming radical during the summer
of her twentieth year. The flaming radical was from
Harvard. Bohemian herself, Miss Theodora Evans had
always supposed that her niece was living in Florida
among artsy types, perhaps on a houseboat. She there-
fore dealt with the gangsters at the wedding as if they
were violently avant-garde, painters maybe or com-
posers.

The vows were exchanged in front of the very monsignor whose picture was on Frank Lopez's wall at the
bakery, shaking hands and wearing a baseball cap. The
monsignor had made a couple of unctuous visits to
Elvira on the yacht, treating her properly like a widow,
which nobody else did. As soon as Tony wrote out a
check for the bishop's building fund, the monsignor
finished his song of sorrows and began to treat Tony
and Elvira as a marriage made in heaven. He would
even gladly officiate, for a well-placed five thousand in
cash.

Manolo was best man. Gina was maid of honor.
While Tony and Elvira wore traditional black and
white, Manolo sported a blue satin tux and Gina a dark
blue ball gown, "Tara Blue" they called it. Of course all
of Tony's payroll was there, down to the ounce-men of
Calle Ocho. Only the police sent no one. The Miami
Chamber of Commerce dispatched a gelatinous man to
give a toast at the wedding feast, but not the police.
Even on such a triumphal day, when differences were
buried, the police were required for the sake of dis-
cretion to maintain the position of silent partner.

Tony and Elvira looked as grave as children when
they made their vows, as if they had stolen the lines

from a much more formal culture, where men and women met in the old way and slowly grew to love one another, till at last they decided to risk their lives. Or was it perhaps that they didn't quite believe the words, even as they said them? A certain glint of irony was in their eyes, of melancholy even, at so much talk of forever. Yet they looked astonishing that day, young and vital and yearning for each other, possessed of a secret place no one else could enter. It was as if they knew they might not have much time, and they mustn't let today slip through their fingers. So they glowed like newlyweds all day long, like real ones.

There was supper under the trees by the quiet canal, mountains of shrimp and Dom Perignon, and an orchestra lush enough to have played Roseland. Tony led several groups to the tropical garden behind the house, where he showed off his wedding present to his bride. Huge wire cages had been set up among the trees, with a wilderness of monkeys in them, gibbons and tamarins and marmosets. Beyond was a lily-padded artificial pond, fifty feet long and kidney-shaped, with a small flock of flamingos promenading. Then there was a birdhouse full of twenty different kinds of parrots and macaws, jabbering as they flared their iridescent plumage.

"Here's the king over here," said Tony, guiding a party across a bright-red Japanese bridge to the orchid garden. They passed through a clump of tree ferns and came to the edge of a moat. Across the water, beneath a solitary banyan tree, stretched a nine-foot Bengal tiger. His stripes shivered as he paced his island. Mama and Aunt Theodora gasped in wonder.

"What is it?" whispered Mama.

"That's the king, Mama," said Tony, drawing Elvira into the circle of his arms. "He ain't scared o' nothin'."

"What are you gonna do with him?" asked the old woman.

Tony laughed. "He's gonna eat my enemies, Mama."

He turned to Nick the Pig, who looked in his rented tux and ruffled shirt a bit like Charles Laughton. "Hey Nick, throw him his cake."

Dutifully Nick unwrapped a paper napkin, revealing a sizable chunk of wedding cake. He tossed it across the moat, where it landed just in front of the pacing tiger. The beast gave it a cursory sniff, almost seemed to sneer, and resumed his pacing. "He ain't hungry, boss," Nick said.

"Maybe he ain't ever been to a wedding," said Tony.

Chi-Chi, who was escorting Aunt Theodora on his arm, piped up: "Hey Tony, let's throw Nick in. He'll like that better."

Aunt Theodora clucked her tongue. "We better not, Chi-Chi," she said. "Nick the Pig would eat the tiger."

Everyone laughed. Just then they seemed extraordinarily like a family—all different shapes and sizes, brought together by a blessed event, wanting only the best for each other. In the end Mama was smitten by Elvira, whose laugh was brighter that day than even the coke could make it. She joked with Mama and Aunt Theodora, fresh as a schoolgirl, gay and irreverent. Nobody mentioned coke at all, and it crossed Tony's mind that for once Elvira was clean. Perhaps it would become a habit. He was wrong, of course—there were dozens of tucks and folds in a bridal gown where a girl could hide her paraphernalia—but he couldn't be blamed for wishing it so. It was the perfect day for pipe dreams.

They trailed back over the Japanese bridge, leaving the tiger to his deeper hunger. Chi-Chi and Nick the Pig bore the old women away to the dance floor. Tony pulled Elvira off the path and ducked among the banana palms. As he gathered her into his arms, the gown whispering about her, he caught a glint of blue out of the corner of one eye. He turned his head and thought he saw Manolo and Gina disappearing among the trees. But then Elvira drew him back to her, nibbling at his lips, breathing into his mouth.

"Is this the happy ending?" she whispered between kisses.

"No," said Tony tenderly, "this is just the beginning."

And they embraced again in the glut of tropical green, the orchids thick around them, the parrots shrieking. It was all a mirage, this paradisal island; but for now, this afternoon, it was lush as the Garden of Eden. They kissed and laughed and kissed again, and they looked in their formal clothes as if they'd escaped from a wedding cake to a place of constant summer. Nothing hunted them. Nothing threatened. Just for a moment they seemed to live in a wilderness all their own.

The Banco Sud di Miami had a beautiful green marble facade that fronted Brickell Avenue. It faced a Barclay's Bank across the street and fitted securely between Payne Webber on one side and Dreyfuss on the other. The Banco Sud di Miami had only been chartered a year ago, but it was no slouch in the money department, able to hold its own quite well among its tonier neighbors. Even the fireplug on the curb out front was brass.

In the parking lot in back, Tony and Manolo supervised as Chi-Chi and Martin unloaded several duffel bags from a Volkswagen van. A bank guard appeared from the rear of the building, pushing a kind of trolley. The Banco Sud di Miami had had to order these trolleys special. No other bank had ever needed one, not in Miami anyway. Maybe in Vegas, maybe in Jersey they used such things. The duffel bags were piled one by one on the trolley, and Manolo went along as the guard wheeled it back to the counting room. Manolo would have to supervise the counting; it would take hours.

Tony headed into the bank proper and was escorted

upstairs to the president's office. He didn't have to wait
ten seconds before the ebullient man himself appeared
to pump his hand. Samuel Taft Eliot Stearns couldn't
have been more than thirty-five. With his razored hair
and his SCUBA tan and the snug fit of his Lanvin suit
he could have been a movie star; he would have been the
first to acknowledge that. He was a man who never
stopped thinking money. On weekends he followed the
Hong Kong money markets on a terminal in his house,
so he would always have a jump on Monday.

He ordered beers for him and Tony. He told a stupid
joke. He thought it was he who had called this meeting,
that what they were getting around to was what Stearns
himself had to say. Perhaps this was why he was so full
of upper-class airs this morning. He fiddled with a pipe.
He kept stretching one arm and kneading the elbow, un-
consciously it seemed, but he acted as if he'd played two
hours of tennis before coming in. His bow tie was tight
as a drum and wobbled when he swallowed. He was
cleaning his glasses, talking about his weekend sail,
about to speak man-to-man, when Tony interrupted.

"Sam, I can't pay this percentage no more. I'm
gonna be bringin' in more than I ever brung in before.
I'm talking maybe ten mill a month. Ten percent off the
top o' that's way outa line. You gotta come down, it's
as simple as that."

"Can't do, Tony," said Stearns, with an irritable
shake of his head. He was annoyed at having his thunder stolen. His pipe went out.

"That's too bad, Sam, 'cause I'll tell you somethin'.
There's other banks."

"Hey, Tony, this is not a wholesale store, sellin'
stereos to niggers. The more you bring in, the harder it
is to wash. I'm sorry to tell you, but we've got to raise
our rates."

Tony stood up and turned to go. It wasn't that he had
so many banks to choose from. Banks were the hard
part; Sheffield had made that clear from the first. But

right now he figured he'd be better off stashing the whole load in a coffee can under the porch. He was that mad.

"Tony, what am I supposed to do? The IRS is coming down real heavy on all of us. The *Time* cover didn't help one little bit. I gotta do it, Tony, I got stockholders." Tony stopped a foot from the door and waited. The deal was about to be proposed. "I gotta go twelve percent on the first ten million. That's if it's all in twenties. I'll go nine percent on tens, six on fives, same as before."

Tony turned, his lip curled in an arrogant sneer. "Kiss my ass," he said.

Stearns shrugged and showed his open palms, thick with tennis calluses. "You're not gonna do any better than us, babe, I'm tellin' you that right now."

"Oh yeah? I'll fly it to the Bahamas if I have to."

Stearns frowned at such obvious naiveté. "You gonna fly it yourself, Tony, on a regular basis? Once maybe. And then what? You gonna trust some monkey in the Bahamian cabinet with twenty million of your hard-earned greenbacks?" He shook his head gently, and his voice grew more and more soothing. "C'mon Tony, don't be a schmuck. Who else can you trust? Ask Sheffield. That's why you pay us what you do—because you *trust* us."

The phone buzzed from the outer office. Stearns flicked a button and took the call. Tony stared at the banker with huge contempt, his mind racing with revenge. Methodically he added Stearns's name to the list in his head of those who would be sorry. Then just as suddenly a wave of weariness washed over Tony. Taking care of all the money was getting to be more than he could handle. The duffel bags piled up in the stash houses with ludicrous regularity. Millions of dollars in tens and twenties amounted to an enormous volume, and then there was the need of guarding it, getting trustworthy people to count it. The whole thing

made Tony crazy—he felt like a two-bit gangster emp-
tying slot machines, the trunk of his car a foot deep in
quarters. He had no time any more. He couldn't keep
track of every phase of the operation and do the laundering too. Being rich was beginning to eat him up.

"I should be done here in a second," said Stearns into
the phone. He glanced at his Rolex as he hung up. He
smiled at Tony. "So what do you say, Tony? Stay with
us, huh? You're an old and valued customer." Three
months was apparently long enough to make you old at
the Banco Sud di Miami.

"Yeah, okay," said Tony sullenly, his face a mask of
indifference.

Stearns grinned. "I knew you'd see it our way," he
said. "Hell, there's enough for everyone, right?"

Tony lay back in his marble gold-leaf bathtub, a Cuban
cigar clenched between his teeth. A color TV was
hooked to one side of the tub, a long phone line to the
other. Within reach across the terrazzo floor were a
stereo console and a portable bar. The bathroom was
enormous, with a great baroque chandelier in the
middle of the ceiling, mirrored walls, a sauna, a steam
room, and a balcony overlooking the zoo. Tony lay
there watching television, while Manolo sprawled on the
sofa across the room, leafing through the racing sheet.
Elvira sat at the vanity next to the balcony doors, slowly
painting her eyes.

Tony was watching the Dolphins game, but just now
they were into a string of advertisements. John Houseman stood in a college lecture hall, books under his arm,
touting the praises of Smith Barney. "They make
money the old-fashioned way," Houseman intoned.
"They *earn* it."

Tony hit the remote control and snapped it off.
"Twelve fuckin' percent," he grumbled. "What kinda
jerk do they think I am? I remember when we used to

knock those places over 'stead of takin' shit from 'em."

"They're too smart," said Manolo. "They got all the angles figured. You steal it, and then you gotta pay to put it back in."

"You know what capitalism is, don't you?" Tony tossed the cigar butt into the toilet. He sounded a bit like John Houseman himself. "Capitalism is Getting Fucked. Everybody gets fucked, ya know? You get fucked in the ass, you get fucked in the face, you get fucked in the ear—"

"God, you're so articulate," said Elvira, reaching over from the vanity and grabbing up the remote control. She snapped on the television and flicked the channel to the cable news. She reached for a vial of coke from among her creams and powders. She began to tap out lines on the mirrored surface of the vanity.

"You do too mucha that shit, you know that?" said Tony. He opened the door of the portable bar and pulled out a slip of champagne.

"Nothing exceeds like excess," said Elvira, bending her swan neck and snorting through a rolled-up fifty. "You should know, Tony. You're the king of excess."

"Ex-what?"

"So why don't we talk to this Jew Seidelbaum?" asked Manolo, folding his paper. "He's got his own exchange, he goes four percent tops. Besides which he's real well connected."

Tony popped the cork and swigged the champagne down like Pepsi. He burped. "Are you kiddin'? He washes for the mob. It's all Guineas." He shook his head thoughtfully. "Fuckin' peasants," he said. "Hey look, there's Keyes."

He pointed to the television. Elvira rolled the volume up. A bespectacled man in a three-piece suit, tall and patrician, was talking to a reporter. He could have been the father of Samuel Taft Eliot Stearns.

". . . the problem can only be solved the way Prohibition was," said Keyes. "We must stop outlawing the substances. Once we legalize them, we can start taxing them. That'll drive out the organized crime."

"How 'bout the organized crime in the police department?" sneered Manolo, shooting the bird at the TV set.

"As a U.S. attorney, Connie," said Keyes, his voice getting breathy like a politician, "I can only tell you it's like having your finger in the dike, down here in South Florida anyway. We can't put a dent in a hundred-billion-dollar-a-year business, not with our budget. . . ."

Tony leaned forward in the tub, so his face was scarcely six inches from the screen. "Yeah, you're right Keyes," he said, "but it'll never happen. Your fuckin' bankers and politicians'll never let it happen. They'll fuck anybody if there's a buck in it!"

"Can't you for Christ's sake stop talking about it?" Elvira shouted, as she snapped the TV off again in his face. "Can't you stop saying fuck? Can't you see it's *boring*?" She turned around to the mirror again but did not look at herself. She bent to the lines and snorted again.

"What's boring?" asked Tony.

"*You're* boring. Money, money, money, money—that's all you ever talk about." She picked up a hairbrush and began to draw it briskly through her hair. "You know what you're turning into, Tony? An arriviste immigrant spic millionaire, that's what. Why don't you just dig a hole in the garden, bury it and forget about it."

"What are you talkin' about?" He swept a wet arm around the room. "I worked my ass off for this."

She stood up, drawing her robe closer about her. She spoke with a certain melancholy as she turned to go. "It's too bad," she said. "Somebody should have given it to you. Would've made you a nicer person. I mean, you probably wouldn't have had to kill a soul."

"You know what your problem is, honey?"

She was halfway out the door. As she looked over her

shoulder, a lock of hair fell across one eye. "Please don't tell me," she said. "I'd much rather be in suspense."

"You got nothin' to do, that's what."

"That's not true, Tony. I do a lot of coke. You said so yourself." And she drifted away into the bedroom, letting the door click shut behind her.

"Aw fuck," said Tony, slapping the water and shooting a stream that splashed against the television screen. He seemed most annoyed at himself just then, as if the squabble was all his fault.

Manolo said dryly: "I guess married life ain't everything it's cracked up to be, huh chico?"

"Yeah, fuck you too."

"Listen Tony, I think we should look into this thing with Seidelbaum. It feels good to me."

"Yeah okay, check it out," said Tony absently.

It was not the first time they'd argued, he and Elvira. Not even the first time that day.

Next morning, about nine o'clock, Elvira left the house for a manicure and a fitting. Chi-Chi drove her in the Continental, and because she was so strung out from the drugs of the night before, she buried herself in the *Herald* and kept her silence. She was still annoyed at Tony. They'd avoided each other all the rest of the evening, and she'd taken a couple of Q's and gone out like a light. She figured he must have slept in his study, since he wasn't in bed when she woke up, and he usually slept in till ten. No sign of him at breakfast either.

As the car came to a halt, she folded up the paper and reached in her bag for dark glasses. Chi-Chi came around to open her door, and she looked up expecting to see the awning of Valmain, the by-appointment-only shop on Riviera Drive where she picked up the lion's share of her daytime clothes. Instead she was surprised to see they had come to the marina. The Continental

was parked on the dock beside the *Elvira*, gleaming in
the morning sun, its motors rumbling. She gave an
irritable look at Chi-Chi, drawing a breath to curse him
out.

"Boss's orders," Chi-Chi said.

Suddenly Gina appeared on deck, waving from the
rail. "Do you know what this is all about?" she called.

Elvira smiled and shook her head, deciding what the
hell. She got out of the car and trotted up the gangplank, still expecting to see Tony himself when she got
on deck. But there was no one except Gina—not including the crew of four in dazzling white, trim as midshipmen, who tossed the lines and immediately got them
under way.

"Limo pulled up at the shop this morning," said
Gina, tossing her dark hair as she settled herself on a
deck mat. "Official instructions from the boss: cancel
your morning appointments. Seems he wants to take me
to the circus. Then they brought me here."

"Where is he?" asked Elvira, moving to the on-deck
bar to mix herself a Bloody Mary.

"I don't know," laughed Gina. "He must've had a
change of plans. Why don't you put on a suit, get some
sun?"

"I'm all right, thanks." Elvira took her drink and sat
in the shade of the wheelhouse. She was still near
enough to talk to Gina, but she couldn't sit out in the
sun herself. Not that she didn't look fabulous with a
tan. But she knew enough about drugs to know the sun
was ruinous to a heavy user's skin. She had seen enough
wrinkled cokeheads in her time. She was still vain
enough to protect herself, skin-deep anyway.

They did not know each other very well, Gina and
Elvira. They had only been together perhaps half a
dozen times. Tony still saw Gina mostly by himself.
Either he stopped by her beauty shop for a haircut, or
he took her out to lunch or shopping. Neither woman

pushed Tony about it, seeming to realize that he needed them for different reasons. But they liked each other and enjoyed each other. The same kinds of things made them bitchy. They tended to roll their eyes at each other if they found themselves standing together in a group of Tony's "friends," Chi-Chi and Nick and the rest.

"So how's married life?" asked Gina, placing a couple of slices of cucumber on her eyes. This sudden mask seemed to free her to ask a sudden question.

"It's okay," said Elvira with an easy shrug. "It's never the same." She sipped her Bloody Mary. A steward appeared with a tray of sushi and placed it on the bar. Elvira watched the ocean, aching blue in the noon sun, till he withdrew discreetly. Then she said: "Well, lately it's kind of the same."

"He drives himself like a maniac, doesn't he? I tell him Tony, whaddaya want to be, the richest man in the graveyard?"

They were heading down the Inland Waterway, past the first small islands of Biscayne National Park. On the mainland side were the clipped flats and landfill of Homestead Air Force Base. Within forty minutes they had reached the sound that ran between Key Largo and the shores of the Everglades. The herons were white as tufts of snow as they bobbed up and down in the surf. Gina dozed off for ten minutes, and Elvira was very quiet. She began to feel more relaxed than she had in weeks.

Because they were heading south-southwest the sun was on her face now, but she made no move to pull back into the shade. She closed her eyes and took off her glasses and let herself bake a little. She had a full gram in her Celine bag, but she didn't need it yet. She was cozy from the vodka and starting to feel hungry. For the moment she couldn't recall why she was so annoyed with Tony. When she thought of his constant profanity and his inexhaustible temper, like he always had to face the world in boxing gloves, it only made her smile and shake her head rhythmically along the back of the deck chair.

When Gina woke up she fetched them both a little plate of sushi. Gina sat cross-legged on the deck to eat, just next to Elvira's chair. They talked about Tony and Mama, laughing at the elaborate dance the old woman went through in her dealings with her son. Officially she still wasn't speaking to him. All the same she would talk to him on the phone if he called for Gina, asking him question after question about his wife, and was she eating enough. If Tony asked her a question about herself, she became quite prim and closemouthed. She had not seen him face to face since the wedding. She lectured Gina often on the evils of her brother's life. She wept and prayed to the Virgin of Guadeloupe.

The steward brought them a pot of coffee, a rich strong Cuban blend that could take a lot of cream. Elvira held her cup close, as if she was warming her hands at a fire. She studied Gina on the floor beside her, stretching her muscles and chatting happily. Though Gina was only four years younger than she, Elvira felt a protective impulse, as one who knew the world a whole lot better. She finally thought there might be a purpose to all the crap she had gone through, if she could only warn someone else.

"So tell me," she said quietly, as they came into Blackwater Sound, heading in to Key Largo town, "what's with you and Manny?"

"Oh, not too much," said Gina quickly, burying her face in her coffee cup.

There was a brief silence as Elvira smiled down at her. Then she said: "That much, huh?"

"Don't tell Tony. Please."

"But it's none of his business." She reached out a hand and feathered the back of Gina's hair. "None of mine either, I might add."

She moved to stand up, and Gina grabbed her hand

and held her in the chair. "No, I want to talk about it, Elvira." There was a pang of great relief in Gina's voice, as if the secret had been a rope around her neck, tightening and tightening. "He's a wonderful man, and I love him, but he's so scared of Tony he don't know what to do."

"Tony'll come around. He loves that man like a brother."

"I don't think so," said Gina with a weary sigh. "He's got this thing about me. Like I'm some kinda virgin princess, and he's gotta find me a prince. What does he think this is, the old country? *Nobody*'s a virgin any more."

The two women laughed, and the tension broke. Elvira stood and held out a hand and pulled Gina to her feet. They moved to the railing, arm in arm. "He certainly is a throwback, isn't he?" said Elvira with gentle irony. "I sometimes think he wishes people still fought duels. Maybe that's a dueling scar, huh?"

At first they thought they were coming into the tiny harbor at Key Largo, which they could see now a couple of hundred yards off to starboard, the rusty pier and the beat-up fishing boats. But the *Elvira* kept sailing past the entrance to the channel, hugging the shore for another half mile. The underbrush was thick as a jungle, and the beach, such as it was, was mostly a tangle of roots and shell heaps. A great cloud of gulls rose off the water as they passed one cove. Though the women hadn't a clue where they were headed, Elvira was glad of the journey, if only because it had deepened her feelings about Gina. She suspected Gina felt the same.

"What does Manny say?"

"Oh, you know," said Gina. "He says he's got enough trouble just running the business with Tony. They're always fighting about something. So I say okay, just give it time. Manolo still sees all his other girls, but I don't care. That's just sex. We see each other maybe twice a week, but he don't ever spend the whole night.

The thing is, I don't wanna go out with anyone else."
She shook her head and sighed. "Same old story, huh?"

Elvira squeezed her arm. "Don't worry. It's like you
said, just give it time. Tony'll stop fighting so hard, and
Manny'll start to stand on his own two feet. You'll
see."

She didn't really believe it. Tony's possessiveness
toward Gina was more than stubborn, it was getting to
be an obsession. And Elvira knew that relations between
Tony and Manolo were increasingly tense. Tony had
grown so paranoid about money that he couldn't seem
to delegate authority. Manolo was feeling shut out. But
she hoped her own worries didn't show as she bucked
Gina up with confident words. She said she was sure
that all four of them would be going out together soon.
Maybe take a vacation, just the two couples. Go to New
York and blow a fortune.

"Wouldn't that be fun?" laughed Gina, and Elvira
saw what a little girl she was at heart. Still unspoiled.
Elvira realized she wanted to keep her that way, just like
Tony did, except in her case she wanted to do all she
could for the secret lovers. It made her feel like a girl
herself.

The boat came around a point of land with a lone
palm tree at the end. Beyond was a wide cove with a
broad, west-facing beach. But what they immediately
noticed were four or five seaplanes dotting the water
like an outsize flock of gulls. The *Elvira* headed in. On
the beach itself they could see a bunch of figures dressed
in bright and gaudy colors. The two women looked at
each other, puzzled.

The crowd on the shore had spotted the boat, and a
cheer went up. Then music began to play, blaring out of
a pair of ballroom speakers perched on a couple of
beached timbers. The *Elvira* stopped about fifty yards
from shore and lowered a boat. Now Gina and Elvira,
squinting into the sun, began to pick out the individual
figures. There were three or four clowns, all dressed up

in motley and tumbling about. There was a girl in a ballerina costume, perched on a white horse. A man in a safari suit held a leopard on a chain. A trio of acrobats tossed each other in the air. A strong-man rippled his muscles.

Indeed, it seemed to be a whole circus, stranded on a desert island.

Gina and Elvira climbed down into the motor launch. One of the midshipmen took the helm, and they roared across the cove, winding their way among the seaplanes. Gina crouched in the bow of the launch, wearing only her bikini, and let the spray douse her. Elvira sat back in a white-cushioned seat, still dressed in a silk wrap and heels. The circus performers were all in motion now, rollicking and strutting. One of the clowns shot a miniature cannon straight at them, and a foam of confetti and streamers billowed out over the surf. Gina clapped her hands with pleasure and called back over her shoulder, laughing:

"A couple of weeks ago he asked me, real serious, what did I want to do that I never did before. And I said: I never been to the circus, Tony."

Neither have I, thought Elvira. She was startled to find how thrilled she was. She'd never once thought about missing the circus, not since she was a kid.

They came in over the waves, and one of the clowns waded out and took the rope and hauled them in to the beach. Gina leaped out and splashed with him in the shallows. Elvira kicked off her heels, hitched up her dress, and hopped down into the soft wet sand. Another of the clowns came over and put a pair of funny glasses on her, with a big false nose attached. Then they led the two women up the beach and sat them down on a driftwood bench. The clowns performed and cavorted, and the tamer put the leopard through his paces, leaping through a hoop of fire. The tumblers tumbled. The white horse pranced.

They laughed until their sides hurt. The strong-man

brought them cones of cotton candy and bins of pop-corn. The clowns set up a conga line and sashayed up and down the beach, coaxing Gina and Elvira till the two women joined the line at the end. After ten minutes they pitched over exhausted into the sand, and when they looked up at the circle of performers grouped around them, they saw Tony walking up the beach, dressed in a ringmaster's outfit—jodhpurs and cutaway, knee-length boots, bow tie, top hat, riding crop. He wore a false mustache big as a walrus's, and he was grinning from ear to ear.

A big banquet was set out among the trees that fronted the beach, and the three of them had a long and lazy lunch, drinking pitchers of margaritas with the circus people. After lunch they all three mounted the horse, Gina in front and Elvira in the middle and Tony in back, and the clowns led them through a grove of sea pines. The trees were full of birds wintering like pensioners. At the edge of a fresh water pond they passed the ruin of an old stone house, and Gina shouted: "That's where we'll all live some day! Okay?"

"Okay!" chorused Tony and Elvira.

And later on he nuzzled his face against Elvira's neck and whispered: "I ain't said fuck once today. You still mad at me?"

"No," she whispered back. "And besides, you can say it once in a while. As long as you really mean it."

All the way back to the beach he couldn't keep his hands off her. She was cradled tight against him, plus there was the rhythm of the horse moving sinuously beneath them. Tony got very hard, and he stroked her thighs and rubbed up against her buttocks. Elvira didn't mind at all, in fact it turned her on. But Gina was right there, cradled between Elvira's own thighs, so she elbowed Tony in the gut to make him stop. This only made him more horny and more playful.

Gina didn't notice. She was holding on to the horse's

mane for dear life, singing a Cuban love song full of fatal love and final kisses. Tony joined in on the choruses, breathing the words into his wife's ear, drunk on the sweat of her, all mixed up with lemon and roses.

When they reached the beach again, the circus people were packing up their boxes, ferrying them out to the seaplanes. The Key Largo cowboy who'd rented them out the horse was pacing impatiently, waiting to lead him away. The leopard was nailed in his cage. They got off the horse and blinked around at the disappearing dream. Tony was so impatient to make love to Elvira that he hardly noticed. The women noticed.

It was still mid-afternoon, bright and dazzling, when they scampered up from the launch onto the boat. Gina, dark as Tahiti already from a day outside, laid out her mat on the roof of the main cabin so she could sunbathe all the way home. Tony pulled Elvira inside, through the main lounge and down to the master bedroom. Elvira grabbed her bag on the way, and as Tony tore the spread from the bed and pulled off his clothes, she drew out her vial of cocaine and began to tap out lines on the bedside table.

"Hey honey," he said, "don't do none o' that, okay?" She didn't even answer him but kept on tapping, four lines altogether. His voice hardened. "Elvira, you don't need that."

"Hey, give me a break, huh?" She was cheerful as hell and feeling just terrific. She drew a half-straw from her wallet. "I haven't even had any yet." Today, she meant, as she bent and tooted two lines.

Tony stood rigid across the bed, naked and hard, clenching and unclenching his fists as if they were taped for a fight. She stood up and spun around, then tossed off her dress in a single wonderful shrug. She came around the bed laughing, wearing a skimpy black lace bra and panties. She looked like a million bucks. Of course he couldn't stay mad at her, his hunger was too

great. As he unhooked the bra she was gasping for it.
She pulled him close and rubbed her panties against his
swelling cock.

"Wanna fuck?" she asked, her green eyes glinting
with laughter.

He lifted her up and set her down on the bed, so
lightly it felt like tumbling into water. He drew off the
panties; they hissed as they slid down her legs. He bent
and kissed along her inner thigh, beginning to grunt
with hunger now. His lips grazed between her legs,
his tongue snaking out to probe, and she groaned and
gripped his hair. She was already wet. He drank her in.

When at last he moved up her body, nibbling at her
flesh, she was crying softly, stung with pleasure, spent
somehow though they'd barely started. She bit at his
lips and whispered his name. No matter how much they
squabbled—hurling accusations, seething with contempt—the trouble always vanished when they were in
bed. Wild to kiss, deeper and deeper, they moaned in
each other's mouth. She dug her nails in his shoulder
blades, begging for him. He could feel her burning body
quivering beneath him, and as he entered her slowly she
arched up against him, whimpering with desire, rolling
her head back and forth on the pillow.

They were lousy at living together. They fought like a
cat and a dog, and they couldn't seem to get out of each
other's way. Sometimes it didn't look as if they could
last another minute. But they made it up in spades at a
time like this, and they knew it. They were twinned like
a force of nature, tidal as the sea that rocked them. Over
and over he brought her up to a pitch, till they were both
balanced on a knife-edge. They went on and on, shifting
places like a couple of dancers, the sweat pouring out of
them. It was as if they had to reach some awesome
height in order not to forget. Sex was the only thing they
still had left that made them prince and princess. They
came staring into each other's eyes, blinding clear like
the light on the water, seamless as the shore.

And when at last they lay exhausted, shipwrecked in one another's arms, they stroked each other lazily and played out all their dreams. They talked about kids, and within ten minutes they'd peopled their lives with three or four, boys mostly, running around and laughing in the walled-in yard, growing up clean and easy. Then Elvira ran down a list of all the places she wanted to see, from the Scottish coast to the Vale of Kashmir. She had a secret wish to be constantly in motion, roaming about the world in a boat like this, without a schedule, without any destination. She slipped to the side of the bed and did another stiff toot. This time he joined her.

"Some day," Tony said, "we're gonna have places all over the place, just like Sosa. California, the Riviera, apartment in New York, you name it. Stick with me, we'll have a place in China before we're through. And hey, Gina can come with us, huh?"

He tickled her under her ribs, and they rolled on the bed and wrestled till she pleaded for a truce. Tony reached for the phone and dialed the steward, ordering up a couple of iced coffees. When he turned back she was sitting cross-legged, her head tilted as she studied him. He suddenly felt very naked, as if there was something she could see in him he couldn't see himself. He moved toward her to kiss her, almost as if to silence her, but she held him back gently and said:

"You have to let her go, you know."

"Who, Gina? She's only nineteen. *Somebody*'s gotta watch her."

"Let her go, Tony. She's got a good heart. Let her ask if she wants some help."

"Yeah, well mind your own business, okay? I don't want her growin' up like you, you know. Fuckin' every gangster in town."

He didn't mean it to sound as hard as it did, and he turned away embarrassed. She winced slightly, feeling it more somehow than she did when they were at home, brawling at each other across the bedroom. As if on cue

they both moved to put some clothes on. He got up off
the bed and went to the dresser and pulled out swimming trunks. She reached to the floor for her bra and
panties.

"I'm gonna go catch some rays," he said, moving
toward the door, one eye shyly watching Elvira as she
slipped back into her underwear.

"Hey, thanks for the circus," she said, bending once
more to tap out lines.

He paused with the door open, looking back at her.
He was filled with an inexpressible sorrow, to think he
could not hold on to the truce they'd reached on the
desert island. Would he have to provide a circus every
time they pulled too far apart? How many circuses were
there? She looked up with a wistful smile of her own,
and they nodded, as if to say they would both go easy.
But as he closed the door behind him and padded up on
deck, neither could have said for sure exactly what it
was they'd lost.

They'd had it there for a minute.

Nick the Pig was frantic. He stood in the doorway of the
greenhouse, talking to Manolo on the phone. "Hey
Manny, I was just playin' with it, y'know? It flew outa
the cage. How'm I supposed to know the Malayan sun
bear likes parrots for lunch?"

An empty birdcage lay on its side on the parquet.
Through a chain-link fence just opposite, Nick watched
as the sun bear licked its paws. Feathers still clung to its
underjaw.

"What the hell you want me to do about it?" Manolo
asked through the phone.

"Tony's gonna kill me, Manny. That's a ten-thou-
sand-dollar bird!"

Nick, it had turned out, was an amateur naturalist.
He liked nothing better than to feed the animals in
Tony's zoo. A professional keeper was on duty three

days a week, but Nick took up the slack, flinging steaks to the tiger, sardines to the flamingos, handfuls of grain to the birds. Tony and Elvira were spending the day out on the boat. Nick was in hog heaven, wandering through the cages, letting the birds perch on his shoulders. Then catastrophe struck.

"Goddamnit Nick," said Manolo, "there's a hundred different birds out there. *He* can't tell 'em apart no more. Forget it."

"It's terrible, just terrible," Nick said soberly, shaking his head.

And out in the street about a hundred yards away, in a steel-gray van with tinted windows, two men in earphones huddled over a console where a tape was running. The two men looked at each other strangely as they listened to Nick and Manolo.

"Tell him the bird flew out the fuckin' window," said Manolo with annoyance. Then he hung up.

The tape in the van clicked off. The two wiretappers looked at each other with a thrill of excitement. One said: "Something's gone wrong. Let's call the chief." And like a couple of kids they threw off the earphones and scrambled for the walkie-talkie.

Tony was at the wheel of his new white Corniche. Manolo sat beside him, scribbling notes on a yellow legal pad as Tony ticked off a hundred things that needed attending to. They glided along the lush and winding streets of Coral Gables. The cypresses hung low, their trunks and outer branches wreathed in Spanish moss. Most of the houses were nestled behind high stone walls and imposing gates. Tony was rattling off figures to give to Sosa as he made the turn on the avenue, heading toward his house.

All of a sudden he said: "Hey Manolo, d'you sweep the house like I told you?"

"Yeah, sure. Last month. The cars too. Set us back

five thousand." He went on making notes.

"What about Seidelbaum?"

"All set," said Manolo. "Next Thursday at ten. We're doing a million and some change. I'll take Nick with me."

"No, I'll handle it. You go up to Atlanta for me, handle the Gomez delivery."

"Why?" Manolo sounded wounded. "Listen, I set Seidelbaum up—"

" 'Cause you're a lousy negotiator, that's why." Tony slowed the car to make the turn in the driveway. "See that cable truck?"

Manolo followed his pointing finger. A panel truck was parked across the street. "Yeah, what about it?"

"Hey, chico, since when does it take three days to rig a cable system, huh?"

Manolo's eyes narrowed. "What are you thinkin'? Cops?"

"Who knows," said Tony with a shrug. "Maybe it's the Diaz Brothers. Maybe they're plannin' to rip us off." He sounded like he didn't really care. It was just another stupid hassle.

"Don't worry, I'll check it out."

"Yeah, you check it out. Then we're gonna blow that fuckin' truck to Bogota." Tony nudged the Rolls up close to the double iron gate, so the wall cameras could sweep them.

"Listen, they're probably buggin' one o' the neighbors," said Manolo. "We're not the only dopers livin' on the block, y'know."

"Hey, don't get casual, chico. Casual means you're dead." The gates began to swing wide. An armed guard appeared and nodded at Tony.

Manolo was steamed. "I told you I'd check it out, didn't I? Look, we're spending too much on this counter-surveillance shit. Seven percent—that's seven percent of adjusted gross. It's like Fort Knox in here!"

But Tony wasn't listening. He was staring into the

rearview mirror, following something with his eyes. The gates were wide open in front of him. The guard was patiently waiting for him to drive on through. Tony said: "See that fat guy?"

Manolo craned around and saw a jogger trotting by along the sidewalk. Very civilian-looking, mid-fifties, dressed in an aquamarine sweatsuit.

"I been seein' him for a week now," said Tony. "Every day. Just joggin' around."

"So what? He's just some dentist or somethin'. Big fat ass, big deal."

A second armed guard had now appeared. They stood on either side of the Rolls, watching the street like hawks. Tony said: "But how do you *know* that, chico? The FBI's got fat guys too."

"Hey, Tony, if he's a cop, don't you think running in circles around a house is a pretty dumb way to watch it?"

"Maybe, maybe not." Tony gunned the Corniche through the gates, churning the gravel. The guards stayed to cover the street as the gates swung slowly shut. Tony's knuckles were white on the steering wheel. He was very, very agitated. "I'm tellin' you we're gettin' sloppy. Our whole attitude. We're not fuckin' *hungry* any more!"

He swept up the long curved drive to the enormous pillared house. A pair of white peacocks went skittering onto the lawn as he zoomed past. Manolo said nothing and sat there sullen. He never knew what to say any more. Whatever he said, Tony was ready to jump him. A gulf was beginning to yawn between them, and they had no time for building bridges. Or maybe no desire.

It was a warehouse just off an exit of the Palmetto Expressway, indistinguishable from most of the buildings for half a mile on either side. A name was stenciled across the corrugated metal: CONSOLIDATED CAR-

RIERS, INC. The name meant nothing, of course, but then neither did most of the corporate titles that stared down dully from the warehouse signs. The white Corniche looked most improbable as it threaded its way over railroad sidings, past the hulks of burnt-out trucks and rusted dumpsters.

Tony drew up close to the warehouse and parked. Nick went around to the trunk and retrieved the duffel bag, which he lugged across to the entrance as if it was a body. Tony pressed a buzzer above the door three times —the signal worked out by Manolo—and it was opened right away by a small, slug-faced man with pale green eyes like grapes. This was Seidelbaum himself, and he stood on no ceremony at all, barely murmuring hello to Tony as he bent to help Nick pull the money in.

There was an office just inside the door, an affair of flimsy partitions in the otherwise empty reaches of the warehouse. Four or five straight folding chairs were grouped around a money-counter. The money was fed through a large plastic funnel, and the machine looked as if it was intended for making sausages. One man, a dark Colombian type named Luis, sat at a desk and held a phone receiver to his ear. He never seemed to speak into it; he just listened. One other man, kind of a nephew version of Seidelbaum, sat drinking a cup of coffee.

They began the process right away; it was going to take four or five hours. Tony and Nick sat on one side of the machine, opened the duffel bag, and drew out handfuls of money. These they began to count and stack, noting the amounts on a yellow pad. Each stack of fifty twenties was then passed over to the nephew, who fed it into the machine. It was slow and tedious work. After the first fifty thousand it was hard not to see double, easy to make mistakes.

They all drank a lot of coffee. Seidelbaum's task was to take the stacks of money from the counter and bear them across to a suitcase on the desk. He put a paper

band around each stack and laid it neatly in the suitcase.
Luis on the phone and the nephew, Ricky, chatted nonstop with one another, even managing to coax a remark
from Tony and Nick every now and then. Seidelbaum
kept his silence, only speaking when they reached a
plateau. "Sixty thousand," he'd announce. "Hundred
and thirty thousand." Mostly he just kept darting back
and forth, puffing with the effort, rings of sweat at his
neck and armpits.

"Oh yeah, I worked in a lotta pictures," said Luis,
still listening at the phone. "I was in that picture *Burn*,
y' ever see it? With Marlon Brando. He's a good friend
o' mine. I was his driver, like."

"Oh yeah?" said Nick, not looking up from his
stacking. Not even listening.

"Yeah sure, in Cartagena. That's where they shot it.
Gillo Pontecorvo, he was the director. Italian guy." No
response from Tony and Nick. A look of contempt
flashed across the Colombian's face. It was as if he
could kill them for not caring. "Yeah, I also know Paul
Newman. I worked with him in Tucson."

Nick perked up. "Tucson, huh? You know a guy
named Bobo Alvarez?"

"Uh . . . no."

"That's funny," said Nick coolly. "Everybody
knows Bobo."

Seidelbaum finished the first suitcase. As he shut it
and turned the key in the lock, he called over his
shoulder to Tony. "Okay, now we'll draw you a company check off Consolidated Carriers for two hundred
eighty-three thousand." He reached up another suitcase
off the floor. "The rest'll be drawn off the bottling
company. Helluva lot o' bottles, huh?"

Tony spoke very precisely: "My figures say two
eighty-four."

Seidelbaum frowned and checked the printout, long
and coiled like the slip from a cash register. "That's just
not possible," he said.

"Okay, we'll count it again," said Tony. And when Seidelbaum groaned with exasperation, he added: "Hey business is business, Seidelbaum. We're talkin' a thousand bucks. I didn't get rich throwin' away a thousand bucks."

"All right, all right," said Seidelbaum. "You keep the change, okay? I don't give a shit."

There was silence after that. They counted and counted and drank more coffee. A second suitcase was filled, then a third. Tony and Nick relieved each other so they could stretch and rub their eyes. After three hours Tony had been issued seven checks totaling one million three hundred twenty-five thousand six hundred dollars. Seidelbaum was drenched in sweat. There were eighty cigarette butts in the ash tray. The boredom had strained relations so, they couldn't even talk to their own men. They were burnt out like factory workers.

Tony pulled the last fistful of bills from the duffel bag. He wet his thumb to begin counting and gagged on the taste of money. On an impulse he tossed the last handful into the air. As the twenties rained down around them, everyone looked up with a kind of glazed astonishment.

Tony laughed. "You think I could take a leak before we do the last batch?"

Seidelbaum sighed, as if he was glad the tension was finally broken. He smiled for the first time, reached around to his back pocket as if he was getting a handkerchief, and pulled out a .38. "I think we got enough," he said pleasantly, training the gun on Tony. "You're under arrest, Montana, under the Rico statute. Continuing criminal conspiracy."

Tony was completely thrown for a moment. The other men now took out their guns. Luis gave a one-word signal into the phone. Tony groaned, then muttered under his breath: "Aw shit." His eyes darted about the office, scrambling for an option.

"Go ahead, motherfucker," said Seidelbaum. "It'll

save me a lotta paperwork.'' His eyes were mean and agile now. He didn't seem quite so fat.

Tony grinned. "You're not kiddin', huh?'' He raised his hands above his head; Nick followed suit. At a signal from Seidelbaum, the nephew stepped forward and disarmed them. Tony said: "How do I know you guys are cops?''

Luis, the budding movie star, flipped a wallet from his back pocket, swaggered forward and shoved it under Tony's nose. "What's that say, asshole?'' he sneered. What it said was that he was a Fed.

Tony whistled. "Hey, that's real good work. Where can I get one o' those?''

Seidelbaum began to drone: "You have the right to remain silent. You have the right to have an attorney present . . .'' The door to the office opened, and several more came in, a couple of them wearing the uniform of the Miami Police Department.

Tony turned to Nick: "Gee, we got lucky. They *are* cops.''

"Hey,'' said Nick to Seidelbaum, "you think we could speed this up? I'm supposed to meet this chick at three.''

"Can I use the phone now, Seidelbaum?'' asked Tony. "I wanna call my lawyer. He oughta get a real kick outa this.''

"He ain't gonna do you a bit o' good, Montana.'' Seidelbaum pointed to a picture of Lincoln on the opposite wall. "That's an eye over there. Say hello, tweetie.''

Now they looked closely, they could see a hole in Lincoln's beard. It looked like a tasteless assassination joke. Tony said: "Is that what you jerk off in front of, Seidelbaum?'' Nick the Pig let out a big guffaw.

"You got about an hour, Montana, before we bring the U.S. Attorney's people into this.'' Seidelbaum sat on the edge of the desk. "They don't make the same kinda deals we do. You know what I mean?''

Tony was suddenly red with anger. "Listen, you fat prick, whaddayou take me for? One o' your whores? I don't make deals with cops, they're too fuckin' crooked. You got no case, Seidelbaum. I'm here changin' dollar bills, ain't nothin' wrong with that. So book me, cocksucker."

Seidelbaum drew himself up to his full five-foot-eight. He strode across to Tony and spoke through clenched teeth. "Have it your way, dickhead. This one's for free—from Mel Bernstein's buddies." And he raised the butt end of the .38 and cracked Tony across the face, right along the scar.

Tony reeled back against the wall. Nick lurched forward like a bear, making for Seidelbaum, and two cops jumped him and dragged him back. Seidelbaum slashed with the gun again, connecting with the bridge of Tony's nose. A great gout of blood came spurting from Tony's nostrils, but he did not raise his hands to protect his face. He stood there, bruises welling on his cheek and his nose, prepared to take whatever was coming. He even seemed to be sneering, though his lips were covered with blood.

"You pigshit, Montana! You're gonna rot this time!" Seidelbaum was crazy. The nephew had to step up and hold him, or he never would have stopped hitting. He seemed to take the whole thing personally. "By the time you get outa jail," he shouted, "you'll be walkin' with a cane!"

Tony leaned over and spit blood in the wastebasket, like a cowboy in a saloon getting rid of a chew of tobacco. He wiped his mouth with the back of his hand, grinned at Seidelbaum, and said: "Wanna bet five bucks?"

The headline in the Miami *Herald* was about two inches high. It looked as if nuclear war was being announced.

It said: DRUG KING POSTS RECORD $5 MILLION BOND. Below this was a photograph of Tony walking out of Dade County Jail, Elvira just behind him on his left, Sheffield beside him smiling at the camera. The next day at the courthouse the press numbered over thirty, with minicam units from all the local stations and correspondents from both major wire services. Tony, Elvira, and Sheffield stepped out into the steamy sun, each of them wearing dark glasses. Before they were halfway down the steps they were mobbed.

"Tony!" cried a gaggle of reporters, "Tony, over here! What's it feel like shelling out five million bucks?"

"Don't worry," Tony said with a cockeyed grin, "I'm gettin' it back. Maybe I'll sue 'em for interest."

Virgil Train, Channel 2's drug investigator, thrust a mike in Tony's face: "What do you think, Tony? You think you got a chance?"

"Hey Virg, how are ya? You kiddin'? We'll knock 'em dead. I got the Fourth Amendment in my pocket."

Sheffield hustled Tony down the steps. A couple of Cuban kids—maybe ten, twelve years old—materialized out of the crowd and held up the *Herald* front page to be autographed. Tony obliged, huddling over the papers and scribbling his name with a flourish as Sheffield opened the limousine door and ushered Elvira in. The photographers crouched and got a picture of Tony with the kids that made him look as fit and wholesome as a pitcher writing his name on a baseball. Virgil Train caught up with him.

"You think you're a scapegoat, Tony?"

Tony stared into the Channel 2 camera and spoke with enormous conviction. "These bums," he said, "they think they can snoop everywhere. It's gettin' to be like Russia. What's America comin' to?"

"Are you proud to be an American, Tony?"

"Virg, I came to this country from a dictatorship.

Every night I thank God—on my knees—that I'm free. This country's done real well by me. I plan to spend the rest o' my life returning the favor.'' He handed the last paper back to the kids, tousled the short one's hair, and turned to the limo.

"Thanks, Tony," said Virgil Train. "Ladies and gentlemen, a remarkable man."

It was that day, between the posting of the bond at the courthouse and the late-night powwow at Sheffield's office, that Tony started using regularly. There was always coke in the house, in five-gram vials in every drawer, like a chain-smoker's cigarettes. He'd been snorting a fair amount at parties, and if Elvira was especially ripped late at night and he felt like making love, he'd toot a few lines with her. But nothing regular. Not half a gram in the afternoon as he wandered among the cages, standing on the edge of the moat in a staring match with the Bengal. Not with a gram in his watch pocket as he left for Sheffield's office.

It was a very tense meeting. Tony paced nervously, smoking a cigar, while Manolo sat in a swivel chair, rocking back and forth as he slugged at a six-pack of Heineken. Sheffield talked through a cloud of Camel smoke, explaining options, charting who was on their side and who was straight. Whenever Tony or Manolo felt like a toot, each brought out his own vial and tapped some out and snorted. They didn't share. Sheffield didn't indulge. But it made no more of a stir than if they'd been eating Life Savers. Nobody noticed Tony was using especially heavily. Everyone they knew did lots and lots.

"The bottom line is this," said Sheffield. "You give me a check for a hundred grand, that's for me, plus three hundred more in cash, and I guarantee you'll walk on the conspiracy charge. But then they're gonna come back at us on a tax evasion. And I'm tellin' ya, Tony, they'll get it."

Tony said: "What am I lookin' at?"

"Five years, maybe three," shrugged Sheffield. "Maybe less if I can make a deal."

Tony whirled around and smashed his fist on the desk. "Three fuckin' years in the can? For what? For washin' money? Gimme a break, George—this whole country's built on grand theft. *I'm* not gonna take the rap."

"Hey, Tony, what's three years? It's not like Cuba here, ya know. It's like goin' to a hotel, for Christ's sake."

Tony shook his head coldly. No deal.

"Come on, Tony," coaxed Sheffield, "I'll delay the trial. A year and a half, two years—you won't start doin' time till eighty-five."

"No way, George." Tony kept shaking his head. He drew the vial of coke from his watch pocket. "They ain't never gonna get me back in a cage. Never. You got that?" He paused just long enough to tap the coke on the back of his hand and breathe it in with a grunt. "Look, George, how 'bout I go another four hundred grand? How 'bout *eight* hundred grand? With that you oughta be able to fix the Supreme Court, huh?"

Sheffield sighed. "It ain't that simple, Tony. Look, the law has to prove beyond a reasonable doubt. I'm an expert at makin' 'em doubt, but when you got a million three undeclared dollars staring into a video camera, honeybaby, it's hard to convince a jury you found it in a cab."

Tony paced back and forth like—well, like a tiger. He could barely contain his rage, and neither of the other men spoke for a moment, for fear he would explode. He looked terribly lonely just then, like a king in exile. Finally he turned to face them. He stared first at Manolo, the closest thing he had to a brother, almost as if he'd never seen him before. Then he leaned across Sheffield's desk and spoke with a savage patience.

"All right, George. I do the three fuckin' years. But lemme tell you about *my* law. There ain't no reasonable

doubt, it's real simple. If you're rainmakin' the judge or
you screw me outa the four hundred grand and I come
in guilty on the big rap, then you, the judge, the pros-
ecutor, the whole fuckin' U.S. Army, nothin's gonna
stop me. I'll come and tear your eyeballs out. Okay?''

Sheffield nodded coolly. "You've made your point.
Where's the money?''

Tony looked at Manolo, who picked up a large briefcase off the floor and set it on Sheffield's desk. As he
flicked the catches and lifted the lid, revealing stacks
and stacks of twenties, Tony turned abruptly and strode
from the office. He was damned if he'd watch them
count it.

Chapter Eight

THE HELICOPTER CAME in over the mountain in dazzling sunlight, landing on the pad as neatly as a Cochabamba butterfly lighting on a flower. Tony climbed out followed by Ernie, who served as his bodyguard now on all international runs. Tony couldn't stand to have bodyguards around him in Miami; they made him feel caged. He walked across the throbbing green lawn toward Sosa's villa. It was his first trip here in a couple of months, his first time out of the country since being busted.

Sosa stood up and waved from the terrace. As Tony approached, he could see there were several men lounging under the arbor having their midday coffee. He didn't recognize any of them. Sosa walked forward with open arms, grinning brightly as he engulfed Tony in a bear hug. They spoke one another's names with feeling, as if they were family.

"Thanks for coming on such short notice," said Sosa, one arm around Tony's shoulders as he led him toward the arbor. "How's Elvira?"

"Great, just great. And Gabriella?"

Sosa sighed with contentment. "Three more months, Tony. I can't believe it." He gave Tony's arm an affectionate squeeze. "How 'bout you, amigo? When we gonna see another little Tony?"

"I'm workin' on it," Tony said with a tight smile.

"I guess you'll have to work harder, huh?" Sosa laughed, but Tony could feel a certain reserve in him, consonant with the other men in the circle under the arbor, who now stood up to greet him. "I want you to meet some friends of mine," said Sosa, starting at the left, rather as if they were going through a receiving line at an embassy. "This is Pedro Feliz, chairman of Tropical Sugar in Bolivia . . . Tony Montana."

"A pleasure," said Feliz, clicking his heels a bit as he shook Tony's hand. He looked like the fly-by-night *presidente* of a dirt-poor banana republic.

Then came General Jorge Navarro, Commander of the First Army Corps, with a breastplate of ribbons and only one arm. Then César Albini, of the Ministry of the Interior, his eyes as blank and pitiless as the jungle wastes he administered. Then Charles Cookson of Washington, crew-cut and Brooks-Brothered. This one even smelled like a government type. They were all very glad to meet Tony, they said.

Sosa called over his black aide and said: "Please have Alberto come out now." The aide disappeared into the house. Sosa gestured Tony to a chair in the middle of the group, and they all sat down. Sosa personally prepared Tony's coffee. As he handed it over, he said: "Tony, I want to discuss something that concerns all of us here."

"Go ahead, Noldo, I'm listening." Tony sipped his coffee and noticed that Ernie had been ushered to the far end of the arbor, where he stood around with a group of four or five brutal-looking men. Suddenly he realized these were the bodyguards of all the big honchos sitting around Sosa's table. This struck him so funny he grinned. The other men at the table shifted nervously. They didn't like the grin.

"Tony, *you* have a problem and *we* have a problem," said Sosa. "I think we can solve yours and you can solve ours. We understand that you're having some difficulty with taxes. It looks like you're gonna have to do some time. This distresses us, Tony. We don't like to see a friend in jail, and frankly, we wouldn't want any interruption in our deal. Mr. Cookson here has some good connections in Washington who tell us these troubles of yours can be taken care of. Maybe you'll have to pay a fine and some back interest, but you won't have to serve any time. How does that strike you?"

All the men's eyes were on Tony. He was startled. He thought he'd come down to renegotiate the monthly flow of the drug. No one had prepared him for this. He turned to Sosa and said: "And your problem, Noldo?"

Just then Alberto, the man they called the Shadow, materialized on the veranda. He focused his venomous eyes on Tony. "You remember Alberto," said Sosa. Tony nodded. The Shadow stood at attention, ready to kill. "Our problem, Tony, is somebody's making a lot of noise in the States about the way we do business down here. This person is very influential. People are starting to listen to him. He's a communist. Alberto here is going to help solve our problem. As you know, he's an expert in the disposal business." Sosa permitted himself the smallest smile, which Tony returned. This was all by way of an homage to Omar. "The difficulty is, Alberto doesn't know his way around the States too well. He needs a guide." Sosa paused to light a cigarette. Tony locked eyes with Alberto, whose eyes were not human at all. "You think you could help us out?"

Tony looked around at the faces of the men assembled in Sosa's arbor. Together they constituted the whole power network of the drug trade in Bolivia. He could see they treated him as an equal. His money, his

daring business sense, his meteoric rise—all of this
assured him a place at the council table. What struck
him here was that he was by far the youngest of them,
by ten years at least. He could see the hunger in all the
men's faces to be as young as he was.

"No problem, Noldo," said Tony, grinning around
the circle.

In the packed auditorium at New York's City College,
Aristidio Gutierrez was just winding up a most passionate address. He was a dark, intense, distinguished-
looking man in his mid-fifties, with a thatch of unruly
hair that looked as if it had never been combed, bushy
eyebrows that jumped about when he talked, and great
baggy eyes like a hound's. Behind him on the stage,
where the white and green Bolivian flag stood adjacent
to the stars and stripes, Gutierrez's wife sat proudly, her
eyes radiant behind thick glasses. Assorted deans and
political types made up the rest of the half-circle that sat
behind the hero. Most of his audience was Latin, exiles
of one stripe or another, and those Americans who sat
among them glowed with a counter-cultural fire. They
could have been attending any leftist rally of the last
forty years. It was surely the first time in the annals of
political oppression that a crowd of idealists had turned
out to protest cocaine.

"This ruthless oligarchy of generals and big business-
men," said Gutierrez, "is dedicated to just one thing—
growing richer and richer. They pour their cocaine
profits into their Swiss bank accounts. They sit in their
mountain kingdoms drinking champagne while the poor
eat rats and smother their starving children. These
pirates have declared war on the Bolivian people! We
will cut them out like cancer!"

The applause welled up, and he shouted in Spanish
the words of a song of liberty, and the crowd broke into
unruly cheering. In Row VV, on the aisle, Tony Mon-

tana the king of Miami sat listening. Every minute or so he touched his nose, as if he had an allergy to populist rhetoric. Beside him sat the Shadow, his face a mask of death. Tony had had that feeling all day long, from the moment they landed at Kennedy—the feeling that he was leading Death around. He never felt this about himself, not even when he was going out to kill someone. But he felt it now with the Shadow. This Alberto was more than a man with a gun. He was like an infection.

"Ten thousand of our brothers," shouted Gutierrez, "are being tortured and held without trial. Another six thousand have simply disappeared. You Americans cannot know what it means to be a disappeared person. In Latin America the rivers run with the blood of the disappeared."

Here Gutierrez began to cough, or he had a frog in his throat, for he reached for the pitcher of water and poured out a glass. The audience was absolutely silent as he drank. There wasn't a single one of them who wasn't thinking hard about what it meant to be "disappeared." Well, perhaps the Shadow wasn't. But Tony was.

Gutierrez cleared his throat and leaned into the microphone and continued: "Unless the U.S. government sets an example soon, by calling for the observation of fundamental human rights, by stopping this endless sale of tanks and bombs and planes to the gangsters who run my country . . ."

The cheering swelled to a fever pitch, practically drowning him out. The Shadow tapped Tony's arm to indicate they had seen enough. They slipped unnoticed into the aisle. Hundreds of people were hurtling out of their seats now, shouting. "Viva Gutierrez!" they clamored. "Viva Bolivia!"

". . . I can promise you not only that the cause of human freedom and dignity in Latin America will once again be strangled in its cradle, but that the sickness is *here* now, on *your* shores. It is worming its way to the heart of your once-proud democracy!"

Pandemonium now. The crowd surged forward, be-
sieging the stage. "Gutierrez! Gutierrez!" they cried.
The Shadow hurried quickly out of the auditorium, as if
the cheering of his enemy made him physically ill. Tony
lingered a moment at the door, looking back once over
his shoulder. Gutierrez had come to the lip of the stage,
where he reached out his hands so they could touch him.
Tony was startled to feel how deep the man had impressed him, and not just because of the heat he created.
He would have stayed longer to watch if the Shadow
had not been waiting.

As he stepped outside in the chilly autumn rain he
drew from his pocket a bullet of coke and snorted, twice
in each nostril. The Shadow stood on the curb, looking
up at the bright-lit buildings with his mouth slightly
open, for the moment as much of a hick as a tourist
from Nowhere, U.S.A. Manolo was parked in an alley
across the street, and as soon as he saw them he streaked
out and pulled to the curb beside them. Tony opened the
door and held it for the Shadow, smiling as the killer
drew his rapt gaze from the giant panorama of Manhattan. Alberto suddenly realized that Tony had seen his
awestruck state, and his eyes now frosted over as he
ducked into the car.

"It's a piece o' cake," said Tony as Manolo drove
away. "Guy don't even have a bodyguard." He shook
his head with distaste. "Real stupid, huh? It's like he's
askin' for it."

"So we're on for Thursday then," said Manolo.

"Yeah, Thursday," Tony said wearily. He turned
and looked at the Shadow in the back seat, who now sat
staring forward with no expression at all. Tony didn't
see why they couldn't just wait in an alley and put a
bullet through Gutierrez as he stepped out into the rain.
Why did they have to go back to Miami and spend a day
making a bomb? It was all getting too political. Killing
was one thing, terrorism quite another. Tony willed
himself not to think about it. He pulled out his coke and

snorted again, thinking only of those three years he would not be in a cage. Yet the phrase kept repeating in his head: *the disappeared ones*. He could almost see their faces. He couldn't see why they had to die for the sake of the drug traffic. Everyone Tony had ever killed had at least deserved to die.

The next night in Miami, Tony and Elvira and Manolo went out to celebrate the three years Tony was about to be given back. He'd spent the whole day doing errands with the Shadow. At Bob's Discount they picked up aluminum baking pans, cookie sheets, black electrical tape, rubber garden gloves. At a Radio Shack they got wire cutters and a soldering iron and slide switch. At a nameless, faceless house off Calle Ocho they met with a whacked-out Vietnam vet who sold them a briefcase full of C4 plastique, with detonating cords and blasting caps. The Shadow was left in the boathouse by the canal to assemble his bomb, with Nick and Chi-Chi guarding him. It wasn't stated out loud, but the bombwork was being done a hundred yards away from the house in case of a slip-up.

By the time they arrived at The Beachhead on Arthur Godfrey Road, Tony and Elvira and Manolo were completely loaded, giggling uncontrollably as they entered the Wasp bastion. The place was full of proper millionaires—developers who'd tossed old ladies out in the cold, proper sorts like that. As the maitre d' led them across to a table, they were slightly weaving and had to hold on to one another. They swayed like a conga line, and a couple of sour-faced diners drew back in dismay. Just as Manolo and Elvira slumped into a booth, Tony recognized someone a couple of tables away. Grinning happily, he lurched over and slapped his hand on the shoulder of a heavy-set man at a round table of six people.

"Hey Vic," said Tony, "I watch your show every day."

The man craned around, with a toss of his leonine

white head of hair. His eyes were glazed with the sort of patrician annoyance reserved for bores in restaurants. "Oh, is that so? How nice," he said, though it didn't *sound* very nice.

"Yeah, I think you got the best drug coverage around. Virgil Train—Channel 2, ya know him?—he's a friend o' mine. Does a real nice spot every coupla weeks. But you got it all over him, Vic. You got drugs on practically every night. We're real proud o' you, pal."

Victor Shepard's face was drained of all color. He didn't know what to say. Tony was talking double fast and pouring on the charm. All the other conversations at Shepard's table had stopped. They were totally intrigued by the man with the scar.

"Just one little thing, huh Vic? You know that two hundred kilo DEA bust you was congratulatin' the cops for the other night?"

Vic's brow furrowed. "Aren't you . . . Tony Montana?" The five rich people sitting around him gasped in recognition.

Tony beamed. "Yeah, that's me." He shook off Manolo's arm, who'd come to retrieve him. He winked around the table at the fatcats. "Hi folks, don't get up. Anyway Vic, you should check it out. I heard like it was two hundred and *twenty* kilos went down. That mean's twenty's missing, right? The way *I* figure, anyway. Why don't you ask your friends the cops about that?" He slapped Shepard's shoulder again. "Hey, keep up the good work, Vic. Don't believe everything you hear, okay? Have a good dinner now. Nice to meet you people."

Waving a cheery farewell, he turned away from the table and sauntered back to his own, Manolo clucking fretfully beside him. "Hey Tony, that wasn't cool," he said. "Shepard's got a lotta friends."

"I don't give a fuck," retorted Tony, sliding into the

booth beside Elvira. "He's an asshole! Never fuckin'
tells the truth on TV. That's the trouble with this country. Nobody tells the truth. Ain't that right?" he asked
the wincing waiter, who nodded fearfully and begged to
know what drinks they would like to have.

And they all laughed at him for being afraid of them,
because he was just a poor Cuban himself. Tony and
Manolo laughed because they remembered huddling in
the linen closet back at the Havanito Restaurante,
looking out through the linen chute at the gold-chained
couples and the coked-up dealers. Elvira laughed
because she was in the mood to find everything funny
about the desperate tacky glamour of a millionaire's
restaurant on Arthur Godfrey Road.

They ordered up a Roman feast. Caviar to start with
and a bottle of the best champagne, here only $280 a
crack, since it didn't have the Babylon Club's markup.
Tony seemed visibly disappointed not to be paying five
hundred. Then they had steaks and french fries, spurn-
ing all the sauces and medallions and game birds on the
menu. The chef nearly wept at steak and french fries,
but he served them up. Everyone at The Beachhead, in
fact, was going out of his way to accommodate Tony
and his arrogant desires. He sent a hundred-and-sixty-
dollar bottle of brandy to Victor Shepard's table, which
Shepard returned untouched.

Tony laughed at the tension he caused, and Manolo
and Elvira laughed along with him, in a vague gesture of
moral support but with less and less conviction. By the
end of the meal the men were sated, weary after all from
the trip to New York the day before, the buzz of the
coke wearing off besides. Elvira got higher and higher,
meanwhile. Surreptitiously she would bring the vial up
to her nostrils wrapped in a hanky, as if she was suf-
fering from some pesky allergy. She did it every ten
minutes. Tony didn't think twice about it, she did it all
the time, but tonight he sat there stuffed with food and

looked over irritably at her untouched plate.

"Why don't you eat?"

"I'm not hungry."

"So what'd you order it for?"

"I didn't. You did."

Silence. It was usually about this time that Manolo would break in and shift the mood, deflecting Tony's anger, soothing Elvira's feathers. But he didn't seem to have it in him tonight. He tossed down another belt of the brandy Shepard had spurned. He figured they'd go at each other for another minute or so, and then Elvira would stalk out, and finally they could leave. But Tony did not fire back at Elvira. Instead he gazed out at the gilded room where the laughing crowd exulted and paraded. His eyes were dead and melancholy. There was no anger now.

"Hey, Manolo, is this it? Is this *all* of it? Eating and drinking and tooting and fucking? And *then* what? You're fifty before you know it, and you got a bag for a belly and your tits sag and your liver's got spots and you look like a mummy. Just like these guys."

"You shouldn't talk like that, Tony. You're gonna bring bad luck."

"You think so, chico? You think Chango the god of fire and thunder's gonna dump two shits on me?" Tony laughed out loud, as if the knot of rage in his chest had finally broken. He reached into his pocket and drew out his vial. He tapped it and flicked the opening and snorted. He didn't bother with a hanky. Then he seemed to drink the crowd in even deeper. "But can you dig it, chico," he said, his voice so soft for a moment they had to hold their breath to hear him. "This is what we worked for. Right here. This is what we kill guys for. For this."

He turned a stony gaze on Elvira. "How many guys did I kill so I could live with a junkie? Who never eats nothin'. Who can't wake up till she's had a Quaalude.

Who sleeps all day with black shades on. Who won't fuck me any more 'cause she's in a coma.''

"Can it, Tony," said Manolo. "You're drunk."

Elvira's eyes were sharp with fury. "Let's not get into who's good in bed, okay? You haven't been winning prizes in that department for some time now."

But he couldn't stop. It was like he had a speech to give. Diners at the tables around them were beginning to cast embarrassed glances in their direction. It wasn't loud enough for them to hear every word yet, but it was wonderfully embarrassing. Tony splashed the last of the brandy in his snifter, filling it half full. Neither he nor Manolo could have said how they drank the whole bottle. Indulgence was second nature now. The razor edge of the coke was fighting the blur of the liquor. It was all a losing battle.

"Is this the American dream, chico?" he asked, a wave of mawkish sentiment welling up inside him. "Is this what happens to Bogart at the end?" He laughed bitterly, staring out at a desert space where the gold had turned to dust. "Fuck it man, I can't even have a kid with her. She's got a womb like a sewer from all the dope. Can't even have a nice little kid."

Perhaps he would have broken down and cried just then, but now it was Elvira's turn. She stood up from the table, lifted the untouched plate of steak and fries, and heaved it at him. It slopped all over his shirt and spattered his face. "You asshole," she said with huge contempt. "You stupid sonuvabitch spic asshole."

They had a black-tie audience now. The diners at The Beachhead, discreet before all else, made no pretense now of trying to listen with half an ear. They dropped their forks and gawked. The waiter—a fine upstanding Cuban-American with a wife and three kids and a mortgage and a Cutlass—hovered near the table, making ineffectual hushing sounds. He had a towel in one hand which he'd have gladly used to wipe up the mess if they'd only stopped and let him.

But Elvira had just gotten started. "How dare you talk to me like that!" she shouted. "You think you're better than me? What the hell do *you* do? Deal and kill, right? Oh that's real creative, Tony, that's just wonderful isn't it. A real contribution to human history. Well, let me tell you something—I don't *want* a child with you. It's the least I can do for the future, you know? At least I won't bring another fuck-up into the world who might grow up like you!"

"Siddown before I kill you," said Tony without emotion. He picked the steak up off his lap and set it on his plate. Then he accepted the towel from the waiter and began to brush at his shirt. He even managed to flash a grin as he said: "Maybe we can have a doggie bag, huh?" It was as if he'd put the whole problem aside. He would just stay drunk and stoned right now.

This only made Elvira madder—and louder. "What kind of home life's a kid going to have with us, huh? With your thugs around all the time, carrying machine guns. Is Nick the Pig gonna be his uncle? Is Chi-Chi the dope fiend gonna take him to the zoo? Oh yeah, I forgot we got our own zoo." Now the maitre d' padded over, and he touched Elvira's elbow gently, murmuring that perhaps if she was feeling ill she should think about going home. She leaped away from him with a hiss, as if he'd burned her. Her voice was a little softer, though, as she turned to Tony again. There was almost a pleading quality as she said: "Oh Tony, don't you see? We're losers, honey. We're not winners." She made a vague and tragic gesture around at the stunned and silent room. "These are the winners, Tony. Not us."

The fury was over for both of them. A curious awkwardness settled on them now. They looked like two actors who'd lost their lines, who had no skill for improvising. Tony said gently: "Go on, get a cab and go home. You're stoned."

"Not as stoned as you are, honey. You're so stoned you don't know it." She stumbled as she reached into the booth to grab her bag. Manolo stood up dutifully and moved to help her. She shook her head firmly, and he stayed away. Without another glance at Tony she turned and wobbled across the restaurant. A hundred eyes were on her, moving back and forth between her and Tony. Once again Manolo moved to follow, as if he couldn't bear to see her watched.

"Let her go," said Tony. "Tomorrow'll be the same old shit. She'll pop another Quaalude and love me again."

She disappeared into the foyer and was gone. Suddenly it was as if the room had had enough of silence. They turned back to their meals with redoubled vigor, buzzing with conversation. Presumably there was but one thing they were talking about, but they couldn't stand to watch it any more, so naked out there in the middle of things. They wanted to turn it into gossip now. They wanted Tony to disappear, the way Elvira did.

Tony stood up and reached in his pocket. He pulled out a roll of cash and peeled off several hundreds. He tossed these on the littered table. As he stepped from the booth he brushed once more at the front of his shirt. Perhaps he was going to leave quietly after all. Manolo waited patiently. The maitre d' and the waiter managed to pull to attention, in case one of those hundreds had a chance of coming their way. Tony took a long look around the room, like he wanted to commit it to memory.

Then he shouted: "You're all fulla shit!"

The room lurched into another silence, this time red-faced and shy, with perhaps an undercurrent of wounded dignity. He had gone way too far. They were not amused any more.

"You know why?" cried Tony. " 'Cause none of you

got the guts to be what you wanna be! You're too fuckin' scared. You need people like me so you can point your finger and say, 'Hey, there's the bad guy.' So what does that make you? Good guys?'' They were listening hard, he could tell. Right then he wished he had an education, so he could show them the kind of hell they were in and make them cower in their seats. He shouldn't have worried. His words were only the half of it. What they could not turn away from was his passionate conviction. ''Don't kid yourself, folks. You're no better than a dealer just because you're buyin'. You get along okay, huh? You know how to hide, you know how to lie. I ain't so lucky. Me, I always tell the truth— even when I lie.''

He began to walk out, past the maitre d' and the waiter, past the pastry cart and the Irish Coffee bar. Manolo kept pace with him, two or three steps behind. The crowd had not recovered from the second silence. They would recover by being offended, if only he would leave. He turned at the door and smiled, then gave them a kind of Sinatra wave.

''Say goodnight to the bad guy now,'' he said. He sounded so much like a man in a show, you wished he had a straw hat. ''Take one last look, 'cause chances are,'' and he laughed like a mad king, ''you ain't gonna see him again.''

And he stepped out into the foyer, and Manolo shuffled after. The room was soundless for one beat more, then it fell into furious protest. Tony hardly saw where he was walking. If he could just get into the car now, he thought, he could have a double toot and clear his head and then they could go where they liked. To the circus or something.

He stood waiting under the awning while a gusty rain swept over the pavement, shiny like diamonds under the streetlights. Palm trees whirred above him. *Make it stop*, he thought, his hands in his pockets because they were shaking. He wasn't cold, he was burning hot.

Make what stop?

He didn't know what. His heart was racing, as if somebody was after him. Any other time he would have just pulled a gun, spun around and faced them. But he knew, with a sickening curl of panic in his gut, that if he turned around there wouldn't be anyone there. He reached in his pocket and grabbed his coke, and it slipped through his fingers and fell to the pavement, just as the carhop sailed up in the Corniche. The bullet of coke rolled under the car. As the carhop got out to hold the door for Tony, Tony dropped to his knees and started to crawl under the Rolls. Manolo yelled at him.

"Leave it alone, for Chrissake! We got more in the car!"

And he gripped Tony's shoulder and dragged him up. Tony's face was white. His teeth were chattering as if he'd caught a bad chill in the rain. He stared at Manolo, then at the carhop. The latter was built like a wrestler, so energetic he seemed to be dancing on his feet. He looked like he meant to conquer the world. He was Tony's age exactly, though he looked a good five years younger. Tony smiled in recognition, and the irony seemed to bring him to his senses. He reached in his pants pocket and drew out his wad of cash. It must have been three or four thousand dollars. He handed it over to the carhop, who looked down stunned at the money, as if a magician had snapped it out of the air.

Tony climbed in the Rolls and took off. The back tire crushed the bullet on the pavement. But like Manolo said, there was more where that came from. Manolo groped in the glove compartment and brought out a five-gram vial. He dumped out a gram in the palm of his hand, pinched some up like snuff, and reached over and held it under Tony's nose. Tony snorted. By the time they'd gone six blocks they were rocking again. The whole episode at the restaurant was forgotten. So was

the panic. The night was young and they had no plans.
Everything seemed the way it used to be, as long as they
didn't stop.

It was as if he'd made a conscious decision: from here
on in he would not stop. No matter how many red lights
there were. No matter how many roadblocks. Now he
was on a roller coaster, reckless and headlong. He
speeded the rain-whipped streets like he planned to ride
to the end of the world.

Alone.

The next day was Wednesday, and they were booked to
fly to New York about six. The Shadow worked on his
bomb all day, putting it together and taking it apart,
making endless tiny adjustments to the radio transmitter
and encoding device. Nick and Chi-Chi watched in a
daze, till the bomb didn't even seem dangerous any
more. It began to seem like the very abstract invention
of an eccentric tinker, and when it was done it would
do something very practical, maybe drink in the sun and
power a turbine.

Tony got ripped over his morning coffee, laying out
long lines on the glass-top table on the balcony above
the zoo, and he stayed as high as a kite all day. He made
a couple of trips out to the boathouse to check on the
progress, but he was annoyed that it took so long, and
the fussing over details only made him irritable. Besides,
they had just brought a shipment into Nashville, and
two of the local dealers there had slaughtered each other
over who controlled it and who should cut it. Tony
had no choice but to send Manolo up there to take
charge of the distribution, which meant that Nick the
Pig would have to take Manolo's place for the New
York run. In addition, Sosa was on the phone fifteen
different times that day—just checking in, he said. It
made Tony spit with rage.

Elvira slept in the guest room Tuesday night, after the scene in the restaurant. They passed in the house a couple of times on Wednesday, but in spite of being 'luded out she didn't profess her undying love. Mostly she froze him, but about three o'clock they met on the stairs. He was just getting dressed to go to the airport. He wasn't feeling angry any more, he was too wired. As she passed him he reached out and tried to clasp her hand. "Hey Elvira," he said softly, "why don't you think of a place you'd like to go. We'll go there, huh? Just as soon's I get back from New York."

"Go to hell," she said in a blur, and stumbled away downstairs.

On the way to the airport Tony told Chi-Chi to run by Gina's shop on Flagler Street. Chi-Chi and Nick and the Shadow waited in the car as Tony went in. The shop was bustling. Gina had a crew of four hairdressers, a manicurist and a shampoo girl, all of them working busily. A thrill of excitement buzzed through the room when Tony entered, for he was both celebrity and godfather here. He nodded and waved to several of the workers, but he saw right away that Gina's bay was empty. He turned anxiously to Pepe, the star stylist, who nodded toward the office in the rear.

Tony strode to the back and through the beaded curtain, aware that he only had a moment before he had to leave. Gina was standing at the full-length mirror beyond her desk, pinning a cluster of gardenias in her permed and frosted hair. She gasped when she saw it was Tony and almost seemed to cower as she turned to face him, as if he'd caught her doing something wrong.

Tony was too preoccupied to notice. "Hi, princess," he said, heading for the refrigerator, where he pulled out a bottle of beer. Gina had recovered her balance by the time he turned to face her again. "Real pretty," said Tony, gesturing at the beige silk dress she wore, with the flounces of lace at the sleeves and collar.

Gina spoke haltingly. "Did we—were we supposed to see each other today?"

"Nah, I'm on my way to the airport. I just wanted to say hi. Long time no see."

"What's wrong, Tony?" she said, as he passed a weary hand over his forehead. She'd forgotten her own nervousness now. She stepped up close and smoothed his unruly hair with her hand. "You need a haircut," she said gently. She was shocked at how tired his eyes were.

He grabbed her hand and brought it to his lips and lightly kissed her fingertips. As she shyly tugged free of his grip, he said: "Gina, let's go away, huh?"

"What are you talking about? Go where?"

"I don't care," he said. "I just need to slow down for a while. I'll be back from New York tomorrow. We could go to Europe—"

"Tony, I can't. I've got too much to do around here." She gave a nervous glance at the clock on the wall opposite. "What about Elvira?"

Tony gave a short, harsh laugh. "Things ain't goin' too good in that department."

"Look, don't you have a plane to catch?"

For the first time he noticed how jittery she was. He felt stupid and awkward all of a sudden. "You got a date or somethin'?"

"Sort of," said Gina, still trying to be light. She threw her arms about his neck and hugged him close. "Why don't you call when you get back from New York? There's some stuff I want to talk about."

"Who with?" he asked coldly.

"What? Oh, nobody. Just some guy. Don't worry, he's real respectable." She tugged his hand and moved toward the beaded curtain.

"Who?" he asked again, his voice like ice now.

"Oh Tony, don't start. Please."

He hated to see the look of exasperation on her face.

Why couldn't she understand it was all for her own good? He had a terrible urge to shake her till she blurted out the name. Why couldn't she wait? He would keep her safe if she'd only let him. If only he could make her see how dangerous life was. Then they could run away together and hide till all the hurricanes had passed. All he wanted to do was talk gently to her—hold her tight and sing her lullabies.

But his rage and jealousy got the better of him. Hating himself even as he did it, he shook his finger in her face and said: "Soon as I get back we're gonna have a little talk, you and me. You got that?"

She pulled away and turned her back on him. Her voice was sad and bitter: "Just go, will you?"

He was so frustrated he wanted to cry out. He needed her so much right now. But his pride was too strong, and something in him was afraid to say the words that were in his heart. It would have to wait till tomorrow now, like everything else. He turned and headed back through the beaded curtain, longing to get in the car again so he could do another toot. Nobody said good-bye to him as he barreled out of the shop. Nobody said hello when he slumped back into the limo.

The world seemed to know when to keep its distance.

He was in a grim mood when he boarded the plane, with Nick beside him in first class and the Shadow back in tourist. He'd had a big fight with Manolo earlier in the afternoon. Manolo had quarreled with the setup of the Nashville run from the first. He argued that you couldn't send a shipment direct from Panama to the hinterlands; it had to pass through Miami first. Miami was part of coke's brand name, almost as much as Bolivia. So maybe Manolo was right, but the argument got ugly. Manolo had stopped just short of saying that Tony was losing control. Tony had cuffed Manolo on the side of the head and called him a coward and a faggot. They both accused each other of being junkies.

Nick was all excited about going to New York. He hadn't been there in twenty years, not since he wasted a Mafia don and went into hiding, only to surface in Florida five years later and a hundred pounds heavier. He took two of everything the stewardess served, and he finished most of Tony's meal as well, since Tony wasn't hungry. Tony snorted coke from a bullet inhaler all through the trip, making no attempt to hide it. He had maybe five grams on him, another ten in his suitcase. He almost seemed to be daring someone to stop him, except it was all unconscious, and anyway no one did.

"Hey boss," said Nick, "we gonna have time to get laid? I ain't had any New York pussy since I was a kid."

"It's all the same," Tony said with a shrug. "It's over in five minutes."

"Come on, boss, it ain't as bad as that. You been spendin' too much time with a princess."

"Yeah, real princess," Tony said laconically, doing a toot in either nostril.

"Never could understand it," Nick observed with a shake of his head. "Guy gets hooked up with an angel— gorgeous, lotta class, like Elvira. Hey, that's terrific. I can hear the violins, ya know? But what's it got to do with gettin' laid? A guy still needs to get laid, boss. You get too serious about it, you'll never get it up. Like Manolo."

"What about Manolo?"

"Aw, he's all fucked up. Real touchy, ya know? I think he's porkin' a married lady or somethin'. It's all a big secret. Pain in the ass, if you ask me."

Tony looked out the window at the glittering lights of New York. They were coming in on a perfect night, crisp and aching clear, with a harvest moon. Tony felt a twinge of melancholy as he said: "It's the first I heard about it."

"Yeah, well he was a lot more fun when he was fuckin' hookers and trash, I'll tell ya that."

All of a sudden his melancholy turned to paranoia. If Manolo was having a secret affair with a married woman, could it possibly be Elvira? Tony would kill them both, he realized, if he ever found that out. The whole idea was patently absurd. Elvira had passed beyond the reach of sex these days, and Manolo was shy as a baby brother in her presence. But Tony was beginning to lose his feel for the absurd. Real was no longer the border of his world, not in any direction. Even if Manolo wasn't fucking Elvira, he was still keeping secrets. What else wasn't he telling? What deals was he making on the side?

When they landed they stayed clear of the Shadow, in case they were being watched. They retrieved Alberto's one deadly suitcase at baggage claim. Then they rented a car and picked him up at the pre-arranged spot, beneath an underpass about five hundred yards from the terminal. As Nick slowed the car, Alberto emerged from the darkness, his eyes as mad for blood as ever. Once again Tony had the feeling that he was escorting more than a simple murderer. It was Death itself climbing into his car. Tony snorted the last of a gram vial and tossed it out the window.

They drove to Manhattan in silence. So urgent was the need to get the bomb in place, they did not go first to the hotel but made straight for the east eighties. The brownstone where Gutierrez lived was on a quiet, tree-shaded street between Madison and Park. The moon shone through the chestnut leaves, and the only people who seemed to be out were evening strollers—walking their dogs, hand in hand with their autumn lovers. Several lights were on in Gutierrez's house, but they knew he was out giving a speech. They parked just down the street from the house and waited, figuring he'd be home by midnight.

They'd been waiting about a half hour, each of them lost in his own thoughts. The only sounds were Nick eating a bag of potato chips and Tony snorting. The Shadow in the back seat was completely silent. They couldn't even hear him breathe. Nick said: "So who *is* this guy? Why's he so important?"

Tony shrugged. "He talks a lot. Lotta people listen. He's some kinda symbol."

"Simble, huh?" Nick poured the last crumbs of the chips in his mouth and paused to mull this over. At last he said: "Is that some gang or somethin'?"

Tony shook his head. "No, it's like when you die your life meant somethin' to somebody, ya know? It wasn't like you just lived it for yourself."

"Yeah?" Nick seemed confused, or at best uninterested.

"Yeah." Tony snorted another line. "Me, I wanna die fast. With my name written in lights all over the sky. Tony Montana—he died doin' it." He chuckled with pleasure, as if the turn of phrase delighted him. "That's what they oughta write on my gravestone, huh? He died doin' it."

"Whatcha talkin' about?" retorted Nick impatiently. "You ain't gonna die. You're too important."

But Tony wasn't listening. He was smiling cheerfully as he spun out the thought. If Manolo or Elvira had been there, they might have said it was the first time he'd looked happy in weeks. "So I'll end up in a coffin," said Tony jovially. "So what else is new? The cockroach who fires the bullet is gonna end up in a coffin too. All I know is, I got further than anybody else from the alleys."

"What alleys?"

"Havana," said Tony. "There's all these alleys fulla garbage. People live like animals." He reached for the handle and made as if to get out of the car.

"Where ya goin', boss?"

"I gotta call Manolo," he said. It was a sudden impulse; he scarcely understood it himself. But if he didn't get hold of Manolo right away and make peace, he was sure they were going to drift further and further apart. There were things that only Manolo understood. Things he knew about Tony that even Tony didn't.

"Sit down, he's coming!" barked the Shadow.

Tony was already halfway out of the car, but he obeyed. He slumped back into the seat and shut the door, momentarily dazed. He tasted blood in his mouth. Gutierrez was just driving up in his modest, grimed Chevette. He drew up to the curb in front of the brownstone, across the street from Tony's car, and idled the engine as his wife got out. He waited till she climbed the steps and unlocked the door and disappeared inside before he nosed the car into the street again and glided off.

"He's gonna park it," said Nick.

"Hurry up, follow him!" commanded the Shadow, and Nick started up the car and did a fast U-turn. Nobody said a word about the fact that Tony had not been the one to give the orders.

They followed at a cautious distance, turning onto Madison when Gutierrez did, then left onto 81st. A space became free as a panel truck lurched away into traffic. Gutierrez stopped, put the car in reverse, and angled into the parking place. Nick kept driving by, and as the car cruised past Gutierrez happened to glance their way and for one brief instant looked into Tony's eyes. Of course there was no recognition.

Nick parked half a block down, just off Fifth. He watched in the rearview mirror till Gutierrez had left his car and disappeared around the corner onto Madison, heading home. Then the three men got out of the car. Nick stayed at the corner to watch for cops. Tony and the Shadow headed back to the Chevette. As soon as they reached it the Shadow ducked to the pavement with his attaché, scooted under the car, and began to work.

Tony was feeling alert again, perhaps because they'd

finally gone into action. As he stood looking up the
street toward Nick, now and then crouching down to
watch the Shadow wind the black tape around the axle,
he recalled how terrorists' bombs were always going off
at the wrong time. For some reason this made Tony feel
light-headed and playful. He fished his vial of coke
from his pocket and tapped some out on the back of his
hand. Two cars drove past as he snorted. He didn't care
who saw him any more, especially now with a game of
Russian roulette going on under the car beside him.

It must have been a good half-minute since he'd
checked on Nick at the end of the street. He hadn't seen
Nick's frantic wave, nor his sudden disappearance into
a basement doorway. By the time Tony pocketed his
vial and looked up with a vacant grin, the cop car was
only twenty feet away, already slowing down to check
him out. He just had time to kick the tire of Gutierrez's
car and hiss the one word "Cops!" when the cruiser
drew up next to him. Tony didn't dare glance down to
see if Alberto had doused the flashlight.

The cop who was driving rolled his window down,
and Tony bent over with a worried frown. "Hey, officer," he said, "have you seen a little white poodle?
He's around here somewhere. Jesus, my kids're gonna
go nuts if I have to tell 'em I lost him. Can you help
me?"

The cop's face glazed over with boredom. In a
patronizing tone he said: "Why don't you check the
SPCA in the morning? They handle that kinda stuff."

Tony gasped. "Jesus, that's not the place where they
chop the dogs up, is it? What'll I tell my kids?"

Already the cop was rolling up his window. "Look it
up in the yellow pages, pal," he said, and the cruiser
glided away.

When it had safely turned the corner, Tony grinned
and whirled around once more to the Chevette. He
banged on the hood three times and said: "Hey jerkoff,

come on outa there! You're under arrest!''

The Shadow slid out from under the car, his gun drawn, the hate in his face so huge he could have opened fire in a schoolyard. His face was drenched in sweat from the tension of the work. He too seemed to understand that a lot of bombs went off before their time. Tony's joke about being arrested wasn't funny to him at all. His eyes blazed with loathing and contempt.

Tony winked. ''Pretty close, huh?''

In that moment the Shadow seemed to mark Tony's name at the top of a list. Tony, who had a list of his own, could see the vow take shape in the murderer's livid face. Then the Shadow inched back under the car to put the final touches on his package. Tony smiled to think they were conscious enemies now, and he pulled out his coke for another toot, almost as if to toast them.

Twenty minutes later they were pulling into the garage at the Sherry Netherlands. Tony had booked a two-bedroom suite, with a view out over the Plaza fountain and the autumn riot of color in the Park. They ordered some food, but the Shadow retired to his bedroom to eat. He didn't want to socialize—not a word had passed his lips since the bomb was locked in place—and he needed a good night's sleep before his big performance. Nick ate like a veritable pig, talking volubly all the while and even making Tony laugh as he laid out lines on the nightstand. It was only fair to give Nick what he wanted on a night like this, and so they ordered him up a hooker. She arrived in a fur coat and looked like Loni Anderson. She seemed disappointed not to be screwing Tony, but sauntered into the bedroom philosophically. Nick charged in after like a fullback.

So the upshot was, Tony was all alone and not the least bit tired. Or horny. He finished another gram of coke and put in a call to Nashville to talk to Manolo. But Manolo had already been and gone, and Tony couldn't rouse him at his apartment in Miami. He was probably with the married lady. Tony flashed on the woman of the barracks, long ago in Havana. He still could see her face the night he shot her husband in the car. He could not remember making love to her.

He dialed his own number in Miami, and he asked the servant woman in Spanish how Elvira was. "Crying," she said. He thanked her and was about to hang up when Elvira's voice came through on the extension. "What do you want?" she said quietly, not hostile for once.

"I don't know," said Tony. "I'm sorry, honey."

"Shh, don't be." He could hear her fumbling with something in the background. For a second he thought she had somebody there. Manolo, maybe. His hands began to shake with rage, then all of a sudden he heard her snort, twice in rapid succession. She was just getting wrecked like he was. She said: "We're too much alike, Tony. That's our problem. Neither one of us trusts anybody."

"Well, so we're made for each other, huh?" He bent over with his rolled-up hundred and snorted a line. "Why don't we give it another try, baby? We got a few mill stashed now. Why don't we sail around the world or somethin'?"

"No thanks, Tony. I've been on that trip before." Another double snort. "I mean, I've been all packed and ready to go a dozen different times. Something always comes up. The boat never leaves the dock. So don't talk around the world, okay?"

There was silence now for a minute or so, but a peaceful sort of silence. They seemed to bear no animosity toward one another. It seemed enough that they were both insomniac and glad not to be alone. Tony watched out the window at the lights of New York. In the bedroom behind him he could hear the furious sounds of Nick the Pig making love. He almost said he was going to be home tomorrow night, and why didn't they all go

out for dinner, Manolo too. Then he realized they'd
already done that. Besides, the rules for this quiet
moment seemed to caution against proposals of any
sort. He was so glad to find they weren't fighting, he
wondered if they couldn't just confine it to phone calls
for a while. He almost said he loved her but didn't want
to press his luck. So all he said was, very softly: "Good-
night, honey."

"Yeah, you too."

He heard the click as the line went dead and stayed at
the window, the phone still at his ear. After a moment
the night operator came on and said: "Can I help you,
sir?" Tony shook his head slowly and replaced the
receiver. He walked across the room to get another
gram out of his suitcase and on the way back flicked on
the television set. Suddenly there was Bogart's face,
curled in a sneer as he told somebody to buzz off.

Tony propped up the pillows to watch. The film was
Petrified Forest, and Bogart was Duke Mantee. It was
already more than half over, and Tony was too coked
out to pick up the thread of the story. Didn't matter. He
was happy to just sit and watch Bogart, with his big sad
hunted eyes and the raw nerve of betrayal in his voice.
Methodically Tony laid out lines. He ordered up a bottle
of scotch from room service, because that was what
Bogart appeared to be drinking.

Before he had watched a half hour he was talking
back to the screen. Duke Mantee would ask a question
of one of his gangster buddies, and Tony would ramble
something in response. "No Duke, the coast ain't
clear," he said. "It's all killers out there. Ain't a good
man left." He snorted and then guzzled scotch from the
bottle. He gave a rueful laugh. "I gotta be honest wit'
you, Duke. I don't think we're gonna make it."

The scotch began to affect him now. As the film
reached its climax, about ten minutes before the end,
Tony began to see double. He tried to lean over for

another toot, but he couldn't get the rolled-up bill to synchronize with the line of coke. He squinted and leaned forward and managed to knock the nightstand over. A gram of coke fell like a flurry of snow on the carpet. Though he still had a king's ransom of it in his suitcase, Tony fell to his knees and leaned down and tried to snort it up.

He happened to look up just then and caught a glimpse of himself in the full-length mirror, crawling around like a pig after truffles. He laughed coarsely and slumped against the bed. He reached for his bottle and took a belt. When he focused on the screen again, he had switched the film in his mind and thought it was *Treasure of the Sierra Madre*. He was crouched beneath an overhang with Bogart, looking out on the pitiless desert.

"I'll tell ya somethin', Fred," slurred Tony, "they all turn on ya. Every fuckin' one of 'em. The only reason they stick around is they think you know where the treasure is." He couldn't see straight to do more coke, and when he grabbed for the scotch he knocked the bottle over. It sank in the carpet like water in sand. "But I don't, Fred. I don't know where the fuck it is." He held his head and tried to shake it clear, but this only made it throb. He was almost whimpering now. "Maybe there isn't any, huh? Huh, Fred? Maybe there ain't no treasure at all."

And then he passed out.

By seven A.M. they were sitting in the car on 81st, waiting for Gutierrez. His speech at the U.N. was at nine-thirty, but they knew he was expected early, for breakfast with the American ambassador. Nick sat in the driver's seat, sipping coffee out of a paper cup and working his way through a bag of doughnuts. Tony sat beside him leaning over the glove compartment, laying out the day's first dose. Nick made no mention of finding him sprawled on the carpet just after dawn, blood dribbling out of his nose and the corners of his mouth, the TV blaring a test pattern. Nick had washed his face and covered him with a blanket, then gone back to bed to snuggle with the hooker. Tony was up before everyone else, hustling the rest of them out of bed, seemingly none the worse for wear.

Now the Shadow watched him with disdain as he bent to snort two lines. In his lap the Shadow held the radio transmitter, a box of wires and circuits, beautifully intricate, with a light that would flash red as soon as Gutierrez began to drive and a detonate button of mother-of-pearl. The Shadow sat aloof from the two clowns in the front seat. He was on a mission that would change the face of a whole country. His eyes glowed like a fanatic.

Tony turned to Nick. "Change places with him, okay?" Then he craned around and grinned at Alberto. "I want you to sit up here, pal. You'll have a better view."

Nick didn't mind at all. He was delighted to see Tony taking charge, and anyway he didn't want the responsibility. He climbed out the driver's side and slipped into the back seat. Alberto was much more rattled by the rearrangement. As Tony slid over to the driver's seat, Alberto cursed under his breath and got out on the passenger's side like he was holding a box of eggs. He settled himself in a gingerly way in the seat Tony had occupied, and when he looked up he groaned with dismay, for Gutierrez had managed to slip into his car unnoticed, and now he was driving away.

Tony shrieked off in pursuit, staying about a block behind once the two cars turned onto Park. The Shadow let out a stream of Spanish: "Thirty meters, thirty meters! If he gets any further away, I lose him!" The red light was flashing on the box.

"Don't worry, pal," said Tony. "When we get to the U.N., he'll be right within range. I'm not gonna fuck it up. It's my chance to be a hero, right?''

But the Shadow was too intent on his bomb to pay any attention to Tony rattling along in English. When they stopped for a red light, Tony took out his vial of coke and snorted. The Shadow exploded with invective.

''Hey, where the hell's he goin'?'' said Nick from the back seat.

For Gutierrez had suddenly slowed and made a turn. Tony followed cautiously. Gutierrez drew up to the curb in front of a church where a small crowd was gathered, chatting with the priest after early Mass. Suddenly from the crowd appeared Gutierrez's wife, two children close behind her. They all began to climb into the Chevette.

Tony whirled around on Nick. ''I thought you said she took 'em to school herself.''

''She *does*, boss. Every day. We've had somebody watching all week.''

''Hurry up!'' cried the Shadow. ''They're leaving.''

Tony put the car into gear and followed Gutierrez, but he said: ''No way, José. No wife, no kids. We hit him alone or not at all.''

''Those aren't my orders,'' replied Alberto stiffly.

''I don't give a fuck what your orders are.''

Alberto was furious. ''Listen, Montana, that bomb is hanging by a little tape. A few bumps and it just might fall. If it does he'll know. There'll be publicity. If we fail, you take the responsibility for it Montana, not me. *You*.''

Tony didn't seem to be listening. ''They must be outa school for the speech,'' he said.

Gutierrez pulled off Second Avenue onto 47th Street. A cab jutted in behind him, so Tony was one car back. The orders were very clear: it had to be done right in front of the U.N. Building, for maximum coverage. The Shadow inserted a key into the mechanism, releasing the safety on the detonator. Gutierrez turned off 47th onto First Avenue, heading into the thick of the traffic in front of the building. Tony's hands were shaking on the wheel, but he darted around the cab and got right behind the Chevette.

"Easy, easy," whispered the Shadow as they inched along.

"What am I doin', Fred?" asked Tony. "What the fuck am I doin' here?" He honked at a truck that tried to cut in between him and the Chevette. About twenty feet away along the curb, a courtly group of officials waited for Gutierrez, waving when they saw him. A special VIP space had been roped off. Tony pulled the bullet inhaler out of his pocket and snorted. "They're all vultures, Fred," he said. "They don't give a shit about nothin'."

Nick leaned forward from the back seat and gripped Tony's shoulder. "Boss, what are you talkin' about?"

The guards parted the roped stanchions so Gutierrez could slip into his space. From where he was following ten feet behind, Tony could see the two kids through the rear windshield, jumping about with excitement. The Shadow was leaning forward in his seat, his index finger on the detonator.

"Bunch of vultures, Fred," muttered Tony. "They don't even have the guts to look him in the eye. What am I doin' here, huh?"

"Shut the fuck up!" said the Shadow.

Gutierrez was nosing the car into the space. Two guards stood on either side of him, directing him in. The Shadow's head began to nod in rhythm, like he was counting down from ten to zero.

"Not two kids and a woman," said Tony. "Hey, Fred, I don't need *that* shit in my life."

And he reached down and snapped the Baretta free from his ankle holster. He swung it up and leveled it at the Shadow. Alberto glanced down bewildered, as if there was some mistake about the weapon for this hit. "Die, moutherfucker," said Tony coldly, and pumped two bullets right into his face. The Shadow's features were blown away, and the body smashed against the door as blood rained all over the car. The death box fell to the floor, its red light still flashing.

"Ohmygod!" cried Nick. "What're ya doin'?"

But it was done now. Tony swerved the sedan out of the curb lane just as Gutierrez and his family tumbled out of the car. The noise of the traffic had muffled the sound of the shots, and anyway they were all too busy greeting Gutierrez to notice a mere aborted act of terrorism. They had their hands full cleaning up after the ones that didn't abort. In a moment Tony was lost in traffic, and nobody seemed to look twice at the rosy streaks of blood that tinted his windows.

Nick was gasping in panic in the back seat, but Tony began to chuckle. "I told you don't fuck with me, didn't I?" he said, taking another snort from his inhaler. "They always forget a man's limits, don't they, Fred? Fuckin' worms, that's what they are. If somebody don't stand up to 'em, they'll eat the world alive."

He began to whistle. He was in a great mood as the sedan cut away off First Avenue and headed into the bowels of the city.

Chapter Nine

THE CAR WAS no problem. Tony drove to the docks and parked it beside a rotting warehouse that seemed to be crawling with vermin, human and otherwise. The Shadow was still slumped against the door as Tony and Nick got out. Tony retrieved the box from the floor and heaved it into the river. He left the car unlocked, with the keys in the ignition. He figured there were water rats who'd steal it without getting squeamish about a hitman with his face blown off. If they didn't steal it, at least they'd strip it within the hour.

As Tony and Nick walked a few blocks west to catch a cab, Nick began to calm down. He had a short attention span when it came to death, and besides, Tony's good cheer was infectious, even if it required a dose every fifteen minutes. They taxied back to the Sherry, and Tony put in a call to the New York police, reporting his rental car stolen. "It's a damn shame," said Tony to the sergeant who took the call, "that a man can't come to New York and have a good time without gettin' ripped off. What's the world comin' to, huh?"

Then they packed the bags and took a cab to Kennedy. They got caught in a tangle of rush-hour traffic, but the cabbie was more than glad to while away the hour getting ripped on Tony's coke. They reached the Pan Am terminal about twenty minutes before flight time. Tony put in a call to Manolo in Miami, but once again there was no one home. Tony had a moment of confusion when he couldn't remember what was on for today. Were they getting the boats ready to unload a trawler off the Keys? Had the half of the coke that wasn't going to Nashville arrived in Miami this morning, or was that next week? Or was that last week?

Tony snorted a double dose from the inhaler and dialed his own number, hoping Elvira wouldn't pick up. He wanted to talk *business*. He needed to be in charge again, so he wouldn't start thinking too hard about the ramifications of the Shadow's death. Chi-Chi answered.

"Hello boss," he said cheerfully. "How'd it go?" At least he wasn't nodding out.

"It went shitty," retorted Tony. "I got Bolivian blood all over my nice gray suit. I look like a butcher. Where the fuck's Manolo?"

"I don't know, Tony. He ain't been around since he got back last night from wherever the hell he was."

"Nashville. You better go find him fast, Chich. 'Cause he's in charge, and if anything gets fucked up while I'm away, I'm gonna hand him his ass. And then I'm gonna hand you yours."

"Boss, whatsamatter? You don't sound too good."

"Yeah, well I caught a little cold." He snorted twice. "Who's he screwin', Chich?"

"I dunno, Tony. He's like a kid he's so happy. Let him go with it, huh? Everything's fine here. The grass came in last night, and it's real pretty stuff. It'll go for a hundred and a half an ounce. We got eighty tons."

"Find him, Chich. I need to talk to him."

The flight was announced to Miami/Lauderdale.

Nick was beckoning from the gate. He clearly wanted to get out of New York posthaste.

"Tony, your Mama's been callin' all day. She sounds freaked out."

Tony only half took it in. He asked about Elvira, who hadn't been out of her room since he left. She'd eaten nothing from the trays that were taken in. Tony issued a couple of orders and demanded that the limo be there to pick them up when they landed. As he hung up the phone he experienced a terrible tightness in his chest, as if he couldn't keep track any more of everyone he'd lost. He was scared of the sorrow that waited to weigh him down. More scared of that than of anyone out there who might have his name at the top of a list.

He loped across to the gate, and he and Nick took their places in first class. They didn't speak the whole way down. Not that Nick was brooding very much. As long as he'd managed to get away, he had no trouble putting the events of the morning into perspective. Because he was not the boss, he didn't have to anticipate the confrontation with Sosa. He ate like a pig again, the very same meal he'd eaten the day before, double helpings.

Tony was very tired, and the only thing that kept him awake now was the coke. He tried to focus on business matters, glancing over reports from his accountants and various memos about his case from George Sheffield. It didn't seem to occur to him that he'd probably blown the deal with the Feds and would have to serve time after all. He didn't seem very connected to the future, or at least not beyond the next twelve hours. What he had to do was find Manolo and sit him down and figure out where it had all gone wrong.

Though it calmed him some to read the numbers and see how much he had, he was having a terrible time with time itself. Was it four months ago he got married? Six months ago that he made his first deal on a kilo? He couldn't seem to put together the twenty million dollars he'd made with the time frame in which he had made it. He got no satisfaction out of being an overnight success, perhaps because the speed of the process had left him no ground to stand on. Besides, time was speeding faster than Tony Montana. He felt old and sick inside. In his mind he kept seeing the man he was when they let him out of prison and sent him into exile. Tough and strong and unstoppable. He couldn't say where that man had gone.

And somehow he kept coming back to Manolo, and he grew increasingly angry and betrayed. Manolo was full of deceit. He'd probably made some private deal and was only waiting now for Tony to come crashing down. Perhaps he was even ready to lend a hand in arranging Tony's fall. Well, just let him try. Manolo was an amateur at death. He would see what a true murderous rage could do if he dared to turn on Tony.

All the way to Miami his mind twisted back and forth, wanting to clasp Manolo like a brother and then wanting to brand him as a traitor. After a while he began to think about Elvira, and half of him wanted to gather her into his arms and love her all night long, and half of him wanted to throw her out. He blew hot and cold. He went from sentimental to paranoid and back again, as if those were the only faces of love he could focus on anymore.

Was it the coke? There was no way of knowing, he was never going to stop it now. He'd been taking a powerful antihistamine for days to clear his sinuses. He spilled more now than he snorted. The rush was still very real, it cleared his head like a vision. The streets were littered with gold again, and all he had to do was scoop it up. It only lasted a minute, of course, but a minute of vision was better than none. At least it was somewhere to go if you had to be all alone.

Martin picked them up at the airport in the gray

stretch limo. Nick, sensing that Tony didn't want company, rode up front with Martin. Tony dialed Manolo's number on the car phone, and he let it ring for twenty minutes, all the way home. No answer. As he held the receiver to his ear, he flicked on the television set to *Kojak*. Then he turned off the sound and turned on the stereo. He opened the bar refrigerator and pulled out a bottle of beer, though he wasn't thirsty at all. It was as if he was checking out all his toys to see if everything worked, to see if they still responded to his touch.

The peacocks scattered as they roared up the drive to the mansion. Chi-Chi was waiting at the door as Tony barreled out of the car. "D'you hear from him?" demanded Tony.

"No," said Chi-Chi, "but Sosa called three times. He sounds real pissed. What happened, Tony?"

"I think he thinks I'm the wrong kinda hero," retorted Tony dryly. He turned to Nick. "Go up t' the office and put in a call to Sosa. It takes a fuckin' half hour to get through. And find me some flake that ain't been cut." He flung the vial he'd been snorting from at the floor, smashing it on the tile. "This shit's so weak, I might as well be sniffin' bakin' soda."

"Boss, that's the purest stuff we got." Nick sounded wounded, as if he'd refined the batch himself.

"Don't argue, will ya?" snapped Tony. "I got a headache the size o' your ass." Nick nodded and then beat a hasty retreat upstairs. Tony turned to Chi-Chi. "She up there?"

"Yeah, she's up there all right. I tried to bring her in a cuppa coffee, and she pulled a gun on me." Tony started to laugh. It was as if he hadn't heard a joke in weeks. "It ain't funny, boss," said Chi-Chi. "She hit the fuckin' door, but she coulda hit me."

Tony's laugh faded to a sickly grin as he grabbed Chi-Chi by the collar and yanked him close. "You got exactly one hour to find Manolo. You got that?"

"Yeah, sure boss."

Tony shoved him away. Chi-Chi stumbled out the door and stood dazed in the driveway, like he didn't know where to begin. Tony had them all on edge now. They tried to steer out of his way, or they shied and shuffled and looked at the floor, which only made him more furious. He stormed through the house complaining, tossing out orders. It was like turning all the dials in the limo. He didn't need the sandwiches he ordered, or his list of dealers or his bank statements or anything else he was yelling for. He just wanted to feel the system responding to his touch. If it hadn't been so late and he didn't have so much to do, he would have gone out and spent money like water, just to show he was still Midas.

By the time he entered the office he was almost his old self again. He made rapid calls to his stockbroker, to the manager of the diamond company, the realty people, the zookeeper. As he listened to brief reports, he attacked the plate of roast beef sandwiches and guzzled a split of Mumm's. In the middle of listening to a list of loans outstanding, he gave a surly nod at Nick.

"Hey, you think we could have some caviar or somethin'? I just got home, for Christ's sake. I wanna celebrate." Nick hustled his ass and disappeared. Tony picked up the phone and wandered with it out to the balcony. Streaks of sunset were on the sky, and a marvelous odor of lemons filled the air. From where he stood he could see the Bengal pacing his island. He never stopped. "Yeah, okay Stan," said Tony into the phone, "I'm sure it can wait till tomorrow. Jesus, ain't this a pretty time o' day?"

Nick came back with caviar, a big Iranian tin of it, and a bottle of Cristal. Tony looked it all over and nodded. He sat down at his desk and took out a sheet of the cream-colored stationery he'd never once used, with the Coral Gables address engraved at the top. He wrote across it in a big clumsy hand: "Would the Queen like to have a drink with the King?" He sealed this in an envelope and handed it to Nick.

"Gimme five minutes," he said.

And just then the phone rang with the call from Bolivia. Nick slipped out of the room. Only now did Tony pick up the vial of coke Nick had set on the desk. He answered the phone and identified himself to Sosa's black aide in Cochabamba. As he waited for Sosa to be summoned, he tapped out lines on the polished mahogany surface of the desk.

"Is that you, Tony?"

"Whaddaya say, Noldo?"

"So what happened, babe?"

"We had some problems."

"Yeah, I heard."

"Somebody sent you a telegram, huh?"

"Not exactly, Tony. Our friend gave a speech today to the U.N. General Assembly. A speech we never expected to hear. Kinda spoiled our day."

Carefully Tony rolled up a hundred. He bent down and snorted two lines, not loudly, but not trying to hide it either. It was getting to be dusk outside, and the light was pearly. Tony made no move to turn on a lamp. In the blue shadows that fell across the room, the cocaine gleamed in a lunar way like gold dust in the sun.

"Yeah, well that guy Alberto was a piece o' shit, Noldo. The situation wasn't quite the way we figured on, ya know. We hadda make some adjustments. Alberto got stuck. I hadda cancel his contract."

Sosa spoke with extreme precision. "He was a very valuable man, Tony. You made a very big mistake."

Tony laughed. "Hey Noldo, no big deal. I can find ya a hundred guys on the street'll kill *anybody*. They'll kill their fuckin' grandmother. I'll go up next week and waste him myself—but not his wife and kids, Noldo. You gotta find scum to do that."

"There's no next week, Tony. They found what was

under the car. Gutierrez has got security up the ass now." The grisly evenness of Sosa's voice finally began to crack. Tony felt a spurt of pride when he heard it. He was younger and stronger than any of them. He *wanted* this man to hate him. Sosa started to shout: "Now all of a sudden the heat's comin' down—on *me*, Tony. Somebody's gonna pay for that! You blew it, you peasant!"

"Hey wait a minute. Who the fuck you think you're talkin' to?"

Sosa's rage exploded now. He was almost incoherent. "I told you the day I met you, you stupid spic! Don't fuck with me! People fuck with me they get burned!"

Tony could hear him panting at the other end of the phone. He flashed on an image of an old man rutting, straining to keep it up. His own voice took on an icy calm. "I guess *you*'re the one made the big mistake, Noldo. You thought I was your bellboy, huh? No way. Nobody tells me what to do. 'Specially scum like you." To punctuate this, he bent and snorted another line.

"This is war, Montana!"

"Great, Noldo, great. Let's have a war. We can flush out the sewers, huh? And then you can kiss my ass."

Sosa let loose with a stream of hysterical bloodlust. Tony dropped the receiver back in the cradle with a cocky sneer, as if he was offended by the Bolivian's lack of decorum. He leaned back in his swivel chair with his hands behind his head, looking out on the mackerel twilight. The door to the office opened, and Elvira walked in. The light from the hallway fell on her golden hair, but her face was all in shadow as he turned to her.

"We supposed to do this in the dark?" she asked. Her voice was wonderfully warm and intimate just then. It was as if she was looking for a joke to laugh at. He loved her laugh.

Tony reached out to the wall and flicked a switch, suddenly bathing the room in honey-colored indirect light. Elvira was wearing a beautiful black silk dress, with her double strand of wedding pearls around her neck. In a way she looked as demure as she had the day she had left Baltimore. Except of course she was high right now. But very much in control: her long slim legs didn't wobble a bit as she crossed toward the desk. Her smile was easy and mocking, completely self-aware.

"Gee I woulda got dressed," said Tony, shrugging almost shyly in his rumpled traveling shirt.

"That's okay, honey. I didn't get dressed for you. I have to go out."

"Oh. Will you have a drink first?"

"Well of course," she said, her smile growing broader. "It isn't every day that I get an invitation from a king."

Tony stood up and went to the bar. As he tore the foil and the wire from the champagne cork, he watched her in the mirror. She knew she was being watched, and she didn't appear to mind at all. As she crossed to the balcony doors, the sultry rhythm of her walk was like something she was whispering to him. Tony popped the cork, and the wine foamed over his hand. As he filled the tulip glasses he said: "Did you think of a place you wanna go?"

"Uh huh."

She stepped out onto the balcony. He followed with the glasses in hand and passed her one when he reached the rail. The lights had come on in the jungle garden below, and a gas torch flamed on the Bengal's island. Elvira lifted her glass and gestured toward the tiger. "To the king," she said, and let her eyes rest on Tony. They clinked and took a swallow.

"Don't matter to me where we go," said Tony, "as long as it's far away."

She looked at him calmly, her eyes roaming over his face as if she was memorizing it. "Where have you never been?"

He thought for a moment, his brow furrowed with

concentration. "I never been to an island," he said.

She laughed. "But you come from an island."

"I mean a real island." He nodded vaguely west, as if he meant to exclude the whole Club Med Caribbean from Nassau to Grenada. "Tahiti or somethin'."

"There is no Tahiti," Elvira said dryly, her lower lip touching the rim of the glass. "I've been there."

"Like I say, it don't matter to me. *You* pick a place."

There was silence now for a moment. Carefully she read his eyes, as if to see how serious he was. Then she looked out at the twilight sky, plotting her course by stars that were only the barest glimmer yet. He reached out to her hand on the railing and covered it with his own. For the space of a breath there was no cocaine at all. Their blood beat with nothing but feeling. The world was as immediate and real as the scent of lemons wafting up from the tree below. And they let it last longer than any moment they'd had together in weeks and weeks. They stood there a good two minutes, leaning slightly against each other and mild as the couple on a wedding cake.

And then she turned to him and said: "I'll be going alone, Tony." He nodded and drew his hand away. She reached out and grabbed it again, lifting it to her face and cradling her cheek against it. "I'm sorry it didn't work."

"Yeah, well . . ." His voice trailed off to an embarrassed silence. It was so much easier when they were yelling. If they weren't going to run to a desert island, if she wasn't going to fall in his arms, then they ought to be raging and throwing things. How else would he ever get over her? He said: "So where you going?"

"Old girlfriend of mine," she replied, tossing off the rest of her glass. She set it on the desk and rang the crystal with a flick of one finger. "She lives in Washington now. Her husband owns Kuwait or something."

"What'll you do?"

Elvira tossed her head and laughed. "Dry out, of course." She patted the pocket of his shirt for cigarettes, slipped out the pack and took one. He lit it for her. "I'm only kidding," she said dryly. "I think Sally and Jeff are Mr. and Mrs. Freebase of 1980."

"When uh . . . ?"

"Oh, right now. Martin's going to drive me to the airport. You don't mind if I use the limo, do you?"

"We could still work it out, Elvira."

"Shh, don't be silly. I don't know what we're supposed to do about the legal stuff, but . . . whatever you want, okay?"

He reached out a hand and stroked her hip, as if he too was trying to memorize something. His voice was husky. "You're still a great-lookin' woman, Elvira."

She shrugged slightly, out of modesty almost. Then she reached through his open shirt and grazed her fingertips in the gypsy hair of his chest. She said: "We looked the best of anyone, didn't we?" She seemed to feel genuine pride in this. "The animal part's no problem, is it? It's the people part."

He didn't know what to say. It was as if there was a cliff right there beside him, and out of the corner of one eye he could see the terrible drop to the darkness below. In one minute, as soon as she left, he knew he was going to have to look down, and then—he didn't know what came after that. He had to say goodbye now, because he couldn't just stand there and chat about why they were falling apart. He would rather kill her.

Awkwardly now he drew away from the touch of her hand and turned toward the desk. "Hey come on," he said brightly, "at least have one for the road." And without first offering her the rolled-up hundred, he reached for the vial and spilled out the whole of its contents, fanning it out in a quarter moon on the hardwood surface of the desk. Four or five grams at least. The gesture triggered a memory, and even as he bent and snorted he thought of Frank Lopez and the five-hundred-fifty-dollar bottle of champagne. Thought of it because he couldn't think of anything he wanted to buy anymore.

He stood up and passed her the hundred. There was something almost formal in her posture as she leaned to the desk and did a double toot. Some ancient tribal ritual whispered about her bowed head. The swan-like curve of her back was like a frozen moment in a dance. She stood up and looked in his eyes. For a single beat they were on that desert island, the one that didn't exist.

"Maybe some day . . ." began Tony, and then he shrugged.

"Who knows?" she said, with a shrug that was the mirror of his own. She bent to the desk again and took up a pen and a sheet of the Coral Gables paper. "Look, here's the address," she said, scribbling it down in a shaky hand. "Call me sometime, okay? Sally'll know where I am." She dropped the pen and looked deep in his eyes, smiling as if for once in her life there were no hard feelings. "Hey, look at it this way," she said. "At least we had the circus, huh? Who ever gets the circus?"

And then she pecked his lips and turned and hurried out, still holding the hundred in her hand. Tony moved to take another hit of the coke, but found he had nothing to toot with. He reached in his pocket for his roll of bills, peeled off another hundred, but his hands were shaking so much that he couldn't roll it up. Then the phone rang. As he reached to answer, he wondered if Nick or somebody had held all calls while he and Elvira were alone together. How long had that been? Ten minutes?

How long did he have now?

"Manolo?" he asked tensely, holding the receiver in both hands.

"Tony, get over here!" It was Mama, and she was hysterical. "She's gone for good now. I hope you're satisfied.'' Then she fell to sobbing, cursing him in Spanish.

He tried to quiet her down, but she wouldn't listen. He said he'd be right over, he needed to see her anyway, but still she would not let go of the phone. He lay the receiver on the desk, bent down and sniffed another dose, then hurried over to the closet.

Inside was a metal cabinet where he kept his cash on hand. It wasn't a safe exactly, more like a double-size locker in a gym. It had a padlock, but they never locked it. They used it as a storage unit, accumulating a bankable amount. When he opened the cabinet he found a couple of half-full canvas bags and a suitcase stacked with twenties in wrappers.

He heaved one of the canvas bags over his shoulder, then grabbed the sheet of paper with the address and stuffed it in his pocket. He rushed from the room. There was no one about as he ran downstairs. It was in his mind to get out of there alone, but as he trotted across the gravel to the garage, he could hear Nick and Ernie running behind him. He didn't care one way or the other now, and he slumped in the rear seat of the Corniche and let them climb in front. Nick drove. Tony called out an address and then sat back in a daze.

About ten minutes later they came to the house in Shenandoah Park. Tony combed his hair in the vanity mirror above the bar and straightened his collar. Then he did a heavy double toot. Telling the men to wait in the car, he hefted up the canvas bag, stepped out onto the curb, and loped up the drive to the back of the house. He waved to the boys who were tinkering with the car, then ducked inside and sprinted up the stairs. It seemed like a point of pride with him that he do this thing with the grace of an athlete.

Just now, as he reached the third floor—not even breathing hard—he looked fit enough to fight for the middleweight title.

Only Dolores and the grandmother and the retarded boy Ricardo were home. Dolores was most upset, for she knew how much Tony liked to go a couple of rounds with Paco. Tony had to reassure her, patting her arm and shushing her. He only had a minute, he said. She had to listen carefully.

"You take this, Dolores," he said, heaving the canvas bag onto the kitchen table, "you hide it, okay? Year from now, you start usin' it to live on. Groceries, gas bill, doctors—whatever you gotta pay, you pay outa here. You understand?"

Dolores nodded gravely. So did the grandmother. They looked soberly at the canvas bag, and it was clear they would follow his instructions to the letter. They would not even open the canvas bag till the year was up.

"That way," Tony said, "you and Waldo can start puttin' half his salary away for the kids. For their education. *Comprende?*"

Once again the two women nodded in unison. They both looked grief-stricken now, as if they understood that Tony would not be back. They did not press him or ask him questions. They were too well-bred for that.

Tony reached in his pants pocket and pulled out the paper on which Elvira had written the Washington address. Tony asked Ricardo to go fetch a pencil, and when the young man brought him one he wrote Elvira's name down twice. Her maiden name and her married name. There was no telling what she would go by later on.

"Some day I want you to contact this lady," he said, handing the paper across to Dolores. "She used to be my wife. You tell her all about me and Paco and Ricardo here, how we met in the ocean. How I got you to take Ricardo in. I want you to tell her she's part of the family too. You understand?"

"Sure, Tony. You can't wait till Waldo comes home?"

"No, I gotta go now." He leaned forward across the table and kissed Dolores on either cheek. Then he kissed the grandmother's forehead. "You just take care o' my boys," he said. "I want Paco to grow up and be President, okay?"

Ricardo stood up when he did, and they shook hands man to man.

"Go with God, Tony," said Dolores.

Tony nodded and smiled and took a last long look around the kitchen. Then he slipped outside and shut the door behind him with a quiet click. He trotted downstairs with a grin on his face. By the time he'd reached the car he was already thinking of the next encounter. He frowned with concentration as he gave the next address and tapped out a couple of thick lines. But deep inside he laughed for a long moment, because he'd finally done something that no one could take away.

Then he snorted hard.

All the way to his mother's house he tried to focus on Gina. When had he set her up in business? When did she leave Mama's house and get a place of her own? He kept thinking that if only he could recover the timing, he'd be able to put his finger on where they had all disappeared to. It was like they were all playing a game, hiding in a landscape full of trees, and he kept forgetting where he'd already looked.

Nick got another gram from the glove compartment and handed it over the seat. Until now he had always waited till Tony asked, but apparently they had reached a new plateau. Tony's snorting now was purely automatic. He did not even pay attention to being high. The rush went right by him, clearing his head for a bit in the process but otherwise leaving no mark. It was as if he needed to do it now to prove how numb he was.

He left the two men in the car, who knew better than to bother a man who was saying goodbye to his mother. As Tony walked up to the front door, he tried to think what the deal was between him and this woman. Was he paying the rent? Or was she the one who'd thrown the money in his face? He could hear her sobbing even through the door. He walked in and followed her grief to the kitchen. She sat with her head in her arms on the table, the receiver of the phone lying helpless there beside her. The line was still open between her house and her son's house, but it might as well have been dead.

"She don't even live in her place," gasped Mama, choking back her tears. Tony hadn't even thought she noticed him come in. She spoke as if they'd been arguing nonstop for hours. He realized he would never be able to fill in the part he'd lost. "One day I follow her in a taxi," Mama said brokenly. "She goes to this fancy condo in Coconut Grove. She don't come out all night."

"Coconut Grove?" Who lived in Coconut Grove? Why was he being so slow? He *knew* now. But he wouldn't let the truth take shape in his head. It was as if some terrible messenger had arrived with a sentence of doom, and the only thing Tony could do was barricade himself within the castle walls. Once he admitted the only possible explanation, time would begin its free fall. He realized he had no coke with him, he'd left it in the car. His hands began to shake again. Sweat broke out on his forehead. He was looking right over the cliff and down.

"Did you go in, Mama?"

"How could I?" the old woman wailed. "If I went in there she'd kill me. She's just like you."

"Where is it, Mama? What's the address?" A voice inside him was screaming: *Don't tell me, I don't want to know.*

"Four hundred something. Citrus Drive. I got it over here." She lifted herself from the kitchen chair and padded heavily to the counter by the sink. She lifted the sugar bowl and retrieved a slip of paper. The wave of sobbing had passed now. She seemed to be drawing together all her strength for one last rational argument. "You gotta talk to her Tony, she don't listen to me. She says 'I'm in love Mama, be happy for me.' So how come she won't tell me his name? How come she has to go there late at night like a . . ." She couldn't say the word. Another squall of tears overtook her.

Tony crossed to her and gently took the paper from her hand. "Don't worry Mama, I'll bring her home."

The paper read: 409 Citrus Drive, #6.

As he turned to go, she reached and grabbed his arm. "Don't you see what you done to her? *Don't you see?* Why do you have to hurt everything you touch?"

"Leave me alone," he snarled, so coldly she drew her hand away. "I never felt nothin' from you—never. I *made* somethin' outa my life, and I did it all by myself. But it ain't good enough for you, is it? I'm the bad boy, ain't I? Your knees are all raw from prayin' for me. Well, thanks for nothin'."

He strode through the house and out the door. She ran after him shrieking. Her grief for her wayward daughter had given way to the fury and contempt she reserved for her son alone. "You got a scar on your soul, Tony! You're gonna burn in hell forever! Make up for the hell you put your people through! I spit on your grave!"

This last curse was flung from the porch, where she stood beneath her beloved trellis shaking her fist in the air. Tony did not turn around but kept walking to the car. Nick and Ernie heard her final savage imprecations, as did the neighbors having a barbecue in the yard next door. As he tore open the car door, Tony yelled back over his shoulder: "Don't you dare come near my grave!"

It wasn't exactly the sort of goodbye that you wore like a locket around your neck.

The Corniche drove off, leaving the old woman weeping on her porch, one hand gripping the trellis for support. First thing Tony did, he took a double hit of coke. Neither man in the front seat said a word, and Nick drove aimlessly around the neighborhood, not sure whether to go home or not, not sure what was there to go home to. At last Tony reached forward and handed the slip of paper to Ernie.

"What's this?"

"The last stop," said Tony.

Once again there was silence, broken only by the sound of Tony snorting. His final scene with Elvira had receded so far into the past he could no longer recall the details. Dolores and Ricardo and the others were faint as the figures in a crumpled snapshot. His mother was someone he'd left long ago in the slum alleys of Havana. All he could be sure of about the evening's encounters was the way they pointed like signposts to the fatal crossroads that lay up ahead in the darkness. Tony picked up the car phone and dialed his number at home. It rang; someone had put the receiver back on the hook. Chi-Chi answered on the fifth ring. Reluctantly.

"Where is he, Chich?"

"See here's the way it is, Tony," said Chi-Chi, very jittery, like he hadn't had a fix all week. "He moved out of his place in Hollywood, maybe two, three weeks ago, only he didn't tell nobody. It's like he's been off the map, ya know? But I found him, boss. I just talked to a dealer's been deliverin' him his junk." Chi-Chi's voice was pathetically ingratiating. He longed for an encouraging word from Tony. "Hey boss, I think he's been doin' some private deal. You want the address?"

"No thanks," said Tony, and hung up the phone.

As they came into Coconut Grove, the streets were broad and lushly planted. Children who always got what they wanted pedaled by on bicycles. The Corniche did not look at all out of place, yet the man watching out of the rear window had a terrible hunger in his eyes—as if the whole suburban world, manicured and proud, lay an inch beyond his grasp. Otherwise his face was totally blank. He seemed dazed by the constant movement. If they'd turned the car over to him and told him to drive home, he'd have sat there clutching the wheel, unable to go ten feet.

No, the fate he was going to meet required that somebody else drive. Tony needed the freedom to cut himself loose from the world of laws. He could never have stayed within the lines, not now. He snorted two heaping spoonfuls, his eyes crinkling up in pain as the drug hit the raw of his sinuses. There was no way to back off now. He was a pure instrument of revenge, betrayed beyond all endurance, hating everything he loved. He did not know why it had come to this, but then he had not lived his life to learn the why of things. His reasons were all bound up in who he was, instinctive like the convulsions of the world. A volcano had no reason. Neither did a hurricane. What did Tony Montana need one for?

The Corniche drew up at 409. It was a complex built around a central court, with a pair of royal palms flanking the iron gates. "Leave it running," said Tony, and right away the other men knew there might be gunfire. As Tony stepped out to the curb Ernie opened his door, making as if to follow. Tony shook his head, and Ernie stayed put in the car. Anyone watching Tony saunter up the walk and through the gate would have assumed the obvious: here was a dealer come to deliver goods. The gramweight was probably tucked in the pocket of his fifteen-hundred-dollar suit, and the cash would nicely fill the empty space once the cocaine was turned over. A figure like this in Coconut Grove was as familiar as a milkman in rural Kansas.

Number six was in the rear, beyond the nightlit pool and a plot of flowering trees. Tony could hear a wistful love song playing on the stereo as he stood outside the door. He rang the bell, and a voice called: "Just a minute. Lemme get my pants on." Somebody seemed to be expected. Only because his heart began to pound did Tony realize he was holding his breath. He expelled it now in a long sigh. He couldn't believe he'd forgotten to bring the vial of coke. He had a sudden mad wish to run back and toot up, to get him through the next thirty seconds. Then he told himself he could have it as a reward. Get through this, and then he would get so high no one would ever find him.

The door opened, and there Manolo stood, stripped to the waist and toweling dry his hair. When he saw it was Tony, he burst out laughing. "How the fuck d'you ever find me?" he asked, shaking his head with puzzled delight. "Leave it to you, huh, chico?"

Tony pulled the Baretta out of his pocket. Because there was no turning back now, no matter how much they laughed. He'd never felt as lonely as he did right now, face to face with the only man he'd ever called his brother. Manolo looked down at the gun, bewildered. But he stopped laughing, because guns were never a joke with Tony. And just then there was a rustle of cloth behind the door, and Gina suddenly appeared in a flowing robe, naked underneath.

"Tony!" she cried, clapping her hands with delight.

Tony said nothing. His face was blank. He held the Baretta pointed at Manolo's abdomen. "Hey Tony, c'mon," said Manolo gently, one hand pushing Gina back, trying to get her behind the door. Now Gina saw the gun for the first time, and she gasped and clamped her hands over her mouth.

Here was the longest second of all, for Tony could not remember now what rage had brought him here. Because his friend had turned his sister into a whore? Because there was some kind of coup being planned, with Manolo at the helm? Couldn't they see that he

loved them? Couldn't anybody see that? The real crime
—and the whole world was guilty of it—was leaving
Tony all alone. Just then he almost saw that he had no
right to kill for that. But still it was only a second, and
Tony was no good at time any more.

He fired twice in rapid succession.

The blood flowered out on Manolo's naked abdomen, and he crumpled. One hand groped in the air
toward Tony, and one hand still held Gina back. His
eyes were full of shock, but there wasn't a shred of
hatred in them. Before his body even hit the floor Gina
was shrieking. Tony looked down at what he'd done,
completely numb, like he'd suffered a stroke. He made
no attempt to quiet Gina's screams, but after a moment
he began to hear the words.

She fell to Manolo's body and cradled him in her
arms, calling his name in agony as if she could breathe
the life back into him. And when she saw he was dead
already she gave a strangled cry of grief, all the more
wrenching because he'd gone before they could even say
goodbye. She wailed at the horror of fate, her hands
mired in her man's blood. She was lost like a widow in a
war-torn country. But at last the words began to tumble
out.

"We got married, Tony," she sobbed. "It was all
gonna be a surprise. He was gettin' outa the business.
He stopped with the dope." She looked up into her
brother's blank face. He could almost hear her heart
break as she said: "We were so happy, Tony."

And then she just seemed to go berserk. She launched
herself on Tony like a madwoman, beating his chest and
dragging her nails across his face. He stood there and
took it. The dead look in his eyes hadn't changed since
the moment he fired the gun. If Ernie and Nick had not
run up she would have scratched his face to a pulp.
Ernie grabbed her around the shoulders and pulled her
off Tony. Nick clamped a hand on her mouth to stop

her yelling. The neighbors had all double-locked their
doors. They were going to sit this one out.

"What do we do, boss?" barked Nick, but right away
it was clear that Tony would not be giving any orders.
He was staring down at Manolo's corpse as if he was
hypnotized. Though Gina struggled against the two men
holding her, unable to cry out, her words went on and
on in Tony's head till he thought he was screaming himself. Ernie managed to lift Gina off her feet, her arms
pinned at her side. Nick tore the belt off her robe and
gagged her with it. Then he gave a gruff command to
Ernie, who bore her away across the courtyard.

Nick leaned down and pushed the body over the
threshold, then shut the door. There was still a great
splash of blood on the pavement, but at least the light
wasn't flooding it now. Nick took the gun out of Tony's
hand and slipped it back in his pocket. Tony was staring
at the door, his head cocked to listen to the stereo playing inside, as if it was terribly important somehow to
identify the song. As if the last two minutes had never
occurred. Nick took his arm and led him away, saying nothing. Tony gave no resistance. He seemed very
drugged—drugged down, not up.

When they reached the car Ernie was already in the
back seat, holding Gina tight on his lap. Nick opened
the passenger door in front and helped Tony in. Then he
ran around to the driver's side, got in, and roared away.
It was only then, as the Rolls disappeared down the
palm-lined street, that the residents of 409 began to peer
around their close-drawn curtains. They had learned,
even in these posh quarters of the city, that they must
not see what was none of their business, or else they
would suffer the consequences. So they let the murders
happen and then let the murderers run off, and they
knocked on wood and thanked their stars that the nightmare had seized on someone else.

And so the nightmare went on and on.

It was not even ten o'clock when they screeched through the gates past the grim-faced guards and up the drive to the mansion. By now Gina was numb with shock, and she dangled like a rag doll as Ernie carried her into the house. Tony sat in the car staring ahead, the scratches on his face livid in the light of the gas lamps that lined the drive. Nick shook his shoulder, but he didn't move. Chi-Chi came out of the house and stood on the steps, wringing his hands. They didn't seem to know what to do if Tony didn't.

An awkward minute passed, Tony still sitting in the car. Finally Nick beckoned to Chi-Chi, indicating that they should go inside and leave the boss alone. As soon as they walked away Tony stepped out of the car, as if he couldn't move at all any more except by way of perversity. He called to Nick as the latter reached the door: "I want all the lights on."

They didn't ask why. They jumped to do his bidding, glad of any order at all. When Tony walked into the foyer he found Ernie patiently waiting, Gina slumped in his arms.

"Where do you want her, boss?"

"Put her in my room," he said, reaching out a hand to smooth her hair. "I ain't gonna be sleepin' there. I'm givin' up sleep." He chuckled ruefully at his own joke, gathering the hair at the nape of her neck as if he was going to make a ponytail. The slight tug stirred her awake. She stared into Tony's eyes, peacefully blank for a moment. Then something triggered her memory, and her face collapsed in agony again. She drew a breath, and it seemed she would scream, but she spat in her brother's face instead.

He stood there and took it, making no move to wipe it away. She sank once more into stupor, as if she could only handle consciousness for seconds at a time. Ernie picked her up in his arms and carried her toward the stairs. As they mounted, Tony looked more shaken than he had all night. He'd lost them all, every single one, deliberately it seemed, but none of them was more innocent than Gina. Her innocence filled his house with horror. She was like a light brought into a slaughter-house revealing all the instruments of death, the rivers of blood, the slabs on hooks, the carrion stench of money.

The lights blazed on throughout the house as he stumbled up to his office. He went to the closet and pulled out a plastic kilo bag of coke. As he slumped on the sofa, a faint cloud of the drug rose off the velvet like a snow scene on a Christmas card. It was in all the creases of the house now, just like it was in his bones. He slit open the bag with a razor blade. Then with a desultory gesture, almost bored, he dumped the whole two pounds on the black marble coffee table. It mounded there like a sand dune, like a strange crystalline anthill.

Tony opened a humidor box where he kept his paraphernalia. He drew out a silver tooter and sat staring a moment at the dope, breathing rhythmically like an athlete psyching up. Nick walked into the room as he bent to snort. Perhaps it was having an audience that made him go for broke. He sniffed up a truly giant amount, burying the silver straw in the mound and breathing in great heaves. He was like a kid with an ice cream soda, greedy to get it all in one gulp. He shifted now to the other nostril and sucked on the straw as if it was pure oxygen he was breathing in. As he burrowed deep into the mound, his face brushed over the snowy surface. When at last he sat up to let it sink in, the cocaine clung to his brows and lashes and patched across the bloody scratches left by Gina's nails. He looked like a man who'd just been baptized, who'd drunk from the waters of the Fountain of Youth.

Nick said: "Hey Tony, why don't you go easy, huh?"

Tony laughed effortlessly, his head rocking back and forth. "You think I oughta save some for my old age? Is that what you think, Nick?"

"What are we doin', boss? What's the plan?"

Tony gestured with the tooter at the mound of coke. "This is the plan, chico."

Nick was fiercely loyal. He wasn't a king, he wasn't even a prince. Mostly he was just an old soldier who followed orders. Now for the first time a shiver of fear passed across his face, like he'd suddenly turned gun-shy in the middle of a pitched battle. Tony was tilting forward toward the table again, ready for another hit. Nick backed away to the door and slipped out, because he didn't know what he might say if he stayed.

About a half hour later it started to rain, a pelting tropic downpour that blew in out of nowhere. The wind swung open the balcony doors, and the rain swept in on the carpet. Tony watched for a while from the sofa, staring dully as puddles began to form in the doorway. He could hear the monkeys screeching in the jungle below, and the cries of a hundred exultant birds who preened their feathers in the rain and forgot they were in a cage, for the moment anyway. Tony found himself leaning forward, craning to hear if the Bengal roared at the tempest.

At last he stood up, drawn to the wildness below in spite of his catatonic state. He bent to the table and scooped up a handful of coke, a whole snowball's worth, and dumped it in his jacket pocket. He sniffed the residue off his hand and stumbled out of the room. When he got downstairs he found Chi-Chi posted at the front door, Ingram in hand. Nick was in the living room on the phone, trying to call in their most trusted men, but as it was late they were all out partying. Ernie was on the front steps in a fireman's slicker, talking into a two-way radio, in constant touch with the guards at the gates.

Nobody made a move to stop Tony as he swayed across the yard and through the hedges to the zoo. It was raining so hard that his clothes were soaked in a minute. Already the coke was melting in his pocket and

running away in streaks down his pants leg. He didn't
seem to notice or care. He went first to the high circular
cage where all the exotic birds were perched in the
branches of a banyan tree. He swung the door open and
left it wide, clapping his hands for a moment to call
their attention. Not a single one flew down to him. The
rain was freedom enough for now. Tony didn't take it
personally—they'd go when they were ready.

The monkeys were smarter. They knew that something was up as soon as they saw him stagger up to the
cage. He pulled open the gate, and a half dozen marmosets came scampering out. They took off every which
way, splitting up so they couldn't be captured in a
clump. The monkeys poured out of the monkey house
and swung through the trees, making for the chain-link
fence that rimmed the whole property. They counted on
the rain for cover as they scrambled away through Coral
Gables, heading home. Home of course was Madagas-
car, but that didn't seem to stop them.

Tony stopped at the edge of the flamingo pond. These
birds were free already; they were here by choice. They
strutted back and forth, stretching their long necks in
the rain. Tony dipped his hand in his pocket, but the
coke was all sop and disintegrated. He sucked his
fingers for a moment, then cocked his head at what he
thought was the sound of a shot. It was only a branch
cracking and falling by the canal, but his mind seemed
to clear for a moment, and he wondered what time it
was.

What he meant was how much did he have left.

He wandered across the Japanese bridge and parted
the tree ferns. Across the moiling water of the moat the
Bengal paced his island. The rhythm of his constant
motion was unaffected by the storm. A jungle burned in
his brain, and in that jungle where he was king the rains
came and the wildfire and the plagues and the hunters,
and nothing diminished his power. His cage was a man's

idea. With the yellow light in his eyes, the roll of his massive shoulders, his bared teeth and his moaning growl, he soared free of the traps of men and the traps of time. Tony drew the Baretta from his pocket and pointed across the water. For several seconds the gun raked back and forth, following the moving target. Then all of a sudden the tiger seemed to understand, and he stopped. He turned his huge head and gazed at Tony on the opposite shore. They saw how alone they were.

Then Tony fired once. The bullet smashed into the Bengal's nose and drove right to his brain. He collapsed with a weird grace, falling over onto his side. The jungle erupted in screeches. Birds came pouring out of the open cage and whirred away through the driving rain. Tony retraced his steps through the zoo, ignoring the rest of the animals. One of the guards had come running around the house when he heard the shot, but he stood back when he saw Tony, asking no questions.

Ernie and Chi-Chi barely nodded as Tony returned to the house. As he dragged upstairs in a kind of trance, he pulled off his soaking jacket and let it fall to the landing. Then he tore off his shirt and flung it behind him. He was shivering with gooseflesh as he regained the office. The rain had soaked half the carpet, and the wind had scattered most of the kilo. The cocaine lay filmed on the marble table and the velvet sofa like an early frost.

Tony closed the balcony doors and went to the closet. He hauled out the other canvas bag and the suitcase full of twenties. Then he retrieved another kilo from the vacuum cabinet behind his desk. He razored this open like the other and once again dumped it on the table. He knelt on the floor, dipped his tooter and snorted. His hair was still wet and his pants, but he felt terrific, like he'd just stepped out of the shower. This feeling only lasted about two minutes, but he acted fast. He stood up and worked open the canvas bag. He dumped the money on the carpet, twisted-up twenties and fifties, here and there a hundred like a Cracker Jack prize. He kicked the pile with his foot, and it flew up and scattered like fallen leaves.

He chuckled as he walked around in it, kicking it further afield till it was spread a couple of inches deep around the floor. But then the high evaporated, and he stood there slightly bewildered, like he'd set up the game and didn't know what the game was. Of course it was a great idea, to see all your Midas money littered around you, but he couldn't seem to get behind the idea. In fact he had started to cry.

"Oh fuck Manolo," he said, sobbing when he spoke his friend's name, "how the fuck do I get outa here?"

Just then, out beyond the trees, the first figure came over the chain-link fence. No one detected his coming because the electronic circuits were all fouled up by the storm. They were relying on nothing more than a grim patrol of the borders, four or five men disgruntled by the rain, and nobody really believed the engine of revenge could act so quickly. This first one had a single terrorist mission, and he darted from tree to tree till he came to the peacock shelter on the grassy slope behind the guardhouse. He took an object about the size of a baseball out of an armored metal container, pulled a pin and tossed it through the rear window.

There was a white explosion, and the roof blew off. The walls were stone and withstood the shock, but both men inside were instantly mangled, and the whole communications system was out. The next second the phones in the house went dead. The noise of the grenade could be heard all up and down the street, but none of the neighbors did anything but draw down the shades. Luckily everyone had enough acreage, and a man could keep his distance.

Upstairs Tony was doing more coke. He had stopped

crying, but all he could think about was Manolo. He didn't really hear the grenade. Oh, he heard it, but only a part of his mind registered it, as if an opponent had nodded to him and murmured: *Shall we begin?* He nodded in acknowledgment, but mostly he bent to the mound of coke and gasped in more and more. And he'd gone beyond his grief now, beyond even his guilt. He spoke to Manolo as if his friend was in the room, the way he spoke to Bogart when they were huddled beneath the overhang.

"You remember what you said, chico? Trust in the gods, huh? Yeah well you were fulla shit, look what happened. What the hell happened, huh?"

Completely disconnected now, he reached for the suitcase stacked with cash. He staggered out the door of the office and made for the upstairs landing.

"I *said* to you, I remember, I said I'll never go crazy, remember? And you said . . ." Here Tony cocked his head as he reached the railing, groping back to a scene that seemed to have taken place a thousand years ago. "You looked at me kinda funny, chico, and you didn't say nothin'. If you knew, why didn't ya tell me?" He looked down into the foyer, where the front door was wide open. Chi-Chi stood on the steps outside, covering Ernie as he made his way down the drive to the guard-house. "Those were the days, huh?" said Tony as he flicked open the suitcase. "Banks, groceries, stores, hey nothin' could stop us. We were the best."

He dumped the suitcase over the railing, and the stacks of twenties tumbled and fell to the floor like a shower of bricks. The loose bills fell like manna from heaven. The wind picked them up and bore some into the living room, some out the door to the rain-swept drive. Tony smiled to watch it snowing money, and he began to descend the stairs to get down there with it.

And just then Gina stepped out of the bedroom, stark naked, holding a Baretta in two hands. Her eyes were

pitiless, full of rage and hate. She walked with the gun
held out in front of her, and when she fired the first time
the bullet went wild, hitting the wall five feet to the left
of Tony. Tony ducked and began to scramble down
the stairs. The second shot clipped the chandelier and
showered the stairs with crystal. Tony jumped down the
last four steps and slipped on the cash and went
sprawling.

"You want me, Tony?" cried Gina. "Why don't you
come and make love to me, huh? Isn't that what you
want?"

She advanced down the stairs, methodically shooting
out the clip. She hit the mirrored wall and shattered a
panel six-by-four. She winged a brass figurine on the
table by the far wall. She got better with every shot.
Tony scrambled to his feet and made a leap for the living room, and her last bullet hit him in the thigh.
He landed hard in the archway, gritting his teeth and
clutching the wound.

Just then a burst of machine-gun fire ripped through
Ernie and flung him off the pavement, so he died fast
and sprawled dead in the fishpond. Chi-Chi turned
around to run into the house, and they tossed a grenade
that blew a five-foot hole in the ground where he'd been
standing. He ran up the stairs and almost made it in, but
a figure with a high-powered rifle took a hunter's aim
and blew him through the front door. He landed in the
money with his guts blown out.

Gina's gun was empty. She tossed it aside and bent to
pick up Chi-Chi's Ingram. Tony was hobbling away
across the living room. Gina stalked through the foyer,
trembling with power. She stood in the arched doorway,
a weird grin on her face, as if nothing in the world was
so sweet as watching her brother run scared. She certainly wasn't innocent any more. But she wasn't a pro
either, and she didn't fire when she had the chance, and
a moment later the first of the hitters stepped in at the

front door. He was a scrawny punk barely twenty years old, but *he* was a pro. He raked his Ingram across her body, and she never even knew he was there. Her torso was ripped to pieces, her spine severed. She was dead before she hit the floor.

The punk darted forward to the living room. Tony had ducked behind the sofa, but he was unarmed. The punk advanced, his face lighting up in a drunken glow. He was going to kill one of the kings, and when the smoke had cleared he would be a kind of king himself. Then suddenly the big picture window exploded as Nick barreled in like a grizzly bear. The punk turned a second too late, just in time to have his head blown off.

"You okay, boss?"

"Hey, never better," said Tony, hobbling to his feet.

A grenade exploded on the terrace outside. There was a rapid exchange of gunfire on several sides at once. They appeared to be surrounded. Nick handed Tony the punk's Ingram, and they began to move toward the foyer. Tony's mood was buoyant now, as if he liked nothing better than a hopeless situation. He had waited all his life for a dead-end standoff.

"We got 'em now, Nick," he said. "We'll eat 'em for breakfast, huh?"

Nick tried to swing the front door closed, but a bottle bomb exploded on the threshold, sending up a roar of fire that sent them staggering back. Nick had no more ideas. He turned and looked into Tony's eyes, terrified at last. Tony didn't even notice. He stood in the foyer almost exulting as the fire consumed the door and began to eat at the silk-covered walls. Two hitters were in the living room now, and they strutted forward, spraying the field with machine-gun fire. Nick, good soldier that he was, managed to heave Tony out of the line of fire, sprawling him on the stairs. Then Nick walked straight into it, kamikaze-style, spraying his own fire. He brought one of them down, and then they got him.

Tony knew his only chance was to get upstairs. As the hitter came around the corner from the living room, Tony sprang for the first landing, not even aware of the pain in his thigh any more. Machine-gun fire exploded up the stair wall, but Tony stayed low and shot through the wrought-iron banister. One lucky bullet hit the clip on the killer's machine-gun, and it blew up in his face. He went screaming out the front door, holding his blinded eyes, and his own men finished him off with a burst of fire because nobody really knew who was who any more.

"We'll get 'em, Fred," said Tony hoarsely. "We'll get 'em this time."

He looked down from the landing at the carnage below. He could see Chi-Chi and Gina and Nick, each twisted up in a knot of death, dark circles of blood under them. The carpet of money was tossed and savaged, but still it lay like a bed of roses beneath the bodies. Tony didn't seem to understand it was his own blood kin down there. He laughed in triumph as if he had witnessed the slaughter of his enemies.

He stood up and shouted, waving his gun in the air. "Come on, you scumbags! Come and get it! I'm gonna fuck you all, you hear me!" He mounted the steps to the second floor, not even limping now.

Another grenade was tossed in at the front door, exploding among the dead and making the corpses dance. The concussion unhinged the chandelier, which fell to the floor below in a great burst of crystal. Tony did not even turn around to look. As he slipped into his bedroom, a squad of three hitters advanced and entered the house.

It was strangely quiet in the bedroom. Not a single window was broken, and the air was still thick with Elvira's fragrance. He crossed to a built-in cabinet in the far wall. He hauled out a shoulder-fired rocket launcher and a canvas bag of refill rounds. It had always seemed an absurd weapon, too cumbersome for the work they had to do, without the handling ability of the Ingram. More suited to war than crime. But Tony had kept it ready the way other rich men in Coral Gables kept bomb shelters. It was the last resort.

He lumbered back across the bedroom, hefting the launcher onto his shoulder. On an impulse he stopped at the bedside table and pulled open the drawer, but there was no coke. If only he could get back to the office, he thought, he could hold them off till dawn and stay wrecked besides. This plan seemed to energize him, and he focused all his attention on it. He had no memory of the slaughter downstairs. He seemed to feel if he lasted the night, the others would all regroup in the morning. Elvira, Manolo, Gina, Nick, Chi-Chi—it was as if they were all in hiding somewhere, waiting for Tony to make it safe.

A grenade exploded just outside the bedroom door, blowing it off its hinges. A couple of the hitters had decided to storm his fortress, and now they advanced in a spray of fire. Tony smiled as he pointed the launcher at the smoking doorway. He fired once, and the shell whined into the upstairs hall, exploding like Armageddon. The two hitters were blown to smithereens, and the whole house shook to its foundations.

"Come on, you scum," taunted Tony, "here I am. Come say hello to my little friend here."

There was silence in the hall except for the fire, clawing to find a way out. Black smoke billowed into the room. Tony walked forward into it, groping his way to the railing above the foyer. The smoke was thinner here, and it swirled about him like a devil's aura, as if he'd materialized out of thin air. He yelled down the stairs as he reloaded.

"You need an army, you hear? An army! I piss in your face!"

A hitter fired up from the front door, and two bullets

thumped into Tony's chest. He felt nothing. He pointed
the launcher downward and fired. The rocket exploded
with a terrific roar, sending up a ball of flame in a kind
of mushroom cloud. The front door was a gaping hole.
The house was on fire in every room. Still not a single
siren broke the night. Tony turned and lurched through
the smoke and managed to gain the office. He was
coughing up blood, but he knew he was safe as soon as
he saw his money and his coke.

While the hitters crept up the stairs he stumbled to the
marble table and bent for a final dose. The blood
streaming out of his nose and mouth splashed on the
dazzling white. With an awesome concentration he
sniffed at the mound like a man taking leave of his last
rose. When the hitters reached the landing Tony was
crouched over, trailing a hand in the cash that littered
the floor as if he was making ripples in a pond. Then he
sprang to his feet and made for the balcony. The hitters
were at the office door.

He reached the balcony rail and saw the empty zoo
below, drunk with the jungle rain. He wasn't afraid. He
wasn't sorry. He began to see there was a reason after
all to be the last one left. It meant he was the only wit-
ness, the only judge. No one was going to pass his story
on. What he saw right now was all he would ever be. It
wasn't something he could put into words. He would
have had to be a poet instead of a king. But he looked
out over his burning kingdom and spoke his epitaph,
brief as a shooting star.

"Tony Montana—he died doin' it."

And he turned with a radiant grin on the ring of men
with their gaudy weapons. They fired every round they
had, and his body began to buck and spin as he came
apart. A bullet hit the launcher, and the rocket blew.
Tony Montana exploded in a ball of fire, pitching over
the balcony rail and hurtling to the ground below. His
killers rushed forward to look, watching the flames

burn out in the riot of jungle plants. The thing was consumed by itself like a meteorite.

And just then the first siren sounded, like an all-clear after a night of heavy shelling. Within seconds the hitters were looting, stuffing the cash into bags, loading their arms with kilos. The rain had almost cleared now, and the Gulf wind blew the bitter smoke away through the clattering palms. As soon as the shooting stopped the half-acre lords of Coral Gables gathered on the curb in their bathrobes, arms wrapped protectively about their wives and eldest sons. They watched with horrible fascination as the guerrillas shrieked off in Tony's fleet of cars, tearing out of the gates on two wheels. But even then, when the place was clearly deserted, they wouldn't venture any closer. All they could see beyond the gates was the flickering neon sign on the lawn: THE WORLD IS YOURS.

And it *was* theirs again. The nightmare was over. They knew it as soon as the police arrived, screaming up the driveway, followed a moment later by the fire trucks and the paramedics. Life was normal again. The lords of Coral Gables turned back to their solid houses with a quickening in their hearts. The real America was safe with them, that dream of money and power that would one day free all men. You could tell by the crystalline moon shouldering through the clouds, tomorrow was going to be bright and clean.

Besides, there was a whole kingdom waiting to be divided.